MW01710863

INQUISITION

BOOK THREE OF THE *LALASSU*

We all hold
our secrets
under our
skin.

Clewis
Can.Con
2019

The characters and events portrayed in this book are fictitious. Any similarity to real persons, living or dead, is coincidental and not intended by the author.

Printed in the United States of America

Published by Past the Mirror Publishing.

ISBN: 978-0-9940121-6-6

<u>INQUISITION:</u>

BOOK THREE OF THE LALASSU

Jennifer Carole Lewis

Praise for Revelations: Book One of the *Lalassu*

"A fabulous and even dangerous heroine, an intriguing paranormal world, a diabolical plan to harness supernaturals AND a sweet romance combine to make REVELATIONS an engaging debut." – USA today Bestseller Deborah Cooke

"*Revelations* is a quick paced novel that changes the common perceptions of the 'hero', with journeys of self-discovery, acceptance and finding romance in unlikely places and people." – Nada, *Nadaness in Motion* (nadanessinmotion.blogspot.ca)

"This is one of the best love stories I have read in a long time!.... The pacing of this story is written so well that you feel like you're a heartbeat away from more action and emotion than you can handle. The characters are so well developed that they have the feel of real people." – Ella, *Writer in Progress* (writerip.blogspot.ca)

"The imagery and descriptions in this book are phenomenal, and I was on the edge of my seat with 'Oh my gosh, WHAT HAPPENS NEXT?!' almost constantly coming out of my mouth…. If a movie ever gets made based on this book, because one should, I would be first in line at the ticket booth." – Lauren, *Romance Novel Giveaways* (romancenovelgiveaways.blogspot.ca)

"This is a seriously cool book…. I loved the plot and twists and mysteries surrounding the gifted …. I want more!" – Maghon, *Happy Tails and Tales Blog* (happytailsandtales.blogspot.ca)

"Absolutely Magical!.... After reading *Revelations*, I haven't been this excited to pick up the next book in a series in a very long time. Jennifer has a true talent & knack for reeling people in. So proceed with caution if you plan on picking up this book, you'll be hooked!" – Jessica, *Taking It One Book At A Time* (takingitonebookatatime.blogspot.ca)

"What a wonderfully imaginative adventure…. There was just something magical and memorizing about this completely original and vivid world of Lewis's imagination." – Beth, *Tome Tender* (tometender.blogspot.ca)

To my parents, who have read every word
I've ever written. Even the steamy bits.

And to my husband, my first Texas Hold 'Em partner.

Lalassu, (Sumerian noun) definition: ghost, hidden or secret

The poker variant, Texas Hold 'Em, has a
number of different stages.
First, players must ante up to play.
Next they are dealt two secret cards.
Now play can begin.

Then three cards, the Flop, are dealt in common.
This weeds out the uncommitted and the unlucky.
Next are two single cards, the Turn and the River.
With each development, the possibilities dwindle and the player must
decide how to play his or her hand.

At some point, the player must take a leap of faith
and declare themselves all in.
After that, there is no turning back
and the cards will determine the player's fate.

Ante Up

Chapter One

"Hey, Detective Cabrera. Good catch today."

The newbie's words caught the attention of the other Perdition police officers bustling around the bull pen. The rustle of paperwork and murmur of conversations dropped, leaving an eager silence.

"Thanks…" Joe Cabrera let his voice trail off, unsure of the kid's name. He knew he should walk away rather than risk tainting this kid's career with his presence. The guy was so new he was practically quivering in his crisply pressed uniform and glistening shoes.

"Rob Salazar." The rookie held out his hand. "If you have a minute, I'd like to talk about the case. How did you track down the firm that makes the weighted dice?" He'd probably read a book on how to introduce himself and create a presence at work. Joe's own eager rookie days were too distant to dig up from his memory. After the last few months, he was too tired and cynical to even try.

"I just followed the leads." *Dammit, it was a good catch.* But he didn't dare brag about the work he'd done to track down the trio of scammers who'd been counting out cards and swapping out dice at the local casinos. He'd managed to catch them before the organized-crime family who ran the place caught up to them. "Nothing special."

"How did you know that one guy would go back to his ex-girlfriend's to hide out?"

The other cops in the precinct were starting to snicker. Joe shook the boy's hand as quickly as he could. *Time to bail.* "Another time, Salazar."

Joe turned and found himself blocked by a tall man whose girth ensured there would be no convenient retreat. Detective Dave Hampton carried a grudge stretching back to when Joe made detective first. Staring at the flecks of crumbs and lint dotting the man's once-expensive wool trench coat, Joe reminded himself not to react and give Hampton the satisfaction of knowing his blows had struck home.

"Don't waste your time, Salazar." Hampton gave a broad grin, clearly eager to delve into old ground with a fresh audience. "Not unless you want a front-page story for the tabloids."

"I don't understand." Salazar glanced between the two of them, eyes round and uncertain.

"Tell him what they call you." Hampton smirked, his grin displaying yet more crumbs caught in his sandy-blond beard. Joe despised the man's slovenliness, especially since it carried over to his police work. Hampton never bothered finding the right suspect if he could beat a convenient one into a confession.

"I wouldn't dream of depriving you of the pleasure." Joe gritted his teeth in a pleasant, professional smile. *Don't react. Don't give him the satisfaction.*

"Creepy Cabrera." Hampton should be in charge of crowd control. He didn't need a megaphone to project his voice. "Guy's a regular X-file."

Salazar shook his head, confused. Joe tried not to roll his eyes. The kid probably didn't even remember *The X-Files*.

"Once they figured out you were loony tunes, they took away the Dalhard Industries investigation and gave it to a real detective." Hampton puffed himself up, tucking his thumbs into the nonexistent gap between his paunch and his belt.

Joe pushed past the bully, not trusting his temper to remain under control much longer. Obedient chuckles echoed down the hall as Hampton proceeded to loudly explain the facts to Salazar. "Creepy Cabrera used to be a hotshot, but no one trusts him since he started spouting off about the little-green-men brigade."

It was psychics, not aliens, you moron. Try to keep your prejudices straight at least. Joe's jaw tightened, and he ground his teeth hard enough to squeak.

The elevator doors slid shut, and Joe let himself slump. If only he'd kept his mouth shut this winter. The ancient machinery whirred in the walls as the elevator ascended slowly, giving Joe plenty of time to brood about what went wrong.

He was open-minded, willing to believe that the universe still held plenty of surprises. Tía Agata was always babbling about positive and negative energy, blessings and curses. He didn't put much stock in such things himself, but he didn't dismiss them either. But what had happened went far beyond a mere surprise.

Seven months earlier, he'd discovered that there were people walking around with the sort of superpowers that belonged in comic books and movies. The discovery hadn't just yanked the rug out from under him—it had shattered the bedrock of his beliefs about the nature of the universe. He'd been doing all right with it, managing to pick up the pieces and fit them back into some semblance of order, until his so-called friends dragged him out to Alaska to hunt down André Dalhard, a man who could control people by touching them. Dalhard had used his skills for murder, kidnapping, extortion, fraud, and any number of other crimes. None of which Joe could prove.

Why did they even bother? He knew the reason. They'd needed his help to track the man down, but then they'd expected him to turn his back while they took care of the problem. Instead, Joe had insisted that even a man like Dalhard deserved due process, and he'd brought him back and put him on trial.

That was when the trouble started. Other officers could mock the tin-foil-hat crowd, but Joe knew that at least some of those dangers were real. He'd begged for enhanced security precautions to keep Dalhard in jail. But he hadn't been able to come up with a rational explanation for why staff should avoid all skin-to-skin contact with the prisoner. Joe had gotten frustrated one day, and it all came spilling out. Two minutes of babbling had ruined ten years of his career and reputation.

His sergeant insisted on Joe seeing a psychologist. He'd gone, and he'd made all the right noises, claiming stress, bad medication, and whatever he thought might make a difference. Of course he understood that psychics weren't real, and he'd been tired and had made a little slip while joking. No big deal.

His verbal footwork had kept his badge safe but hit his pride hard. Cops were worse than frat boys for holding on to an embarrassing joke. At least frats only lasted through college, though. He'd be Creepy Cabrera until the day he retired. Especially with Hampton stirring the pot at every opportunity.

Even worse was the knowledge that his brothers in blue were

walking out there, ignorant of the dangers that Joe now knew existed. Keeping it to himself made him feel like a traitor, but how could he convince them of the truth if they hadn't seen it for themselves? Joe's eyes had been forced open, and slipping back into the shadows of ignorance wasn't an option any longer.

The elevator doors dinged as they began to close, and Joe realized he'd been standing there, staring into space like a shell-shocked trooper from World War I. Grabbing the door to keep it open, he gratefully realized no one seemed to have noticed. *I need to go home and start working on the end table for Mamá and try to forget that I'm the only one who knows we're balancing on the verge of some kind of superpowered apocalypse.*

"Detective Cabrera!" his sergeant, Fran Modnik, called out before he could escape, her blond ponytail swinging like a hangman's noose as she stalked across the lobby.

Shitshitshit. "Sergeant," he replied politely.

"We need your help on something." Modnik passed him, her sensible flats squeaking softly against the linoleum. She didn't bother looking back to see if he would follow her as she made her way to the tech department without a single wasted step. A great believer in efficiency, Modnik didn't use makeup or wear fashionable clothes or indulge in idle chitchat. Dark slacks and a department T-shirt were her uniform unless she was forced into something else by political necessity. Some cops didn't like working for her, finding her cold and unforgiving. But Cabrera was impressed by her Sherlock-worthy detective skills and hoped the department would continue to recognize her incredible potential.

I was almost home free. He kept a discreet distance behind the sergeant. As they opened the door, the temperature rose—too many machines and too little air conditioning. The sheer number of storage units, tables, and monitors made Joe twitchy. They blocked his lines of sight and could potentially hide a half dozen intruders.

"You've heard about the series of break-ins at data-storage facilities across the state?" Modnik logged into the main terminal, powering up the large central screen.

"It was in the morning briefing," Joe said cautiously. The higher levels were frustrated and spreading a wide net, asking local cops to keep an eye out for anything that might be connected.

Modnik nodded. "Lockbox here in Perdition got hit yesterday. The thief is a pro—set the cameras on a loop, disabled the alarms. The only thing she tripped was a routine maintenance alert, which noticed the missing file."

"She?" Joe's interest perked its ears. His sergeant didn't drop details like that by accident.

"Thanks to the alert, we knew the file was removed at 2:13 a.m. The security cameras at Lockbox were affected but not the street cameras." Modnik delivered the news with grim satisfaction. She always told her officers to be patient, because criminals were invariably sloppy. They made mistakes, and then the cops could reel them in.

"A big oversight for a pro to make." Joe frowned. After the last few months, what others called "easy" smelled more like a trap to him.

"She didn't know about the red-light camera at the intersection of Roosevelt and Third. Tourist blew through the light at 2:16, and look what we found." Modnik pointed at the high-resolution traffic photo. The prominent feature was a grey sedan midway through the intersection, but Joe focused on the area behind the car.

The steel doors to Lockbox had the company name and logo clearly stenciled on them. A woman wearing a long, cream-colored designer coat over a grey business suit held them open. The photo resolution was sharp enough that Joe could see a flash of coral pink on her painted nails and the heavy stitching on her slim leather briefcase.

"Any chance she's an employee working late?" Joe asked.

Modnik shook her head, a smirk curving her pale lips. "Nope. Checked the employee records, and there's no match. And no record of anyone in the building either. That's our thief."

"It's a nice clear shot of her face." Joe leaned in. She'd be easy to identify. She looked more like a model or actress than a criminal. Her makeup and dark hair were even done up like one of those fifties pin-up girls, emphasizing big eyes, pouting lips, and sharp cheekbones. "Were we able to track her movements?"

"The bank on Roosevelt has twenty-four-hour coverage of the street. Same with the drugstore on New Orleans Ave." Modnik began typing again.

"Then we've got her." Joe started to warm up to his sergeant's enthusiasm. The two streets were a block apart and close enough to Third to have partial coverage of the area in front of Lockbox, although they were at the wrong angle to see the actual building.

"You'd think so." She split the screen into two views, one from the bank and one from the drugstore. As the timestamp crawled from 2:10 to 2:25, the streets remained deserted except for the grey sedan roaring through the light and a homeless couple, both bundled so heavily against the cold that their features were impossible to pick up. The man was definitely African American, with a worn knit cap pulled low over his forehead. The woman was dark skinned as well, possibly Latina, with filthy bleached-blond hair. They meandered over to the dumpster in the alley across from the drugstore and picked through it. Modnik paused the playback. "They go through the dumpster for another half hour and then wander off. No sign of our Jane Doe."

"How?" Joe's mind began to click through possibilities. "She'd have to pass at least one of the cameras. Could the feeds have been tampered with?"

"No. The sedan confirms the recording isn't from a previous night. I'm still having tech go through it to make sure, but it looks clean. Our mystery lady simply vanished into thin air." Modnik clicked off the screen and faced her detective. "That's where you come in."

"Me?" Joe tried to keep his voice nonchalant while his heart sank deep below his belt. *Another weird case for Creepy Cabrera.*

"Too many cops get focused on what they expect to see. You keep an open mind and follow the evidence. I don't need someone screaming ghosts or conspiracies. I need someone to find out what happened. The truth, no matter how strange."

His reluctance seeped through his professional mask. "I'm not sure I'm the best choice."

"Because they call you Creepy Cabrera?" Modnik hit the nail with a blunt-force sledgehammer. "I don't care about a bunch of status-happy idiots poking at you because they haven't heard a good joke in a while. You're a good detective, Cabrera. You find the connections—you find the bad guys."

"And what about the other stuff? This isn't going to help my reputation, Sergeant." Joe decided to be equally blunt.

"Trust me. You want this case." Modnik paused, glancing around the room to make sure they were alone. "The data firms that have been hit all have a client in common: Dalhard Industries."

Joe's head snapped up. He wanted to ask if the sergeant was sure, but she'd take it as an insult. *Careful.* Dalhard's lawyers had already slapped Joe with a police-harassment suit.

"I see I've piqued your interest," Modnik said dryly.

"Hampton is the lead officer for the Dalhard investigation." Joe forced his shoulders down, trying to appear relaxed.

"Officially, that's not going to change." She held up one finger to forestall any reply from Joe. "I've known you long enough to trust your gut instincts. This is too big a coincidence to leave unchecked, and I'm offering you a chance to prove what you've been saying. Find this thief, and you might find your evidence against Dalhard." She offered him the slim file.

"Find a thief who disappears without a trace. Easy. And what should I do after lunch?" Joe accepted the file.

Modnik smiled briefly, and the weary sergeant morphed into an attractive woman. "Could be worse. The department is also asking for someone to look into that shapeshifting viral video."

No need to ask for details. Joe suppressed a wince. He'd caught the live version of the event during his trip to Alaska. "It's fake. Probably a publicity stunt for some movie."

"It's caught the attention of some very prominent people. All sorts of experts are insisting the footage hasn't been tampered with. Now I'm having to field ridiculous calls asking what I plan to do if we catch a suspect with unusual abilities." She rolled her eyes. "If they find out about our mystery thief, I could end up having to handle a crackpot task force. So don't thank me yet."

"So you need me to keep this quiet." Could their target be one of the *lalassu*? Was invisibility one of the possible powers? Joe made a mental note to get in touch with his best friend, Michael, to ask. After years of bringing Joe useful tips, Michael had found the secret society of people with an astonishing variety of supernatural gifts, and he'd dragged Joe down the rabbit hole after him.

Modnik nodded. "Whatever you find, you bring to me. And one more thing—stay away from Otisville."

That was the prison where Dalhard currently lived. "Understood."

"I mean it, Cabrera. This is your one chance, and you have no margin for bullshit. You don't talk to Dalhard again until you have enough to hang him with." Modnik delivered her final orders and stalked into the hall, ready to take out her irritation on the next hapless victim who crossed her.

Enough to hang him with. Only a figure of speech, but the words echoed what the other *lalassu* had suggested for Dalhard back in Alaska: a summary execution. Joe had stopped them, but lately, he wondered if his ethics had trapped him into making a fatal mistake.

CHAPTER TWO

Cali stretched her aching muscles, her old scars pulling like weighted ropes as she climbed the stairs to the third floor of her apartment building. A half dozen IDs in as many names were hidden in various pockets sewn into her jeans and long-sleeved blouse. She'd never known her birth name or whether her drug-addicted mother had even bothered to register the birth. That uncertainty left her a ghost, haunting the edges of society. The position suited her, freeing her to do what was necessary rather than shackling her with polite expectations.

She wriggled her fingers against the rust-speckled handrails, trying to force warm blood back into her numb tips. Without her agile digits, she would have starved a long time ago. *I might be out of practice when it comes to picking pockets and lifting wallets, but I haven't totally lost it.* She'd picked over three hundred dollars from various pockets, all for her neighbor Speranza. Cali had plenty of money coming in for herself through other, less respectable sources.

Speranza's door was one of the few with apartment numbers still attached to the deep brown metal. Cali tapped on the door, calling softly, "It's me."

"Cali!" The door pulled open to reveal an angelic little girl with her dark hair in thick braids and her black eyes sparkling. "Guess what?"

"What, *querida*?" Cali knelt down, smiling at Carlotta. The little girl's faded pants rode high, revealing tiny ankles, and Cali reminded herself to pick up a couple of new pairs next time she was out.

"Daddy came, and we had a game of hide-and-seek, and I stayed quiet the longest!" Carlotta announced proudly.

Cali kept her smile in place with grim effort. Speranza was trying not to frighten the girls and had turned hiding from her abusive ex-husband into a game. "Good for you!"

The little girl's grin drooped. "Daddy sounded mad and scary."

"I know, *mi corazon.*" Speranza appeared in the doorway, holding the youngest, two-year-old Zara, who clung to her mother with chubby fingers. The young mother's bruises might have healed long ago, but the hunted look in her downcast eyes would take longer to vanish. "I think he'd be proud of you for how good you were, not making a sound. I know I am."

Carlotta's confidence returned. "Zara cried a little, but I made faces at her."

"You're a great big sister." Cali hugged the little girl. "Give me a minute with your mom, okay?"

"Can I watch TV?" At her mother's nod, Carlotta danced off through the scattered toys. Zara made a little noise, and Speranza put her down to toddle after her big sister.

"How long was he here?" Cali asked quietly, keeping her voice low.

"Over an hour." Speranza's voice wavered. "I kept thinking he would break in, but the locks you gave us held."

"They'll hold back an elephant in full charge. The wall will give out before that door does," Cali said with grim satisfaction. "You still have the Taser I gave you?"

"*Si*, in the safe room. Out of reach of little hands." Speranza glanced over her shoulder, an automatic maternal check-in. "Rodolpho has always been so strong—"

"A thousand volts running through his system will shut him down no matter how strong he is." Cali pulled out the cash-laden envelope. "Here's the money for this week."

Speranza wouldn't accept it right away. Cali put the envelope on the polished kitchen counter, following the dance they'd established almost two months earlier. Her neighbor didn't have much choice. Her ex-husband had terrorized her, showing up at any job that Speranza managed to find. He would brutalize her and threaten her coworkers, costing her any chance of continued employment. Cali had offered to move Speranza and her kids out of the city, but Speranza wouldn't abandon her mother, who was dying of cancer in a local hospice.

The situation was heartbreaking and frustrating in equal measure. Divorce paperwork and restraining orders might be slowly creeping through the legal system, but the local cops and Rodolpho ignored them. A lifetime of watching bullies and thugs made Cali certain that things would only get worse. Speranza still believed her ex would one day see reason, which left Cali biting her tongue hard enough to bleed while Speranza and her kids played "hide-and-seek" and Cali dropped off enough money to cover their bills.

Kids should never be afraid at home. I wish she'd let me send Hood or Red Willa after him. Intimidation or elimination—either would take care of the problem. But the one time that Cali had gently suggested that route, Speranza had refused to talk to her for a week and then forced her to promise not to pursue it. Maybe there was another way. "I know of some empty apartments in the neighborhood. I could move you someplace where he wouldn't know to find you and you could still be close to your mom."

"He would find us again. He always does." Speranza shook her head. "I won't give up our home."

Personally, Cali didn't see a reason to be particularly attached to a two-bedroom apartment in a neighborhood that might someday aspire to be a slum, but she could understand how sometimes it was necessary to stop running. She wouldn't be the one to strip away Speranza's pride if that was all she had left. "Lucky me. Without your cooking, I'd starve."

"You don't eat enough," Speranza scolded, pulling a repurposed margarine container out of the fridge. "I worry about you."

The smell of creamy sauce, fish, and rice wafted out, making Cali's mouth water and her stomach grumble. "I can take care of myself." Cali accepted the container, holding it close so it pressed reassuringly against the snug bands of her arm harness. Having to wear long sleeves in all weather was a small price to pay for the security of her hidden knives. Some might prefer guns, but knives never jammed or needed to be reloaded. "And I eat plenty."

Speranza's scarred lips twitched. "You are such a liar, Cali. But a good-hearted one. Always ready to protect everyone else and forgetting to care for yourself."

Cali secretly liked Speranza's mothering tendencies. Knowing that someone cared whether or not she came home was a nice change of pace. It soothed an old ache in her heart.

"I had nearly given up that there were such people as you still in this world." Speranza's smile slipped as she checked again on her children.

I'm no hero. She was too coldly practical for heroism. Heroes got themselves taken down because they were too busy doing good to remember to watch their backs. And then the people who needed them ended up in worse situations because no one was left to protect them. *Not going to happen on my watch.* "Thanks, Speranza. See you tomorrow."

Leaving the family to find what peace they could, Cali climbed the stairs to her own apartment, trying to ignore the bone-deep ache in her joints. She couldn't get to her warm shower and bed fast enough. Her body allowed her to do some amazing things, but it also left her vulnerable to the stresses of everyday life. Like a contortionist or dancer, she was threatened with arthritis and the limitations of cumulative fractures despite not having reached her thirtieth birthday yet.

Someday, she promised herself, the word a shorthand for a long list of promises. Someday she would retire to someplace warm and flat where the cold wouldn't torture her. Someday she would put her training and skills aside and find something she could enjoy doing. Someday she'd find the peace she longed for. *Just not today. Not while there was still work to do.*

Her tiny apartment looked more like a squatter's lair than a proper home, but it was hers. No one stepping inside would guess that it was owned by one of the most successful thieves in New York State. Exactly how she wanted it. The living space was completely empty, with only a few old newspapers lying on the old parquet floor. Cali avoided stepping on them as she locked the door behind her. She'd hidden narrow pieces of thin glass underneath so the crunch could alert her if anyone came in.

The round container of food weighed heavily in her hand. She should eat. She knew her body needed the fuel, but the siren call of her shower was louder. *Later.* She stepped high over the invisible tripwire stretched across the hall's entrance. Once inside the brightly lit bathroom, she secured the three locks and finally allowed herself to breathe. Undoing her rough bun, she allowed her blond hair to fall loose and brushed out the tangles.

After carefully folding her clothes, she put the margarine tub on top of them. Twisting, she checked in the mirror to see how her most recent scar was healing. The closed gash on her left hip was the result of not ducking properly during a knife fight a few weeks earlier. She'd stitched it up herself and was relieved to see the redness fading. Next time, she'd be more careful.

She balanced her own knives on top of the plastic tub, in easy reach if she needed them. Only then did she allow herself to finally step into the shower and let the steaming water pour over her body. The heat relieved the bone-deep chills and aches, bringing her back to something resembling human again. She braced her hands on the worn and chipped tiles, letting the pounding cascade wrap around her head, neck, and back.

Her breath escaped from her lungs in a long, sustained exhalation. Another day had passed without a crisis, without the other shoe dropping. The shoe always dropped—it was inevitable. So Cali tried to savor the calm in between.

The water started to chill, and Cali reluctantly shut down the shower. She toweled off and dressed quickly in old, battered sweatpants and a snug T-shirt. Gathering her knives and her food, she unlocked the bathroom and swiftly crossed into the deceptively empty bedroom. She pried open the heavy doors to the room's walk-in closet. The landlord would undoubtedly be pissed if he discovered she'd reinforced the closet frame and hung steel doors, but what he didn't know wasn't going to cost Cali any sleep.

The closet held a futon, a heavy down comforter, and thick pillows as well as Cali's tablet and a small heater and fridge. Heavy locks would hold the door in place against any assault, and if they didn't, a magnetic strip over the minifridge held over a dozen throwing knives. Switching on the light, she wrapped herself in the comforter and began to eat Speranza's casserole while scanning the local papers on her tablet. Still no mention of an increase in stolen wallets and purses in the high-end malls. Sooner or later, her targets would talk to each other and put pressure on the city, but until then, she could keep flying under the radar.

There was also no mention of a break-in at Lockbox, which was a huge relief. She could still see the pop of light from the red-light camera as she emerged from the building. The records she'd stolen were safely on their way to her partner, where she could ensure they'd stay buried rather than be used against Mr. Dalhard.

She'd have to visit him in prison the next day in order to deliver the various legal papers that his lawyers had given her. The spineless bastards were too afraid to see him themselves, just like the rest of his "friends," who were pretending he'd never existed. If it weren't for Cali, Mr. Dalhard would have been completely abandoned. Anger flushed her pale skin, turning it ruddy and blotchy.

The trial had been a farce, featuring doctored paper trails and nonsense about tax evasion. No one even cared that the police had gone after him in Alaska in a blatant disregard for jurisdiction. Mr. Dalhard had remained confident the charges would be overturned—right until the judge passed sentence after less than two days of trial. Cali's heart had broken as she watched the first person who'd ever protected her being led away from the courtroom with his hands shackled at his sides. Someone had figured out Mr. Dalhard's gifts and didn't want to give him an opportunity to use them. Cali could guess who.

"Local Detective Joseph Cabrera Breaks Card-Counting Ring," the headlines had said. There was the shoe dropping. A small one, a slipper on a carpet, but it still counted. *Cabrera should be the one in jail.*

Cabrera was still after Mr. Dalhard, trying to bring new charges to pile on to the relatively inoffensive white-collar conviction. The detective had been slapped with a lawsuit, but Cali knew it wouldn't stop him. He'd presented evidence for a kidnapping charge. *Mr. Dalhard saved that little girl.* What was her name? Betty? Bernadette? Mr. Dalhard had saved her from a mother more interested in pushing pills down her daughter's throat than in realizing that the child possessed a supernatural talent. The mother had signed her parental rights away and then tried to claim she'd been tricked. Mr. Dalhard said she'd probably received a higher cash offer for her daughter.

Neither the child nor her mother was anywhere to be found these days. Cali hoped that the detective had them stashed somewhere, waiting to testify. *If the mother took another offer, who knows what happened to the little girl?* People were so disgustingly predictable. They might freak out when they discovered someone different, but two seconds later, they were searching for ways to use that difference. At least Mr. Dalhard cared enough to try and give his charges something of the life they wanted. Without his help, Cali would probably have been long since dead on the streets.

I'm done playing by the rules of polite society. She'd begun to collect what she would need to make those responsible for the mess pay for it. Meanwhile, she'd take care of Mr. Dalhard and support him however she could. She knew he was a good man, one who understood the necessity of operating outside society when dealing with circumstances that the world considered more legend than fact. Whatever he needed, she would make it happen.

André Dalhard frowned at his cellmate, a giant of a man who had taken full advantage of the weights in the yard and the tattooing skills of his fellow inmates.

"I'm sorry, Mr. Dalhard. I'll get out of your hair." Dodger ducked his head and scrambled to get out of their shared accommodations.

Dalhard watched his cellmate go without allowing himself the slightest change in his expression. His idiot lawyers were trying to convince him to petition to be moved into a lower-security facility. As if he would trust their advice again when they'd lost the damned case to begin with.

Prison had been intimidating, but the advantages quickly became apparent. His persuasive influence ensured he emerged at the top of the local food chain. Within a day, he'd obtained a contraband cell phone and other creature comforts. Within a week, he'd gained the respect of the various internal gangs.

Settling onto the double-thick mattress, he began to skim through the latest batch of information. Cali would come to visit the following day, and he needed to have her instructions ready to begin the next phase of the operation. His body would block the papers from casual view if any of the guards made it past his early-warning circle of hastily bribed inmates. That precaution was tedious but necessary.

Or was it? Dalhard frowned, considering. All his life, he'd kept up an appearance of decorum, a cloak to hide his illegal activities and socially questionable choices. He'd struggled to maintain the illusion throughout his trial but had been proclaimed guilty anyway. Since arriving at Otisville, he'd seen another side of society.

The casual and efficient brutality of his fellow inmates had been an eye opener. Out in the real world, respect was bought with money and power, an ephemeral miasma that depended as much upon illusion as reality. Dalhard could play the role of successful businessman perfectly, wearing designer suits, donating to the right charities, and appearing at significant cocktail parties and gala events. He'd mastered it and had even believed it was who he truly was.

In prison, respect came stained with blood and violence. Its perceived absence was brutally punished. Offences over breakfast meant someone would be taken to the hospital ward by lunch. The power was tangible, raw, and heavy on the shoulders of those who wielded it. To his surprise, Dalhard liked it. It felt far more solid and real than his life outside. He imagined how his business partners and society colleagues would react if they saw the predator he knew he could become. He could destroy their illusions of security and show them that their precious power was as false and intangible as the fashions they followed.

As satisfying as it would have been to rip the smug masks off their faces, he needed to keep his rage focused on the targets who deserved it—his treacherous former assistant, Karan, and the insufferable police pawn, Detective Joe Cabrera.

I should have killed the detective when I had the chance. A single bullet would have greatly simplified Dalhard's current life and perhaps even entirely prevented the trial and conviction. Dead men did not investigate. But Dalhard had wanted to maintain some plausible deniability in the policeman's death, so rather than shooting him, he'd left him to be crushed in an imminent building demolition. Somehow, in a chain of events more suited to an action movie than real life, the detective and his friend had managed to escape and free Dalhard's other acquisitions.

He would not repeat that mistake. Thanks to his mother's Siren gifts and his proximity to the criminal class, a brief touch would yield him a new source of power: ruthless, brutal men eager for violence and bored from inaction.

Deep voices shouted in the distance, cutting across the usual bass rumble of muffled conversation. Dalhard listened, evaluating. It was not a disturbance he needed to worry about.

An army lay inside these walls, savage and terrifying. And more potential recruits waited outside, ripe for his influential touch. Criminals, thugs, gangsters—they could all be his. If they unified under his leadership, could any aspect of civilization survive a coordinated assault? He could become truly untouchable. Already, his collection of inmates allowed him to draw on substantial connections, reducing the thick and forbidding walls to mere inconveniences.

Caution reasserted itself over pleasant daydreams of vengeance. He was still vulnerable to forces outside the walls—Karan and Cabrera. They understood who he was and what he could do. Cabrera had influence within the justice system and could potentially thwart Dalhard's plans. Karan had already shown his willingness to draw blood in their contest for supremacy. They both needed to be removed. Then when his lawyers finally succeeded in releasing him, Dalhard would rule unchallenged. The streets would rise up and ensure every last person who betrayed him would meet with utter destruction.

Chapter Three

As the clouded glass door to the restaurant opened, Joe tensed, wondering if Michael would stand him up. Their last talk hadn't gone well, devolving into a shouting match over the best way to handle the Alaskan shifting video. Joe still thought passing the shapeshifting off as special effects and waiting for the attention to blow over had been the right decision.

A pair of young women came squealing through the restaurant to join another group chattering in the corner, and Joe realized he'd forgotten to exhale. Forcing himself to sample another lungful of air, Joe fixed his gaze on the flickering ESPN feed that silently showed game highlights.

"Hey, Joe." Michael's quiet voice cut through the mix of music and conversation filling the air.

Joe's hand twitched toward his weapon before he could convince his body that he didn't really need an adrenaline surge at that moment.

"Sorry. Didn't mean to startle you." Michael held up his gloved hands in surrender.

"Guess I'm preoccupied. Good to see you." Joe stood as Michael took off his long trench coat and draped it over the back of his chair. As they both sat back down, Joe noticed that Michael had left the thin leather gloves in place. Not a big surprise, since his friend could pick up resonances and information from both objects and people if he touched them. Joe rarely saw Michael's bare hands.

"Good to see you too. Should I make this quick?" Michael nodded toward the party of women, all talking loudly and gesturing broadly with their hands.

Joe shook his head. Six months before, a part of his mind would have always been on the ladies in the room, picking which ones to approach. He'd been a master flirt, enjoying the game and careful not to leave any broken hearts in his wake. Lately, all of that seemed superficial. "We've got too much to go over. We should get to it."

"Agreed. I've been talking to a few people about creating other shifter videos. Some solid fakes should help discourage public opinion." Michael pulled out his tablet and a stylus.

Joe couldn't actually bite his tongue, but he rubbed his eyes.

"Everything okay?"

"Just a headache. Too much on my mind these days," Joe said, letting his hand drop to the table.

"Work giving you trouble?" Michael pushed the long hair back from his face. Joe preferred his own trimmed close to his skull. That way, it required less fuss, and it fit neatly under a riot helmet if necessary.

"Same shit, different day." Joe tilted his glass, letting the amber whiskey roll inside it. "Still fighting the good fight, but it's harder now."

Michael whispered, "Once you know what's out there, you can't ever go back to ignorance."

Then why the hell couldn't you leave me alone? Joe didn't let his thought escape. It wasn't Michael's fault. Joe had insisted on joining in, afraid his friend was getting into a deep and dangerous situation. He just hadn't known how deep and dangerous that particular rabbit hole could be. Now he was stuck on the far side of the mirror, where the old rules no longer applied.

"Things are going to get worse." Michael glanced around to make sure no one could overhear. "Dani's getting warnings."

"Is that direct from the source?" Joe gestured toward the ceiling with his glass. Accepting that Michael's girlfriend could directly contact a god—one that was not Jehovah the Almighty—had taken a fair bit of mental work to reconcile with Joe's Catholic upbringing.

"We don't know. It's all vague and irritatingly portentous. I don't know if there are too many pieces in the air or if the Goddess is deliberately keeping information from us." Michael stopped abruptly as the waitress approached to take their orders. For a few minutes, they both played the role of two friends meeting casually. Michael held the menu tightly as if it held the answers to the universe. He stammered over his order. Lying was not one of Michael's talents.

Joe waited until the waitress had disappeared into the kitchen. "What about Vapor? He's got to have an opinion. He sees everything with that computer shit."

"We can't reach him. Dani says he does this sometimes—disappears for a few months. Except never before during a crisis." Michael hesitated. "I went to his apartment to try and figure out where he was, and I couldn't find anything. No resonances to pick up on. It was completely blank."

Hell no. Joe did not want to know anything more about how that freaky world worked. He had enough nightmares. Vapor was a big guy and had the skills to take care of himself.

"I don't like him being out of touch. We could use his help." Michael fidgeted with his place setting, minutely adjusting the glass and cutlery. "Gwen's getting more visitors."

Joe winced. That was not the direction he wanted the conversation to take. Visitors and Gwen meant ghosts. But he needed to know. "How bad is it?"

"There have been a half dozen over the last month, all murdered. Before they died, their attackers demanded to know the names of others like them. The ones in contact were desperate to warn friends and family, which makes me wonder how many others simply vanished." Michael stubbornly shook his head. He'd always cared too much about things he couldn't change. "Something tells me there's more to this than random attacks."

Their greasy pub food arrived, but Joe couldn't have choked it down if his life depended on it. "You think the kills are government approved? Is this a warning?"

Michael frowned, and Joe gestured toward the ceiling again. Michael sometimes got flashes of psychic insight that pushed him into various situations such as meeting with Dani.

"No. I haven't gotten one of those since we stopped Dalhard." Michael sounded frustrated. "I don't know if the government is involved or if it's people panicking. No one likes to find out the world isn't what they thought."

Yeah. No one except you. His friend had been thrilled to learn that his beloved comic books might be based more on reality than anyone could have guessed. But Joe knew most people wouldn't be eager to embrace the *lalassu.*

Time to change the topic. "I've got a possible lead that might let us get some more charges nailed on Dalhard. Someone is stealing information from secure sites, probably someone looking for leverage against Dalhard Industries." Joe quietly explained about his disappearing thief. "Are there people who can make themselves invisible? I already checked the tapes to see if they were tampered with, like Nada used to do."

Michael leaned back in his chair, considering. "I haven't heard of any powers like that, but I'm only at the beginning of understanding how diverse the *lalassu* truly are. Sometimes it seems like I learn of a new lineage every time I turn around. And frankly, none of us can predict the results when the lineages mix."

"It's a damn mess. Suspicions that a werebear might be real are bad enough. Add in the Invisible Man, and we'll be lucky if Homeland Security doesn't shit a brick." Joe pushed aside his still-full plate. The idea of his friend disappearing into some black-site prison due to a bureaucratic panic killed the remnants of his appetite. "Speaking of bricks, how's Vincent doing?"

"Still not talking to any of us. Andrew says we should give him space." Michael glopped ketchup over his crispy fries.

So much for safe topics. Dani's brother had barely spoken on the way back from Alaska. Joe thought occasionally about dropping by to see how the man was coping with his return, but Vincent had a way of discouraging visitors. And surprising a man strong enough to rip through walls wasn't an option for anyone who wanted to collect a retirement pension.

"Andrew doesn't think he'll ever be ready to testify about what Dalhard did to him. He still refers to Dalhard as the Beast."

Joe speared a mouthful of fried cod but couldn't summon the energy to eat it. "I'm not asking him to testify anymore."

Michael's face immediately softened with contrition, leaving Joe feeling as if he'd kicked a puppy instead of defending himself.

"Look, man, I don't want to argue about it. If we want Dalhard to stay in prison, then we need better charges than money laundering," Joe said. That had been their fight before the one about the video—whether or not Bernie and Martha could be brought out of *lalassu* witness protection to testify about how Dalhard had kidnapped the girl without her mother's consent. "I'm trying to figure out a way."

"I know. Sometimes it's hard to remember that we're all on the same side." Michael drained his water. "We all have to work together."

Another point of contention. Joe made himself smile, although he didn't like it. Michael was a civilian, no matter how gifted. He shouldn't be going into dangerous situations. Luckily, Dani possessed both strength and cynicism enough to keep Michael safe from himself. A cop shouldn't take comfort in knowing someone was willing to break the law to protect a friend, but with Michael, Joe was a friend first and a detective second.

Michael suddenly grinned. "If it makes you feel any better, Dani and her mom are driving me crazy. Virginia wants Dani to get pregnant yesterday and continue the Babylon legacy."

Joe seized on the new topic with relief. Complaining about girlfriends and in-laws was the core of any bro-lationship. "I can't see Dani being too happy with that kind of pressure."

"Sometimes I think Virginia's about two steps away from breaking into our apartment at night to offer constructive criticism on our techniques."

Joe chuckled at the joke. "You definitely hit the jackpot for crazy in-laws. And it gets worse. Mamá's been on me to have you and Dani over to dinner. She's eager to feed you again and get a look at the girl who'd better be treating you right."

"Tell Mamá that we'll be there soon. And don't worry—I'll warn you in plenty of time to duck and cover."

That conversation felt like old times. Joe's mother had adopted Michael into the family circle when she discovered his own family wasn't in town. In Mamá's world, making someone eat alone was a federal offence. "Having you around always makes it easier. Keeps Mamá and the tías off my case and gives them someone else to focus on."

"I'll figure out when Dani's next night off is," Michael said.

"Have you told your folks about her?"

And the comfort of old times vanished along with Michael's grin. "They're touring Europe for the next eighteen months. I've tried calling and emailing, but I'm not getting anything back except their travel postings."

Assholes. Even though Joe spent a fair chunk of his life trying to carve out some space from his overinvolved family, he couldn't imagine walking away from them. Any family that voluntarily abandoned one of its members didn't deserve the name of *family.* "I can't believe your mom is leaving you hanging."

"She's always told me to keep what we can do secret. I don't think she ever forgave me for trying to tell Dad." Michael toyed with his water glass, slowly rotating it in place on the table. "Maybe it's for the best. I'd hate if Dalhard went after them. I've touched his mind, and obsessive doesn't even come close to describing it. I don't think he'll ever stop coming after us."

He's not going to get you. Not on my watch. "I got your back, Bro. He's going to have to come through me to get to you," Joe said. Michael was one of the few genuinely good people out there. If the universe held any justice, he'd get a happy ending. But the expression on Michael's face meant he was considering a leap back into the hero business. Lone crusaders against the darkness might work in comics, but in real life, idealists were buried in paupers' graves. *Time to head off any heroic impulses.* "I'm on this. Don't get any stupid ideas."

Michael laughed weakly. "Do I ever have any other kind these days?"

Chapter Four

His conversation with Michael stayed in Joe's head long after they finished dinner, echoing over and over as he climbed the stairs to his apartment. *What else could I have said?* Michael seemed to be trying to keep him at a distance. It was probably for protection, but Joe wasn't sure whose. Was it an effort to protect Joe's career by keeping him out of more quasi-legal events? Or could there be another surprise down this rabbit hole? *I miss the days when remembering my paperwork was the hardest part of taking down bad guys.*

When he reached his door, Joe stopped, his internal alarms going off. There was nothing obviously wrong with the closed door, but there were fresh scuff marks on the cheap, industrial hall carpet. The marks led into his apartment.

Not again. He eased his gun in the holster, checking to make sure he could draw quickly just in case he was wrong. *Nothing like getting your gun caught in your coat during a shootout to ruin your day.*

He turned the key as quietly as he could, listening for any sound from inside. He heard running water and a faint slapping noise.

"Hey, Mamá."

"Pépé!" Mamá greeted him with the same broad smile and open arms that had welcomed him home from school each day, dropping the rag she was using to wipe down his granite counters.

He leaned down to hug her. Mamá might be tiny, but she was a Mexican firecracker through and through, larger than life and twice as vibrant.

"I brought you enchiladas and some of Tía Agata's cornbread. I'll fix you a plate." Mamá shooed him to one of the barstools.

"I already ate," Joe protested, knowing it wouldn't make a difference. He saw the vacuum perched in the corner, not where he'd left it. He wished his mother didn't feel the need to come over to clean his place and stock his fridge but knew better than to fight it anymore. Every time he brought it up, she laughed and pinched his cheek and told him that when he had a wife and they produced some grandbabies, then she would stop. *Probably because she'll move in.*

As expected, his mother continued preparing a plate for him, placing two enchiladas dripping with cheese next to the crumbly cornbread speckled with jalapeno peppers. "Your cousins miss you."

"I know." With his crazy work schedule, he'd missed the last few weekly family dinners. Time to hop on the guilt train. "I'm sorry. I'll be there this week, I promise."

"Tía Ximena brought her neighbor's daughter last week. A lovely girl, she plays the violin for an orchestra in Brooklyn and works as a teacher at an elementary school." Mamá slid over a fork and knife.

Whoa! Need a derailment here. "Mamá, I told you I'm not ready for the blind-date thing. I don't need the tías to bring women to dinner. I can find my own."

"Hmmph." Mamá sniffed, folding her round arms across her chest. "The women you find, you don't bring home."

"Only because the only woman I've ever truly loved is you, Mamá." Joe grinned at her. "What other woman could compare?"

"Pah." She waved away the compliment and pulled out a Tupperware full of chocolate chip cookies, adding one to his plate. "You can't spend all your life working, Pépé. You need to settle down, have a family."

"I will one day." He wasn't faking agreement with her to avoid arguing. He'd always intended to settle down once he found the right girl. He remembered how his father used to bring home flowers and other little presents for Mamá just to make her smile. Joe wanted to make his girl smile when she saw him. When he passed by the street vendors selling jewelry, he wished he had someone to buy such things for just because the sparkle reminded him of her eyes. He dreamed of his own family and holding little hands on the way to Mamá's. His kids would be spoiled with love as soon as they stepped through her door.

"One day doesn't happen on its own," Mamá said.

"Mamá, please trust me on this." He took her hand in his to

emphasize his words. "It's not the right time for me. There's so much going on right now that I can't even think straight." *Don't ask me for details. I can't drag you down this rabbit hole too.*

She squeezed his hand. "Someday, a girl will knock you off your feet, and it won't matter what else is happening. It happened to your father." Mamá crossed herself and gestured briefly at the ceiling. "It will happen for you too."

I hope so. Joe took a bite of the cornbread. As soon as he started eating, Mamá began tidying up again, clucking because he'd left his woodworking tools out. She started putting things away in random places, and Joe resigned himself to not being able to find anything. *Family. Can't live with them but wouldn't want ever to be without them.*

Family sucks. Vincent stared at the cheap calendar fastened to the dingy apartment wall—"Birds of North America" or some shit like that. It hadn't been touched since March of the previous year and seemed like a perfect metaphor for his life, a man trapped by an inescapable moment from his past.

"I'm telling you, man, you've got to get out of this place," he whispered softly to his brother. Eric lay in a narrow twin bed, thin wires connecting him to a bunch of machines, all beeping in a muted electronic chorus. Vincent recognized the quilt with its riot of clashing colors as one of his blind mother's creations.

"Healers say I have to be patient." Eric was propped up on pillows. His body had wasted away. The arms resting on top of the quilt were half the size they'd once been. "Can't push myself too hard—I could still drop."

"Healers are full of bullshit." Vincent finished shuffling the cards and began to deal out new hands.

"Isn't Andrew teaching you medical stuff?" Eric chuckled, sorting his cards. Mr. Know-It-All Andrew, High and Mighty Shaman, had decided Vincent needed something productive to concentrate on during his recovery.

Vincent shrugged, keeping his expression cool. "I tried to convince the werebear to let me study tequila shots, but he didn't go for it."

"What sort of stuff does he have you doing?" Eric asked, his voice thin.

Vincent stared at his cards without seeing them. It was like his brother was fading away in front of him instead of getting better. "Emergency stuff. Stitching up cuts, fixing broken bones, frowning in moral disapproval, useful shit."

"Sounds interesting."

Of course he would think that. Eric wanted to pretend to be "normal" and go to a nine-to-five job. Vincent was happy being a freak, free of the burdens of society and their associated boredom. "Oh yeah, I'm thinking of taking my newfound knowledge and playing a doctor on TV."

"It still doesn't qualify you to decide when I can get out of this place. They're giving me the good Jell-O here, and I'm not going to risk that by being a pain in the ass." Eric dropped the six of clubs face-up onto the table.

"Damn, you should have told me about the Jell-O first. I wouldn't have bitched." The cards in Vincent's hand all seemed to blur together.

"Are you okay?" Eric asked, his voice positively dripping with brotherly concern.

I am so damn tired of people asking me that. Vincent played the eight of hearts. "I'm outstanding. Rediscovering my love of the minimum-wage shuffle."

"Please tell me you didn't take a service job." Eric looked up, his hand frozen in the act of pulling out a card.

Vincent couldn't blame Eric for his alarm. Vincent's brain-to-mouth filter wasn't strong enough to risk the temptation of dealing with the public. And in the tourist town of Perdition, almost everything required playing nice with the people and their money. "Don't worry. It's a job in a warehouse, shipping out orders. No contact with others except for my fellow drones."

Eric relaxed and played the ten of diamonds. "Sounds unbelievably boring."

"Keeps me out of trouble." Vincent shrugged. "Your hand."

Eric collected the cards on the table and dealt. "How's the new roommate?"

Way better than you at keeping her mouth shut. Evonne didn't want to talk about the husband she'd left in Alaska, and Vincent didn't want to talk, period. It was a match made in heaven. Vincent admired her for having the courage to leave everything she'd ever known. "I'm getting spoiled. The girl can cook. Man, Evonne cried when she saw the supermarket here. She loaded up two whole carts. I think she's determined to experiment with every non-caribou recipe she can find."

"You're behaving, right?"

Vincent rolled his eyes. "Sheesh, dude. What's with the concerned-older-brother shtick? No, I'm busy seducing her every night because I love taking advantage of vulnerable young women—you know, right after I tie them to train tracks and stand beside them cackling and twisting my mustache."

"Maybe you should do the train thing after seducing them. Otherwise, that's kind of sick."

"Duly noted. I'll bring up your suggestion at the next monthly bad-guy meeting. Right after they tell us where we can all get matching black hats. Can't be a bad guy without a black hat." *If only it were that simple.* Vincent threw down his card.

"I don't think I remember that particular rule." Eric folded his cards together and set them aside.

"Well, you're a good guy. You're not invited to the meetings." Vincent pointed at the table. "You gonna play?"

"You can't play a three on a jack." Eric's voice barely registered above the beeping equipment.

"Oh. Yeah. Damn, now you know my secret reserve weapon." Vincent tucked the three back in his hand. He wished they were playing cards back at their old apartment. *I want my old life back.* "Your hand."

Eric made no move to claim the cards. "Want to talk about it?"

"What are you, Dr. Phil? I'm talked out. It doesn't change anything." Vincent slumped in his chair. "I should feel like shit after what happened."

"It wasn't your fault, Vincent."

"I know, dammit. But it doesn't change the fact that you got your brain fried, we made an enemy who is determined to hunt us to the ends of the earth, and I got myself broken past the point of repair. Forgive me if I'm not big on playing the look-on-the-bright-side game here." People kept trying to cheer Vincent up, and he hated it. His life sucked, and some sulking went with the territory.

"I'm the one who wanted a normal, legal job," Eric replied. "I was the one who applied to work with Dalhard."

"True. I guess that does make it your fault. Congratulations. Hop on the guilt train. Makes stops at Regretville, Stupid-Decision Town, and Tequila-Shot Station. I'll find you a black hat somewhere. Meetings are every second Tuesday of the month."

Eric laughed weakly, lying heavily against the pillows. "I'll put it in the calendar."

"Guess I should let you get some sleep or something." Vincent collected the cards and stood up.

"Thanks for coming to visit."

"Yeah, well, you should be grateful. This place sucks, and you need to get out of it. I'm sick of coming here." Vincent watched his brother's eyes start to slide closed and realized it was much later than he'd thought. He shouldn't have kept Eric up so late. The healers were all very specific about him needing rest to recover.

Carefully, Vincent adjusted his brother's pillows and pulled the heavy quilt up to keep out the chill. Eric was already asleep, his bruised eyes standing out against his pale skin in a stark reminder of how badly Dalhard had damaged him.

At least you fought, Bro. Eric could have surrendered to the Beast's psychic influence, but instead, he'd chosen to resist, letting Dalhard rip his mind apart rather than surrendering. In the weeks right after the attack, Eric had lain in a coma, and no one could say if he'd ever come out. It had been the worst time in Vincent's life.

The memories were a blur. Vincent hadn't resisted. Like a lost puppy trailing its owners, he'd been ready to run after the man who'd destroyed his brother. He knew his mind had been tampered with, but it didn't make the memories any easier to bear.

"See you tomorrow." Vincent left quietly. His sharp hearing could pick up the coughs and murmurs of the half dozen patients sleeping or recovering in the rooms lining the halls.

Mishler used his *lalassu* healing gifts to run the off-grid medical facility for anyone who didn't want the hospitals getting involved and could pay a pricey sum—at least, for the patients he agreed to treat. Mishler had taken one look at Vincent and flatly refused to get involved. He'd accepted Eric, but no amount of pleading or threatening could make him allow Vincent to stay. If Andrew hadn't agreed to come with him and Evonne to Perdition, there would have been no one to knit up Vincent's bitter soul.

"Do I need to remind you of the rules, boy?"

Speak of the devil. Vincent turned to face the man himself, standing in a doorway, his stethoscope draped over a faded white T-shirt. There was no point in making excuses for the late hour. Mishler didn't want him around, even to visit his brother.

"You and your damn family. All you do is bring trouble on us and expect us to fix it." Mishler folded his arms over his chest, glaring as if he wanted to pin Vincent to the floor and begin a premature autopsy. "You push him, it'll drive him back into a coma. And this time, he wouldn't wake up."

Vincent didn't bother with a reply. He could guess why the man despised him, but he wasn't going to stop seeing his brother.

"Nothing to say?" Mishler taunted.

"It won't happen again," Vincent said quietly. That intimidation crap might work on gangsters and thugs trying to hide bullet wounds from the authorities, but it didn't impress him. The worst had already happened, which gave him a sort of Zen lack of concern about threats.

Something about Vincent's nonchalant reaction must have unsettled the healer. His next rebuke didn't hold the conviction of his previous efforts. "See it doesn't."

Vincent turned and walked away without another word. His acute hearing easily caught the increase in the healer's heart rate. Mishler wasn't as confident as he wanted to pretend. *Fine by me. As long as he helps Eric.* And if he didn't, then the healer would find out what a real problem looked like.

CHAPTER FIVE

"I'm telling you it looks real."

Cali winced at the woman's increasingly shrill insistence. She'd been listening to the woman and her friend talk about that viral shapeshifter video for the last twenty minutes. Cali gritted her teeth and hung onto the metal bar as the bus bounced along the road. *The joys of riding public transit.*

The number of people who believed in that clip was rising to alarming levels, though. Those things always attracted a number of I-want-to-believers and conspiracy theorists. But more and more people were weighing in on that video, and attempts to discredit it were failing.

If the damn thing was real, the exposure could undermine everything she'd worked for. She could end up on some black-market auction block, offered to the highest bidder for her "special" skills.

Not happening again. I'm not a scared kid anymore. The reminder didn't help the way it used to. She might not be a kid, but she had responsibilities. If she up and disappeared, what would happen to Speranza and her children or Mr. Dalhard? They were depending on her, and she wouldn't let them down.

The bus pulled into the prison lot. It was the weekly visitation run for those without a private means of transportation.

Cali stepped down onto the cracked pavement, careful to keep her concentration up. She couldn't afford to break character and draw attention to herself. Her stooped shoulders, mousy-brown ponytail, and cheap, poorly fitting clothes had all been chosen to portray a classic lifelong victim, one without enough spirit left to be worth poking—she hoped.

The guards ignored her as they dug through her worn leather bag, searching for potential contraband. Pretty girls who visited the facility were subjected to long, leering glances or outright propositions. She offered a silent prayer of relief that the disguise worked. Flattening out her natural curves always helped when she wanted to be unnoticed, but she was surprised how effective bulking out her nose and cheeks had been. Adding a clunky pair of glasses might not have been entirely necessary, but she wouldn't abandon them now.

The guard handed her back the bag and tersely reminded her of the rules. No physical contact except at the start and end of the visit, no giving the prisoner anything, hands in sight at all times. Cali nodded rapidly, trying to appear intimidated and frightened.

She joined the line of waiting visitors and trudged in behind them. Automatically, she catalogued the position of all the video cameras, adjusting her posture to avoid giving them a clear shot of her face. She wouldn't be able to avoid being seen entirely—there were too many surveillance cameras. But she didn't need to make it easy. Not after the fiasco at Lockbox.

Claiming a table bolted into the corner, she searched the room for Mr. Dalhard. The flaking pale-green paint on the walls revealed grey concrete blocks beneath. The chill crept up into the soles of her shoes. Men were filing in, shuffling like caged animals in their orange and green prison clothes. But Dalhard wasn't among them. *He'll be here. It's not like he has another engagement.* Still, her isolation was beginning to draw notice. A few prisoners were eyeing her table as if considering taking it away from her. If they forced her to resist them, she'd draw even more attention.

Mr. Dalhard sauntered into the waiting room as if entering a five-star restaurant, his dark hair loose instead of properly oiled back. A slow, sardonic smile curved his lips when he spotted her. "Colleen, so nice to see you again."

"Mr. Dalhard." She ducked her head, playing shyness to the hilt.

"Any trouble with picking up the paperwork I asked for?" He settled himself in the chair, his bright-orange jumpsuit the only jarring note in an elegant picture. Cali's worry jumped as she saw that he'd lost weight and muscle. His powerful frame seemed diminished.

"Only two more packages to pick up." Unfortunately, neither would be easy. Both were in private hands, and Karan held one. At least there would be no more industrial data centers with inconvenient traffic cameras.

"I knew you could do it." His easy smile was the one she remembered from her childhood, but it disappeared quickly. "I can't tell you how comforting it is to be able to rely on you. I'm so proud of how you've turned out. I always knew you had the potential to be the best."

His praise warmed her. "You can always count on me, Mr. Dalhard."

"I've never doubted it for a second." He reached out to pat her hand but stopped under the disapproving eye of the guard.

"Are you… all right?" Cali lowered her voice and leaned forward. "Is anyone giving you trouble?"

Mr. Dalhard inhaled deeply. "You don't need to worry about me. Now that I have some relative freedom to talk and interact with others, things are moving much smoother. In fact, I've found some intriguing possibilities."

He smiled again, but it was more of a predatory flash of teeth than shared affection. Cali's instincts flared. Mr. Dalhard looked more like one of the predators she'd learned to evade as a child than the man who'd rescued her from them.

He must have noticed her discomfort. "What's wrong? Has Karan been causing trouble?"

"Karan is also searching for the packages. I intercepted one of his agents at the second pickup." Cali took comfort in the familiar pattern of reporting to him, even if the news wasn't entirely pleasant. "I've infiltrated Right Hand Man, as you requested. But I think Mr. Fuentes hid the package."

"He was told to keep it safe until I return." Mr. Dalhard's fist clenched.

"His family disappeared two days ago, and he's been getting strange phone calls since then. His wife's work and the school say that they're ill, but there's no one at their home."

A burst of shouting interrupted their conversation. Mr. Dalhard leaned forward, putting himself between Cali and the large black man with the shaved head who was yelling at another inmate with bare arms sleeved in intricate tattoos. The guards immediately separated the two, escorting them from the visiting area. An elderly woman remained at the table, looking nervously after them. She seemed helpless and confused about what to do next. Cali wanted to go over and offer help, but it would have been out of character for her Colleen persona.

"We don't have much time left." Mr. Dalhard turned back to Cali. "Find out what's happening. I wouldn't put such a thing past Karan, but he's never had the proper vision to understand what is needed. You will be able to outthink him."

Another inmate stalked past their table, glaring at them in a blatant challenge. Cali wished she could have worn her knives. As she lowered her gaze, she saw Mr. Dalhard returning the glare, chin lifting to meet the implied threat.

"Cowering before predators is never an option. It only delays the inevitable," he murmured to her. "You can look up now."

"You need to be careful." She knew prison and how quickly things could go badly if someone caught the wrong kind of attention. Prison and the street had a lot in common, and she'd seen men in both places preparing to do violence to defend their reputations. "Maybe we should ask for protective custody again."

"I'm not without resources. And I understand what part I must play." Mr. Dalhard stretched his fingers. "I won't go back to isolation. Trust me."

She wanted to believe him. If anyone could resist the toughening kiln inside these walls, surely it would be Mr. Dalhard. His gifts would provide protection. But it would still be better if she could get him out quickly.

The guards began calling out that visiting hours were over.

"Focus on the packages," Mr. Dalhard continued. "I know I can leave matters in your capable and beautiful hands." He rose to his feet, smoothing his uniform tunic just as he'd always smoothed his suit before buttoning it.

"Of course, Mr. Dalhard. You can count on me." She made her promise to his retreating back, noting how the other prisoners shied away from him. Not a good sign. She would talk to his lawyers and make them push forward with their appeal.

As she waited in line, she scoured her memory. There had to be some kind of legal technicality they could exploit. The damn cop had followed him across the country, way out of Perdition's jurisdiction. The Alaska police had picked him up. There had to be some violation of protocol there. She'd push the lawyers until they found it.

Karan Samil should be the one in jail. He'd betrayed Mr. Dalhard. If she ran into Mr. Dalhard's former assistant, she would scratch his eyes out without hesitation before unleashing the demons accumulated during her grim childhood—the sort they made television movies about. She knew how to make someone suffer for a long time, how to make them pray for the release of death. It would be a shame to let all that knowledge be for nothing.

I can't go directly after Dalhard. Fine. Joe accepted the limitation. It happened all the time in police work. A suspect might be too powerful, too connected, or too public to risk tipping an investigation's hand early on. It didn't mean everything stopped. It meant getting creative.

And that meant tracking down Miss Colleen Avila, the only name in Dalhard's prison logbook. She'd been visiting him at least once a week since his arrival. He'd gotten a copy of her driver's license from the prison logs, and he doubted they were romantically involved. The address on her license was fake, making him also doubt that she was a legitimate business acquaintance.

If he could find her, he might be able to convince her to testify against her boss. Then he wouldn't need to worry about Vincent or Bernie. *As long as she's not one of Dalhard's zombies.* Even if she were, Andrew should be able to help break the compulsions.

Miss Avila made her weekly visits by bus, so Joe only needed to wait at the downtown drop-off and follow her. He studied the enlarged license photo again. With mousy brown hair, thick glasses, and pale lips, she looked as if she'd jump in fright at a whispering breeze. *Should be easy enough to spot.*

The bus pulled up and disgorged its passengers. Joe straightened up, ready to pounce as the small herd of milling people began to disperse. *Bingo.* Juggling a large paper cup of coffee and a battered leather satchel, the pale woman myopically peered at the bus signs. Her worn coat was too thin for the chill spring air. *Hello, Miss Avila.*

He joined the dwindling crowd, hanging back. His target never looked around as she waited under the sign for the crosstown bus. *I hate trailing people on public transit.*

At least they didn't have to wait long. He followed her onto the bus, sitting several rows behind her. She seemed ill at ease, clutching her bag as if afraid someone would wrench it away. *She can't be one of his zombies. Maybe he's got something on her.* That would be ideal. He could handle blackmail a lot easier than psychic coercion.

Joe was used to women who were louder than life—bright, flashy, and aggressive. This one could have faded right into the worn plastic seats. Her brown hair wisped around her face, the thin strands pulling loose from the ponytail at the nape of her neck. Her clothes were so unflattering that whoever sold them to her ought to have been prosecuted for malicious mischief. The thick glasses were perched on her nose as she peered out the window, her hands clenching the bag.

Except he wasn't sure if she was really as nervous as she seemed. Something seemed off about her, a false note somewhere in her appearance and behavior. His instincts screamed at him to hold back and pay attention. She was hiding something.

Even if she is, it doesn't matter. If she was hiding something, it would likely be exactly the kind of information he wanted or something he could use to get that information.

She pulled the cord and scrambled off the bus, leaving her half-empty coffee behind. Joe slipped out, finding a food truck to stand behind while he watched her.

He finally realized what was off. *She's not scanning the crowd.* Someone as nervous as she pretended to be would have been constantly searching her surroundings. But Miss Avila simply gathered her things and opened the door to an office building with the logo for Right Hand Man prominently displayed. That same company had served as a front for the group that had kidnapped Vincent and Eric for Dalhard, which meant Joe would be Miss Avila's new best friend, at least until he found the leverage he needed.

His badge got him past the secretary at the lobby desk. She

recognized Miss Avila's photo and told Joe to check the archives on the second level. Joe quickly climbed the stairs, wondering what he would find. Right Hand Man's website claimed they provided trained and bonded bodyguards at hourly and weekly rates. They had to offer some of that to maintain the illusion of legitimacy. But he suspected that a fair number of candidates ended up in Dalhard's experimental labs.

Maybe Miss Avila had been involved with the kidnapping. Maybe she was a human trafficker, a modern slave runner. Joe's pulse quickened in anticipation of the hunt. Starting an investigation was like having a first date. Everything was unknown, and all the potential was up for grabs. *Showtime.*

The archives consisted of a long room full of file cabinets behind a glass wall. Joe's target stood at a computer mounted on a pillar in the middle of the room. He hung back, watching her carefully. Her worn coat lay on top of one of the cabinets, her bulky bag resting on it. She didn't seem nearly as nervous about it now. *First tell*—a loose thread to tug on and unravel her disguise.

Despite her clumsiness in the street, her fingers danced gracefully over the keyboard, not wasting a motion or missing a beat. The movement was mesmerizing, at odds with her awkward image. *Second tell.*

She smiled briefly at something on the computer, and Joe froze. When she smiled, she transformed. The mouse vanished, leaving a sleek little kitty in its place. She pushed her glasses back into place, fiddled with the arm hinge for a moment, and resumed the illusion of dowdiness. *Third tell.*

His dormant hunter's instincts were coming back into play with a vengeance, urging him to strip away the false layers and find the true woman beneath. His instincts were that the woman underneath the keep-away persona would be a lot more interesting than her disguise. *First, concentrate on the job*, he told himself, rapping on the archive door.

She jumped, scrambling to adjust her glasses and peer at him through them. "Can I help you?"

"Sorry to frighten you." He offered a medium-grade smile, mostly professional with a hint of flirtatious dazzle. "My name is Detective Joe Cabrera, I'm with the—"

"Perdition Police Department," she finished, arms settling into an impenetrable folded barrier.

Crap. He should have guessed she'd recognize his name, and not for a good reason.

"Are you looking for Mr. Fuentes?" she asked, glaring at him. Joe couldn't help noticing her eyes were gorgeous, haunted shades of green. She should get contacts and stop hiding behind her glasses. He began to think of her the way he saw his home renovation projects—with an eye for the amazing potential hidden behind a faded or garish exterior.

"Actually, I'm looking for you, Miss Avila. I wanted to talk to you." He kept his tone very casual and nonthreatening. *Nothing to worry about here.*

"And you thought stalking me to my work was the best choice?" Her lips twitched, lifting at the corners as if she was trying to fight back a grin.

A sense of humor. Points for her and one point for me. He upgraded to the charming smile. "Is that a yes for talking to me?"

She responded, and his masculine internal sensors all pointed to the green. Then she must have remembered who she was dealing with and shut herself down. The hint of a smile vanished, and her arms tightened. "I don't have anything to say to you."

Time for the big guns: selective honesty. "I know you don't like me. In fact, you have some good reasons not to like me."

"You put my boss in jail." She glared. If the words had been bullets, he'd have six chest wounds.

Joe refused to take her bait. He needed to talk her back down. "He put himself in jail. I was just the one who found out what he'd done."

She folded her arms, looking like a stern librarian. "Unless you have a warrant or a subpoena or some other legal document saying I have to cooperate, I'm not talking to you."

CHAPTER SIX

"If you don't want to talk, then just listen." The handsome detective held out his hands as if begging Cali not to throw him out. "Yes, I put your boss in jail for money laundering and tax fraud. But that's only the tip of the iceberg. He hurt some friends of mine."

Does he want revenge? Cali wiped her damp palms on her skirt, checking the distance to the exit. The detective was between her and the door, but she could make it if she charged and took him by surprise.

He kept talking, the hypnotic rhythm of his voice lulling her. "He kidnapped a little girl—"

That's it. Cali's temper snapped. "That's a lie! He tried to save her."

Her hand flew to her mouth, covering it, as if her fingers could snatch back the words. Her control was better than that.

Joe looked at her, holding very still—one of those classic moves that cops made when they were trying not to escalate the situation. "Did he tell you differently?"

Next, he'll tell me that he's open to listening to my point of view. Colleen wouldn't challenge him. I can't let myself slip again. Cali rubbed at her neck and hung her head, giving herself time to regain her composure.

Joe held out his hand. "Why don't you let me buy you a cup of coffee, and you can tell me his side of things?"

I should say no. It would be the smart choice. But if she went with him, perhaps she could learn something that would help her boss. There must be some dirt hiding behind those gleaming teeth and sparkling dark eyes.

"Please, just five minutes, and then I'll go if you don't like what I have to say." His hand hung between them, waiting for her to make or break the connection.

She could resist the impulse to claw his eyes out for five minutes. "All right. Start talking."

"Is there somewhere we can talk in private? Maybe out of the office?" He glanced around as if expecting a spot to leap into existence.

Out of the corner of her eye, Cali saw Mr. Fuentes staring at his telephone, despair tugging his face downward. She couldn't risk getting a cop interested in what was happening in the office. "There's an atrium downstairs. I usually eat lunch there."

"Sounds perfect to me. Shall we?" He bowed like a fairy-tale prince. Cali had never seen someone achieve that pose in real life, and despite her intention to dislike him, she couldn't help a quick smile.

Grabbing her clunky leather bag, she shooed him ahead of her. A hint of a roguish grin teased the corner of his lips, and once they were outside the archives, he held back to let her precede him. His warm hand settled in the small of her back, and Cali fought the urge to twitch away from the casual touch. It triggered too many bad memories.

To her surprise, he withdrew his hand a moment later. She studied him as unobtrusively as she could, wondering whether he'd noticed her reaction or pulled back for his own reasons. He kept a careful distance in the elevator, but every time their eyes met through a reflective surface, he grinned at her.

White-haired Tony waved at her as they approached the coffee cart. "Hey, Miss Colleen. It's early for you. Who's your friend?"

She smiled at him as he poured coffee into two cups. The elderly little Italian baristo had been a fount of useful information. He knew everything about everyone in the building and was more than happy to share it. "This is Joe. Joe, this is Tony. He makes the best coffee in the city."

"Too kind, too kind." Tony waved off the compliment, handing her a coffee with a splash of milk and two sugars. "This one, she is the best tipper in the city. And the nicest—always willing to listen to an old man ramble. Joe, do you take cream and sugar?"

"One sugar, please." Joe pulled out his wallet and handed Tony a ten. "Don't worry about the change." Cali wondered if he'd done it because of Tony's comment about the tipping or if he was naturally a spendthrift.

"A keeper, this one!" Tony gave him the cup. "You come by later, Miss Colleen. I have pictures of Ronnie from the science fair. She got top marks. Myself, I couldn't understand a word of it, but the judges were impressed."

"Sure thing, Tony. Save me one of your grilled-tuna specials." From some of the hints he'd dropped earlier, she suspected Tony knew something useful about Mr. Fuentes. She fidgeted with her cup, twisting the paper insulator, suddenly uncomfortable. This wasn't quite how she'd imagined an encounter with Detective Joe Cabrera would proceed. He seemed nice, even genuinely personable, and she wasn't ready to see him as a person instead of an adversary.

"What was the science-fair thing about?" Joe asked as they sat down on the wide stone rim of the burbling fountain.

"Tony's granddaughter is competing for a college scholarship. If she gets one of the top three places, she'll get full tuition." And if not, then Cali would see to it that an anonymous donation or two made its way to the family.

"Good for her. There must be stiff competition." He sipped his coffee, and his eyes widened with surprise and pleasure. Cali hid a smile. She hadn't been kidding about Tony's baristo skills.

Too bad she couldn't indulge. She needed to keep all of her attention focused on her companion. Reluctantly, she put her untasted cup aside. "The whole family has been focused on it for weeks. And your time is ticking away."

"Maybe I'm just enjoying the coffee." Joe grinned, saluting her with the cup. "And the company."

A surge of frustration reminded her that they were on opposite sides. He'd used a predictable manipulation tactic and expected her to fall for it because everyone knew that plain-Janes couldn't keep their brains when confronted with an attractive man. "Please don't make fun of me. I'm not an idiot."

His grin drooped and vanished. "I never said you were. I don't understand."

Cali's patience disappeared. Forgetting her role as Colleen, she pinned Joe with her gaze. "Then forget the flirting, and tell me why you're really here. You're a cop investigating Mr. Dalhard. I'm the only one who visits him in prison. It doesn't take a genius to connect the dots. You want dirt to take him down."

Joe swallowed. He hadn't expected Colleen to challenge him directly. And yet it didn't surprise him. He'd guessed that the mousy, frumpy exterior was a disguise. Now the real Colleen Avila was stepping forward, forest-glen eyes snapping with fury.

All right. The direct approach. He put down his cup. "You're right. I'm hoping to find evidence I can use to keep him in jail so that I don't have to ask a traumatized child to testify. Bernie and her mother have enough to deal with."

Colleen's hands tightened into fists. "Enough to deal with? The girl needed proper help, not the drugs her mother pushed on her. She needed to be rescued."

Understanding dawned. Joe had seen his fair share of awful situations as a police officer. Colleen's nervousness, her vehemence about Bernie, and the tension at physical contact, it all pointed to abuse. *Have to be careful not to frighten her.* "Her mother did the best she could. True, she didn't understand that her child was speaking to ghosts instead of hallucinations, but really, how many people would that explanation occur to?"

He watched her eyes carefully. No flicker of surprise. She knew about the *lalassu.*

"I can understand why you might think your boss was being noble. You know about what he can do." Joe leaned forward slightly. "Maybe you thought he was trying to protect his own kind from the ignorant masses. But nothing changes how he used his abilities to convince an exhausted and desperate mother to give up her only child, a child she'd devoted her life to."

"She still gave her up." Colleen's fingers folded and unfolded a pleat in her skirt.

For an assistant, she knows a lot of details about Bernie's kidnapping. But he didn't think she'd been privy to everything. It was time to poke her with an uncomfortable truth. "I know Martha, Bernie's mom. She gave up a six-figure career, her marriage, and her home all in a desperate attempt to make sure that Bernie had the best help possible. Nothing mattered more to her than her daughter's safety and happiness."

Colleen looked down at the creases marring the front of her skirt. "Love isn't always enough. It doesn't make what she did right."

"See, I can't agree with that. Love doesn't mean that someone won't make mistakes, but it does mean that they care enough to try. Which counts for a lot in my book." Joe saw the tiny pinch at the edges of her eyes and mouth, evidence that his words had struck a tender spot in her soul. He decided to see if his hunch was right. "You obviously care about André Dalhard. Otherwise you wouldn't visit him in prison."

She took the bait. "He took a chance on me when no one else would. Gave me a job when no one else would even take my résumé. He needs my help."

Joe didn't let his inner satisfaction seep into his expression. She didn't sound like a mind-controlled zombie. Every answer gave him more puzzle pieces to put together, and he was starting to see the edges of difficult times lurking in her past. He held still, wanting to avoid spooking her. "What does he need your help with?"

"I'm his liaison with the board of directors for Dalhard Industries."

A lie—a good one, but definitely a lie. She held her chin steady and looked him right in the eye, but it was the only time she'd done that without being angry. He needed to push just a little to keep her off balance if he wanted to keep getting the truth. "I thought Karan Samil took over the company."

Bingo. Mouth tight, chin lifting. "There are still people who are loyal to Mr. Dalhard."

Good to know. "Like you. I guess you feel that you owe him something, right?"

"He saved me." Her hand flew to her mouth again, the same way it had when she'd had her outburst in the office upstairs. Joe had seen the reaction before when people said more than they'd intended.

He let it slide, pretending not to have noticed. "Okay. I can understand that. I'll be honest with you, Colleen. I don't think that Dalhard acted alone, and I need your help if I'm going to prove it."

"I've seen what you're willing to do for proof. I shouldn't have come." The venom in her voice could have dropped a bull. Her fingers curled into fists. For a moment, her hair seemed brighter under the lights, but when Joe looked closer, the golden highlights vanished. *A trick of the light. Too bad—she'd make a cute blond.* He wanted to take her hair out of that ponytail and watch it fall over her shoulders before he began to kiss them then maybe slide her ill-fitting blouse to the side… he caught himself. *Not the right time.*

"Please don't go." He held out his hand, careful not to touch her for both her sake and his. "Even if you don't agree with me, you can't be okay with everything that Dalhard has done. I wasn't kidding before when I said that he tried to kill me."

She hesitated, visibly calming herself down. "You mean that? As in the literal truth?"

From the way her hands were twisting tightly together, she hadn't wanted to ask the question but had done it anyway. *Five points for courage.* "Yes. He caught me sneaking onto his property to rescue Bernie. The assistant, Karan, wanted to shoot me, but Dalhard didn't want to leave direct evidence. They knocked me unconscious and left me in a building that was wired with explosives. If a friend hadn't gotten me out, I'd have vanished under the rubble. I doubt anyone would have ever found my body, or if they had, they wouldn't have been able to identify it."

He'd had plenty of close calls in his life, some before the uniform and some after it, but that day had come closer than most to being his last one. The memory still left him unsettled. *What if Michael hadn't woken up? What if the bomb had been set for twenty seconds less?* He shoved the endless round of possibilities aside to concentrate on Colleen, who was watching him with something akin to sympathy.

"Are you sure? If you were unconscious—"

"I heard him give the order. And you know that he has ways of making people do what he wants." He watched her to see if she was aware of Dalhard's psychic abilities. She showed no surprise, no confusion. She knew.

"He only uses them when there's no other choice. He was trying to protect the little girl and stop you from taking her." Colleen stood up.

Joe's time was almost up. If she walked away without agreeing to help him, he wouldn't get another chance. The more that he talked to her, the more he suspected that there were some unexpected depths to Colleen Avila—depths he wanted to explore in a way he hadn't experienced since before Michael told him about the *lalassu.* "Please, Colleen. All I care about is making sure that people are safe."

Her eyes narrowed. "You really mean that."

It hadn't been a question, but Joe answered it anyway. "I do."

"What about catching the bad guys?" She settled back onto the fountain rim, watching him. The klutzy, dowdy secretary was gone, leaving behind a passionate and vibrant woman. *Why does she hide herself away? It's criminal.* Joe gave himself a mental high five for penetrating the mask but held off on any further congratulations. The encounter could still go sideways.

"Stopping criminals is one way to keep people safe. But the best way is to make sure that civilians don't need to act on their own." Joe hadn't ever admitted that to anyone else. Cops were supposed to live for the arrest, but he'd always found more satisfaction in giving a helping hand than in whipping out handcuffs. "I won't lie. I still think your boss has hurt people and needs to be off the street. And I don't think he was the only one."

He held his breath as she considered his tentative partnership proposal. He'd put his last card down on the table, and either he or she would walk away with all the chips.

Finally, she spoke. "I'll help you find information on Karan. But I won't help you persecute Mr. Dalhard."

"Just keep an open mind. If I'm wrong about him, I'd like to know." *Will you be willing to be wrong about him, Colleen?*

She picked up her coffee cup again, running her thumbs along the plastic lid. "So how does this work? Do we set up a secret email account or something?"

Too many movies. He hid his smile. She might still storm off if he offended her. "Well, I'll give you my card so you can call me, but mainly, we find a nice, plausible excuse to meet up frequently. Like dinner."

He caught a flash of forest green as she forgot to avoid his gaze. "What do you mean, dinner?"

"You and me, going out. Garden Delight makes some of the best eggrolls you'll ever taste." He grinned as she glared at him. The more he got to know Colleen Avila, the more he liked her. The girl had a spine of steel.

"I've asked you not to make fun of me. It's obvious I'm not your type of girl."

"And what do you think is my type?" Joe teased. She hadn't stood up again, so he was willing to bet that part of her liked his flirting. He'd never pursue a woman who wasn't interested, but he did enjoy a gentlemanly coaxing every now and then.

"Gorgeous model types," she replied quickly, eyeing him up and down. "I'd bet you usually go for the prettiest girl in the club. Though she doesn't last long."

Joe shrugged. "I haven't been a long-term kind of guy."

"But you'd like to be." Her nails tapped against the stone parapet surrounding the fountain. "Someone close to you found love recently, and it's eating you up inside. You're trying hard not to be jealous, but since then, the bimbos don't cut it anymore."

Joe was impressed. She was one hell of a cold reader if she could pick up so many details from his body language.

She tilted her head to one side, the overhead lights glittering off her glasses. "Actually, it's more than that, isn't it? Something hit you hard recently, something that made you want to reevaluate everything in your life. But it wasn't nearly dying in that building—it was something else that happened afterward."

Suspicion coated his spine with frosty breath. Her examination of him was moving deeper than he wanted to go.

"Except that's not what you asked me." A pleased smile curved those plain lips, and Joe found himself wondering what they would taste like. No flavored lip gloss or lipstick to get in the way—just her pure, natural taste. He forced himself to pay attention as she continued to talk.

"You like flirting, and you want to be seen with the hottest girl in the room, someone who is equally sexy whether she's dressed in a gorgeous dress or jeans and a sweatshirt. When the job gets to be too much, you want to be able to talk to her and have her understand. You want someone with an edge, a little dangerous and able to color outside the lines. Someone strong but who still needs you. And you're waiting for fate to deliver her to you. How'd I do?" She gave a wicked little librarian's smile from behind those glasses.

"You should do horoscopes." Hiding his discomfort behind a joke, Joe couldn't completely suppress a twinge of uncertainty about his plan. With that kind of insight, Colleen could creep past all of his well-constructed barriers.

She stood up, obviously satisfied. "It's just observation. Comes in handy in my line of work."

"Cops need to be able to read people too. But I'm having a hard time figuring you out." He handed her his card. "See you tomorrow at seven?"

"Until tomorrow." She tucked it into her pocket and walked away. From what he could see through her ill-fitting clothes, she had a spectacular body, one that curved in all the right places. She was a mystery, and no cop worth his badge could resist a mystery. *See you tomorrow, Miss Avila, and then we'll find out who reads whom the best.*

DEAL

CHAPTER SEVEN

Still in disguise as Colleen, Cali watched Ken Fuentes pretend to work in his office. He stared at his computer screen, his fingers clasped in a steeple and braced against his lips. *He doesn't want to talk about whatever is preoccupying his thoughts.* When he wasn't doing that, he was fidgeting—toying with papers and pens or picking them up and putting them down without looking at them. *Nervous energy to burn.* And he studiously avoided the photo of his family on the wall, but if he did catch sight of it, his face briefly crumpled into despair. *Something is wrong at home.*

If he hadn't been distracted, Cali wouldn't have been able to just show up and pretend to be the new administrative assistant. She glanced at the clock. It was almost eleven thirty, which meant the daily phone call should be coming into the office at any minute.

She'd installed a bug in Fuentes's office telephone the previous night. With luck, the calls would lead to both the missing data and to Karan Samil. She could picture the pleased smile on Detective Cabrera's face. *Stop that.*

The man was annoyingly distracting even when he wasn't present. She'd armed herself thoroughly against him, but he hadn't turned out to be a self-important, petty bully. His story about the mother, Martha, held a ring of truth. He believed it without any doubt or hesitation. Mr. Dalhard must have been wrong, at least in part. *He'd be horrified to learn that he made a mistake.*

Or would he? The number of "mistakes" that she'd noticed over the last few years was growing too rapidly for her comfort. Had he really left the detective in a building wired to explode? If so, then Cabrera's persistence in tracking Mr. Dalhard down was understandable.

Her thoughts kept going back to the detective. She'd been unable to get away from him since their encounter that morning. His warm smile and easy laugh dug holes in her protective layers. *I should cancel dinner.* She was perfectly capable of doing her own investigation, and if Detective Cabrera wasn't the enemy, then she should concentrate on retrieving the data and getting Mr. Dalhard out of prison. But she'd inexplicably said yes, and even more inexplicably, she was reluctant to change it to a no. As much as she told herself that accepting had been a practical decision, an opportunity to gather intelligence, she knew she was lying to herself.

I can't afford this kind of distraction right now. She pushed on the tiny earbud to make sure it was still securely lodged in place. As soon as Fuentes picked up the phone, she would be able to hear everything.

The phone rang, and Cali braced herself, deliberately slowing her breathing to keep her composure.

"Hello?" Fuentes began.

"Do you have what I asked for?" The second voice was male but nondescript—no trace of an accent, medium timbre, not distinctively young or old.

"Not yet, but I will soon, Mr. Samil. I swear it." Desperation wrung all the depth from Fuentes's voice, bringing it perilously close to squeaking.

Karan. Surprise flooded Cali's system. She'd only allowed herself to hope for a flunky, someone she could follow up the chain to the former assistant, not the man himself.

"Your family will be very disappointed. They have not been enjoying my accommodations." Karan's threat twisted a knot in Cali's stomach. She couldn't take the data and leave innocent people caught in the crossfire.

"Please don't hurt them," Fuentes pleaded. "I'm doing everything I can to get it as quickly as possible."

"I am not certain that is entirely true. My proposition is not unreasonable, and you agreed to my terms, promising delivery in two days."

"Two or three. Please, just don't hurt them," Fuentes begged. Cali closed her eyes, anger building a controlled simmer in her gut.

"This conversation is becoming tedious and repetitive. Do as I ask, and your family will be fine. Attempt to be clever or to betray me, and they will suffer. Am I clear?" He sounded bored, as if repeating a lesson for a particularly stupid student.

"The courier says it will be here tomorrow. Please let me talk to them." Fuentes's demand showed he wasn't completely broken. Cali didn't think that Karan would be ruthless enough to kill hostages rather than going through the trouble of keeping them captive, but it was best to be certain.

There was a brief pause and then a pair of clicks on the line. "Dad?"

"Matt? Are you okay?"

"I'm okay. Mariana's okay too. Mom's still asleep, but she looks okay." From his high voice, he sounded like a prepubescent boy of about twelve.

"Okay. I need you to be strong, Matt. I'm going to do everything I can to get you home soon, I promise." Fuentes's words to his son broke Cali's heart. A family who cared about each other was a rare thing in her world and should be protected.

"I trust you have sufficient confirmation that I am not reneging on my side of the bargain," Karan said.

"I do." All the vitality had drained out of Fuentes's voice, leaving it small and withered.

The line went dead, and Cali went into action. She'd planned to keep her partner, Hood, out of her investigation into Fuentes, but now she needed their mutual resources—in particular, his husband, Harley. She quickly filled Hood in on the situation.

"Shit," Hood's resonant voice said over the line. His Jamaican accent always grew stronger when he was upset. "What can we do?"

"We have to find them. Ask Harley to start running the computer stuff and get the entire crew searching."

"You know we will, but this is beyond our usual skill set. Raiding pawnshops and clubhouses is one thing, but these people are dangerous."

He was right. *Dammit.* She couldn't send street kids into situations where they might come into direct confrontation with someone like

Karan or his thugs. She quickly reconsidered. "Tell them to keep their eyes open for anything unusual. We'll pay them their regular salaries just to be aware of anything that could lead us to Karan or the Fuentes family, but we won't be accepting any more commissions until this is settled."

"They won't like being held back."

"They're too smart not to recognize the danger. If they find something and get caught, then we still won't know where to find these people. Put it to them that way, and they'll listen." Cali mentally ran down the list of commissions. "We found the watch for Mr. Carro and the ring for Mrs. Schild. There shouldn't be anything else outstanding."

"Any ideas where they should start looking?" Hood asked.

"If I did, this whole situation would be moot." Cali rubbed the bridge of her nose. Maybe Fuentes hadn't been as oblivious as she'd thought. If he'd suspected her, then he could have moved the data to keep it from her. Which meant anything that happened to his family was partly her fault. "Karan must have them stashed somewhere relatively nearby. He wouldn't want to transport hostages too far away—not if he's planning to return them. Too much chance of an escape during the transition."

"That's a big if. He might not be planning to return them at all." Having spent his life off the grid, Hood had thrown some work Cali's way before Mr. Dalhard had rescued her from the street. Together, Cali and Hood had built a network, giving street kids other options besides joining gangs or becoming pimps.

"I know." Both of them were all too familiar with how quickly things could go badly without the protections of accepted society. An idea dawned on her, and she couldn't decide if it was terrible or brilliant. "I might have another option."

"Detective Hampton, we pay you a substantial amount of money to ensure these sorts of errors do not occur." Karan Samil allowed himself the luxury of glaring at the portly Perdition police officer.

"Hey, I told you about it, didn't I?" Hampton lifted his hands inside his long trench coat. "Without me, you'd never know the thief was targeting you."

The detective was lucky that Karan did not have the time to teach him a lesson on the drawbacks of being smug with one's superiors. Instead, Karan studied the photograph. The image was surprisingly clear for something captured with a government camera. He could even see the woman's eyes beginning to widen and her mouth opening in surprise from the red-light camera flash.

"The sergeant didn't even realize all the data firms had you as a common client." Hampton jammed his thumbs into his belt, obviously proud.

"Do you know who this woman is?" Karan asked.

"Just one more scumbag out to make a profit. I'll find her. I could use the overtime." The detective probably thought his approach was subtle. He wanted more money. Agents always wanted more money. Such requests thinned the herd, purging it of the stupid ones. Unfortunately, Karan recognized the woman and knew what must have been stored at the data centers. *The other parts of the list.* Not to mention information he needed to run Dalhard Industries properly.

"She is somewhat above the level of scumbag. Her name is Boomerang, and she is one of the most successful thieves currently operating on the East Coast."

The detective frowned. "So how do I find her?"

Karan briefly considered allowing the detective to do the search. The fool was greedy for the acknowledgment of his peers although too lazy to actually put in the necessary work. If he had recognized his limitations, he could have been quite useful, but Karan suspected the idiot would inevitably try blackmail. He would jump ahead, never realizing that he was leaping off a cliff and onto the rocks. Karan did not believe in second chances, but he also did not believe in unnecessary risks. He had his own plans in place to recover the stolen data. "You do not find her. You continue to concentrate on ensuring that André Dalhard remains incarcerated for the foreseeable future."

"Sure thing, Boss." The obsequious smile on the detective's face was repulsive. He accepted the folder of material that Karan had provided. It included further evidence of Dalhard's crimes, ensuring he stayed in prison and out of Karan's way. The detective could claim to have found it and gain the credit for a skilled investigation, earning promotions if he was smart.

But something about the insolent way the man picked up his grey fedora and put it on his head made Karan decide to issue a more direct warning. "Detective, I do not encourage misguided initiative by my employees. If you attempt to improvise, then I will be displeased."

His reputation for efficient brutality must have been sufficient. The detective blanched and nodded. *A fool but a useful one.* Hampton liked to present himself as a rogue, willing to break free of the unnecessary red tape and regulations that kept modern police from protecting their cities. But one predator could always recognize another.

Karan dismissed the detective from his mind as soon as the man left. Either the detective would perform the task adequately, or he would fail. The contingency measures would be in place for both.

As he checked his email, annoyance threatened his careful mask. When he'd assumed official control of the company, he began having difficulty maintaining his usual rational composure. Many members of the board and others in key positions were men and women who were still under the influence of Dalhard's Siren gifts. They were beginning to show signs of independence as Dalhard's psychic influence waned due to time and distance, both of which weakened a Siren's hold.

Mapping out the extent of his former employer's psychic failsafes was taking longer than expected. Subconscious commands prevented a target from implicating Dalhard in anything illegal, encouraged him or her to follow Dalhard's instructions, and kept the victim from taking any active steps against the man. But even without breaking the compulsion, there were limitations and loopholes that threatened to undermine Dalhard's commands, rendering them useless and even giving them the potential to backfire. One of the Harris siblings had actually called the police despite being apparently "controlled" at the time. Karan had spent months searching for those kinds of loopholes.

A dozen or so subjects had been sufficient to allow him to plumb the depths of the failsafe. He knew where the pressure points were, the ones that would break a man before allowing him to violate Dalhard's instructions. More importantly, he knew how to navigate around them. Perhaps one day he would find out how McBride had broken free of the failsafe, but fourteen suicides and fatal accidents in the last four months had left the employees shaken. Karan could continue his research later.

I could still arrange an accident for Dalhard. The thought tempted him, whispering with seductive caresses. Even with his boss's Siren powers, money could buy a convenient assault or accident that would result in Dalhard's tragic death. Karan had not longed to destroy a man so thoroughly since his sister Priya had been murdered at the hands of their family's employer when they were both children, and Karan had taken revenge. His sister had been too trusting, too convinced the rules would protect her. The man responsible had died too quickly. He never got a chance to reveal what had happened to Priya's body, leaving Karan's parents in anguish and providing a costly lesson in the dangers of righteous haste. Karan never required repetition for his lessons.

He needed to make sure Dalhard did not have any surprises waiting, particularly ones that would be triggered after an untimely death. Once Karan could be certain the venom was drained, he would enjoy crushing the viper under his boot.

Chapter Eight

Joe rubbed at his aching eyes. *Join the police force, catch the bad guys, watch a twenty-second video clip more repeatedly than a feature-film animator. Feel the glamour.* With a sigh, he queued up the video again. There had to be some trace of his thief there—a reflection, some kind of visual break in the film. He pounded the desk in frustration. It didn't help, and he considered whether or not throwing something would be a career-limiting choice. Hitting play, he stared at the screen, trying to find what he'd missed. He'd gone to the site to try and find a sewer entrance or some other way she might have gotten out without crossing the camera's path. But there was nothing. The thief would have had to pass in front of one of the two cameras.

The footage finished without any eureka moment. Time for a new tactic. He pulled out the red-light photo and tried to make himself see it with fresh eyes. This thief was careful, disabling the security system like a pro. *Okay, let's say I'm her. I'm walking out the front door because it's the easiest one to deactivate the alarm on. Probably how I got in too. I'm feeling good, thinking I've covered all my bases, when a flash goes off in front of me.*

Her face showed surprise in the image. Either she hadn't known about the red-light camera, or she hadn't been able to access the system. Joe continued mentally walking in his suspect's shoes. *I know I need to get away, but I also know I have some time. The alarms didn't go off, but now there's a chance someone will see this picture and realize that I'm not supposed to be there. I need to make sure I don't appear in any other footage.*

She'd succeeded spectacularly. Joe had gone through the security tapes in a six-block radius and hadn't caught a glimpse of her. Of course, coverage was spotty. This wasn't London or Vegas with more CCTV cameras than people. She could have easily taken a path that avoided further cameras once she got past the intersections at Roosevelt Drive and New Orleans Avenue.

I can't go up—unless I can climb walls like Spider-Man. Joe wasn't ruling it out yet, but a normal person would need specialized equipment to get up the buildings across the street from Lockbox. And his thief wasn't carrying coils of rope or other climbing gear.

I can't wait for a distracting car. The streets were empty, and the longer she loitered, the more likely she would be noticed.

I need to go east or west along Third, or I need to go down Roosevelt or New Orleans. Those were the only options, and either meant exposing herself to one of the cameras. But which one did she choose? After a moment's thought, he discarded the footage from Roosevelt. Once the sedan went through the intersection, there was no more movement. If his thief had gone that way, the tapes were useless. She'd scrubbed them or hacked them to set up a loop—except Joe's instincts told him that she hadn't planned on altering footage from cameras outside Lockbox. Otherwise, she would have dealt with the red-light camera. *I'm too smart to get caught in a trap. The more systems I alter, the more risk I have of getting caught. I planned the Lockbox job to avoid being noticed. If it had gone as planned, the outdoor footage would have vanished for recycling before the theft was noticed.*

Joe went through the New Orleans Avenue footage again. Whoosh—a grey sedan. Then the homeless couple stumbling down the block and poking through the dumpster. No classy pin-up business girls. "I'm missing something."

Again. Sedan. Homeless couple.

Again. Sedan.

That time, he saw the detail that had been nagging at him subliminally since he'd first watched the tape: the woman's shoes.

They were only in the frame for a second or two—pale high heels. No homeless woman wore high heels for a dumpster stroll. Sneakers, boots, and even rags were common. Homeless people needed footwear that let them stay on their feet for days and nights without causing problems. Even if she'd found high heels somewhere, she wouldn't be wearing them.

Other inconsistencies popped out. Her filthy coat hung loosely over her arms and dragged on the ground, far too large for her. That wasn't necessarily a red flag on its own. After all, the homeless didn't get a lot of fashion choices. But a closer look at the man showed he didn't have a coat, just layers of sweaters and shirts. The woman's coat would have been a good size for him. Joe stared at the screen, not quite ready to commit to his suspicion that the homeless woman was the thief.

The scenario stayed plausible on first examination. The thief could have noticed the homeless man and offered him money to use his coat and walk with her until they got past camera range. She'd have to keep her shoes on, but it was low risk. Not many people paid attention to footwear. A quick scrub of her makeup and a little dirt on her face would complete the disguise, making her skin appear darker. The only flaw in his theory was the blond hair.

There was no way she'd been carrying a blond wig, and he was willing to bet his pension that the homeless guy wouldn't happen to have one on hand either. Joe scraped his hand across his scalp, his close-cropped hair rustling under his palm like brush bristles. He couldn't go to Modnik with this theory. He needed something solid.

Before he left, he printed out a photo of the homeless couple. Tracking the man down would be a challenge, but if Joe could find him, then maybe he'd have the evidence he needed. He tidied up the archive. It always drove him nuts on TV when cops found a lead and then ran off, leaving everything scattered across a desk. That was a great way to ensure the chain of evidence got broken and thrown out of court.

"What are you doing here, Creepy Cabrera?" Hampton's loud question caught Joe off guard as he put away the last box.

Even so, Joe refused to show any weakness. He kept his voice casual. "Reviewing some footage for a case."

"Yeah, the glamorous life of sending out parking tickets." Hampton smirked. "Too bad they don't let you work the big-boy cases anymore."

Joe didn't doubt that Hampton was enough of an asshole to be taking a poke at him despite the lack of an audience, but something was off about the man. Sweat shone on Hampton's forehead as if he'd been running. *Or hiding something.* "Is there something I can help you with?"

"So you can screw it up the way you did your own cases? Hell no."

Hampton sneered, but Joe spotted the sudden clenching of his fist. Before Joe could call him on it, Hampton continued. "I don't know how you tricked the shrink into giving you your badge back, but nutcases like you are a disgrace to the uniform."

That blow struck at Joe's core. He clamped down on his reaction and left the archive. Replying to a bully only wasted time, and he was ten times the cop that Hampton could even dream of being. Joe's teeth locked together, and every angry stride sent them clashing together. He'd made one mistake, and it dogged at his heels. Hampton did sloppy work quarter after quarter, making the job twice as hard for the decent cops on the force, but scandal never stuck to him. *I need to get out of here and cool down.*

He snagged his coat as he walked through the bull pen. The rookie, Salazar, saw him and then deliberately turned his head away. The kid's cheeks were red with embarrassment, but he'd already grasped an essential rule of thumb—don't glom on to the guy at the bottom of the pecking order unless you want to join him. *Not my problem.*

Joe's temper didn't cool until he was stalking down the sidewalks. He wasn't even sure where to go. *Away is enough of a destination.* Joe made himself stop and breathe. He couldn't let Hampton get to him. *The opinion of idiots isn't worth improving.* His mom had told him that years ago, after his father was killed and the reaction of his schoolmates nearly drove Joe into dropping out. He couldn't let Hampton chase him out of this job, not when he'd worked so hard for it.

As his brain started to pick up again, Joe realized he'd played into Hampton's agenda. The other man had deliberately driven him out of the archive. Maybe he should call the sergeant and warn her, get someone to check on Hampton.

His phone vibrated in his pocket, and Joe fumbled it out, nearly dropping the slick brick. He missed big receivers that were firmly attached to a wall. The number was unfamiliar, but he cautiously answered. "Hello?"

"Detective Joe Cabrera? It's Colleen."

Joe immediately straightened, hoping she wasn't calling about having second thoughts or to break their date. Her next words drove everything else from his mind.

"I need your help."

Cali held her breath as she waited for Joe to reply. She'd walked five blocks to find a working pay phone. Creating a record of this call at work would have been incredibly stupid.

"What's wrong? What do you need?" Joe asked.

"It's about my boss, Mr. Fuentes." She explained what she'd overheard on the phone, though she made it sound as if she'd accidentally picked up the line instead of deliberately listening in.

"Shit!" The expletive burst out of Joe's mouth like a gunshot. "Does he know that you heard?"

"I don't think so. I waited, and then I snuck out of the office to call you from a pay phone. I checked, and no one has heard from his wife and children for several days." She scanned the street, checking to see if anyone was paying undue attention to her conversation.

"You have to be careful." His rough concern surprised her. It didn't sound like a cop worrying about a source but rather like a man worried about a woman.

This isn't supposed to happen. Her Colleen persona was designed to be essentially asexual and anonymous, someone everyone could rely on and no one remembered five minutes after she left. *Keep focused.* What mattered was rescuing the Fuentes family and destroying Karan's leverage before Fuentes handed over the list. And if she wanted Karan to pay officially for what he'd done, she needed the detective's help. "Do you think you can find them before something horrible happens?"

"There are a lot of places to hide someone if you don't want them to be found. And I don't think I can count on Mr. Fuentes cooperating with me. If I knew where they'd been taken, I'd have a better chance of knowing where to look."

Cali's fingers tightened around the heavy receiver, disappointed. "I see."

"Colleen, please don't give up. I'm not saying I won't try, but I don't want to break any promises to you." His breath razzed against the microphone. "I'll need more details, like a timeline of what happened."

"I could help with that." She already had most of the information. And Harley would have more soon.

"You can't," he said quickly then slowed to a more reasonable verbal pace. "I mean, I'd be more comfortable if you stayed out of this. Karan is dangerous, and if he thought you were interfering, he'd make you disappear in a snap."

Don't-trouble-your-pretty-head dismissals usually had Cali seeing red, but somehow, Joe's adorable concern had her fighting a smile. He had no idea of what she was capable of. Still, she wasn't about to let him get away with casual chauvinism. "You need my help. There's no missing-person report, no official reason for you to get involved, and it could be seen as an extension of your vendetta against Mr. Dalhard and his people. Stop assuming that I'm helpless, and tell me what I can do."

Softly buzzing static filled the empty line. Cali wondered if she'd gone too far and blown her cover. But she couldn't stand by and let innocent people be hurt.

"You know, I like it a lot better when you show me the real Colleen instead of hiding behind your office-mouse mask." Joe's warm voice seeped through the phone line like liquid sunlight. "All right. Here's what you're going to do. Check the office records and see if you can find the telephone number of the person who called. Find a timeline of what happened and when the wife and kids disappeared. Send me the information, and I'll see where I can go from there."

Cali's cell phone buzzed with an update from Hood. One of their crew thought that she might have spotted the Fuentes kids at a cheap diner near the train tracks.

"Colleen? Are you still there?"

She shoved the phone back in her pocket. "I'm here. I'll get you what you need."

"Just be careful. Because I am definitely looking forward to dinner tomorrow." His sunlight-filled voice threatened to illuminate parts of her that she preferred to keep in shadow.

"Me too," she whispered and hung up quickly, before Joe could snarl any more of her emotions into tangled knots. *Why did I say that?* She could lie to herself and pretend it was all part of a plot to draw him closer, but she'd never been big on any kind of manipulation. Her continued interactions with Cabrera were rapidly changing from a sneaker on linoleum to a clog on hardwood—a sharp rattle that startled and set nerves racing but hadn't caused any damage. Yet.

Her heart pounded, her system poised to run or fight. How could she possibly get through dinner if a phone call affected her like this? *I should have kept the boundaries clear.* But they needed his help if they were going to track down the Fuentes family.

He's not one of the bad guys. Recognizing a slick charmer who hid sickeningly evil intent behind an alluring and attractive mask was a skill she'd mastered before puberty. Joe seemed to possess a full share of charm but also integrity. As much as he seemed too good to be true, part of her wanted to find out if a man like him could really exist.

She could keep her disguise as Colleen Avila as a protective layer between them, giving her the option to vanish if it went badly. Meanwhile, there was work to be done, and time wasn't on her side.

CHAPTER NINE

Vincent shoved open the apartment door and froze, keys in hand, when he heard an unexpected voice from the kitchen.

"The sequins keep coming off during turns." His sister Dani must have come by. *Just what I need—another attempt to save me.* Between Andrew and his family, he was saved out. Maybe he could quietly exit before someone came down the long hall and spotted him.

"The fabric is weak here. I'm not surprised it's not holding the thread," his roommate, Evonne, replied. Silken material whispered, probably one of Dani's dancing costumes. Vincent eased the apartment door back open just as his keys slipped out of his hands to clatter on the linoleum floor.

He mentally cursed, mouth and arms moving as he silently expressed his frustration. *She probably already knew I was here.* His sister's senses had always been sharper than his, and he could clearly hear the people moving in the next apartment. Closing the door, he smoothed his expression and sauntered past the closed bedrooms to the kitchen.

Evonne and Dani were seated at the tiny table with clumps of black fabric covering its wooden top. Dani's dark eyes glinted with repressed irritation as she greeted him. "Hey, Vincent."

Vincent found himself missing the days when her eyes would glow red when she got pissed. Becoming the High Priestess might have fulfilled their parents' fondest dreams, but he preferred his old, unconnected big sister who'd yelled at him constantly but still bailed him out of whatever trouble he got into—the one who'd held his hand when he couldn't sleep in the dark and his parents were too wrapped up in their own trauma to notice.

He grabbed a beer out of the fridge, stealing another glance at the table. To the casual observer, the two women could have passed for sisters with their long dark hair and tan complexions, but Dani had that hint of Mediterranean olive to her skin, while Evonne's glowed ruddy from Native roots. "Don't let me interrupt."

Evonne, not catching his subtle hint, picked up the fringed skirt and shook it to make it hang straight. "It's no trouble. I've got what needs to be done. You two should have a visit."

"I don't know," Dani drawled. "I assume he's planned a busy day of sulking and staring at the TV."

"I'm planning to get drunk too. Helps to keep the drama going for *Say Yes to the Dress*." Vincent caught the hint of a smile on his sister's face before she lifted her nose and chin in haughty disdain.

"You never take anything seriously." Dani slowly pulled her big leather purse toward her. "I'll see you later, Evonne."

"I take plenty of things seriously." Vincent took a swallow of beer. "Like those poor people in Nigeria who need my help to get their money out of the country. I've got some big paydays coming."

"Enough." Evonne stood up, locking her gaze on each of them in turn. Neither of them was willing to push many social boundaries with the petite seamstress. She folded the skirt over her arm. "You're family."

"So Mom and Dad insist. Personally, I thought we should run DNA tests to be sure." Vincent shrugged.

Dani glared at him, her mouth opening to let the venom fly.

"You can't keep going like this. You need to talk to one another." Evonne headed for the doorway. "I'm going to my room to fix this fringe, and you two are going to work out your differences. Understood?"

"After that, I can still watch TV, though, right?" Vincent called after her. He was not surprised when she ignored him.

Dani made a visible effort to calm herself, closing her eyes and taking a deep breath. "She's trying to help you." Hints of his old big sister came through with the measured words. "It won't kill you to talk to me."

"But if I talk to you, I won't be watching TV. Which would be bad." The pose of indifference came easily even as he sat down at the table. "Talking won't solve our differences."

Dani's red-lacquered nails curled into claws. "How would you know?

You haven't even tried to contact us since you came back."

Vincent abruptly decided he was tired of avoiding the elephant in the room. "You all sent me up to the North to die—from cold, by suicide, or at the hands of the Guardians of Bear Claw."

Dani's fists curled tighter with fury, but she managed to keep her voice level. "Is that what you think?"

"I don't think it. I know it. Hell, I even agree with you." He took another long swallow, hoping the cool alcohol could wash away the lingering ache. "I'm dangerous as long as the Beast has his hooks in me."

"You can fight him. McBride did." *And you didn't.* The unspoken implication sliced between them.

"Damn. Why didn't I think of that? Yeah, I'll take care of it this weekend." Vincent chugged down the rest of the beer and stood up to toss it into the sink. "Great talk. Very big-sister inspired. You should write some cards or shit."

When he turned around, Dani stood between him and the exit, hands on hips and fury in her eyes. He hadn't heard her move at all.

She jabbed a finger at him. "Don't you dare walk away. Maybe everyone else wants to tiptoe around poor, wounded Vincent, but I care too much to let you flush your life down the toilet. You need to pull your head out of your ass and get back in the fight. We've all got scars, dammit. No one walked away."

Vincent stared down at his sister. She'd always been stronger and faster, even before becoming High Priestess. When they'd fought as children, she'd made him eat his share of dirt. But when someone or something from the outside threatened, they'd always had each other's backs. The look in her eyes said she wanted that brother back. *Hell, I want to be that brother again.* None of his family understood that the old Vincent was long gone. *I won't fight alongside you, Sis, because I'm a liability, not a protector.*

Pain and threats meant nothing to him. It didn't matter how dire. He knew the video of Lily shapeshifting had ignited concerns and fears worldwide. He'd heard the rumors of a bounty on his head and Dani's. The *lalassu* were crouching behind stones as the bright searchlights probed the darkness. Any slip could wipe away the defensive secrecy of millennia.

He understood the consequences. And he still didn't care. It all washed over his numb soul, leaving him unmoved.

"We need you, Vincent." Dani reached out for him.

Vincent grabbed her hand and twisted it before it could touch him. The reaction was instinctive, a legacy of the Beast.

Dani gasped with pain, and Vincent released her. "I'm not the person you need anymore. It's better for all of us if I stay away."

"I can't accept that," Dani whispered, moving away from the door.

"Not my problem." He stepped back. "Thanks for bringing over the outfit. Evonne can use the work."

He left the kitchen, heading to his room before she could say another word. Unfortunately, he'd forgotten she wasn't the only woman left in the apartment.

Evonne waited in her doorway. "I thought you weren't giving up anymore and understood you didn't deserve what happened to you."

"I didn't deserve it. Doesn't change what happened." The darkness brooded and built inside Vincent like a volcanic island rising out of the sea. He tried to keep it tamped down with jokes and irreverence, but those defenses had fallen away. "The Beast broke me. If I try to fight, he will use me against each and every one of you. The only way I can stop that is to make sure I'm nowhere near the final conflict."

"You can't be sure of that," Evonne pleaded. His sharp ears caught the faint scrape of Dani's shoes from the kitchen. She was listening. Or maybe getting into position to take him down if he attacked Evonne. *Either way, doesn't matter.*

"I'm not willing to take the risk of coming back to my senses and seeing all of you dead on the ground in front of me." The image haunted his dreams night after night. He'd be fighting his enemies and winning, only to see the masks melt away and discover he'd slaughtered his friends and family while the Beast laughed. *I'll take myself out first.*

"Mamá, I know that Tía Ximena is upset because I don't want to date her neighbor's daughter, and I'm sorry about hurting her feelings." There was more to his opinion, but Joe wasn't dumb enough to say it out loud to his mother.

"What harm could it do to meet the girl and eat a meal together?" Mamá was in her relentless mode. He could get shot, and she wouldn't consider it a valid excuse for disappointing the family.

Joe scanned the street, searching for his quarry. He should have known better than to call his mother while he waited for Sticks to wander back. At least it kept him from thinking too much about Colleen and wondering if she was getting herself into trouble with her search. "It's just not something I'm interested in pursuing right now. I don't want to give this girl a false impression."

"Not every woman falls in love with your big brown eyes at first sight. And how will you find your true love if you don't take chances?"

"It's not—" Joe cut himself off before he could say anything damning. Too late. His mother seized on it like a terrier on a rat.

"You have met a girl." Mamá began speaking in rapid-fire Spanish, sharing her news with whoever was lingering in the kitchen.

"Not exactly…" He needed to make the effort to stop the rumor even though he knew the familial avalanche had already begun.

"Not exactly?" Mamá returned her full attention to him, and her voice suddenly softened. "Pépé, are you trying to tell me something?"

I'm trying not to tell you something. Joe saw a disturbance moving up the street among the tourists. Maybe he'd be saved by the informant.

"You know you can tell me anything. It's not like the old country. If you have found a man to love, then you know that we would love you and support you both. Does he like *tortas*? I can ask Tía Agata to make some for this week. And if you're worried about your tías, don't. It might be a surprise, but they care about you too much to hide such news from them."

The disturbance came close enough for Joe to spot its cause—a skinny, pale man in a loud Hawaiian shirt, holding out a paper cup to the crowds.

"You can always adopt to have children. Or perhaps we can find a surrogate. He must be a handsome man to match you, Pépé." His mother's ramblings over the last few moments suddenly came flooding back into Joe's awareness.

Joe planted his hand over his face. "Mamá, I haven't fallen in love with a man. That's not the problem."

"Then it is a woman." Mamá switched gears easily enough. After all, the goal was to get him happily settled with a partner and starting a family. The other details were entirely flexible. "Bring her to dinner. A nice girl will want to meet your family. Or a nice boy."

"Mamá, we'll have to talk about this later. I have to go. It's work." Joe couldn't quite picture springing his family on Colleen. He'd hoped to have time to build up the relationship gradually, but now that his family suspected, they wouldn't rest until they'd met her. If he didn't bring her to dinner, they would arrange to "accidentally" bump into him and Colleen.

"Be safe, Pépé. I will let the others know." Mamá hung up, leaving Joe to wonder what she thought he'd promised. *I'll figure it out later.*

He got out of the car and cautiously approached the panhandler. "Hey, Sticks. How's it going?"

Sticks peered blearily at Joe, his expression wary until he recognized the policeman. His skinny, wrinkled face lit up in a grin, revealing the rotted stumps of his teeth. "Goin' good. Not causin' no trouble."

"Glad to hear it. Here, man—they gave me an extra lunch." Joe held out the paper bag. Inside were two bacon cheeseburgers, two large fries, and one of those deep-fried pie things. Sticks never turned down a meal, but he wouldn't cooperate if Joe implied it was charity.

Sticks immediately pulled out one of the burgers and began to devour it with messy gusto. Joe leaned against the building. A few tourists gave him and Sticks dirty looks, but they moved along quickly enough when Joe shook his head and shifted to flash his badge at them. *Too bad for them if they're offended by an old man's lack of table manners when he's starving.*

"That hits the spot." Sticks belched noisily, wiping at the fresh ketchup and mustard shining on his stained shirt. "You need me to keep an eye out for something?"

"For someone. This guy." Joe held out the photo of the homeless man from the surveillance footage. Hopefully, Sticks would be able to pass it around, and the lure of another free lunch would reel in Joe's target. "He's not in trouble, but he saw something, and I need to talk to him."

Sticks frowned. "You sure he's not in trouble?"

"Yeah, I'm sure." A tingle of adrenaline threaded through Joe's nerves. He made a point of never lying to Sticks. Otherwise, the homeless man would never have trusted him again. "Why—does he have a history of causing problems?"

"Nah. That's Doggy Dan. He ain't too bright. Somethin' wrong in his head, you know. Like a little kid. Likes to hang out in the parks and pet the dogs. Freaks out the families." Sticks clucked his tongue disapprovingly. "Keep tellin' him to keep his hands to himself, but he can't remember."

"You know where I can find him?" Joe asked.

"He's not here no more. He was all excited a couple of nights ago, said he met this pretty lady and she gave him a ticket to go south. Said he could find all kinds of nice dogs down in Kentucky or Georgia or somewhere. I'd have thought he made it up, but he had the bus ticket, and we ain't seen him since." Stick handed back the photo.

Damn. The "pretty lady" must have been the thief. She'd anticipated that someone would look for Doggy Dan and made sure he couldn't be found. Joe hoped the bus ticket had been real and not a ruse to lure the man to some anonymous grave. "Thanks, Sticks. If you hear from Doggy Dan, make sure you give me a call. I'd still like to talk to him."

"Yeah, man. I'll do that. Thanks for the food." Sticks glanced around as he tucked the grease-stained bag into his backpack. "Hey, do you think you could get me a place to sleep for a few nights? Like, maybe a shelter or something?"

Joe straightened in surprise. Sticks hated the shelters and, if forced to go, usually ended up doing something disgusting or violent so they would make him leave. "I can talk to the folks at St. Michael's. They usually can find room if I ask. But why?"

"Something's going down lately. I can feel it coming, like a thunderstorm. Everybody's scared about these freaks and worse. Someone's offering money for freaks, and word is that they ain't too particular about who they grab." Sticks rubbed his skinny arms together. It might be spring, but it was still too cold to be walking around without a coat.

"Don't worry—I'll find you a spot. If not at St. Michael's, I'll leave word there about where to go. Sound good?" Joe's brain filed away the information. Dalhard had collected *lalassu*, and he probably wasn't the only one.

"Yeah, man. I'll do that." Sticks shuffled off to rattle his coffee cup at more tourists.

Wonder if I can get someone to run down dog-related arrests or incidents in the southeastern states. The department wouldn't do it. Vapor would have been useful, but since he wasn't in a mood to play well with others, Joe would have to see who else might be able to help. *Maybe Colleen has good computer skills. She's into spy stuff.* The memory made him smile.

He hoped she was being careful investigating what happened to Fuentes's family. Fingering his phone, he wondered if he should call her just to check in. His phone buzzed, and he pulled it out to see an incoming text from Colleen. *Speak of the devil*, he thought

The message read, *Mrs. Fuentes went to yoga on Tuesday morning, her usual class, but didn't show for work. The schools say she showed up in person to take the kids out of school that morning, 10 for the girl and 10:15 for the boy.*

Joe's eyebrows lifted in appreciation. Colleen was a heck of a researcher to have found out so much so quickly. Before he could reply, a second text came in with the phone number from the company records. Finally, something he could officially investigate.

Good work, he texted back.

Don't sound surprised. Talk when I have more, she replied.

Joe chuckled and said out loud, "I'd bet the house on that."

CHAPTER TEN

"What exactly does this have to do with the data thief?" Modnik rested her weight on her hands, leaning forward on her desk.

"A family could have been kidnapped. We have to look into it." Joe soothed his professional conscience. He hadn't stopped investigating the theft, but with his leads gone cold, focusing on the Fuentes family wouldn't hurt.

"We don't have a missing-persons report. And according to your source, we can't count on Mr. Fuentes's cooperation." Modnik shook her head wearily. If Joe hadn't known that her frustration with the bureaucratic restrictions equaled his own, he'd have begun violently rearranging the furniture.

"No one has seen the family for days," he reminded her.

"If the story is true, we don't want to put them at risk. Who is your source, anyway?" Modnik straightened.

"She's reliable. She works at Right Hand Man." Joe wasn't ready to reveal Colleen's identity or his own suspicions that she was only playing a role.

"One of André Dalhard's people?" The sergeant's eyebrow quirked. "I thought I told you to stay away from that investigation."

"I'm not investigating Dalhard," Joe replied. Creepy Cabrera didn't have any leeway in the department anymore. He'd really managed to screw himself over.

"Find me something objective, something I can bring to a judge." It was a dismissal. Modnik had bent the rules as much as she could.

"By then, it could be too late." Joe knew how much the words would hurt but was unable to hold back. He believed in the law, but the bureaucratic process left a lot to be desired sometimes.

"That's enough, Detective." Modnik never got angry, but only an idiot would miss the cold steel backing her warning. "Walk away. I don't want to see you back here before tomorrow."

Joe caught the implied invitation and nodded. He left the police precinct quickly, ignoring the curious looks from his colleagues. He couldn't afford to wait and go through procedures. His gut told him that things were going to move quickly, which meant he needed someone who could move even faster.

Dani, Michael, and the other *lalassu* would help. He could ask if Gwen had heard from the family, which would tell him if they were still alive. Maybe she could ask the ghosts to search. He sent a quick text to Michael and got an immediate reply. He and Dani were at the burlesque club. Joe suppressed a wince and got in his car. He hated going to the club, but the missing family wasn't something to discuss over a phone line.

Night had fallen by the time he reached The Blue Curtain Club. The bouncer recognized Joe and waved him in. Making his way backstage, Joe ignored the pretty girls fastening corsets and securing pasties. His nonchalance was not because his mother had raised him to be a gentleman but because their painted charms held no appeal when compared with the memory of a pair of forest-green eyes hidden behind thick glasses.

Colleen wasn't like any woman he'd ever met. Her combination of firecracker and fragility hid dark secrets. He'd loved watching her ignite in a passionate, righteous rage, and when she'd tried to hide it behind her shy persona, he'd wanted nothing more than to bring it all out again. He wanted to give her a safe place where she didn't have to hide anymore.

He hadn't ever felt like that about a woman before. It struck him that it must have been what happened to his father when he met Mamá. Colleen had taken over his thoughts. Relief and hope lightened his steps for the first time since he'd first learned about the *lalassu.*

"Good to see you, Detective." Dani was dressed in a shimmering, black-beaded corset with her black curls piled on top of her head.

Joe didn't have time for games. "I need to talk to you and Michael."

"He's helping Ruby with her costume." Dani flicked her obsidian nails toward the back of the dressing area. "I'll join you once I'm done on stage."

Joe waved absentmindedly as he followed Dani's casual directions. He found his friend chatting with the strawberry-blond Ruby, offering tips about the best way to get the dancer's preschooler to sleep easily at night.

"You have to be firm. Letting her have an extra story or drink of water may seem easier in the moment, but you're only setting yourself up for long-term problems," Michael explained as he helped Ruby fasten bright-red sprays of ostrich feathers onto the clips attached to the woman's corset.

"You're right. She asks for more every night, and it takes longer to settle her down." Ruby spotted Joe in the mirror. "Hi, Detective Joe."

"Hi, Ruby." Joe smiled, but he didn't give it his usual reflexive flirtatious hint.

The dancer straightened her skirt. "I'll leave you to talk. Got to get on stage."

Michael waited until she was out of earshot. "How bad is it?"

"Pretty bad. I think Karan might have kidnapped a family." Joe quickly explained what Colleen had told him.

"She works for Dalhard?" Michael frowned. "This could be a trap."

"Can we take the chance that it's not? I need a way to find them quickly."

"I'll talk to Virginia and see what we can do. If Vapor were here to help…" Michael shoved his gloved hands into his pockets. "But he's not, and we can't always rely on him, I suppose. That family doesn't deserve to become collateral damage in the conflict between us and Dalhard."

"Or the one between him and Karan. I'm losing track of all the sides." Joe rubbed his nose.

Michael hesitated before continuing. "You trust this woman? Colleen?"

"There's something about her." Joe felt his mouth stretching into an involuntary smile. "I know I don't know everything about her, not by a long shot. But I can't wait to find it all out."

"We're missing something." Cali chewed on her fingernail as she stared at a map of Perdition. The few sightings provided by her crew had turned out to be false leads. Wherever the Fuentes family was squirreled away, Karan had chosen well. She, Hood, and Harley had been working from their headquarters for most of the night.

"Stop hovering," Harley muttered, his sharp eyes scanning through footage and code on his computer screen. His narrow, nimble fingers flew over the keys. The glow from the screen made one of three islands of light in the windowless office space.

Hood hid a grin, ducking his chin as he listened to the recording of the phone call again.

"I'm not hovering. I'm supervising." Cali twisted around to glare at Harley. "And I'm not even looking at you."

"It doesn't matter. I can sense you hovering." Harley's eyes never twitched away from their target.

"You're just grouchy." It was petty, but sniping with Harley was the only immediate outlet available for Cali's frustrations. He was doing the same, and they'd forgive each other when it was all done.

"Right. Grouchy. Because I should be overjoyed to be here into the wee hours of the morning instead of curled up in bed with my husband."

"Behave, Harley." Hood pulled off the headphones. "Cali is right. We did miss something."

"What?" Cali spun around, and Harley stood up so quickly that he knocked over his chair. A few hours earlier, she might have been incensed at the idea of having failed to catch every nuance of the call, but now she was desperate for any kind of help.

"I think the children are being held separately from their mother. The boy says that his mother is still asleep but looks okay. He doesn't mention having spoken to her or pass on any message." Hood rubbed his forefinger along his jaw.

"Still asleep." Cali's tired mind seized on those two words. "What if the mother is being kept sedated somewhere?"

"Makes sense. Kids won't run without their mother, and if she's unconscious, she's not plotting escape or acting to protect them." Bitterness stained Hood's words. He might have been knowledgeable about the darker ways of the world, but he still hated them. Cali always admired how he kept his integrity despite the temptations of their work.

"Keeping someone sedated can't be easy. They don't put doctors through years of medical school for no reason." Harley put a comforting hand on his partner's shoulder.

"Maybe that's not it, then," Hood said.

Cali wasn't sure they could dismiss the idea so easily. It felt right, but her brain could be fixating on it in her exhaustion. "How would we search for them if the mother is drugged? She could be anywhere. We have to get them all. We can't leave her in Karan's hands."

"We won't." Hood lightly touched her hand on the table. He knew why she didn't like physical contact and wouldn't push further. "You need to rest."

"We have to keep looking," Cali insisted.

"We're going to need Boomerang in the morning. Which means that you need to sleep, or you'll never be able to keep up the disguise." Hood pointed to the small room off their work area. Barely large enough for a cot, it was the only other place that Cali could sleep besides her closet. "I'll wake you if we find something."

"Go. I'll keep searching," Harley said with unexpected kindness. "Maybe I can find out more about what's needed to keep people sedated without killing them."

Cali opened her mouth to object, and Hood stopped her. "Go."

Outflanked by caring, Cali had no choice but to agree. "Get me as soon as you find anything."

She locked herself into the side room, telling herself that she was perfectly safe. There were two heavy bolts securing the door, and she had her knives if they failed. No one wanted to attack her, and even if they did, she could count on Hood and Harley to protect her. Curling up on the cot, she stared at the narrow strip of light underneath the door, unable to stop herself from watching for telltale shadows.

As her eyes grew heavy and sore, she found herself wondering how the dinner with Joe would go. He said he liked the real her, but she wasn't sure which version of herself was the real one. Boomerang, the professional thief who ran the street crew? Colleen, who existed as an infiltrator and aide? Or Cali, the leftover bits between the two of them?

A tap on the door jerked her out of a light doze. Her mouth was horribly dry and tasted as if she'd been licking a shoe all night. She stared at the clock, trying to understand why it was suddenly four hours later. A second tap yanked her sleep-dazed senses back to awareness.

"Boomerang, we've found something," Hood called through the door.

"One moment." Calling her Boomerang meant someone else was there. She would need her game face on before opening the door.

Taking a deep breath, she opened up her bag and pulled out an expensive designer watch done in heavy silver. Her father had taught her how to use multiple personas for cons and thefts, but he'd also taught her how to keep them all straight. Colleen had her glasses and frumpy clothing. Boomerang wore designer clothes and a watch that could be mistaken for a wrist cuff at first glance. A black suit jacket hung on a hook in the room, which she'd discovered could be quite useful. She rinsed out her mouth with water, smoothed down Boomerang's black locks, and touched up her makeup before opening the door.

Hood and Harley were standing beside the computer along with a boy she didn't recognize. He couldn't have been more than fifteen, and his grimy, tanned skin suggested he'd been on the street for a while.

Hood nudged the boy. "This is Billy. He saw something interesting, and Red Willa sent him to us."

"I was hanging out at the park near the river. There's a food truck there that gives out food if it gets too burned to sell." Billy's gaze swung wildly between the three of them. "I wasn't causing any trouble."

Cali gestured for him to continue. Hood handed her a large cup of steaming coffee, well aware of how she didn't wake up well. She sipped the bitter liquid, needing the jolt of caffeine.

"I saw another kid come running through the park. He was a couple years younger than me. A guy chased after him. He looked really mad, so I hid behind a bench, but I was still watching. He grabbed the kid and dragged him to a van. The kid looked really scared." As did Billy, his eyes wide and his thin fingers clutching his worn backpack.

"Did you get the license plate of the van?" Cali asked.

Billy shook his head. "It was dark blue. That's all I saw."

"All right. It's a start." Cali smiled, hoping to put the boy at ease. "Go with Hood. He'll get you something to eat and a safe place to sleep."

Billy swallowed, obviously afraid of the large man but not ready to turn down food and sleep. All of the kids who came to them were suspicious at first. The trusting ones didn't survive long enough to find help. Eventually, they'd win his trust. Hood escorted him out.

"The park by the river is still a hell of a lot of territory." Cali took another gulp of coffee, scorching her tongue.

"I might have a way to narrow it down." Harley logged into the computer and began typing rapidly. "If I'm right… yes!"

"What is it?" Cali held herself back from peering over his shoulder. *No hovering.*

"Exactly what I would need if I was going to hold someone in an artificial coma." Harley grinned, his narrow features lighting up. Then he suddenly frowned. "Which I would never, ever do. Because it would be wrong."

Hood snorted as he came back into the room.

"Do I need to hit you to get you to finish?" Cali grumbled.

"It's right beside the park. Riverview Mental Health and Recovery. Everything you'd need to keep someone drugged and compliant." Harley brought up the facility's website. It showed an impressive modern structure of stone and glass set in picturesque landscaping.

Cali finished her coffee. "Then that's where we need to go."

Chapter Eleven

"Any luck?" Joe asked into his phone as he picked over the plate of huevos rancheros he'd found in his fridge that morning.

"I'm not sure how much Gwen understood," Michael replied. "So far, no luck. Dani and I are on our way into town. She's going to talk to some people, and I'm going to pretend I don't know she really means she's going to hit them."

"Only if they don't talk back," Dani called out, clearly audible over the connection.

Joe grinned. "As a duly appointed officer of the law, I didn't hear any of that."

"Ask him about the girl," Dani shouted again.

"I haven't heard from Colleen yet today. I'm hoping she's not going amateur investigator on me the way you did." Joe kept his tone light, but he'd been up most of the night worrying about it. He'd wanted to call her to make sure she was okay but hadn't wanted to frighten her by coming on too strong, too quickly.

"That all worked out." Michael laughed.

"Nearly blown up in a building," Joe reminded him.

"Key word, nearly." Michael sounded happy, freer than Joe could ever remember his friend being before. Dani had brought that into Michael's life, and maybe, if Joe was lucky, Colleen would bring some of it into his life too.

His phone buzzed with an incoming text. Joe's spirits lifted when he saw it was from Colleen and then immediately sank when he read it:

Found out the mom is at Riverview Mental Health and Recovery. On my way.

"Shit!" Joe grabbed his keys.

"What is it?" Michael asked.

Joe told them Colleen's news. "Please say you're close enough to help. If the pattern for the phone calls hold, the kidnappers will be there in half an hour. I can be there in ten minutes."

"We're in the city. Assuming Dani doesn't get us killed in traffic, we'll be at the center in twenty minutes." Michael swallowed audibly. Joe understood why he'd be nervous. Dani didn't just have a lead foot—she had an entire lead leg and took chances that would leave NASCAR drivers shaking their heads.

Joe hung up and dialed Colleen, hoping to persuade her to stay put. The call went immediately to voice mail, and Joe cursed, hurrying to his car. If Colleen was right about the timing, the kidnappers would be arriving soon for the daily phone call. He needed to get there before she put herself in danger.

He drove as fast as he could to the center. Subconsciously, he still expected all asylums to be crumbling brick and wrought-iron Victorian structures like the ones in the movies, but Riverview was a modern hospital with a dedicated staff and superb reputation. So how did a state-of-the-art facility end up housing a woman drugged against her will? It occurred to him that perhaps Mrs. Fuentes had voluntarily checked into the facility and Colleen had been wrong. But if so, the children's absence and the phone calls no longer fit.

He immediately went to the receptionist, a serious young man with heavy glasses that reminded him of Colleen's. Joe hoped she was all right, but he tried to keep his caveman protective instincts in their proper place. He still asked the receptionist to hold Colleen back and keep her in the lobby when she arrived. "Tell her that I'm already here."

The receptionist directed him to the head psychologist, Dr. Evelyne Clavier, a petite woman in a white lab coat and with her auburn hair tucked into a neat bun. "How can I help you, Detective Cabrera?"

"I'm looking for a patient who might be here. I think she may be in danger. Her name is Anita Fuentes, but I don't know if she registered under that name." He hoped the good doctor would be more concerned with the woman's well-being than with patient confidentiality.

Dr. Clavier searched the records and shook her head. "I don't have anyone named Fuentes here."

Okay, time for a long shot. Joe showed the picture he'd downloaded from Mrs. Fuentes's social media site.

"I do know her." Dr. Clavier paled. "She's in a coma. They transferred her from another hospital a few days ago so that she could be closer to her family. Her husband visits twice a day and brings the children every day to see her."

"I have reason to believe that the man claiming to be her husband might actually be her kidnapper." Joe used his best crowd-control voice, the one that projected calm and competence. "I need to see her."

"Her paperwork was all in order. Are you sure?" Dr. Clavier began to walk before waiting for his answer.

"Frankly, I'm not sure whether to hope that I'm right or wrong." If he was right, a kidnapped woman had been successfully hidden in a hospital. If he was wrong, then the Fuentes family was still out there. "Is it possible to keep someone artificially in a coma?"

"Well, yes. But the drugs have to be carefully administered on a regular basis. It would require medical training." The doctor led Joe through a long, brightly lit corridor. Her rapid pace drew attention from the scrub-clad staff, leaving Joe wishing he hadn't been quite as direct. The last thing he wanted was to alert his suspect.

The doctor stopped near the end of the hall and quietly opened the door to a private patient room. It was much nicer than the ones Joe remembered from his infrequent hospital stays, painted a pleasant shade of green with a large window overlooking a mature tree. In summer, it would be beautiful to watch the sunlight filter through the leaves. A woman lay on the bed, covered in a soft, cream-colored blanket, her dark hair neatly braided to one side. The medical equipment must have been discreetly hidden away in the wooden cabinets. Only the slender IV pole and adjustable bed betrayed the true purpose of the room.

"Can you check to see what she's on?" Joe asked, visually confirming that the woman was either Anita Fuentes or an unknown twin sister.

The doctor began to examine the bags hanging from the IV pole when the door opened again, admitting a nurse in pale-blue scrubs who backed in with a rolling tray. Joe stepped backward into the corner, hoping she wouldn't see him.

"Nurse, I need you to—who are you?" Dr. Clavier blurted.

"I'm a transfer from Perdition Hospital," the woman replied smoothly. She seemed familiar to Joe, not to mention far too gorgeous to be a nurse. Her dark hair was pulled back in a bun, emphasizing her sharp cheekbones and wide, dark eyes. She wasn't wearing any makeup, but her lips were still a soft, kissable pink. The thought surprised him and brought a hot flush of embarrassment creeping up his neck. *This isn't supposed to be happening.* If Colleen was the one, he shouldn't be thinking about kissing some other woman or imagining her lips as red instead of pink.

The connection hit. The thief from Lockbox. *Oh, shit.* He reached for his weapon, and her eyes went wide.

"Stay there, and keep your hands over your head." He couldn't spare a glance for the doctor. Hopefully, she would keep out of the line of fire.

The thief lazily raised her hands to either side. She purred her reply. "Detective Cabrera, such a pleasant surprise meeting you here."

Her sultry voice ignited fresh fires under his bubbling libido. Luckily, guilt helped him to keep a firm lid on that treacherous pot. *Not going to act on this.* "Step away from the door."

"Whatever you say." She shrugged as she complied. "Now what? I'm unarmed."

Joe moved to stand between her and the door. "I don't think I'll take your word for it."

A delighted and sensual grin curved her lips. "Why, Detective, we haven't even been introduced. We should at least exchange names before moving on to groping."

"Why are you here?" Joe wondered if she was stalling for time. She didn't seem particularly concerned about being caught.

"Probably the same reason you are. Returning that woman to her family." The thief nodded toward the figure on the bed. "I'm Boomerang, by the way, since you haven't been polite enough to ask."

"You'll forgive me if I don't believe you." Joe reminded himself that he should not be enjoying foreplay-esque banter with a suspect.

"I'm horribly crushed." She pouted briefly. "Her husband offered a substantial reward on the Darknet. Is it easier to believe if I'm in it for the money?"

Joe let go of his gun with his left hand and pulled his handcuffs out. "Turn around."

"Shouldn't we have a safety word first?" She did as he asked, allowing him to snap the cuffs on her left wrist and then pull it down to cuff the right one as well.

Something about her wasn't adding up. The sultry-vixen thing was too determined and stylized—effective as a distraction but without the sincerity that would have made it dangerous. He turned her around and repeated, "Why are you here?"

Her liquid dark eyes softened briefly as they flicked toward Anita Fuentes, lying silent and wan on her hospital bed. If Joe hadn't been watching her carefully, he would have missed the sliver of a hint. *She's not as indifferent as she wants me to think.* He didn't have a lot of time to explore his insight. If the pattern held true, then the kidnapper would be here soon with the Fuentes family.

"Keep an eye on her," he ordered Dr. Clavier, who stood in the corner, eyes wide and hands shaking and looking completely overwhelmed.

Joe opened the door to the tiny bathroom. It was just big enough for a shower, a toilet, and a tiny sink. No windows, vents, or other exits. Perfect.

He sent Dr. Clavier back to her office with instructions to stay out of the way and alert the police if she heard a commotion. Then he hustled Boomerang into the bathroom. He wasn't going to let her out of his sight, and he needed to stay there to catch the kidnappers.

As the chill of the tiled floor seeped through his thin-soled dress shoes, it occurred to him to wonder if she was one of the kidnappers, maybe sent early to check the situation. It was plausible, but his instincts violently rejected the idea. Whatever had brought Boomerang to that hospital room, it wasn't to keep Anita Fuentes there against her will in order to coerce Ken Fuentes to do her bidding.

She shifted in place, bringing his attention to how close her body was to his in the tight confines of their hiding place. A fantasy began to play in his mind. He could reach over and turn on the shower, letting a sluice of warm water cascade down over them both. It would quickly soak the pale-blue cotton. The darkened fabric would cling to her body as he pressed her against the wall and thrust his tongue between her candy-pink lips.

Head in the game! His fingers tightened around the textured handle of his gun, the crosshatch pattern imprinting itself on his skin. He enjoyed women, but he'd never found himself so immediately fantasizing about one except for Colleen. *I have to get myself under control. This is just the result of too many months of celibacy.* The last thing he wanted to do was hurt Colleen and confirm the horrible way she must see herself.

His self-recriminations needed to wait. Footsteps echoed in the hall outside the room, and the door began to slide open.

Chapter Twelve

"Mommy?" A boy's voice broke the silence. Through the narrow slice of view between the door and the frame, Joe saw a child of about twelve run to the bed and grab one of Anita's hands. A young girl, probably a few years older than the boy, followed him. She looked more frightened, with her arms clasped tight to her body and her long dark curls shining with grease. She kept turning toward something or someone that Joe couldn't see, located by the main door.

"Stay close, kid. We don't want another misunderstanding like yesterday," a gruff voice snarled. Joe recognized the undercurrent of glee in the bullying tones. The speaker knew he frightened people, and he enjoyed it. The girl grabbed her brother and held him tight. Through his grip on her, Joe felt Boomerang tense.

"I won't let you hurt him," the girl said, terrified but defiant. Joe wished he could let her know she wasn't alone.

"I thought you said she'd be awake today," the boy pleaded.

"That depends on your dad." The kidnapper stepped forward into Joe's view. He was an older man with close-cut grey hair and a bland, forgettable face. "Time to give him a call."

"We have to stop this," Boomerang hissed, her voice barely clearing the audible threshold.

He turned his head slightly to answer her. "I will. At the right moment."

The kidnapper pulled out a slim phone. *Hands are busy, no weapon.*

Joe leaned in to whisper in Boomerang's ear. "You wait here. I'll get them."

"Yeah. I got 'em here." The kidnapper hit the screen. "You better have good news for me."

"I have what you want." Ken Fuentes's voice was clear though slightly tinny coming through the speaker. "I want to see my kids."

"Like hell. You need my help," Boomerang insisted. Fortunately, she spoke quietly.

"Smile for Daddy." The kidnapper held out the phone to take a picture. Joe couldn't wait any longer. He shoved Boomerang aside and burst out of the bathroom, weapon raised.

The kidnapper dropped the phone in shock, and Joe got close enough to press his gun into the man's scowling face. "Perdition Police. You're under arrest."

"Matt! Mariana?" Their father's voice shouted from the floor.

Joe hesitated. He needed to secure the kidnapper, but his cuffs were still locked on Boomerang's arms. He settled for moving behind the other man to physically hold his wrists.

"Allow me." Boomerang knelt, picking up the phone. "Come on, Mariana and Matt. You can tell your father that everything is all right now."

The kids looked stunned, standing next to their sleeping mother and clutching each other. Boomerang smiled again and whispered conspiratorially, "It's been quite the daring rescue, hasn't it? You should thank the nice detective."

She held out the phone to the girl, who reluctantly released her brother to take it. "We're okay, Dad."

Joe approved of her caution. She wasn't ready to trust them yet. Then his eyes snapped to Boomerang's bare wrists. "Where are my cuffs?"

"Those?" Her eyes were wide and innocent. "I assumed they were mainly for dramatic emphasis." She held them out, letting them dangle from one finger. "Would you like them back?"

"You know how to use them?" Joe asked her before focusing on the kidnapper. "You're under arrest for kidnapping, extortion, and whatever else I can think of to throw at you."

Boomerang expertly cuffed the kidnapper, allowing Joe to put his gun back in its holster. A quick search discovered an IV bag identical to the ones the hospital used, but Joe guessed it wasn't for an approved treatment.

"What's going on?" Ken Fuentes demanded from the phone.

"My name is Detective Joe Cabrera, Mr. Fuentes. I've arrested the kidnapper, and I have your wife and children here. They're all safe. Can you meet us back at the station?"

Fuentes quickly agreed, and Joe told Mariana to hang up the phone.

"My work appears to be done here, and your involvement means I can say good-bye to any hope of payment." Boomerang shrugged. "I'll be on my way, then."

The door to the room burst open. The kids shrieked, and Joe knocked the kidnapper to the floor, reaching for his holstered gun. Then he recognized Dani with Michael entering a step behind.

"I take it we are not arriving in the nick of time." Dani flipped her thick, dark braid over her shoulder in irritation.

Boomerang straightened up from her protective crouch in front of the Fuentes children and their mother. Joe caught a gleam of metal near her hand. *A weapon?* The thief raised an eyebrow. "Friends of yours, Detective?"

Michael hurried to the bed, tugging off his gloves. Joe nodded at Boomerang to let her know it was all right. She moved aside, ushering the children with her. Michael took Anita Fuentes's hand in his and closed his eyes. "She's struggling to wake up. She's dreaming of searching for a way out among endless corridors."

Joe hauled the kidnapper up by the man's shoulder and collar. It was not a gentle move, but he was in the mood to take his irritation out on someone. "Hell of an entrance, guys. You could have knocked or something."

"Wastes time." Dani's gaze snapped and locked on Boomerang. "Who's this?"

Boomerang was still standing protectively in front of the children. Her smile could have triggered the next ice age. "The one who arrived in time to be useful."

Dani's eyes narrowed, and her bright-red nails disappeared into fists.

Joe interrupted. "We need to get these kids to the station to meet their father. He's going to be frantic." Stepping into the middle of a potential catfight wasn't a bright idea, and he just hoped to survive and keep his manhood intact.

The kidnapper tried to squirm out of Joe's grasp, but the detective held firm, glaring at Dani. Her hands were still clenched and her mouth tightly closed, but she didn't seem to be on the verge of attacking anymore. Boomerang held her ground, leaving Joe feeling as if his team had won.

"What about Mom?" Matt asked. His sister looked hopefully at the adults.

Once again, Boomerang stepped up. She knelt in front of the boy, cupping his face. "I'll go get the doctor, and she'll be able to help your mom. I'm sure it will be all right if you go meet your dad. He's been worried sick about you. All right?"

"Okay." He nodded, and Mariana wrapped protective fingers around her little brother's shoulders.

As Boomerang stood, Joe heard a faint crackle and pop. His *abuelita* had arthritic joints, and they sounded like that when she straightened her legs. But the thief didn't display any signs of pain as she moved fluidly toward the door.

"Hold him." Joe shoved the kidnapper at Dani. "Try not to kill him."

"No promises." Dani grinned, the eager smile of a tiger spotting a fresh steak.

Joe followed Boomerang out into the hall. "Wait."

She turned, looking over her shoulder at him. "You do enjoy being in command, don't you? I wonder how you'll do at taking instruction."

"I still want to talk to you about the Lockbox break-in." *Especially how you managed to escape.*

"I imagine you do." She winked. "Give me a call sometime. My number is in your pocket."

Joe stuck his hand in his jacket pocket and found a crumpled slip of paper. He pulled it out and started to ask Boomerang when she'd put it there—only to discover that she had vanished during his brief moment of inattention. There was a blond nurse walking away, wearing the same pale blue scrubs as his thief. Joe wondered if it might be a disguise but dismissed that idea. The nurse wasn't as full figured as Boomerang, and while the thief might have had a blond wig hidden away somewhere, he doubted there had been time to swap out padding. She'd ditched him.

He wanted to go after her, but he needed to get Anita Fuentes and her children to safety. Suddenly, he remembered Colleen. She was supposed to be on her way. He hurried down to the lobby, but there was no sign of her anywhere. That meant he'd been ditched by two women that day. He felt an unprecedented sting of rejection. But there was no time to lick his wounds—he had a job to do. And maybe he could try to figure out what exactly had happened.

Cali spotted Harley and Hood's van loitering outside the hospital and quickly climbed in.

"Problems?" Harley frowned.

"Kids are fine. They're with Joe. He came through." Cali began to strip off her scrubs and change into her Colleen clothes. "He told Fuentes to meet him at the station, so we've got a limited window to retrieve the data."

Hood pulled away smoothly. Cali stared into the narrow mirror mounted onto the side of the van. She'd been Boomerang for a long time, but she wasn't quite as comfortable in Colleen's skin yet. The mirror would make sure she got the details right.

Her dark mahogany hair began to lighten, brightening to a soft sandy blond. The hollows under her sharp cheekbones filled in, rounding her face. Her nose plumped, and her lips narrowed and paled. Settling the thick-rimmed glasses on her nose, Cali assumed the persona of the meek assistant.

No one challenged the three of them as they went to Fuentes's office. The staff was buzzing about the abrupt departure of Mr. Fuentes. Cali closed the office door and drew the blinds across the windows. "Let's go."

They searched quickly and efficiently, careful to leave no trace of themselves behind. Amateurs and bullies dumped out drawers when searching. Professionals put everything back exactly where they'd found it. Unfortunately, the search came up empty.

"Blast. He must have taken it with him." She'd hoped that Fuentes would be overwhelmed by the rescue and leave the data file behind.

"If he did, he will probably give it to the police officer." Hood closed and relocked the office door behind them, giving the handle a quick swipe with his handkerchief. "We will get it."

"I should do it." Cali kept her voice low. Her coworkers were distracted, but she didn't want to provide fresh grist for the rumor mill.

Harley shook his head. "You're more useful as a distraction. He's taking you to dinner tonight. It gives us a good window of opportunity."

"Assuming he doesn't log it as evidence." Cali rubbed at the back of her neck, trying to ease the tightness pinching the skin. The air conditioning in the office always made her scars ache. She told herself the pain was the only reason that her spirits were sinking faster than the *Titanic*. It certainly had nothing to do with the idea of having to deepen her deception with the detective.

Cali sent the two men on their way. She had another meeting, and it didn't promise to be very pleasant. She hailed a cab rather than walk the short distance. Her bones and back were both aching badly from overextending her morphic abilities. She needed to spend some time in her own face soon.

The look on his face when I handed him the cuffs was worth it. A smile blossomed despite her preoccupations. She hadn't imagined the hint of approval and masculine appreciation leaking past Joe's official cop face. He'd enjoyed watching the show as much as she enjoyed giving it. Boomerang was the persona that let her go wild, creating a larger-than-life reputation to ensure that she became legendary. Boomerang didn't have to worry about consequences, at least not ones past the five-minute mark.

Whereas Colleen does nothing but deal with consequences. Cali stepped out of the cab at the law offices of Adler, Chatton, and Higgins, the firm on retainer for Mr. Dalhard. Time for the faithful handmaiden to go to work once more.

The administrative staff recognized her and immediately escorted her to a comfortable conference room and offered her food and drink. Cali declined and settled herself to wait for Donald Chatton, hoping he wasn't taking an extended lunch.

It didn't take long. Mr. Dalhard paid the firm handsomely to give him and his representatives prompt attention when necessary. Which made its recent actions all the more surprising.

"Miss Avila, what an unexpected pleasure." Chatton greeted her with a smile but didn't try to approach for a hug or handshake. She'd made it clear during their first meeting that she had no interest in creating an illusion of friendship. This was business.

Cali pulled a thick folder out of her bag. "Thank you for fitting me into your day. I am concerned about the progress in Mr. Dalhard's appeal. The deadline for—"

"Didn't Mr. Dalhard tell you?" The lawyer paused in the middle of sitting down, his hand on the back of the chair.

"Tell me what?" Cali kept her temper on a short leash. Colleen Avila would not lash out at a man in a superior social position, no matter how irritating he was being.

"Oh dear. This is rather awkward. I realize that you and Mr. Dalhard have a special relationship, but we must respect attorney–client privilege." Chatton managed to look both regretful and smug at the same time, and it made Cali want to smash in the caps on his teeth.

"Mr. Chatton, I am Mr. Dalhard's assistant. I am acting as his representative while he is indisposed. You drew up the agreement." Colleen might not be aggressive, but she wasn't a pushover either. Cali wasn't about to let the lawyer get away with dismissing her.

"Yes, well, I suppose so." A thin layer of sweat gleamed on Chatton's temples. Something of her true self must have slipped past the façade of handmaiden. He folded his hands on the desk and faced her. "Mr. Dalhard instructed us to cease efforts on the appeal."

"What?" She kept her expression professional and polite. She must have misheard.

"His wishes were very clear. He did not want to waste further time and money on the appeal, although his terms were rather more pejorative." Chatton reached out as if to pat her hand but must have thought better of it and pulled back. He interlaced his fingers once more.

It's worse than I thought. Drastic efforts were necessary.

Chatton apparently took her silence for a dismissal. "I'm sure this must be a shock. Perhaps we can call someone to get you."

Cali raised her eyes and pinned him in place with her glare. He stopped talking and visibly swallowed. She delivered her instructions, never relinquishing his gaze. "He isn't himself. The prison is warping him. You need to get him out of there as quickly as possible. Find a technicality, whatever you have to."

"Without further funds…" Chatton trailed off, aware his caveat would be unwelcome.

"You'll have them." Cali pulled out her phone and made a brief call to her banker. When Chatton overheard the amount, his eyes widened.

Cali didn't care about the money. Dalhard paid her handsomely for her work, and she'd made some prudent and timely investments. And that wasn't even touching her Boomerang funds. If money was what it took to get him out of prison, then she'd happily beggar herself.

"Are you sure?" Chatton asked.

"Very. Do whatever you have to. Get whatever you need." Cali stood up, holding her slim leather portfolio in front of her like a battle shield. "Keep me informed."

"Of course. It will be our top priority."

For what I paid, it bloody well better be. She left the office, hoping she wasn't grasping at straws. Surely, if there had been a way to prevent Dalhard from going to prison, the lawyers would have done so during the trial. But he'd been reeling from Karan's betrayal and ranting about shapeshifters and supersoldiers. Not the most helpful information for a trial.

She might be comfortable operating in the shadows on the fringes of society, but Mr. Dalhard wasn't like that. He was ruthless in business and a dabbler in criminality but not hardened the way the street needed a person to be. Or at least, he hadn't been before he went to prison. *Please don't let me be too late.* Once someone's eyes were opened to the ease of violence, it became far harder for them to pretend to be blind.

Joe watched from the partial concealment of a newspaper stand as Colleen came out of Adler, Chatton, and Higgins. After seeing Mrs. Fuentes safely installed in a proper hospital and the kidnapper delivered to the precinct, he'd gone to check on Right Hand Man, hoping to find her. He'd been worried that she might have been hurt and instead found her coming out of the office with two black men, one large and powerfully built and the other leaner and watchful. He'd watched as they spoke briefly with each other before splitting up. All three had seemed upset and agitated.

Why had she gone to the office instead of the hospital and then gone to Dalhard's lawyers? It didn't make any sense. He didn't want to believe she was involved in the kidnapping, but he was more than willing to believe Dalhard could have orchestrated something like this even from behind bars. *She could be trying to stop anyone else from getting hurt,* his optimistic side pointed out.

The deeper he probed into the mystery of Colleen Avila, the more the pieces he found didn't seem to make sense—and the more determined he was to put together the whole picture.

CHAPTER THIRTEEN

I know what you're looking for.

Karan frowned at the words glowing on his computer screen. They had appeared while he was going through the accounts for Right Hand Man, trying to eliminate any lingering references to Dalhard's previous recruitment drives.

Vapor. How typical of his old partner to break months of silence to deliver yet another lecture.

A new line of text appeared. **You won't find it. Not the way you've been searching.**

The phrasing did not match his old partner's. Besides, if Vapor knew about Karan's search for a database of files for hundreds—if not thousands—of *lalassu,* then he would not be taunting him online. He would be desperate to stop Karan no matter the cost.

I could help you, the stranger continued.

"I need something more than vague references and a virtual monologue." Karan switched the computer off rather than reply. He refused to trust anyone unless absolutely required to. He had paid too dearly for the lesson to throw it aside.

Whoever had sent the messages was correct about one thing: his attempts to gain the information had all failed thus far. Dalhard's paranoid insistence on dividing the data had made what should have been simple into a difficult and frustrating exercise. The first retrieval went smoothly enough, but then the other three were stolen. The final portion had been kept at Right Hand Man, but Ken Fuentes had inexplicably decided to send it away and refused to return it to the rightful owner. Such a distasteful lack of respect had forced Karan to resort to stronger measures.

Now the capture of his agent forced his hand in a different direction. The man could decide to reveal what he knew to the authorities, thereby leaving Karan vulnerable.

Boomerang's involvement was predictable. He had guessed she was the one to remove the data files from storage even before he saw her picture. But he had not anticipated her choice to involve the police. *Perhaps it will simplify matters.* His tame police detective should be able to hunt her down and retrieve the stolen data.

The telephone rang. "Mr. Samil, we've been reviewing the information you've sent. The possibilities are intriguing."

"I am pleased you share my vision." Karan stood up to watch the boat traffic moving on the busy waters of the bay. So much activity for so little purpose.

"This must be handled very carefully. We already have delicate feelers out in high places. People are frightened and need the reassurance that their government will protect them."

Karan was not surprised that the caller had advised caution. Small minds were careful. Those people like him who could see the big picture relied on proper preparation for all circumstances. "It will be critical to harvest their fear without letting it devolve into chaos. You read through my proposal?"

"How will you get him to agree?" the other man asked bluntly.

"I learned a thing or two about persuasion from my former employer. Trust me—he will cooperate."

"She probably staged the whole thing to get some attention," Detective Hampton loudly announced at the nurses' station, oblivious to the angry looks aimed at him as they tried to manage the late-afternoon shift change.

Joe hung back, wincing as his obnoxious coworker decided to add insult to injury by ostentatiously checking out a pretty brunette's breasts before smiling at her. *Never piss off a woman with access to medical drugs and a syringe.* If Joe weren't already on the lowest rung of the totem pole, he would report Hampton. The idiot's actions gave cops a bad name. Never mind that the vast majority of the department neither encouraged nor endorsed that kind of behavior.

Hampton's phone rang loudly, attracting more irritated looks from the nursing staff. Joe's own phone was on silent mode. When he arrived, he'd sent Colleen a text to update her about the Fuentes family. He was curious to see how she would reply. Would she admit to having gone to Right Hand Man instead of Riverview?

Hampton pulled his cell out of his jacket pocket without a hint of apology, grinning with self-importance. Until he looked at the screen. Whatever the man saw on the caller display wiped the smug arrogance off his face faster than a bucket of water could clear a chalkboard. He immediately walked away, talking on the phone in hushed tones.

Joe waited a few minutes to make sure the idiot wasn't going to reappear then moved to the nurses' station. He waited until the one in charge, an older Latina woman with her dark hair pulled into a bun and a no-nonsense attitude, took a break from rearranging charts.

"Hi. I'm Joe Cabrera, Perdition Police." He held out his badge.

Her eyes narrowed suspiciously, and Joe caught the subtle shift as her shoulder muscles tightened. "We've already spoken with the police."

Hampton had really pissed them off, which meant Joe needed to up the charm at least two levels. "I'm not here officially. I'm the officer who found Mrs. Fuentes. I wanted to check in on the family."

The nurse's face softened with each sentence, but Joe knew he hadn't overcome all the barriers.

"I saw the detective who was here before, and he's a jerk. I'd protect my patients from him too if I were you." Joe lowered his voice and leaned in. When she did the same, he knew he only needed to give her a good excuse to bend the rules. "That family has been through enough. I just want to make sure they have what they need."

"Ten minutes. No more." The nurse glared at him like one of the nuns from his elementary school. They always knew he was working them, but it somehow never made a difference.

"Of course. Thank you." He allowed a hint of flirtation to warm his smile and enjoyed seeing a responding flush under her dusky skin. She scowled and waved him off, probably to preserve her dignity. He didn't press the matter but winked at her before sauntering down the hall to where Anita Fuentes was recuperating.

Joe knocked lightly on the open door and poked his head inside the room. Anita lay on the bed, her skin pale and bruised and translucent enough to show the veins underneath it. Her thin arms firmly cuddled her two children, one lying on each side of the hospital bed. Ken Fuentes sat beside her, holding his wife's hand as if he'd never let it go. Joe could only imagine what the man must have gone through over the last few days. At least he'd gotten his family back, although there would probably be challenges as they adjusted back to ordinary life after going through such a trauma.

"Hi. I don't know if you remember me—" Joe began.

"You saved us," Matt chimed in, lifting his head from his mother's shoulder.

"I don't know how to thank you." Raspy and weak from lack of use, Anita's voice could barely be heard over the monitoring equipment.

"I'm just glad that you're all safe." Joe turned his attention to Fuentes. "I know why you didn't call the police when your family first went missing. It's because this isn't an ordinary situation, is it?"

To his credit, Fuentes didn't try to pretend not to know what Joe was talking about. "There have always been rumors about what happens downstairs. The special recruits that they have me search for."

"You know that your boss also has abilities beyond what ordinary people have, right? I don't know if Karan Samil has them too, but given how he effectively managed to push André Dalhard out of his own company, I wouldn't bet against it." Joe carefully avoided saying the word *lalassu*.

"I know. I once watched Mr. Dalhard change the mind of a corporate CEO who was being stalked. A brief conversation and a handshake, and suddenly, the argument over the costs of services was over." Fuentes looked over at his wife and squeezed her hand. "I knew they had eyes and ears in the police department. I couldn't risk you and the kids."

"What did Karan want from you?" Joe asked.

"This." Fuentes reached into his collar and pulled out a slim thumb drive on a narrow chain. "I don't know what's on it, but Mr. Dalhard gave it to me with strict instructions. I was never to let it out of my sight, not for a moment. He would be in touch to retrieve it once he returned from overseas."

Blackmail material? Evidence against Karan? Joe's curiosity practically clawed its way over his caution in its eagerness. "Why not give it to him after your family was taken?"

"I didn't have it." The corners of Fuentes's mouth trembled, and his wife clamped her fingers tighter over his. "There was a new girl in the office, Colleen Avila."

Joe drew on more than a decade of poker practice to keep his gaze steady and his expression politely interested as his stomach decided to try skydiving into his toes.

"She used to work closely with Mr. Dalhard. When she came to me a few weeks ago, she claimed the company had reassigned her, but I didn't believe it." Fuentes fidgeted with the thumb drive. "I caught her snooping around, and I decided to protect myself."

Joe held up a hand to stop Fuentes from continuing. Poking his head out into the hall, Joe made sure it was clear before closing the door to keep anyone from overhearing. "How?"

"I mailed the drive to myself through a high-end courier company. I thought that way I couldn't be tricked or drugged into giving up the data. Except my clever plan backfired. They never would have taken my family if I hadn't sent it away." Fuentes's head dropped to stare at his own shoes. "I only got it back this morning."

Joe couldn't let him wallow in guilt. "From what I know, they probably would have gotten it and then killed you."

The kids gasped, but Joe figured their right to know outweighed the risks. These kids had learned that bogeymen actually did lurk in closets, ready to grab them. If they could understand why it had happened the first time, they would be less afraid of it happening at some random point in the future.

"I suppose you want me to give you the drive now." Fuentes didn't make any move to pull the chain over his head.

"I'm working with some friends, people who have been hurt by Mr. Dalhard. They're trying to make sure that he can't hurt anyone else. They can protect you, take you all into hiding and give you new lives."

Anita's fingers tightened over her husband's. "They'll come after us again, won't they?"

"If you save the information for Dalhard, then Karan will come after you. If you give the information to Karan, then Dalhard will come after you. Either way, once you don't have the information, you become a liability, and I would not give good odds of you surviving into next year. If you keep the data and go with my friends, both Dalhard and Karan will be after you." Joe hated being so blunt, but the family needed to understand their options. "The only way to protect yourselves is to give us the data. Then there's no reason to go after you, and if anyone does, my friends have experience in keeping themselves and others safe and hidden."

"It doesn't sound like we have a choice." The bitterness in Fuentes's words was too familiar. Joe had heard it in his own voice often enough. They'd both been caught up by forces they hadn't known about or asked for, and their lives had been irrevocably changed.

"I'm sorry. I wish I could offer something better." Innocent people shouldn't be the ones to suffer while criminals walked. It offended Joe's sense of professional purpose.

Fuentes yanked the chain over his head and held out the slender thumb drive. "Protect my family."

Joe pulled out his phone to call Michael. He gave a brief outline of what had happened. If someone was tapping his phone or had him under surveillance, he wanted that person to know that Fuentes no longer had the data. "Any luck tracking Vapor down? This should be right up his alley."

"Still no word. They keep telling me that this is how life on this side works sometimes. People have to disappear or lay low for a time. But something tells me this is more." Michael cleared his throat. "I don't suppose you could…"

"Find Vapor if he doesn't want to be found? I doubt it, but I'll see what I can do." One more thing for the impossible to-do list.

"We'll be there in a few minutes to pick them up."

Joe hung up and told the family to gather their things.

"So soon? Anita hasn't been cleared by the doctors." Fuentes's protest died off as the implications of his choice hit him.

"What about my friends? My stuff?" Matt's wide eyes flicked back and forth between his parents.

"Shut up. Is your stuff worth dying for?" Mariana snapped.

Tears welled up in the boy's eyes, and he buried his face in his mother's side. Joe reached over to gently squeeze Matt's arm. "It's not fair, and it's not okay, and you have every right to be mad and sad and whatever else is going on in your head. But you're going to have to stick together now, which means taking care of one another."

Anita mouthed "thank you" to him, holding her children tightly to her. Joe pulled back, the softened edges of the thumb drive pressing firmly inside his clenched fist. The device was such a small thing but still enough to tear apart this family's life. As soon as they were safe, he was going to find out what the hell was on it. And then he would make sure that no one else's life would be destroyed over it.

CHAPTER FOURTEEN

"Are you sure we should be bothering him with this?" Joe asked as he and Michael pulled up at the crumbling motel on the outer edges of South Perdition. His stomach grumbled, reminding him that they needed to hurry if he wanted to make his date with Colleen. She'd texted him a quick thank-you for the update on the Fuentes family but hadn't mentioned Right Hand Man or the lawyers. It left Joe uneasy about the forthcoming evening.

"With Vapor still missing in action, Eric is the next best hope at deciphering what's on the thumb drive." Michael's patience was showing some wear around the edges. Joe supposed he deserved it. They'd already gone through that conversation twice. But the thought of involving a man who was still confined to a hospital bed just chafed Joe. It seemed like a bad idea.

The two men picked their way across a parking lot dotted with cracks and potholes like some kind of demented Morse-code message. Between the lack of upkeep and the location, it guaranteed that no tourists would be desperate enough to stop there. Joe guessed that was probably the point. He wondered how many other abandoned and run-down buildings served secret purposes, hiding in plain sight.

The hinges on the door to the main office were thick with rust, and as Joe yanked on them, he wondered if the entire thing would come off rather than yield. Inside, a flickering bulb reluctantly illuminated the sparse office and its surly occupant.

"What do you want?" The squat man glaring at them from the other side of the counter didn't look like a doctor. His hairless pate shone with grease and sweat, and he wore a faded grey undershirt that had seen cleaner days.

"Hello, Mishler. We're here to see Eric." Michael kept his hands tucked close to his side to avoid picking up any psychic impressions from this place. Joe couldn't blame him. *I wouldn't want to relive the sorts of things that happen here either.*

Mishler grunted and went back to whatever he'd been doing on his computer. For a split second, Joe thought an expression of rage and disgust briefly curled the man's features, but it vanished so quickly that he wasn't sure he'd really seen it. Easing the strap on his holster, he followed Michael down the narrow internal corridor to Eric's room.

Dani's brother looked much healthier. Some color lurked underneath his pasty skin, and he sat up in bed rather than relying on pillows for support. Joe recalled that the healer had recommended intensive physical therapy to retrain Eric's brain to use his body properly. Dalhard's mental attack had severed the connections, leaving Eric with no more control over his body than a newborn babe.

"This is a surprise," Eric said, laying his book aside. "What's the problem?"

Michael explained, offering the thumb drive and a laptop. Joe leaned against the door, keeping a wary eye on the corridor.

"Worried about Mishler?" Eric asked. "He's been edgy lately. So have the families who've come to visit. I hear them talking in the hall."

"We're all worried about being exposed by this video." Michael set up the computer on the rolling hospital table.

"It's not just the video. I think someone is approaching *lalassu*—maybe threatening them, maybe bribing them, but in either case, it's got people whispering in corners." Eric's hand shot out and blocked Michael before he could plug in the thumb drive. "Hold on. Let me shut down the transmitters."

"Why?" Michael looked over at Joe as if he might know the answer.

"If I had a secret file, I'd install a program to tell me if anyone else accessed it. If I make sure the computer can't talk to any networks, then there's less chance of the bad guys screaming down on us. It's less dramatic but probably safer." Eric tapped away at the computer. "Okay, it's ready."

Joe felt the virtual executioner's axe hanging above them as Michael plugged the tiny unit into the laptop. All three men tensed, waiting, but no alarms blared or flashing red lights went off.

Eric clicked on the drive. "This is strange. It's not even encrypted."

Tech stuff was not Joe's cup of tea. There was a whole department to deal with those kinds of things. He just wanted to catch the bad guys and protect the innocent. *Is that too much to ask?*

"It's a list of names and other details, like dates of birth, addresses and—oh, sweet Goddess…" Eric leaned forward, scrolling rapidly through the data. Michael gasped, leaving Joe irritably in the dark.

"What?"

"Ferrokinesis, clairvoyance, shapeshifters… this is a list of *lalassu*," Michael whispered.

Realization congealed in Joe's gut like a lump of fast-food grease.

"There's over a hundred names here." Eric quickly began to type. "No ferals. Nothing about our family."

"If Dalhard had a list like this, why wasn't he using more *lalassu* before? Why kidnap you and Vincent? Why not use these people instead?" Joe's mind fired questions at him faster than he could ask them out loud, whirling around to fit the new puzzle pieces into what he knew.

"He wanted ferals," Eric said slowly. "He kept talking about it with me and Vincent. He mentioned casually that he knew of a number of people with supernatural gifts, but most of them were unsuited to the kind of work he wanted to do. He talked about seeing our father in his father's laboratory when Dalhard was a boy and how he wanted the same kind of power under his control."

"Maybe it's about blackmail." Joe tapped his fingers against his belt. "The *lalassu* need to keep their existence secret. Anytime you have a group with a secret, that group is vulnerable to blackmail. Even if their gifts aren't useful, Dalhard can use them as rats to find others or coerce them into doing whatever else he needs."

"A hundred people isn't a lot," Eric said grimly. "He'd need more."

"He might have them. Someone has been stealing files from companies holding data for Dalhard Industries. What if this is only part of a larger list?" Joe's mind clicked away, putting the puzzle together.

"Why steal them if he already has them?" Michael asked.

"Because he doesn't control Dalhard Industries right now. Karan does." It all made sense. And it meant that his pretty little data thief was up to her neck in trouble.

He wasn't sure what to believe about her. She'd figured out where the Fuentes family was, but she'd also automatically protected the kids. She'd helped him take down the kidnapper and then vanished into thin air. She stole information from Dalhard Industries, including what was apparently a list of *lalassu*, but went out of her way to help a homeless man after using him for a disguise. His instincts told him that she was one of the good guys, but those same instincts were also claiming that both she and Colleen were the one for him.

How did I let myself get into this situation? He'd never had trouble keeping his head over a woman before, and now two of them were tying his brain in knots. He couldn't even have the satisfaction of following in his father's footsteps in finding the woman who was meant to share his life because unless he moved to Utah, he was going to have to choose between two of them. Boomerang was a criminal but seemed to have a heart of gold. Colleen was an intriguing mystery but was also firmly in André Dalhard's camp. No matter which woman he chose, he would be in for a rough time trying to reconcile his feelings and his principles. But they'd each claimed residence in his mind and heart, threatening to break both.

Cali stood in front of the mirror, trying to decide what to wear on her date with Detective Cabrera. *It's not a date. It's an informant and a cop exchanging information.* Except that she didn't want it to be all business. But she should keep it all business. If he was a decent man, then he didn't deserve to get caught up in the mess of her life. She groaned at the pain of twelve feet of indecision crammed into her eight inches of skull.

I can't afford to get emotionally entangled. There was too much to do. The next day, she would visit Mr. Dalhard and tell him what she'd done with the appeal. She still needed to find where Fuentes had hidden the missing data and figure out how she would get the portion that Karan held. Involving a policeman in her life might be the stupidest decision she'd ever made. *So why can't I walk away?*

Would her choice be clearer if her mother had stuck around to explain relationships instead of focusing her parenting efforts on pickpocket skills and fooling people into giving up money? Cali somehow doubted it. Maybe she'd be doing better if she'd had girlfriends to talk to in her teens instead of Hood and Harley. She loved the guys, and they were devoted to each other on a scale that she hadn't thought existed outside of movies, but they'd already been together when Hood first noticed her on the streets in her early teens. She'd never seen them go through the awkward-courtship stage.

Time to make a decision. She held up the two dresses that Colleen Avila owned. The first one was black with white lace at the cuffs and collar. Perfect for serving dinner as one of the catering staff or going to a funeral. The second was grey and pale blue and could have been a costume from *Little House on the Prairie* if it had a slightly longer skirt. She'd picked both up at secondhand shops precisely because they fit the character of someone meek and unsophisticated.

A reflection of deep blue in the mirror caught her attention. The sheath dress hanging from the bathroom's narrow clothing rack was one she'd picked up for herself. It cupped all of her curves like a lover's caress while still keeping an illusion of modesty with its high collar and long sleeves. It covered everything she wanted to hide, especially her arm sheaths. She told herself she was being ridiculous but still put the frumpy dresses aside and carefully lifted the sheath dress off its hanger.

The soft, silky fabric whispered along her skin as she tugged it into place. In the shop, she'd thought it looked fantastic and beautiful, and it hadn't lost any of its charms since then. It made her feel alive and vibrant, and she almost forgot the dead flesh clamped along the back half of her body. *Forget it. Concentrate on the now.* The instructions were old and automatic by that point. Dwelling on the past only kept her trapped by it. She refused to allow her bastard father to define any more of her life than he already had.

The dress was beautiful but completely out of character for Colleen. Cali stared at her reflection, watching as her blond hair slowly darkened to a dull light brown and her cheekbones rounded out. The shade and fit of the sheath suited Colleen's coloring. Twisting, she watched how the hem clung to her thighs, showing off her long legs in their dark tights. Definitely attractive.

Except Colleen wasn't supposed to be attractive. That was reserved for Boomerang. Her hair darkened even further, to a rich chestnut brown, and her nose and face slimmed to glamour-girl sharpness. Her lips plumped and reddened, creating a dramatic splash of color. Studying herself in the mirror, Cali frowned. Boomerang's beauty was part of a trap, a way to manipulate targets and cause others to underestimate her. *That's not the face I want to show to Joe.*

She concentrated on reshaping her features back to Colleen's, settling the thick-rimmed glasses back on her nose. *I should change back into the pilgrim dress, or else I'm going to be late.* And yet she continued to stare into the mirror. Slowly, she began to pull her mousy brown locks into a smooth bun.

If I act as if I don't know the dress flatters me, it wouldn't be entirely out of character. It was an excuse, and she knew it, but somehow, she couldn't bring herself to stick with Colleen's meek persona. The detective was proving more dangerous than she'd expected, cracking decades of discipline. *I should break things off.*

"You are two seconds away from arguing with your own reflection like Gollum," Cali muttered as she applied her lipstick. "I can do this. He's a means to an end, like any other mark."

It was too late to second-guess her decision anymore, not if she wanted to be on time at the restaurant. She pulled on her coat and hurried down the stairs. As she passed Esperanza's apartment, she decided to talk to the other woman in the morning. Maybe the young mother would have some advice on this whole dating nonsense.

A cab was slowly cruising down the street as she stepped out. *At least one thing is going right tonight.* Cupping her cheek in one hand, she brooded, staring at the lights flickering past the cab's windows. Ordinary people managed to date without complete catastrophes. Surely, she should be able to manage it if she wanted to. Except she wasn't ordinary and never would be. No one had ever understood that except Mr. Dalhard—who Joe wanted to keep in jail. *Way to pick an impossible mess for your first infatuation.*

There were a hundred reasons why she should stop the cab and walk away, yet she still found herself walking up the short ramp to Garden Delight. As much as she told herself that having dinner with Joe was necessary to accomplish her job, she doubted she could walk away under any circumstance. Somehow, Joe Cabrera had worked his way past her defenses, and the only way she could go was forward, hoping it wouldn't hurt too much.

She stumbled over the restaurant's threshold, catching herself from falling by grabbing the hostess stand. That bit of awkwardness was certainly in Colleen's character.

"Table for one?" the pert and pretty little Asian woman asked, an artificial smile covering any personal amusement at watching a potential patron nearly do a face-plant on the floor.

"I'm meeting someone." Cali spotted the detective nearby at a cozy nook of a table surrounded by decorative ferns. He lifted his hand to wave at her, an easy smile brightening his face. Unlike the hostess's polite greeting, it wasn't an act. He seemed genuinely pleased to see her.

He looked gorgeous, more like a model than a cop. His white button-down shirt set off his tan skin perfectly while the leather jacket over it added a hint of edginess and bad boy. His smile was devastating, an unregistered lethal weapon. *I am so screwed.* Cali straightened. *Time to get the shoe in the air.*

She allowed her coat to slip down her arms, catching it in one hand just before it could hit the floor. It was the perfect reveal for her outfit, and Joe didn't disappoint. His eyes widened, a circle of white framing the dark irises, and his mouth dropped into a shocked and unsteady grin. *Nailed it. A solid hit. High heel on concrete.*

CHAPTER FIFTEEN

"Colleen." Joe heard his voice crack slightly and swallowed to regain control. "It's great to see you."

Colleen's eyes sparked in feminine triumph before she lowered her lashes to hide it. "You too, Detective."

So she wants to play. Joe had a few cards of his own to add to the game, but it was damn hard to concentrate with her right in front of him. Her blue dress was the perfect blend of sexiness and modesty. It clung to her tightly while hiding every detail, giving a man ample opportunity to use his imagination. He needed to keep his focus. "I was worried about you today."

"Why?" She cradled her water glass, keeping her gaze on the clear liquid.

Joe leaned closer to her. He'd asked for that table specifically. Due to a weird trick of acoustics, it was impossible to be overheard in the little nook. "Things were pretty bad at the hospital today when I found the Fuenteses."

Her eyes flashed forest green as she forgot to hide them. Joe smiled in short-lived triumph. Her fingers tightened around the glass. "I thought you said they were okay."

"They are. Now." Joe stretched his hand across the invisible divide between them. "But I said I was worried about you. Not them."

He'd expected some guilt, maybe even a secret smile of deception, but instead, Colleen gave a sudden harsh intake of breath, her eyes wide. As if frightened.

She reasserted her mask quickly, playing the role of the shy assistant once more. "I never got past the parking lot. I was too afraid to go inside."

Time to change the rules of the game. "I think we both know that's not entirely true."

Colleen put down her water glass and met his gaze squarely, a silent invitation to air his evidence.

"You went to Right Hand Man." Joe kept his voice quiet, just loud enough to be heard over the cutlery clinks and conversation around them. "You waited until Ken Fuentes left for the hospital, and then you searched his office. Probably for the data drive that Dalhard gave him. Then you went to Dalhard's lawyers."

"You followed me." It was a statement, not an accusation. She was still waiting for the rest of the hand before placing any bets. Her calm impressed Joe, raising his already high opinion of Colleen Avila.

"I did. So I know what you did but not why. There are a lot of people interested in the data, including at least one professional thief. So why were you trying to find it?" Joe had done a lot of thinking that afternoon, and he'd come to some difficult conclusions. Whatever Colleen said next would decide which plan went into action.

The little mouse had vanished. The woman sitting across from him stared at him with cool confidence. "You're right, Detective. I was searching for the data. It's the reason I went to Right Hand Man to begin with. It's information that Mr. Dalhard needs."

"I've seen what's on the drive. Have you?" He couldn't pursue a relationship any further if she'd knowingly targeted people whose only crime was being born different.

Her head snapped back in surprise, and she started to shake her head before catching herself. "You have the data?"

He crossed his arms, resting his elbows squarely on the table. "I do. So you can let your boss and anyone else know that there's no point in pursuing the Fuentes family."

"And what if they come after you instead?"

Was it his imagination, or did he detect more than a hint of concern in her question? "Let them come."

Her gaze dropped back down to the tablecloth, and she fidgeted with the cutlery. "That's quite a bold statement, Detective."

"Call me Joe." He reached out and put his finger on the other end of the fork she was twitching around, careful not to make physical contact. "Will you pass on my message?"

Colleen nodded, releasing the utensil to his custody. She half turned and picked up her coat from the back of her chair.

"Please don't go." Joe held his breath. If she left, he'd never see her again. He'd bet the house on it.

"Did you have more that you wanted to say?" Her voice held more than a trace of bitterness.

"I did, actually. But I won't make you stay and hear it. If you want to leave, I won't stop you." He hoped she would trust him.

She let the coat drop and faced him once again. "I told you before, I won't help you hurt Mr. Dalhard. That stands no matter what you intend to do to me."

Oh, shit. He'd known he needed to be careful, but if she thought he was threatening her, he hadn't been careful enough. Thirty-odd years of guilt-induced parenting to respect and honor women threatened to rise up and smack him. He took a deep breath. "Please, that's not what I meant. I've been doing a lot of thinking since I saw you come out of the office today. At first, I was hurt, more hurt than I should have been."

"I'm sorry," she whispered. Joe guessed that she hadn't meant to say the words out loud.

Cards-on-the-table time. "There's a connection between us, and I think you feel it too. It's why you can't hide behind your mask with me and why I couldn't rest until I knew you were safe. But right now, we're on opposite sides, with you supporting Dalhard and me knowing that he needs to be kept in jail to keep other people safe. The fates haven't been kind to us by only putting us in each other's paths under this kind of circumstance."

"You believe in fate?" Her hands trembled, the movement barely enough to detect against the cloth.

"I do." Joe didn't hesitate in his answer. He could finally be completely honest with her. "All my life, I heard the story of how my father was a real player before he met my mother. He had a different girl for each night of the week, but once he saw her, he said all the other girls disappeared for him. She was the only one he saw every day for the rest of his life. So I spent my life waiting for the same flash of clarity to happen for me. And finally, it did. With you."

Cali took a long drink of water to ease her dry mouth. This was the sort of awkward moment when it would have been very convenient to have some food to pick at and keep her hands busy. Of all the things that Joe could have said, she'd never expected him to profess a connection with her.

Except it wasn't with her. It was with Colleen, who didn't exist.

"I've shocked you." He didn't seem terribly displeased but gave a smug little grin, flaunting his perfect teeth.

Shock was too mild a word for what felt like a construction boot crashing into glass. Cali's expectations had shattered, leaving her uncertain where to move next without getting sliced by the shards. "Why me? I'm not anyone special."

"I disagree. But then, I'm not interested in the corporate-assistant disguise. It's the woman behind the mask who draws me. And even though we're on opposite sides, I don't think we're actually so very far apart where it counts."

He had no idea how true his words about disguises were. And he was right about making her slip. She'd completely failed to realize that she'd agreed to show up at the hospital as Colleen instead of Boomerang until he'd mentioned her absence there. It was an inexcusable and dangerous lapse.

He was still talking. "… care about the Fuenteses, even though it would have been better for your boss if I'd never gotten involved. And the way you took the time to get to know Tony and his family shows that you're a good person. I don't think you know half of what Dalhard has been involved in."

"I know enough. I'm not a sheltered innocent." She couldn't let him put her on a pedestal. She knew Mr. Dalhard could be ruthless, but until recently, it had always been to protect his people.

"No, I suppose not." He paused. "I'm proposing we put our differences aside. We can leave them behind at the door and just be Colleen and Joe. We don't have to have any lies between us." He cleared his throat uncomfortably. "Which is why there's something else I have to tell you about the hospital today."

Had he figured it out? Colleen's hands felt as if they were carved out of ice, sucking the heat out of her body.

"There was a woman there. A thief. I think she came for the data."

Boomerang. Cali knew she shouldn't be jealous of someone who was essentially herself, but it didn't stop the green-eyed monster from pinching and twisting her confidence.

"There was something about her, something that I didn't expect to feel again after meeting you." Joe picked up her hand with his warm one. "She was beautiful and sexy."

Of course she was.

"But there was something hard about her. I think she's a good person underneath, but I would rather be with you. You're real in a way that she wasn't." His skin was pleasantly warm against the coolness of hers. Her hands and feet were always cold. She suspected it was because of the peculiar biology that allowed her to morph from one face to another.

Cali suddenly realized that he was touching her and it wasn't triggering any unpleasant reactions or memories. Somehow, Joe's hand on hers felt right—protective instead of a display of ownership.

"This would be an awesome time for you to say something before I start to babble from overwhelming nerves." Joe's smile started to crack at the corners.

"I don't know what to say." She stared at his hand enfolding hers, and he immediately withdrew. Cali missed the warmth of his skin but couldn't help being impressed with how he'd let her go as soon as she'd begun to tense.

"Do you want to give us a chance?"

She rubbed her thumb against her fingers, trying to recapture the warmth. "My life is complicated. More than you know."

"I can deal with complicated." He smiled in relief. "And maybe I shouldn't have been so blunt, but I've learned the hard way that pretending something doesn't exist only makes things worse. I'd rather face this on my own terms than try and run. I'm hoping I didn't frighten you off."

"I don't frighten easily." But she couldn't share his optimism. "I'm not sure this is a good idea."

"Of course not. Good ideas are overrated. Bad ideas are the ones that pay off big." Joe's lips curved in a sexy grin. "Don't give me a final no right now. Take some time. Get to know me. I won't push without a definite yes from you."

She looked down at her hands again. "Somehow, you don't strike me as the passive type."

"I didn't say I wouldn't be working to persuade you to take a chance." He winked. "But you don't have to worry. My mother raised me to be a gentleman rogue."

Too much. Her mind kept searching for an angle. He had to be after something. He couldn't be tempted by Colleen's meager charms.

"You really find it hard to believe, don't you?" Joe asked. "I want to be outraged on your behalf, but I can't help feeling like I've discovered a hidden treasure, and I'm just glad not to be fighting off competitors."

A bark of rough laughter escaped her lips, and her hand flew to her mouth to hold it back. "No, we're only fighting each other."

"Hey, like I said, we'll leave that all behind and just be Joe and Colleen." He held out his hand. "I'd like to touch you again if it's okay."

She nodded, and his strong hands folded around hers again. His thumbs and fingers kneaded her palm gently, the calluses pressing into her padded flesh. Heat burned in her cheeks as he held her hand up, palm outward, and used his thumbs to caress upward from the bottom of her life line to the base of her ring finger. He grinned at her as his fingers feathered along the back of her hand, leaving tingling after-trails in their wake.

"I figure your hands must get sore from all that typing." He applied firm pressure to the edges of her palm and lifted it closer to his mouth.

Cali thought he was going to kiss it, but instead he blew on it, warm air followed by more soothing caresses. *Oh God, that feels good.* All of her joints, big and small, ached constantly, and the warmth and relaxation spreading through her hand began to echo elsewhere, reducing the underlying tension.

He lowered his voice and leaned forward, continuing to massage her fingers. "You know, to get the full effect, you'll have to let me give you a full-body massage someday. I have very talented hands." He winked at her.

Cheeks flushed, she looked around to see if anyone was watching them.

"Say the word, and I stop."

He paused, giving her a chance to end the moment. The place was too public for such an intimate exchange, but the same blaze of exhibitionism that drove Boomerang's in-your-face sexuality kept Cali silent. She crossed and recrossed her legs to alleviate the uncomfortable twinges dancing through her gut. "Go on."

"I think I'd start in your hair for a scalp massage." He spoke barely loud enough for her to hear and continued to caress her hand with his strong fingers. "I'd start at the temples with gentle circles with the tips of my fingers while my thumbs start loosening the knots that must be at the base of your skull."

His hands were probably wide enough to do that. She swallowed, trying to visually measure their width.

"I'd move into your scalp, letting your hair tumble free around your shoulders." He gently set down her hand and pointed to the other one. "May I?"

She nodded, and he picked up her cold hand and began the entire dance over again.

"Once you started to relax, I'd move my hands down your neck with the lightest of touches. Enough to warm you up." He winked at her again. "Then I could begin on your back."

That word dashed a bucket of cold water over the fantasy.

Joe immediately stopped, concern replacing his flirtatious grin. "What's wrong?"

Cali couldn't answer. Too much whirled and ripped at her mind as humiliation replaced arousal. *I am such an idiot.* She never let anyone see the scars covering her back, ugly dead flesh that refused to shift at her command. All the banished tension returned tenfold, clamping her muscles into rigidity.

"Colleen, talk to me. Please."

He doesn't even know my real name. Another mental reality slap. Words failed to come. Her brain felt oddly hollow and fragile as if Joe's touch had drained her. She opened eyes that she hadn't realized she'd closed and met his gaze. Rather than the usual frustration or predatory anticipation of weakness, there was only quiet comprehension. His gaze left her stripped and vulnerable as it penetrated deeper than she allowed strangers to invade.

"I told you I won't do anything that makes you uncomfortable. That's a promise." Joe had released her hands. They lay limp on the table like pale sacrifices to an unknown god. "But I'm not going to give up either. You can count on me to be there when you need me, no matter what."

"I… I don't usually like to be touched." She forced each word out through her numb lips. Not much of a confession, but it seemed to crack the ice holding her in place.

"All right." His easy agreement left her feeling hollow as if she had denied herself something vital. He tilted his head to one side. "But you seemed to be okay with the hand massage."

"I was. At first." Her fingers curled around her napkin to keep them from trembling.

"Too far. At least for our first time. Understood. Now it's my turn to share. I like touching. My family is always hugging or giving each other pats. I'm very comfortable expressing my affection physically. But I'll respect your boundaries. You decide when you're ready."

She believed him. There wasn't the slightest sliver of deception anywhere to be seen. As incredible as it seemed, he really was equally determined to pursue and protect. If she could make herself say the words to send him away, he would go and never bother her again. *How can this end in anything other than heartbreak?*

The Flop

Chapter Sixteen

Cali stumbled off the prison bus, features firmly fixed as Colleen despite the anxiety chewing through her typical steadiness. Her dinner with Joe kept running through her mind. After the hand massage, they'd finally eaten, keeping the conversation light. She'd learned that Joe was an only child, although he'd grown up with a dozen cousins of various ages. His pride and love for his mother shone through with every story he told about his family, even the embarrassing and exasperating ones.

Of course, Cali couldn't do the same. So she listened and ate and tried not to feel too guilty, trapped by her own lies in an unbreakable web. Joe might not want any deception between them, but she doubted that he would ever be able to accept all of who she really was.

He'd insisted on booking another date for lunch the next day, and he'd already sent her a few text messages wishing her a good day and letting her know that he was thinking of her. *I should cancel.* Colleen could disappear. It might be a pain coming up with a new face and identity to continue her work with Mr. Dalhard, but she could do it. She could get the last two portions of the list and walk away from this whole mess. Running away had never seemed so tempting.

But it would be impossible. She couldn't abandon Hood, Harley, and the kids from the crews. They depended on the money that Boomerang brought in. Cali shuffled through the metal detector, arms outstretched to show that she wasn't concealing anything.

Would it really be so bad to let this thing with Joe play out? She needed to stay close to find out what happened to Fuentes's portion of the list. *It's not like it will hurt any less to walk away now than later.* She'd already missed the exit that would have protected her heart, so no matter when she left, it would hurt like hell. So why not enjoy what she could while she could?

There were a bunch of logical reasons why not, but the buzzing hum of growing infatuation drowned every single one of them out. *I'm starting to sound like an addict.*

"Miss Avila." Dalhard's voice made her jump.

"Mr. Dalhard." Cali rapidly scanned him. The corners of his eyes were tight along with his mouth. His annoyance sent her adrenaline pumping, causing her mind to play tricks. The walls seemed thicker and the air thinner. Everything moved in crystalline-precise clarity, letting her note multiple small details simultaneously.

"I trust your preoccupation is not a sign of difficulties." Dalhard took his seat, one arm resting along the tabletop. The fingers of his hand were curled inward but not tightened into a fist. A good sign.

"Personal matters, sir. I apologize for my distraction." Cali kept her voice formal the way she'd always done for the thugs and bullies growing up.

"I'm sorry for snapping." Dalhard's voice softened, and his face relaxed. "Do you need my help for anything? More money? Contacts?"

Cali shook her head, relieved. That was the Mr. Dalhard she recognized. One who cared about his people, protecting them from all threats. "I can handle it for now, but I'll let you know if the situation changes."

"Very well. I trust you, Colleen." Mr. Dalhard rolled his broad shoulders, his eyes scanning to make sure no one was close. "I worry, though. You've always been inclined to take too much on your shoulders and not ask for help."

"Old habits die hard." Cali smiled, her body settling back into safe mode. "Besides, that's one of the reasons you can trust me. You know I'll do my best and not slack off, waiting for someone else to do the work."

"True. Your resourcefulness has always been impressive. I'm particularly impressed with your latest tactic." His head inclined in a proud nod of acknowledgement.

What latest tactic? Cali's palms dampened. Had the lawyers contacted him? She'd hoped to tell him herself about reopening the case.

"Developing a relationship with Detective Cabrera is a brilliant move. It could give us a connection straight into the heart of our enemies." His pleasant demeanor slipped, letting a hint of obsession leak through. "You'll know exactly what they're planning, and we can use him to plant disinformation, leading them to disaster and ruin."

"Ah." Cali folded and refolded her fingers, wondering who had told Mr. Dalhard about her involvement with Joe.

"We have bigger issues to deal with, however. Have you procured the final packages?" Mr. Dalhard tugged on the cuffs of his orange jumpsuit.

Cali's gaze flicked to the cameras mounted along the walls and the guards patrolling the lines of cheap, bolted-together tables and chairs. "Not yet. There were some complications."

"Not the news I expected to hear." The hard edge returned to his voice. Cali braced herself for an explosion.

Instead, Mr. Dalhard surveyed the room, where the prisoners were desperately trying to cram in a few minutes of normalcy, the guards watching with bored alertness between dull, institutional walls painted with behavior codes and warnings about physical contact. "I'm not sure why I spent so long being afraid of this place."

"It's prison." Cali kept perfectly still, moving as little as possible. Every instinct and memory of her childhood told her that the man opposite her was a dangerous predator.

"It's inconvenient certainly. Though I'm beginning to believe that my time here was necessary. I needed to understand how the world truly worked, or else I would always have been vulnerable." His eyes tracked across the room, dead but alert like a shark's.

"I've told your lawyers to push on the appeal and get you out of here. It's important to keep your head down." Cali held her breath as she offered him the hope of freedom. *Please be enough.* "You can take back the business and have the resources of Dalhard Industries again."

He was going to hit her. Cali had seen that look in men's eyes before. If he struck, that would mean the man she knew was lost. She held his gaze with her own, refusing to back down.

The simmering anger tightening his eyes and mouth blazed at her attitude of disrespect. In prison, respect was the only protection. A person needed to meet any violation with a furious attack or they'd face a short slide into victimhood. If her mentor chose to embrace the prison code, to dive in and submerge himself in the culture of violence, then she was too late.

Abrupt laughter barked out of his mouth. "You're right, of course. I've learned what I can from in here, and it's time to emerge back into the world."

Relief flooded through her tense limbs. He understood and wasn't upset.

Mr. Dalhard leaned close, keeping his voice low. "I know you've been worried about me. There are certain roles I have to play in here even if it's not entirely what I would have chosen."

Maybe it's not too late. He might claim that his callousness was part of a calculated ruse, a disguise to help him survive. But Cali knew better than anyone that spending too much time behind a mask changed someone. Sooner or later, all illusions stopped being temporary. Still, she couldn't abandon all hope. "Just be careful."

"Once I'm out, we'll make sure that our enemies can't hurt us again. Keep close to Detective Cabrera, and learn what you can about him. Meanwhile, you have other duties to attend to." He patted her hand.

She felt a crackly slip of paper slide between her palm and the table. She lifted her gaze to meet Mr. Dalhard's eyes.

"I know you'll keep on taking care of me. Visiting hours are nearly over. I don't want you to miss the bus." Mr. Dalhard got up, tugging his uniform tunic straight. "I'll see you next time."

Cali nodded dumbly. He leaned down and kissed the top of her head before regally walking away. She watched him go, seeing the same violence-backed swagger that the top thugs always used. It broke her heart to see him moving that way.

Her fingers automatically tucked the paper away, keeping it moving during the pat-downs and inspections of the exit protocols. *Everything will be okay once I get him out.* She clung to her hopes, repeating them over and over like a spell.

Once on the bus back to the city, she pulled out the paper. It held eight names and addresses with amounts beside them—instructions for money transfers. *Probably for protection.* She'd take care of it that morning, and then she'd stop by the lawyers' again and find out what they'd decided to do. *Everything will be okay once he gets out.*

Ready to talk? The invitation appeared on Karan's computer as soon as he logged in. He had struggled most of the night, deciding how best to handle his mysterious intruder. He needed to draw the person out and find out what they knew and why they had chosen to target him.

It only took a moment to enter his reply into the chat window. **I do not do business with people I do not know.**

You may not know me, but I know you. I've been watching you for a long time.

No surprise there. Not many people understood his true position within the hierarchy of Dalhard Industries. Even now, most dismissed him as an administrative assistant.

I know you want proof of what I know. In Alaska, you provided documents to the police to ensure that André Dalhard was convicted. Since then, you've been working with Detective Hampton in the Perdition Police Department to keep your former employer in jail. You've been searching for the list of *lulassu* that you compiled for him, but the need to stay undetected by your former partner, Vapor, has hampered you.

An impressive list of accusations without any proof to back them up, Karan responded. This intruder demonstrated intelligence and skill, guaranteeing Karan would not dismiss any offer of help out of hand, though the hacker was treading perilously close to being too dangerous to allow to survive.

Of course without proof. You aren't a fool, and you covered

your tracks well. As I said, I've been watching for a long time.

"So what do you want?" Karan asked softly. It did not seem like the traditional approach to blackmail. Nor did it seem like a trap set by Vapor or his ilk. A thrill of excitement sent an intoxicating trickle meandering through his careful control. He so very rarely received the privilege of a challenge.

What would you do if you didn't have to worry about hiding? the hacker asked.

I could have what I seek within a few days. He could divert more resources and take more risks without the threat of tipping off his old partner.

Then start planning your celebration. A webcam image popped open beside the video chat. A man sat in a chair, blue-grey tattoos gleaming through the stubble covering his head. A thick black blindfold covered his eyes, and Karan could see where plastic ties bound him to the chair. Skeptical, he searched for evidence of a trick. But he could not deny it—the man was Vapor.

He needed to handle that very delicately, as with any sensitive negotiation. Karen typed, **It could be a recording. Or he could have posed for this.**

Pick a television channel.

Karan chose a local news station, using the remote to put it up on the television in his office. A moment later, a television clicked on in the video, showing an identical broadcast. Not a recording.

He's been my guest for the last month and will remain so indefinitely, the hacker continued.

What is it you want? The implied threat was clear. If he did not do as his intruder asked, then Vapor would be released. It seemed impossible that his old partner had been captured and held, but it would explain his uncharacteristic silence.

Only to help you. I saw him speak to you on the rooftop in Juneau. If he had left you alone, I would have left him alone. But he threatened your hard work, and I couldn't allow it.

Karan doubted his intruder's altruistic claims. All people made choices that benefited themselves. **Very well. I still need a way to**

contact you and a name to use when speaking to you.

You can call me Naya Jeevan. And I'll be in touch. The computer went silent.

Naya Jeevan. It meant "new life" in Hindi. *Very well.* If his intruder wished to continue to play games, then Karan would indulge them. Meanwhile, he would take advantage of that latest move. He contacted Detective Hampton. "Are you still interested in extra compensation to recover the data I seek?"

"Sure thing, Boss. You said the gal who stole it was called Boomerang, right? I can go after her right now." The detective's eagerness to play the bully meant he had not done any research on his target. Karan was not surprised, but the man would need to be carefully guided.

"Do not go after Boomerang directly. She is prepared for such an attack. Instead, focus on her partner, a man they call Hood. He has a daughter, Eva." Karan hoped he would not have to spell things out further. Was a little native intelligence too much to hope for in his operatives?

"You want me to take the daughter? Rough her up unless they give us the data? She's not, like, a little kid or something, is she?"

How interesting. It appeared the detective might still have a vestigial conscience after all. "She currently attends South Perdition High School. Threaten the daughter, and Hood will make Boomerang give you the data. Once you have it, you will be paid appropriately."

Threatening family members or other loved ones was always more efficient than directly threatening another player. Karan hung up the phone. The detective would bumble the operation, but he would flush Boomerang out of hiding. All of that was part of the game, and Karan never lost once he chose to play.

Chapter Seventeen

Joe's morning-after, post-date buzz abruptly crashed as he saw the phone call from his sergeant. *Come on.* Surely the universe should give him more than a few hours to enjoy his memories of Miss Colleen Avila. Even though they'd spent most of their meal keeping things light and he'd gone home alone, he'd never enjoyed a date more. He'd made the right decision. She was a woman he could spend the rest of his life with.

Repressing a curse, he put down his coffee and accepted his duty. "Cabrera here."

"We've got a problem." Modnik's usual brisk manner had sharpened enough to feature in razor commercials, but she was keeping her voice low. "The footage from the Lockbox theft is gone."

"What do you mean, gone?" Joe's training kept his brain from leaping ahead to conclusions.

"I mean gone. It's been erased, and the physical copies have vanished." The sergeant spat out each word like gunfire. "I've got Internal Affairs crawling up my ass here."

"I'm a suspect." It wasn't a question. IA wouldn't be on his side after his "breakdown" or his trip to Alaska. He'd tripped the bad-cop alarm, and it looked like his hopes for everything to blow over were going up in flames like an ex's photos in a trash can.

"You were the last one logged in to see it."

"I put it all away, and then I ran into Hampton…" The other detective's suspicious behavior suddenly became clear. Or was it? Hampton was a lazy, loudmouthed jerk, but would he cross the line and destroy evidence?

Modnik continued. "I need you to stay away from the station until I can get this calmed down. Luckily, I've got a good excuse to keep you out of here—I need a Spanish translator."

Joe closed his eyes. "Sarge, you shouldn't do this. I'll come and turn myself in. I know I didn't do it, and the longer I wait to talk to them, the worse it will be."

"I know you didn't do it either, and I'm telling you to stay away," Modnik hissed, the words barely audible. "IA isn't alone. They've got two guys in suits. They smell like Feds but haven't identified themselves. They're real interested in your caseload and in your stories about psychics and superheroes. I don't trust them."

Shitshitshitshit. He'd been afraid that his outburst would attract whatever secret government agency dealt with the *lalassu.* Dani's family kept insisting there wasn't one, but he'd been sure it existed. He couldn't be the first cop to stumble onto the secret. He couldn't take the risk of leading them to Michael and the others.

"Stay away from the station. Go and help Salazar. He got called in on reports of shouting and heavy crashes, and now he has a heavily battered woman who only speaks Spanish and is refusing to go to the hospital. She's got two kids with her." Modnik rattled off an address.

"I'm on it." Joe hesitated, unsure if the sergeant would take his next words as questioning her legendary competence. "Be careful, Sarge. Don't put yourself at risk to protect me."

"It's not just for you. Now, get going." Modnik hung up without another word. Joe's post-date vibes were definitely smashed beyond redemption by that point. *Think it through.* If unknown Feds were at the station, they might also be sniffing around his phone or his apartment. They might even go after his family if they couldn't find him.

Joe hurried to help Salazar, his brain rapidly sorting through and discarding possibilities. She'd said the two Feds weren't talking, which meant they wanted to keep a low profile but also wanted to be on site so they could snatch him up without causing a fuss. Their actions suggested they didn't want to alert anyone to their intentions. If they had the resources, they would probably track him, but he should be safe from aggressive action, which would only serve to tip everyone off. He'd have to find a way to pass a message to Michael and the others—one that couldn't be tracked easily.

No suitable ideas had presented themselves by the time he reached the apartment building. Parked out front, the shiny white paint on Salazar's cruiser contrasted sharply with the faded and cracked concrete façade of the building. Although the structure itself was cheaply built and poorly maintained, the balconies still blossomed with flowers and vegetables, and the windows held brightly colored curtains fluttering in the wind, showing that the residents hadn't completely given up hope.

Joe expected to hear shouting as soon as he stepped inside, and the relative silence triggered further alarms in his head. He took the stairs to the third floor and found the apartment door open. Cautiously, he looked inside, a hand on his weapon. Salazar stood in front of the tiny kitchenette while a woman perched on the couch, two little girls tucked beside her. Bruises dotted her face and arms, and neat stitches sealed a long slice along her upper left arm.

He introduced himself in Spanish and asked if everything was okay. "*Hola. Soy el Detective Cabrera. Todo está bien?*"

The woman said nothing, staring straight ahead as if deaf. Joe glanced at Salazar, who took it as an invitation to report. "The neighbors reported a disturbance. I arrived along with the EMTs. She let them stitch her up but wouldn't go to the hospital. They think her ribs are broken."

Joe watched the woman out of the corner of his eye. From the way she stiffened at Salazar's words, Joe guessed that she understood English perfectly well. She probably spoke it as well. But she'd been pretending otherwise, either to encourage Salazar to leave or to buy time for someone else. "I've got this if you want to head out."

"Are you sure? Whoever did this might come back." Standing tall, Salazar looked ready to do his heroic duty, but Joe's attention stayed on the family. One of the little girls whimpered at the rookie's words, her grip tightening on her mother.

"I've got it. I'll call if I need you." Joe ushered the other cop out of the apartment before turning back to the family. He spoke in Spanish, not wanting to trip the mother up. "Is it okay if I stay and we talk for a while?"

"Do I have a choice?" Her diction was awkward through her split lip, but it didn't diminish her inherent dignity.

"Of course. If you really want me to leave, I will. But I hope you'll talk to me so that I can help you and your girls." He kept his voice light, not wanting to do anything that might trigger her to feel threatened.

"You can stay." She shrugged as if indifferent. "But nothing happened. I was in a car accident."

"Okay. Can I ask your names?" He smiled at the children, hoping their mother would relax.

Her expression softened as she looked down at the two little girls. "Speranza Mechoso. This is Carlotta and Zara."

"*Hola.*" He waved at the girls. Carlotta, who looked about five, buried her nose back in her mother's side. Joe noticed Speranza wincing. The EMTs were right about her ribs. The other little girl was only a toddler, and she stared at him with wide black eyes over a firmly inserted thumb.

"Can you tell me where the car accident happened?" He pulled out his notebook. Her story was a lie, but she needed to believe that he believed her.

She named an intersection nearby. "A taxi hit me as I crossed the street. It left after, and I did not see the license plate."

"Were the girls hurt? Even a small hit with a car can cause big damage." He noted the pattern of bruises on her arms. Round and evenly spaced, they were more consistent with someone grabbing and shaking her than with a collision.

Speranza's arms tightened around her girls. There could be no doubt about her devotion to her daughters. "No. They were already across the street."

That didn't make sense. Zara could barely toddle. She was way too young to walk on her own.

"I took good care of her." Carlotta announced proudly. In English.

"Good for you." He answered her in Spanish, pretending not to notice. The little girl preened under his praise.

Whatever really happened, Speranza had known it was coming. She'd sent her children ahead while she stayed behind to confront it. Or rather, him. Joe would bet his annual salary that this was a case of spousal abuse. There was no sign of a man living at the apartment, but any cop could tell stories about ex-spouses who went crazy after someone finally got the courage to leave.

"Speranza? What happened?" A woman's voice interrupted, speaking English.

Carlotta's eyes lit up, and she scrambled off the couch. "Cali!"

Joe turned to greet the new arrival and got hit with a double gut punch. First hit, she was stunningly beautiful, with long blond hair and wide blue-green eyes. She was dressed in a simple, professional nut-brown suit and a high-collared white shirt and carried a briefcase. Her clothing showed off every rounded curve and would make any red-blooded man indulge in boardroom fantasies. Second hit, she stared at him as if she recognized him, and while he would have sworn he had never seen her before in his life, there was something intensely familiar about her. A sense of intimacy and trust made him want to tell her everything.

"What are you doing here?" Cali blurted out, her inflection making it quite clear that she meant him in particular rather than the police in general.

"There was an accident," Speranza answered in perfectly clear English. She shot a defiant glare at Joe, daring him to call her on her pretense of ignorance. "I've told him everything is fine. He can go."

Joe wasn't about to do that. Not until he figured out who Cali was and why he felt so drawn to her. *First Colleen, then Boomerang, and now Cali.* If this was another test of his newfound determination, then the universe lacked all sense of proportion. He watched as she picked up Carlotta, cradling the child and holding her close. The sight of a child in Cali's arms made him acutely aware of how much he wanted a child of his own, a little boy or girl to protect, cherish, and teach.

"Detective?" Cali's prompt made him realize that he'd been staring.

"Ah, yes." He looked down at his notes, buying time to chase down his meandering thoughts. "Ms. Mechoso, I know you didn't want to go to the hospital, but I'm concerned about leaving you here all on your own with your girls. You might be hurt worse than you realize."

Speranza straightened and regally lifted her chin. "I can take care of myself."

"I can help," Cali offered, rocking slightly to soothe Carlotta. "I live in the building. I can check on her."

And what happens when whoever did this comes back? Even if his own conscience and professional ethics allowed him to leave these women alone and vulnerable, his mother would personally kick his ass if he walked away. "Ms. Cali, could I speak to you in private for a moment?"

She nodded, putting Carlotta down. "I'll be back in a minute."

They stepped out into the hallway, and Joe carefully closed the apartment door behind them. It was heavier than he'd expected, and a number of fresh scuff marks dotted the paint. Noting that for later consideration, he turned his attention back to Cali and immediately realized he'd made a tactical mistake. Being alone with her in the dimly lit hall got his lower brain considering all sorts of possibilities it had no business imagining. *Keep it professional!* "It's very generous of you to offer to help your neighbor out, but I don't think you know what you're getting into."

Cali's generous mouth thinned and tightened. "I understand better than you think."

"I don't think this was a car crash." He wished he could have access to Speranza's records.

"Of course not. It was her ex-husband, Rodolpho Mechoso. He's put her in the hospital five times in the last four years. They have a restraining order, but it doesn't stop him from coming by to yell at her through the door at least twice a week." Cali's folded arms and defiant glare told him that she hadn't been impressed by the system's efforts thus far.

"I'll be honest. I'd love to go and arrest him right now, but since she's insisting on having been hit by a taxi and I don't have any other witnesses to say otherwise, my hands are tied." Joe ran his hand over his close-cropped hair. "Can you talk to her—convince her to make a statement, or even just call me the next time her ex stops by to harass her? If there's a restraining order, I can take him away without having to involve her or the kids."

He held out his card. Cali looked at it warily, as if it might explode on contact, then slowly took it from him. She turned it over in her delicate fingers. "I'll see what I can do. Neither of us has had great experiences with the police."

"So call me. Not 9-1-1." He was moving into more dangerous territory. Visions of riding to the rescue were best left to television, not real life. Of course, maybe he could stop by to check in from time to time. That would be responsible. *Stop it.* "I'll ask the local cops to keep a lookout for her ex."

"They won't do anything to stop him." Cali bit her lip as if she wanted to trust him but wasn't sure about it.

"They can't arrest him, but they can ask for his ID and start recording his trips to this neighborhood. In my experience, bullies don't like official attention." He was making a lot of glib promises, especially considering how his sergeant had specifically told him to lie low, but he needed to erase the distrust from her eyes. "Please think about what I've said."

She nodded, setting her golden mane of loose curls into motion. He wanted to reach out and wrap them around his fingers while making her moan his name.

He stepped back too abruptly to pretend it had been anything except a retreat. He needed to get out of there before he did something horrible and stupid.

CHAPTER EIGHTEEN

Cali watched Joe practically stumble over his feet in his desperation to get away from her. When she'd arrived and noticed the open apartment door, she'd immediately gone inside. Seeing Joe standing in Speranza's kitchen stunned her like a blast from a Taser. He'd gotten a look at her naked face, and then it was too late to shift into one of the personas he knew.

Compartmentalization was the key to keeping her different lives and personas intact, but they all seemed to be colliding together into a giant muddle centered on the detective. *Maybe I should tell him the truth.* Her sardonic inner voice replied, *Good idea. And then he can tell the nice men in the white coats that you're a certifiable lunatic.*

Or maybe not. The video of the woman shifting into a bear had opened up all kinds of conversations. Maybe he would believe her, and she'd end up in some kind of government black site, coerced into being a spy. "One thing at a time."

Talking to yourself is still one of those signs of crazy. Cali gathered her mental faculties and unlocked Speranza's door. Finding her neighbor and the girls still on the couch, she asked, "What happened?"

Speranza tried to stand, and her face immediately twisted in pain.

Cali hurried over. "Stay put. I'll take care of the girls."

Zara's diaper puffed out, nearly ready to burst, and Cali took her to the bathroom to change her. Speranza leaned back on the couch in relief. "They need to eat. Their snacks are ready in the fridge."

Diaper dealt with, Cali found the plates of prepared fruits and vegetables in the fridge and set the girls up with a video about animated singing cats. Then she confronted Speranza. "Let me have a look."

Speranza patiently held still while Cali checked over her injuries. The paramedics were right. She had bruising, broken ribs, and some small cuts that didn't need stitching. They'd already wrapped the ribs, leaving nothing for Cali to tend. "Okay, start talking."

"I took the girls to see my mother. I checked with Rodolpho's cousin, and he was supposed to be working. It should have been safe." Speranza stared down at her folded hands. "We were almost back at the apartment when I saw him."

I should have been here. There were too many things pulling on Cali's attention.

"I told the girls to hide by a newsstand. They did very well." Speranza smiled sadly at her children. "I hurried across the street, and that's where he found me. He tried to make me tell him where they were."

"How did you get away?"

"A man in a truck got out and grabbed Rodolpho. I broke free and ran to the girls, then we all ran as quickly as we could back to the apartment. Rodolpho followed us, and we got the door closed just in time." Speranza shuddered, burying her face in her hands.

"Where was your Taser?" Cali asked.

"I left it here. I didn't want one of the girls to get hold of it."

Cali bit her tongue. After Rodolpho's last visit, she'd told Speranza to keep it with her at all times. But the last thing her friend needed at the moment was criticism.

"Someone must have called the police. Rodolpho left when he heard the sirens. It is all so embarrassing." Speranza rubbed her forehead with both hands.

"It's not embarrassing. He hurt you." Cali could have crushed the man's throat with her bare hands if he'd still been there. She respected Speranza and her desire to handle the situation with quiet dignity, but if the idiot came back, she would make sure it was the last time. "I think you should call the detective if he comes again."

Speranza shook her head. After the cops in her old precinct had refused to believe her, she wouldn't trust the police.

Cali wasn't going to let Speranza bet her own life and the lives of her daughters on an assumption of Joe's incompetence. "He's a good man. He cares what happens to you and the girls. He said to call him the next time Rodolpho bothers you."

A raised eyebrow told Cali she'd gone too far. Speranza leaned forward. "You know him."

"I've run into him a few times. Enough to know he's a good man and a good cop." Cali put Joe's card on the table, trying to remain casual.

"You like him." Speranza's smile split her lip again, and she dabbed at the blood with a tissue.

Cali grabbed ice from the freezer and wrapped it in a towel. Speranza held it to her mouth and motioned for Cali to continue.

What can I say? "I like him, but we're too different."

A knock at the door shattered the girl-talk mood. Speranza's hands tightened on Cali's arm, her blunt nails digging painfully into Cali's flesh.

Untangling herself, Cali pulled one of her knives from her sleeve sheath and crept silently to the door to peer through the peephole. "It's okay. It's a friend of mine."

Speranza collapsed back onto the couch, wincing in pain.

Cali opened the door. "Harley, what are you doing here?"

"You aren't answering your phone." Harley pushed past her, his usually animated features frozen in a rictus of grief and fear.

Cali pulled her phone out and frowned. Four missed calls in the last half hour. "What's going on?"

"Some detective came to the apartment, claiming to be investigating with social services. When Hood let him in, he demanded to be given the files you stole or else he would hurt Eva." The words exploded out of Harley. Hood and Harley had adopted Eva when she was only a toddler, rescuing her after her drug-addicted mother was shot. "I listened from the office. Hood left, pretending to play along, and I tried calling you."

Cali's anger broke like a summer storm, ready to enact some devastation once she found the right target. How dare someone involve Hood and Harley's daughter in that mess? "Where did they go?"

"Headquarters. He made sure to say it loudly enough for me to hear. The detective wanted him to call you, but Hood insisted it wasn't necessary." Message delivered, Harley sank down, bracing his hands on his knees.

"He's buying time. The files aren't at headquarters. Have you talked to Eva? Is she okay?" Cali asked.

Harley nodded. "I called her phone, and she said she was pulled out of class by a police officer. He's still waiting with her. She didn't say anything, but if I call the school or the police, she could be killed."

"I need to think." Cali was being pulled in too many directions. Speranza needed her. Hood needed her. Mr. Dalhard wanted the data, and Joe wanted the data. Now this new guy wanted it, and she was starting to think it was too dangerous to allow anyone to have it. As soon as Hood and Eva were safe, she would figure out exactly what was on the drives she'd stolen. A professional blind eye was valuable, but not when people started shooting at her from the blind spot.

"Your friend, he needs you," Speranza said. "Go. Both of you. We can hide in the safe room."

A reinforced master closet, the safe room was meant as a last resort and would be torture with two bored and frightened children—not to mention with broken ribs. Harley straightened up, puppy eyes pleading with her to fix the crisis.

"Okay. Speranza, you won't need to hide. Harley will stay with you until I can come back." Cali held up her hand to forestall his protest. "I know you want to come with me, but this isn't your forte, and the fewer people I have to keep track of, the more chance of getting us all out unscathed. You know the only way I'll let anything happen to Hood or Eva is over my cold, dead body. Speranza needs someone to keep an eye on her and help out with the kids. You can do that. Speranza, Harley is one of my oldest friends, and I'd trust him with my life. He'll make sure you're all okay."

"I don't like it, but you're right. Just please hurry." Harley made shooing motions with his hands.

Cali turned to Speranza. If she was too gun-shy to trust a strange man in her house and with her children, then they'd need to come up with a plan B. Fear pinched the battered woman's eyes, but she slowly nodded. She was willing to trust Cali.

"I'll call as soon as I can. Meantime, don't let anyone in the apartment. If someone knocks, pretend you're not here." Cali barely waited for acknowledgment before sprinting out to the street. Thank God she'd gone with a flexible wardrobe that day. The drab brown skirt and jacket were perfect for Colleen but would also work for Boomerang with a few adjustments. Ignoring the cab driver's widened eyes in the rearview mirror, Cali stripped off the conservative blouse to reveal the scarlet, lace-trimmed camisole underneath. She pulled out a clip and tied back her hair in a hasty bun.

The cab didn't linger after dropping her off in Sow-town, giving her more than enough time to finish the final touches of her transformation into Boomerang. She slipped the heavy watch onto her wrist and walked briskly down the streets. Any other young woman walking alone would have attracted a multitude of catcalls, but Boomerang was known and respected. When people noticed the barely controlled fury in her walk and face, they discovered sudden urges to head inside or to another part of the city, which suited Cali just fine. *Fewer potential sources of collateral damage.*

A short walk brought her to the abandoned three-level apartment building their crew used as their headquarters. The brick façade lacked a fair amount of its mortar but still stood strong.

Avoiding the broken front door, Cali went around to the locked side entrance. Using the front would trip a sensor, alerting her people to an intruder. Hood had wanted booby traps, like a weakened floor that dropped trespassers into the moldy basement. But hurting some street kid or homeless person looking for shelter wasn't an acceptable risk in Cali's book.

The thought reminded her of the homeless man who had loaned her his coat in exchange for fifty dollars and a bus ticket south. *I hope he made it safely to Atlanta.* She'd check with her southern contacts after things settled. She climbed the stairs, which were lit by sporadic flashes from the few bulbs still hanging from their swinging cords.

Only one more flight to go. Cali took a deep breath and crept up as quietly as she could, hoping to overhear something that might give her a clue about what she was walking into. But she couldn't hear anything, not even the normal sounds of business. Hood must have cleared everyone out, which was a very bad sign.

At the top of the stairs, she opened the door as quickly as possible, hoping to gain some advantage by using the element of surprise.

"Drop it!" a harsh voice barked from nearby.

Cali blinked against the brightness of the lights, lifting her hands to show they were empty. As expected, the large, windowless loft was deserted except for the two men in the center of the room.

Hood sat at his desk, his big shoulders slumped forward. A paunchy pale man in a long trench coat and fedora stood behind him, a gun pointed at Hood's head. "I thought you said she was away on business."

"I returned early. I'm not accustomed to reporting my every movement to my subordinates. Nor am I accustomed to having a weapon pointed at my people in my own office." Boomerang's arrogance settled around Cali like a shield. It usually worked to put people off balance, and this cop was no exception.

"Sit down. You, get the files." The cop prodded Hood with his gun.

"I told you—they're in the safe, and I don't have access." The lyrical lilt to Hood's words told her that things hadn't been going well.

Hoping to distract their intruder, Cali took a seat at her own desk, crossing her legs to make sure their unwelcome guest got an eyeful. "If you're holding us hostage, it seems like the polite thing to do would be to introduce yourself."

"That's real funny, a thief like you caring about manners." The gunman's grey beard bristled.

"He's with the police. Detective Hampton," Hood said, earning himself a cuff from the gunman's free hand. Unfortunately, the gun didn't waver from its position near Hood's skull.

The situation was too tense. Detective Hampton wasn't a professional thug, and Cali would have bet this was the first time he'd tried to bully someone so overtly. She needed him to relax to give Hood a chance to get away from the weapon. She smiled graciously and saw the detective immediately focus on her red-painted mouth. He couldn't seem to look away. *Gotcha.* "How can we help you, Detective? We're quite happy to cooperate."

Hood's eyes narrowed, and his finger tapped once on the chair. Good. He understood the plan.

"I'm looking for the data files you stole from Dalhard Industries." Detective Hampton's chest puffed out, one more sign his internal peacock had been activated. *Strut and display to impress the lady.* A hint of a promise of sex worked on most petty bullies.

"I see. You do realize that I am an information broker. I'd be more than happy to provide the files to you for a price." She smiled in cold flirtation.

"He has my daughter," Hood interrupted. Cali lifted her left hand, briefly touching her ring finger and thumb together to let him know Eva was still safe.

"A fair price. The girl for the files." Hampton preened, enjoying his walk on the dark side. "And don't do anything cutesy, or I'll shoot him."

"Understood." The threat awakened a fresh burst of cold fury, making her hands shake. She walked slowly to the safe they'd built into the wall and spun the combination. Easing the heavy metal door open, she pulled out a flat, portable hard drive. "All the information you want is on this."

"Toss it over," Hampton ordered.

"No. Release the girl, and you get the drive." This wasn't Cali's first negotiation at gunpoint. Unfortunately, based on the way Hampton was chewing his mustache, it might be his. She needed to explain further before he did something stupid and unnecessary to show his toughness. "Once I know she's safe, I'll give you the drive. If I fail to cooperate, you can still shoot one or both of us."

Hampton nodded and pulled out his phone. "Hey, Robbie. It looks like the potential threat to Miss Bateman is settled. She can go back to class."

"Let me speak with her," Hood demanded.

Hampton held the phone to Hood's ear. "Eva, are you safe?"

The answer was evident as Hood sagged in the chair and closed his eyes. "I'm sorry to have upset you. I think the school will understand if you leave early to go to Grandma's. She'll be worried about you."

"Grandma" meant a safe house instead of home. Eva knew the sort of work her fathers dealt in and understood how easily she could become a target. She'd disappear.

That meant Eva was safe now, which changed all the rules. The muscles in Hood's neck and shoulders tensed, ready to move, as

Hampton hung up the call and smirked. "Satisfied?"

"Quite." Cali tossed the drive up into the air as she lifted her foot from the release switch in the floor, filling the room with dense artificial fog.

CHAPTER NINETEEN

Cali dove beneath the fog layer, wincing as her fragile knees smacked hard into the carpet. They needed to get softer floor coverings for the office. The carpet might as well have been laid over concrete. Three gunshots blasted out, and she rolled, trying to get away from wherever the detective might be aiming. He was shouting insults at the top of his lungs.

Does he think I'm going to get offended enough to stand up and surrender? An inappropriate urge to giggle swelled her lungs, trying to burst out and betray her location.

She opened the trapdoor built into the wall beneath the safe and slid inside, closing it behind her. A pole dropped her straight into a closet on the first floor. Faint echoes of shouting from upstairs told her the detective was still searching for her on the upper level. Hood would be making his way out via one of the other escape routes they'd built when they'd taken over the building.

The closet door opened, and Cali instinctively braced for an attack.

"Did he get you?" Hood asked, his dark skin gleaming under the flickering bulbs.

Shaking her head, Cali led the way to the concealed connecting door between her apartment building and the one next to it. She pulled off her jacket and yanked the sleeves inside out. Reversible clothing and Velcro were a godsend to someone with morphic abilities. "Did he get the drive?"

Hood nodded. "I saw him scrambling for it as I escaped."

"Good. I'd hate to have wasted the effort." The drive was a dummy, full of encrypted data that concealed a virus that would overwrite any device it was plugged into. Cali had palmed the real drive from the safe. She held it out to Hood. "Harley is at my neighbor's apartment. Go to him, and take this with you. I can't afford to have the drive on me if he catches me."

"I should make sure you're safe." Hood folded his arms.

Great. He's going to argue with me. "There's no time. If you want to be even more useful, call Red Willa, and tell her to get her boys over here." Willa's "boys" included street kids of both genders, and they were more efficient than locusts. They'd have the building stripped within thirty minutes, leaving no trace if Hampton decided to come back.

Hood frowned, and Cali repressed an urge to start shouting at his stubbornness. Heavy feet thumped down the stairs next door, suggesting their guest had abandoned his search. She dropped Boomerang's watch into her bag and pulled out heavy gold earrings. After sliding them into her ears, she ripped out the clip holding her hair back. "I'm going to follow him and see if I can find out who ordered this ridiculous raid."

She closed her eyes to concentrate. She felt a tugging in her hair as if a soft breeze whispered between the strands. Morphing was always a little harder to judge without a reflective surface.

"That's good. Bottle blond." Hood knew what she could do, and he'd been the one to suggest keeping separate personalities for the street and her real life.

Detective Hampton burst out onto the sidewalk, flailing as he searched for his targets. Cali and Hood stood perfectly still, watching him through a tiny gap in the newspaper covering the window. The detective stormed away from them. Cali slipped out the door, her shoulders back and her hands stuffed in her pockets. Just another girl working the block.

Hampton was cursing, the profanities interlaced with bouts of coughing. *Serves you right, bastard.* She'd been dealing with the criminal side of Perdition since childhood and had witnessed all sorts of nastiness. But threatening family and friends wasn't done unless someone wanted to spark an all-out war. *Do you know what you've started, little man?* Hood wouldn't forgive or forget the threat, and neither would Cali.

That was the problem when the so-called law-abiding people crossed over to the dark side. They had no idea where the boundaries were or how to handle things with respect. People in Cali's world were vicious and quick to anger, but there were rules. When friends and family were the only people in the world to turn to for help, they became sacrosanct.

The cursing subsided, and Cali peeked around the corner. Hampton shouted into his phone. "I got what you need. Transfer the money."

Cali shook her head at the man's naïveté. He hadn't checked the files and was already demanding money from whoever had hired him. A long and profitable criminal career wasn't in Hampton's future.

She began to move as soon as he dropped the phone into the right-hand pocket of the trench coat. If she didn't catch him before he reached his car, her ruse wouldn't work. Hurrying, she raised her arm as if signaling someone in the distance. Hampton half turned at the clacking of her heels on pavement, and she pretended to stumble.

He caught her, proving he wasn't entirely lost to depravity—although he did cop a quick feel of her breast as he helped her up. Keeping her eyes wide, she launched into Operation Bimbo. "Gee, mister, are you all right?"

"I'm fine." He offered her a hasty grin, obviously torn between delivering his ill-gotten goods and taking the opportunity to flirt with an attractive young girl. Cali also noted that he quickly patted his left trench coat pocket, telling her exactly where the drive rested.

"Thanks." She forced a flush of blood into her cheeks, imitating a shy blush.

"You're the first good thing to happen to me today."

The predatory glint in his eyes brought up the sour taste of bile, but she kept up her mask. Giggling, she straightened his coat with both hands. "That's sweet."

"Where are you headed?" He leaned closer, overwhelming her with the scent of stale deodorant and old food. *Lucky me.*

"To do some school stuff at the library." She shrugged, using her right hand to finger the lapel of his trench coat while her left dipped into the pocket. *Bingo.*

She managed to slip the phone into her own pocket, laughing and flirting to keep his attention away. Next came the dangerous part. Most thieves screwed it up by hurrying away to inspect the loot, thereby drawing attention to themselves. Cali would let the scene play out naturally.

Not gagging was a challenge as she let him escort her to the subway platform, regaling her with how important he was at the police station and dropping hints about being single with money to burn. Cali kept her eyes wide and her smile insipid, pretending to be absorbed in his every word.

A group of youths came up from the platform, and Cali saw an opportunity. She leaned to one side, and Hampton did the same, which put him in the perfect position. Two of the sullen guys bumped into him, swearing in Spanish. Hampton puffed up his chest, trying to act like the hero. His attempts to intimidate them fell short—the boys didn't even slow down as they climbed up to street level.

"No respect." Hampton shook his head. "In my day, a man gave a lady right of way."

Not rolling my eyes. Not rolling my eyes. "Sounds so chivalrous," she murmured. "Maybe you could text me your number so I can call you once I'm done at the library."

"Now, that is a good idea." He reached into his pocket, and his predatory grin abruptly vanished. His mouth twisted down as he checked the other pocket.

Cali waited patiently like the good little airhead she was pretending to be. *Come on. The shoe's in the air.*

His eyes went wide, and it took all her training not to smile. *Shoe just dropped.*

"Those bastards stole my phone!" He spun around as she opened her eyes even wider.

Hampton charged after the boys, shouting. Cali allowed herself a little smile and continued down the stairs to the platform as the train pulled up. Slipping between the sliding doors, she made her escape.

"I'd ask you if you're crazy, but I know that's a sensitive subject right now." Michael pinched his nose with his gloved fingers.

Joe tilted his beer glass, watching the amber liquid roll. He'd asked his friend to meet him for lunch in the hopes of getting some advice to figure out what to do next. His strong reaction to Cali had broken his confidence. "I thought a guy who ended up in a whirlwind relationship with his lady love would be a little more supportive. Or at least less hypocritically judgmental."

"She's a suspect, and you asked her out." Michael spread his hands wide. "I know you like playing the field, but did you think about the consequences at all?"

"I'm not playing the field." Before, his relationships had been casual, fun, and convenient. No woman had ever hit him like a bolt from the blue, shaking his world down to the foundations, let alone three of them in less than a week. Colleen had yanked him out of Planet Casual's orbit, and after months of being emotionally shut down, Joe had happily followed, but now Boomerang and Cali were tugging on him with equal gravity.

"Then what is it?" Michael was studying him in genuine concern.

So much for my poker face. "Ever since I got dragged down this rabbit hole, things have changed. Everything seems more real, and I can't compartmentalize like I used to. I haven't been on a date since we went after Dani." Joe took a long swallow of liquid courage.

"I'm sorry. I didn't know." Michael's stricken face meant a long-winded apology was coming, but Joe waved it off.

"You had your own shit, man. And it's been great for the condo. I sanded and stained all the cabinets in the kitchen, made built-in bookcases in the bedroom, and rewired the surround sound in the living room." Joe drew random lines in the spilled beer, not willing to see the pity on his friend's face. "I tried going out, but I found myself scoping out whatever room I was in, wondering which of the pretty girls were *lalassu*. Heck, maybe there's even something else out there that neither of us knows about yet. Maybe Dani's Goddess is the vanguard for an alien invasion or something."

"She's been watching over humanity for millennia. I don't think she's planning to move in anytime soon." Michael paused. "How does Colleen fit into this?"

Joe's mouth stretched in a smile. "When I met Colleen, none of that mattered anymore. I thought it was finally happening to me like it did for my dad. I'd found the right woman. When I'm with her, suddenly the other stuff doesn't seem so big. I look at her, and it's like I'm seeing a woman for the first time. I notice all kinds of little shit like the different greens floating in her eyes or how the light sometimes catches hints of gold in her hair. She really doesn't see how pretty she is. She's smart too. She's not afraid to call me on my bullshit."

"And this Boomerang? And Cali?"

"Boomerang has this whole sexy and saucy thing going, a real forties glam girl with the attitude of Rita Hayworth. And Cali—I've never seen someone so protective. She looks like this frail little thing, but she was ready to stand up to her friend's abuser, no reservations."

"But Colleen works for Dalhard, Boomerang is a professional thief, and you don't know anything about Cali, not even her last name," Michael pointed out, crushing Joe's buzz. His friend tapped his fingers against the table, a tell that Joe had figured out a long time ago: bad news to come. "The strength of your feelings for all three of them might be a bad sign."

"What do you mean?" Joe's stomach muscles clenched in an unconscious shield to ward off the coming blow.

"There are *lalassu* who can make you feel things. Sirens, like Dalhard. And the Lilitu, like Dani, who can produce pheromones to induce sexual euphoria. And the Bastites, who can make people think that they're in love. Those are just the ones I've found so far in the High Priestess journals." Michael pushed his long hair out of his eyes. "What if one of them is a *lalassu*, and she's manipulating you?"

"Whoever it is must be doing a piss-poor job if I'm attracted to three women at once." *I should have figured the universe wasn't done laughing at me yet.*

Michael leaned forward. "Or she's fighting something powerful. Think about it. Colleen works for Dalhard. She's not exactly your type, and you're still ready to throw everything away to be with her. Doesn't that seem a little odd to you?"

"I think it's exactly like what you and Dani did." Joe bristled with anger. Michael had found someone. How dare he spit on Joe's feelings.

"I know you don't want to hear it, but she could be like Dalhard. She could be manipulating you." Michael stayed calm in the face of Joe's anger, delivering his message like the professional therapist he was.

"What the hell am I supposed to do? It's not like there's a test for *lalassu*. There's no way to know." Joe was back where he started, unable to trust his own reactions. Except now he wasn't content to hide in his apartment, doing renovations. He couldn't walk away from how he felt.

"There might be. Andrew should be able to tell if she's *lalassu*. It's part of being a shaman. All he needs is to be able to study her in person for a while. But he wouldn't be able to tell what kind she is. Even if she is, it doesn't mean that she's manipulating you, especially not on purpose. Dalhard could be controlling her. The fact that you feel so strongly about all three women could be a side effect of her trying to protect you."

"So what you're saying is that even if Colleen is *lalassu*, no one can tell me whether what I feel is real." Despair threatened to wrap Joe in its clinging tentacles and drag him down.

"Andrew can't, but I can. I can read her secrets." Michael held up his gloved hand.

The offer should have been touching. Joe knew how much Michael hated invading other people's secrets. But all Joe could summon up was anger. "Because you can't trust my opinion anymore now that you're a part of this muckety-muck secret society."

If Michael had been anyone else, those words would have been cause for a friendship-ending fight. Joe would have bitten out his tongue to tuck the accusing syllables back behind his teeth if that were possible.

Luckily, Michael wasn't one to let surfaces distract from the core of an issue. "Because I don't think you're reacting rationally. This isn't like you."

"Not really looking for a lecture from the guy who took up with a gal whose criminal record is longer than my arm. And that's only the shit we know about." Joe was fighting the wind, and he knew it. "My instincts tell me she's not like Dalhard. She'd never be okay with kidnapping a child like Bernie or leaving people to die in a collapsing building."

"And your instincts are good, so that says a lot. But we can't afford to be second-guessing ourselves. You need to find out for sure. Let

Andrew take a look. If she's one of Dalhard's victims, then we can help her break free."

Trust Michael to see this as a white-knight mission. Joe's protective instincts demanded he defend Colleen, but he swallowed the impulse. His friend was right—this was bigger than his personal life. The rules of life were different now, and Joe couldn't assume his mind was clean. Any out-of-character behavior needed to be checked out. "I'll set something up."

Michael nodded, taking the reluctant promise for what it was. "It doesn't have to be obvious. He and I could be at the restaurant the next time you meet her. If she's clean, she never has to know."

CHAPTER TWENTY

"This is not what I paid for." Karan had rarely been tempted to physically throw something as part of a temper tantrum, but the urge to test the false hard drive's aerodynamic qualities was strong. Luckily, for the detective's sake, Karan's will was stronger.

The man seemed to have finally realized his grievous error. He stammered, promising whatever he thought Karan might want. Unfortunately for him, all Karan wanted to hear from this particular subcontractor was permanent silence.

Signaling to his bodyguards to remove the man from his presence, Karan turned his back on the flurry of cursing and protests. *Clever girl.* He had not expected Boomerang would easily give up the list. Despite his foolishness, the detective had done what was required, forcing the woman from the tidy hole that she called home. She would seek a new burrow, and people in transit left traces, especially when they were in a hurry.

There were several new bursts of activity within South Perdition. Karan could eliminate a few as known gang hangouts, although the level of activity was higher than normal. The cause for such seething in the underworld was not clear. It couldn't have been his offers in exchange for information or capture of one of the Harris siblings. Those had been on the open market for over a month and would be unlikely to spark new interest after so much time had passed. He was fairly certain of the location of one of the siblings—an underground hospital run by a *lalassu* healer. His instructions to his people were clear: wait until after the announcement before moving on the target.

Karan studied the anomalies. Boomerang was sentimental. She ostensibly employed a number of teens and young adults, but she made few demands on them. Instead, she supported them in escaping their old lives on the street. Wherever she chose for her new location, it would be convenient for her to continue such work. Which meant that the most likely choices were the old movie theater on MacDougal Avenue or the half-finished subway terminal intended for St. Nicholas Drive.

The theater served as a front for several pimps, providing a steady stream of traffic in and out. It would be easy to hide Boomerang's people amid such traffic, but it would likely put them at risk, something such a sentimental woman would never tolerate. The half-finished subway station had links to the underground tunnels, providing multiple entrances and exits, as well as links to the city's power and communication grids. It would be the perfect choice.

Time to bring in a professional. It was a shame not to be able to utilize Boomerang's particular talents, but the conflict of interest was unavoidable. She was not the only professional thief in the area, and Karan could choose one who would not be limited by Boomerang's peculiar moral blinders.

That left the decision of what to do with the troublesome Detective Hampton. Karan could not afford to attract official notice just yet. Leaving the man alive to attempt an escape could yield disaster, but if he was immediately eliminated, there was no guarantee Hampton's body would not be discovered at an inconvenient juncture no matter how many precautions were taken.

Joe put his weight behind the sander, stripping off the old layers of varnish on the wooden chest he'd found at the flea market over the summer. He'd intended to refinish it and put a new inlay pattern on top for his mother's birthday, but one thing or another kept interfering. As the crackly varnish disappeared, it gave him the perfect distraction from his thoughts, letting him concentrate on his hands instead of his heart.

Is anything I feel real? Philosophers could argue about whether the only requirement for "reality" was to feel real, but Joe's standards of judgment were much simpler. The high from a drug like cocaine was fake—artificially induced and quickly vanishing into addiction. The high from running a marathon was real—earned through sweat and training. If he felt strongly about Colleen because of some chemical or psychic effect, then that was fake regardless of whether or not she'd intended to influence him.

Pale natural ash emerged from under the scrubbing disk of the sander. Joe held it steady, not wanting to gouge the surface. *And what if it is fake? Do I go after Boomerang or Cali? Or do I need to walk away from the whole thing?*

From the way his gut tightened at the thought, Joe suspected that walking away wasn't going to be as easy as it sounded. Aside from his tangle of emotions, his mother was in full parental coercion mode. He'd come home to four messages containing not-so-subtle hints to bring his new girlfriend to family dinner. Not to mention the plate of *tortas* and rice sitting on his counter along with a note letting him know that his window of respite was closing. If he didn't call Mamá soon, she would sic the tías on him. No man could withstand the fussing of three Mexican matrons for long.

He turned off the sander and set it aside, getting a damp cloth to wipe down the accumulating sawdust. The telephone rang loudly in the new silence. Joe checked the call display and then immediately picked up. He owed Michael an apology for their fight earlier. "Hey. I'm glad you called. Sorry for being a jerk at lunch."

"Apology not necessary, and not why I called."

Joe straightened, setting aside the cloth. "Then what's up?"

"Turn on the television."

"What channel?" Joe picked up the remote.

"It won't matter."

Michael didn't need to explain further. The presidential seal hovered over the shoulder of a dignified news anchor with the words "Shocking Presidential Announcement" prominently displayed on a red banner. Joe turned up the volume as the shot switched to the president standing in front of a podium, grey hair glinting in the camera lights. "Thank you for coming. I'll be brief, and I will not be accepting any questions. Of late, we have all grown concerned with the recent claims of strange and unusual activity. We created a special task force to investigate these claims, and to our surprise, some of them have turned out to have substance."

"Holy shit," Joe said.

"It gets worse," Michael replied grimly.

The president stared into the camera, looking dignified and sober in his pressed suit and carefully coiffed grey hair. "In response to this information, I am creating a new enforcement agency to deal with such individuals, the Bureau of Special Investigations. Further information about the agency will be provided at the end of this conference. I want to reassure the American people that we are not taking this new threat lightly and that they do not need to worry. Thank you."

The predictable media pandemonium was cut short as the shot returned to the news anchor. "The president's startling announcement an hour ago has sparked reactions ranging from outright disbelief to calls for preemptive incarceration for anyone identified as having abilities beyond the human norm—"

Joe turned off the television, bile rising in his throat. "This is really happening."

"We're nowhere near ready for exposure on this kind of scale." Michael paused. "I need your help. I've tried contacting Eric to warn him, but there's no answer from him or Mishler."

He didn't need to explain further. Joe grabbed his weapon and badge. "I'll meet you there."

The streets were eerily quiet as Joe drove to the underground hospital. From experience, he knew the quiet wouldn't last. Right now, people were in shock, but as the enormity of the situation settled in, there would be citywide riots. Maybe countrywide. The rabbit was definitely out of the hole, and people wouldn't be sure what to think or believe. And if the president thought a thirty-second speech would calm them down, he and his advisors were dreaming.

Joe spotted Michael at the wheel of Dani's GT convertible and followed him into the rundown parking lot. "Any idea what we're walking into?"

Michael stepped out of the car, unnecessarily smoothing his gloves. "Not a peep. Things were in an uproar before this announcement. *Lalassu* have been disappearing all over the country. Having seen the list, I suspect certain people and organizations have been watching us for a long time. Among the *lalassu*, there's a real backlash against Virginia and Dani for having cut off contact with the Goddess."

"Any word from Bernie and her mom?" Joe asked as they slowly approached the office. He couldn't see any signs of other people there, but every police instinct he possessed was screaming at him. The empty street didn't feel abandoned—instead, it was as if an armed mob hid in the unseen shadows.

"Nothing. And I think they might have Vapor. I went by his place to try and track him down, and everything I could use has been stripped." Michael folded his mouth into a thin line. "It must be deliberate. It was too thorough."

"Bernie's a smart kid. And she's got the ghosts to warn her." Joe could not have imagined ever uttering those words as a reassurance, but there they were. He signaled to Michael to hold the office door open while Joe went in first, gun drawn.

The office was abandoned, and Joe caught the familiar musty, copper scent of dried blood. Joe cleared the room and then started down the hall. Michael stripped the gloves from his hands, staying a few steps behind. His slender build might have looked more suited to a poetry reading than a street fight, but the combination of years of martial-arts training and the ability to read his opponent's intentions with every blow exchanged made Michael a potent fighter.

As they reached Eric's room, the signs of struggle were obvious—the door lay in pieces in the hallway with a few chunks dangling from the misshapen hinges. Holes and cracks dotted the plaster along with specks and dabs of maroon dried blood. Inside, Eric sat on the edge of the hospital bed, pulling on pants. Andrew stood on the other side, wrapping a bandage around Vincent's arm. Blood had already leaked through the first few layers, but Vincent's attention was on Mishler, crouched in the corner, his white shirt dotted with irregular dark flecks.

"The cavalry has arrived," the Native shaman said sardonically, tying off Vincent's bandage.

"Too bad the show's over. But you can still watch Mishler do his bullfrog impression." Vincent's bruised and bloodied knuckles and swollen eye testified to what had occurred. "He blows himself up like a puffer fish on helium. It's pretty good. He should take that shit on the road."

"Get out of here! And take that damn Indian freak with you," Mishler snarled.

"You don't deserve the title of healer if you only choose to offer service where it is convenient." Andrew's scorn was loud enough to travel down the hall.

"Are you guys going to tell us what happened?" Joe said before Andrew and Vincent could continue trying to outdo one another in sarcasm.

"Vincent came as soon as the president's announcement hit the air. I told him he was being paranoid, and Mishler tried to throw him out, but Vincent refused to go." Eric looked at his younger brother with a combination of surprise and pride. "Andrew came a little while later. I think Mishler called him to try and bully Vincent into leaving."

"He was gravely disappointed to discover I did not share his view of the situation." Andrew folded his arms to stand in front of Mishler. Beginnings of alarm rose in Joe as he noticed Vincent slumping. Eric might be proud of his brother's actions, but Vincent wasn't. He was avoiding everyone's eyes, trying to occupy as little space as possible.

"About forty-five minutes ago, some *lalassu* came," Eric continued. "They were frightened and demanding answers from us. I said I didn't have any. Things started to devolve quickly, and some of them said they were going to drag me out as an example."

"An example of what?" Joe asked.

"I don't think they knew. They just wanted to do something other than cower in fear." Eric shrugged.

"No. They had a plan." Michael's bare hand was startlingly pale against the broken walls. "They were going to trade him for others who have been taken. They thought he would be worth more to the captors.

Mishler knew about it."

"That's not good." Eric paled further, his skin going grey and blue as if he'd been dead for days.

The healer grinned, keeping his mouth shut as he became the focus of the group.

Vincent chuckled without humor. "You keep being surprised by this. Of course the Beast is still hunting for us. Did you actually believe prison would stop him or even slow him down?"

"I don't think this was Dalhard." Michael frowned, closing his eyes to concentrate. "I think it's Karan Samil, the assistant. I'm getting a faint trace, more of a hint than anything else."

"He's going to take us back to where we always should have been," Mishler burst out. "We shouldn't be scrambling in the dirt, fighting over scraps. We used to be gods! If it weren't for that bitch pretending to be High Priestess—"

A sharp crack cut off the man's insults. Michael gracefully put his foot back down, having snap kicked Mishler in the jaw. Vincent uncurled his unnecessary fist, looking sheepish.

"What do we do with him?" Andrew asked, eying Joe.

Probably wondering if I'm going to object to a vigilante solution.

There was nothing they could do. Psychic evidence wasn't exactly valid in a court of law. Joe shoved his frustration aside. There were people to protect and get to safety. Fixing injustices would have to wait, especially if there were *lalassu* who might return, seeking revenge. "What happened to the people who attacked you?"

"One of them died." Michael used a wet-nap to scrub the traces of blood from his fingers.

"He had a gun. I got it away from him, but he wasn't ready to let it go," Vincent said dully. "A couple of the others had knives, and they were all crowded around me. The gun went off, and then they scattered."

Shit. That meant Joe was standing in a crime scene. A homicide. "Where's the body?"

"I don't think you truly want to know the answer." Andrew picked up a bag. "We need to go."

"Say hi to Mom for me." Vincent got to his feet.

Eric grabbed at his brother's arm. "You need to come home with us. It's not safe out there."

"Good thing I'm not safe either." Vincent gently pulled his arm out of Eric's grasp and looked over at Andrew and Michael. "Take care of him for me. I'll make sure Mishler doesn't cause trouble."

"We will talk later about continuing your medical training. You show a remarkable grasp of basic anatomy." Andrew nodded gravely. Joe winced, guessing the shaman referred to Vincent's lethal effectiveness.

Joe and Michael supported Eric as they proceeded down the hall. The tension kept stretching, paradoxically getting thicker as it grew, until Joe half wished for the attack to happen so they could get it over with. It hurt Joe to walk away without calling the crime in, but this wasn't a time to be a cop. Bigger issues were at play, and he could only hope he and his friends weren't all swallowed whole.

CHAPTER TWENTY-ONE

Mamá's home had always been the family refuge in times of trouble. And it looked as though tonight would be no exception. The small, whitewashed house with its brilliant flowerbeds and lacy curtains was boxed in by cars, which were lined up against both curbs and jammed into the driveway. Joe parked far down the street and walked back, listening to the excited conversation and music spilling out into the quiet neighborhood. Mamá's windows were the only ones blazing with lights, and he was willing to bet she was hosting every household within a three-block radius.

I could try sneaking into the kitchen and just making sure everyone's okay. His arms and back ached with fatigue, and his brain raced with worry. Colleen hadn't returned any of his texts, and he needed to know if she was okay before he could collapse into his own bed. But he also needed to be sure his family was all right. The president's announcement meant a visit to Mamá shifted from optional to mandatory. He quietly opened the kitchen door around back.

"*Pépé!*" Mamá dropped the spoon into her red ceramic cooking pot. "Thank goodness you are safe." She wrapped him in a hearty embrace, her head level with his chest and her arms snug around his waist.

He dropped a kiss on her salt-and-pepper locks. "I told you not to worry, Mamá."

"Pah!" She pulled away and slapped his upper arm. "Tell the sun not to shine. You'll have more luck."

As a child, he'd believed his mother was an unmovable force capable of shattering any barrier. He knew better as an adult but still treasured her dynamic and determined personality. She shouted news of his arrival to the others, triggering a general roar of welcome.

"You must be hungry." Mamá snatched at a skinny teenage boy as he helped himself to sweet churros. "Adán, get Pépé a plate."

Adán scampered off to the dining room, where Joe could hear the rest of the family talking loudly in a mixture of Spanish and English. From what he could tell, most of them were arguing about the latest football match along with complaints about plot twists on a popular *telenovela.* A few were discussing the president's announcement and what it might mean. He could hear Tía Agata saying, "I told you so."

"You look pale. You'll be more yourself once you eat." Mamá pushed Joe down onto a chair at the kitchen table beside his Tía Ximena, who was busily shredding cheese, and a neighbor from down the street who was dusting sugar over cookies before they went in the oven.

"I'm fine, Mamá. It's going to be busy after the announcement today." He wondered if Modnik would call him in with IA sniffing around. She'd probably need every hand she could get.

Mamá ladled a hearty helping of her famous black-bean stew into the empty bowl. "Here. If you'll be busy, you need to eat. You can tell me if I've lost my touch."

Joe grinned. His mother's stew was his favorite, and despite his numerous attempts to make it himself, the dish never tasted as good as when it came out of her battered red stewpot. "You'll never lose your touch, Mamá."

Adán returned with a loaded plate. Tía Ximena immediately reached over and added one of her empanadas to it. The pastry, filled with meat, cheese, and vegetables, sent a direct hit of *home* to his hindbrain. After the events of the day, he needed the comfort even if it came with strings attached. He quickly polished off his bowl of stew and three empanadas.

"Tía Agata brought charms against *brujería* to hang about the house," Mamá said quietly.

Joe's hand froze halfway to the fourth pastry.

"Pah. The other world will leave you alone as long as you don't go poking after it." Tía Ximena sniffed.

I wish I'd listened to that advice. "You've never let her put up charms before."

"What am I to think when the president says there are men who can crumple steel with a touch or walk through walls? How can I be sure that Agata's charms are not necessary or helpful?" Mamá twisted a dishcloth between her hands. Joe wouldn't have believed anything could unnerve his mother if he wasn't seeing it for himself.

"It's foolishness, and the president is even more foolish for saying such nonsense." Tía Ximena's narrow hands and crooked fingers waved it all away.

"Tell us the truth, Pépé," Mamá demanded.

The empanadas didn't taste nearly as good coming back up as going down. Joe coughed and grabbed at a glass of water, trying to think of something plausible.

"Don't try and lie to me, my boy. You were never any good at it." Mamá folded her arms. "There is more to this than you have told me."

Joe rediscovered the joys of unrestricted breathing. "There's more to this than anyone knows."

The women stopped their food preparations and gave him their full attention. Joe had never seen them do that before, not even when the house across the street caught fire and the sirens echoed painfully through the walls. They'd kept on with their work, certain more food would be needed before the night was over.

"But you know." Mamá wiped her hands on her apron.

I should bring her down to the station and put her in charge of interrogations. "I learned some things in confidence. The world isn't like we thought it was."

Mamá's harsh stare softened, and she reached out, pulling him into the kind of hug he'd thought he'd long outgrown. Despite being almost a foot taller than her and an armed police detective, being cradled in his mother's arms brought Joe a sense of peace and protection. He savored her solidity and strength.

She'd offered him comfort that way all his life. He'd be upset or hurt, and she'd stop questioning him and just hold him. It didn't matter if he needed a few seconds or a few hours—she wouldn't let him go until enough of the hurt drained away to make it tolerable again.

"I won't ask any more questions. None of us will." Mamá glared at the other two women, though neither showed any sign of jumping into the conversation. "When you are ready, you can share what you know. And until then, I won't complain about Tía Agata stinking up the house with her charms." She bent him down and delivered a warm, maternal kiss on his forehead that promised to banish all the darkness.

"Thank you, Mamá." He straightened and gave her a grateful return kiss on her cheek.

She patted his cheek, her wedding ring cool against his skin. "Now, tell me about the woman you've been seeing."

"It's complicated." He resisted the urge to check his phone again to see if a new text had appeared. He was a grown man, not a teenage boy.

"It's never too complicated to introduce a woman to your family. She should know us before you make her fall in love with you." Mamá nodded emphatically, and the other two women murmured agreement.

I wish I could make her fall in love with me. The thought bounced immediately into his mind. But which *her*? And could he trust it if she did? He took refuge in practicalities. "There's too much going on right now. I'll barely have time to think for the next few days."

Mamá frowned. "That is why you must talk to her and bring her to the family. Your partner should be there to help you in such difficult times."

"He'll do the right thing. He's a good boy." Tía Ximena patted his arm. "Now, eat up. You're going to waste away to nothing."

Joe accepted another empanada, taking the opportunity to relax in the warm shelter of food and family.

Creaking noises drew Cali out of unsettling and jagged dreams. Light burned where the closet door met the floor. She hadn't left any lights on in the rest of the apartment when she'd gone to sleep. Her panting breaths echoed in the closet, threatening to reveal her hiding place. Panic curled around her body, twining tightly around her limbs and freezing her in place. No matter how hard she struggled against the paralysis, nothing moved. She felt as if the nerves connecting her terrified brain to her limbs had been severed.

More crunching noises. Someone was stepping on the thin shards of glass she'd left scattered on the floor to warn her of intruders. A shadow broke the line of light as the intruder drew closer.

She tried to mute her breathing, though a scream threatened to claw its way through her numb vocal chords. The thin line of light under the door blurred and multiplied as her eyes refused to focus, leaving her effectively blind. *He's here.* No, it couldn't be him. The ones who'd hurt her had all died years before. They couldn't be here now, searching her apartment.

Heavy footsteps vibrated against the floor, and the vestiges of logical thought disappeared under an avalanche of primal fear. *I need a weapon.* Her cramped fingers pawed at the magnetic strip full of throwing knives, sending them clattering to the ground.

The footsteps stopped as the chorus of metallic pings rang out. Cali fumbled for the knives, which seemed to have disappeared into the folds of her duvet. A moan escaped her stiffened lips as she heard a low, animalistic chuckle from outside the door. The strip of light began to vanish as the intruder's shadow cut across it.

He's coming for me. Too late to fight, she had to escape. A trap door beneath her futon would drop her into the empty apartment below, but her body wouldn't obey her. Every movement felt as if she were pushing her way through a thick, smothering liquid. Pinned by her own panic, she could only choke on her own rising sobs of panic as the shadow completely blocked the light. Helpless.

No. No. Nononononono. She wasn't a helpless child any longer. She could fight back. She would not be a victim again.

But it was as if all her training had never happened. Her body wouldn't listen to her. She was a prisoner in her own dead flesh. Trapped and afraid, she was no more of a threat than when she'd been too small and weak to fight.

The closet door rattled as the intruder tested the locks. *Please hold.*

The door slammed against the wall, and the shadow of a man reached down for her, his fingers glistening with shiny blood.

Cali woke up screaming and trying to run. Her legs were tangled in her coverlet, and she bashed hard into the wall of the closet, unable to catch herself. Knives crashed to the floor with a metallic clatter that threatened to send her back into the nightmare. She still saw the shadow man reaching for her, superimposed over the dim outlines of her closet refuge. She flailed as if her brain had saved up every movement she'd failed to make in her dream and was trying to act out each of them at once.

It took a long time for her mind to wake up enough to make an effort at control. Her heart slammed against her chest as if it wanted to run free from the prison of her body. Her lungs refused to accept new air, leaving her dizzy and light-headed. Fresh bruises covered her hip, thigh, and arm from losing her balance and hitting the wall. Every joint ached as if she'd just run a marathon and fought in a mixed-martial-arts tournament.

Slowly, real memories returned, replacing the dissolving terrors from her sleeping mind. She, Hood, and Harley had worked late into the night, examining the data on the drives she'd stolen under Dalhard's instructions. They found multiple lists of *lalassu* along with addresses and pictures, more than enough to identify them. Such a list would be invaluable in the wake of the president's announcement. It unnerved them all even after they'd locked the drives away in the new safe. Cali was already working on more secure options.

There's no danger here. She sat on her futon, arms resting lightly on her bent knees and the back of her head supported by the closet wall, trying to wrestle her body away from the panic. The apartment was empty and dark, just as it had been when she went to sleep.

Clicking on the small light she used to read, Cali clucked her tongue at the disaster wrought by her nightmare. The futon and duvet were twisted into a Gordian knot. Luckily, she'd managed to avoid hitting her tablet, which was perched on top of the minifridge when she fell, but about half of her throwing knives were gone from the magnetic strip beside the squat unit. She knelt and began picking them up with numb fingers. The sleep-driven paralysis faded, and as movement grew easier, the lingering panic began to lose its grip on her. She wasn't helpless. Not anymore.

Resetting her bedding, she stretched out again. She wouldn't be going back to sleep anytime soon, but maybe she could relax enough to not be completely exhausted and useless the next day.

She hadn't gone through a nightmare like that in months. Most of the time, her dreams woke her and sent her heart racing. Her body would tense and ache, but the actual visions faded as she opened her eyes. The blurring of nocturnal terror and reality wasn't an experience she was eager to repeat.

Her phone shrilled, and she bolted upright again, fumbling for the slippery rectangle. She didn't recognize the number, and her first thought was to wonder if something had happened to Joe. "Hello?"

"I trust I didn't wake you."

Mr. Dalhard's voice dried Cali's mouth and set her mind to instant, painful alertness. He wasn't calling through the prison network, which meant he was using a smuggled cell phone. He sounded smug and reckless as if he was drunk or high. Her father used to sound the same way when he had a line on a particularly big score. *Not a good sign.* "I wasn't asleep."

"Excellent. I knew I could count on you to see the opportunity. I'll need everything set up by tomorrow evening. And do air out the bedroom. I can't abide sleeping on musty bedclothes," Mr. Dalhard instructed.

"Tomorrow? Did you hear from the lawyers?" Cali wondered if this was another dream. Or nightmare.

"Lawyers are irrelevant, particularly after today." He laughed and hung up the phone, leaving Cali staring at a blank screen. Was he high? Or could he really be planning to break out of jail?

Do I try and stop him? She could call Joe and let him know what she'd learned. *Or do I try to help him?* Her resources as Boomerang were nothing to sneeze at. It was all too much. Mr. Dalhard would never forgive her if she tried to stop him, and if she didn't stop him, he'd never forgive her for letting him fall—assuming he even survived long enough to know how bad a choice he'd made. Either way, she would lose everything.

If Mr. Dalhard gets out, he'll go after Joe. Her boss was definitely operating on prison instincts: crush all opposition. The only way to keep them both safe was to ensure Mr. Dalhard stayed in prison. But then the pressure-cooker environment would continue to transform her mentor into a man she could no longer recognize. Cali curled up in the corner of the closet, her fingers buried in her scalp.

She would have to tell Joe what was happening, and then Colleen would have to vanish. He might think he was falling in love with her, but Colleen had never been real. Better to make her disappear mysteriously than reveal herself as a traitor and a spy. *He'll hate me.* Tears grated over her swollen and sore eyelids at the thought of the warmth in his eyes disappearing. Her knees jabbed into her chest, and her arms clamped on either side of her legs as she buried her face in her knees, trying to make her body constrict into a tighter and tighter knot.

CHAPTER TWENTY-TWO

Chaos reigned over the police station as Joe arrived. People rushed up and down the short flight of steps, and sirens blared as cars pulled up and away from the curb. He hung back, trying to look casual. A baseball hat jammed low on his head concealed his face, and he slouched in his leather jacket, sipping a paper cup of coffee.

"You better have brought another one for me." Modnik popped up at his left elbow, and Joe inadvertently swallowed a much larger mouthful than he'd intended.

Sucking in cool air to ease his burned tongue, he moved aside. "Sorry."

"Damn. Large, black," his sergeant ordered.

The kid at the truck opened his mouth, and Modnik glared at him. "If I wanted sugar, cream, or a flavor shot, I'd have said. Do your job."

She collected her coffee and continued issuing orders. "Walk with me."

Joe jogged to catch up as she led him to the private back entrance they used when they wanted to bring someone into the precinct without drawing attention.

"Is it as bad as it looks?" he asked.

"It's worse," Modnik replied grimly. "I have a kid in the morgue. Tried to rob a convenience store last night, claiming he could shoot lasers out of his eyes. The store owner shot him, and his damn lawyer is arguing that lethal force was justified on a kid with no visible weapons because the laser-eye thing might have been real in the wake of the president's announcement."

"Shit." If dead bodies were already in the morgue, riots couldn't be far behind. People were scared, and scared people did stupid and unpredictable things.

"The mayor and the governor are both screaming down my ass. Half of my guys are convinced this is all a big scam, and the other half might shoot someone for twitching. Not to mention the number of idiots who figured this would be a good day to just not show up for work." Modnik hurried him through the back door and into a private interrogation room, one without a camera system attached.

Once inside, she confronted him. "I need to know everything you know."

Words deserted Joe. She couldn't be asking him to tell her about the *lalassu.* How had he ended up in the expert chair? Despite his mother's promise not to push, he'd spent several hours the night before trying to explain the *lalassu* to his family, but he hadn't expected to do a repeat performance at work.

"Don't play dumb. You were talking about people with strange powers during your breakdown, and now we've got the government freaking out about the same thing. You've never been a conspiracy nut or into fantasy shit, which means you believed what you were saying." Modnik's fingernails chimed against the metal desk. "And even though you've tried to pretend otherwise since, I can see that you still believe it."

"I found out a few months ago," Joe said, hoping he was doing the right thing. She still might think he was crazy, but he had to at least try to educate his fellow officers about the real dangers of the *lalassu.*

"That source of yours, Michael Brooks. I always thought it was suspicious for a child therapist to see so much criminal activity in so many different parts of the city. He wasn't a conventional witness, was he?"

Modnik's shrewd deduction threatened to topple Joe's precarious balancing act between his job and the *lalassu.* He couldn't pretend that the old rules still applied anymore, but he didn't know what the new rules would be. Half the country still didn't believe the president's announcement. The country could still slip back into ignorance as soon as the next big scandal caught their collective attention. He took another sip of coffee to buy himself time to think.

"You need to trust me, Cabrera." Modnik stopped her tapping. "I've got a lot of scared people out there, both cop and civilian. If I can give them a taste of solid reality again, we might be able to get through this with minimum casualties."

"I don't know a whole lot," Joe said. "I don't think laser eyes are a thing, but I've seen men and women strong enough to bend steel with their hands. Ghosts are real, and there are people who can talk to them. And there are people who can mess with your head, make you do whatever they want."

"That's why you kept insisting on the special precautions for André Dalhard. He's one of them." Modnik rapidly scribbled notes. "What else?"

"They've been around for a long time. They have their own underground society and rules. It's more a mob-law, Wild West type of attitude. They keep to themselves because they're mostly afraid of what we'll do to them." As he talked, it grew easier. He began to feel useful again, setting the record straight and banishing prejudice and fear.

"So they're going to be scared and desperate. Not good." Modnik closed her notebook. "Joe, there are some men here that I think you need to talk to."

The door opened, admitting two men in dark suits. Joe tensed, realizing that they must have been monitoring his conversation with the sergeant. His good feeling vanished, and he cursed himself for his oversight. Just because there was no camera didn't mean someone couldn't listen in.

"Detective Cabrera, I'm Investigator Davis from the new Bureau of Special Investigations," the slightly taller one said. He indicated his grey-haired companion. "This is Investigator Lockett. I'm afraid we don't have our proper credentials yet."

"Hard to do when the president announced the agency less than twelve hours ago. I'm frankly surprised they've already made staffing choices." Joe leaned back, folding his arms.

Davis chuckled, taking a seat. "I won't play games with you, Detective. Although we only became public a short while ago, we've existed in one form or another since the colonial days. Most governments have a similar group and for precisely the same purpose: to deal with these *lalassu.*"

Joe swallowed, trying to keep the motion discreet. Was this the moment his friends disappeared into black sites?

"We will be happy to brief your officers on the various groups and their abilities, Sergeant Modnik," Davis said. "In these early days, it will be important for us to work with local law enforcement. To that end, we have an offer for you, Detective Cabrera."

"What kind of offer?" Joe's suspicions were tapping at the top of the meter. He snuck a glance at Investigator Lockett, whose hatchet-faced, silent glare did nothing to alleviate the detective's worries.

"A job offer. We've been impressed with how you've handled your introduction to the *lalassu*. You have several influential friends within their community, and we think you could be a valuable liaison in our efforts to convince them that they don't need to be afraid of us." Davis leaned forward. "Our job is going to be to catalogue what the *lalassu* are capable of and begin preparations to integrate them into human society in a more consistent way. It's in their interest to cooperate with us rather than continuing to do things through vigilante justice and mutual obligation."

Joe wasn't buying. "Sounds a little too good to be true, if we're being honest with each other, Investigator."

Lockett's narrow mouth tightened in offence as Davis chuckled again. "I don't blame you for being suspicious. We're not the Men in Black from Internet lore, but after several decades of fringe theories, we're going to have a lot of that kind of thinking to overcome. Even if you don't entirely trust us, this gives you the opportunity to be a part of the process. You could make sure we're on the up-and-up."

"I need him on the ground right now. We're short on manpower," Modnik interrupted. Joe could have kissed her for giving him the perfect excuse to avoid making a decision.

"We understand completely." Davis rose smoothly to his feet. "Take the time you need to come to the right decision, Detective. I'll ask you not to discuss our offer too widely. Public perception is a difficult balance at the best of times."

The two Feds left, and Joe felt as if any sense of normalcy walked out the door with them. Was he too warped from movies and television to even consider that a secret government organization might be anything other than a corrupt puppet master? What they said made sense, on the surface of things, but he couldn't believe it would be that simple. The government wasn't known for its fair and evenhanded reactions to minority groups in the face of greed or fear. The Japanese internment camps of World War II, the systematic extermination of Indians during the settlement process, the off-book prison sites for people suspected of being Islamic terrorists— none of them were reassuring items on the historical résumé. *Could I make a difference if I joined?* Or would he be caught up in forces beyond his control?

"Do you trust them?" he asked.

"Trust is irrelevant right now. We need to know what they know." The sergeant stood up. "They promised to get rid of the IA investigation if I gave them the chance to talk to you. Welcome back to the team."

Modnik left, and Joe followed. She hadn't understated the barely suppressed panic among the other police officers. Wide eyes and jerky movements spoke louder than the hushed whispers hissing through the precinct. And if the cops were already tucked into a powder keg, Joe could only imagine how much worse the civilians were reacting.

Modnik began issuing orders, picking out individuals to ride patrol to discourage looting and suggesting that others use their contacts to spread reassuring or threatening messages to try and keep the situation stable.

Joe was about to volunteer for patrol when someone tugged at his arm. Rob Salazar beckoned for Joe to follow him into the deserted break room. Joe did, curious about the panic in the kid's eyes. Instinct said he was concerned with more than the announcement.

"Detective Cabrera, I think I need your help," Salazar said abruptly.

I'm suddenly popular. After months of being a pariah, Joe didn't cherish any illusions. The other cops were scared and desperate enough that they'd take help from the devil if he'd appeared with answers. "What's up, Salazar?"

"It's Detective Hampton. I was assigned as his partner, but he kept going off without me. Frankly, I'm worried about what's been going on." Salazar took a deep breath. "Yesterday, after I left Ms. Mechoso's apartment, he called me and asked me to go to South Perdition High School and take a student into protective custody. He said there was a threat against her, that she'd witnessed a drug deal. But when I talked to her, she didn't know anything about it. Less than an hour later, Detective Hampton called and said the threat was resolved and the girl could go. Since then, I haven't heard from him. I've checked his home, and he hasn't been there or contacted anyone here at work."

"You've told the sergeant?" Joe asked.

Salazar nodded. "She marked him down as one more no-show. But I think there's more to it. A few days ago, I overheard him talking about a big payday coming his way. And he was making a lot of secretive phone calls."

Things were pointing toward corruption. All that convenient evidence Hampton kept bringing in against Dalhard had to be coming from someone. He could have been working with Karan. *Damn. I don't have time to deal with this right now.* "All right. For the record, I think you're right and something may have happened to him. If so, this could be bigger than we're prepared to deal with right now."

"So what do we do?" Salazar asked.

"We keep our eyes open and work the evidence to figure out what happened. We can't afford to make assumptions. And right now, the city needs us to keep everyone safe, so we can't let them down. Hampton is like a bad penny—in the past, he's always turned up again before too long. Hopefully, this time is the same." Joe didn't like to consider the alternative. Even if the man had been corrupt, he didn't deserve to be rotting in a shallow grave somewhere.

"What if one of those… those freaks got to him?" Salazar's hand twitched toward his holster.

"Those freaks are people like you and me." That kind of thinking needed to be nipped in the bud, and Joe wasn't about to let it slide. "They want the same things we want—to get through the day safely, be with their families, and have the freedom to pursue their own interests and pleasures. Don't assume they're all opportunistic criminals."

"But the things they can do—why wouldn't they take advantage of that?"

"You have a gun. Would you take it out and shoot someone to get ahead in line?" Joe fixed Salazar with his gaze, refusing to let the rookie wriggle out until he started thinking about the situation rather than reacting emotionally.

"No, of course not." Salazar leaned back, his lip curling in affront.

"You've done the martial-arts training with Rosie, right? Would you expect her to go around beating people up to get what she wants? How about cashiers at the bank? Do you expect them to help themselves to the money in the vault?"

Salazar shook his head.

Joe drove his point home. "Everyone gets opportunities to take advantage of the system. Most people have some skill or access that would let them break the rules. And the vast majority of them don't. Not because they couldn't use the money or the power but because they know it would be wrong. It's just not an option for them. It's no different for the *lalassu.* Some of them have extraordinary gifts and could help themselves to whatever they want, but they don't. A few do take advantage, like any other criminals. And we'll treat them like the ordinary criminals they are because it's not their abilities that are the problem—it's their rejection of society's rules."

"But—"

"No buts." Joe had spent months not being sure how to resolve his own feelings about the *lalassu* and their abilities, but with Salazar's words, it all settled into place, crystal clear. "Don't make the mistake of lumping them all together because you're afraid. We need to be better than that."

The sting to Salazar's professional pride worked. "You're right, Detective. I won't let you down."

"Good man." Joe slapped the rookie on the back and sent him to get an assignment from the sergeant. Enjoying the latest high on the day's emotional roller coaster, Joe felt ready to conquer anything and everything. Even his love life. If Colleen was one of the *lalassu*, it didn't matter. He could make it work, and he wouldn't let his fear get in the way.

Chapter Twenty-Three

Cali hurried toward Joe's precinct, her features firmly fixed as Colleen for what would likely be the last time. Settling into the new headquarters made for a difficult morning. She wasn't used to the rumbling of the subway shaking the floor and walls every few minutes. It would be difficult to detect someone approaching.

The real problem wasn't the headquarters. She couldn't stop worrying about the lists of *lalassu*. Somehow, she doubted they were part of a recruiting drive for Mr. Dalhard. She needed to find someone or somewhere to keep them safe, but with the newly created Bureau of Special Investigations hanging over everyone's head, volunteers would be slim.

At least Joe had agreed to see her earlier than their planned lunch date. He'd sounded so eager on the phone, and it had nearly broken her heart. *I wish I could really be Colleen for him.* For a few minutes, she indulged in an impossible daydream. She could let Joe believe he'd persuaded her to his way of thinking, and he'd never have to know how deep her connection with Mr. Dalhard went. They could be happy. *Until the night he wakes up and sees your true face.*

It took effort to keep her face and body shifted but not a huge one—it became close to subconscious with the right preparation. But once she slept, everything went back to what she'd been born with. How would Joe react when he woke up and found himself next to a stranger and Colleen mysteriously absent? At best, there'd be copious amounts of shouting.

I need to make this quick. For both our sakes. The police station was getting closer, so she smoothed down her dowdy skirt and tugged down the cuffs of her pilgrim-inspired blouse. Joe stood by the food cart, two loaded hotdogs ready to go in slim paper trays. He looked so confident and handsome standing in the sunlight, like a fairy-tale prince ready to slay the dragon and rescue the princess. If only she were actually a princess.

He spotted her and smiled, a delighted grin that said the mere sight of her made his day. Cali's heart did a little flip, burying itself between her ribs so it wouldn't have to see the carnage that was sure to follow.

"Hey, beautiful girl," he said. "It's great to see you. Things are kind of crazy right now."

"I can imagine." She accepted her hotdog from him and followed Joe to a vacant spot on the precinct's steps.

"I still hope we'll have time for a meal together later. Maybe dinner instead of lunch. I need your smile to get me through." He stretched out on the steps, his long legs sprawled out like a teenager's.

"I wish you wouldn't say things like that." It made what she needed to do so much harder.

"And I thought we were past the whole believing-you-aren't-attractive thing. No one puts down my girl."

My girl. The two words stabbed at her soul, and it was only a matter of time before she would bleed out and lose her courage. "There's something I have to tell you. Mr. Dalhard called me last night."

Joe sat up. "Are you okay? Did he threaten you?"

Cali shook her head, wishing she'd left her hair loose to hide behind. Her throat was so dry that she could barely whisper what she needed to say. "I think he's planning to escape today."

To his credit, Joe didn't ask her to repeat herself or if she was sure. He accepted what she said and trusted her enough to know she wouldn't have said it otherwise. "Did he give you any details?"

"He just told me to have his place ready to go by tonight." She made herself lift her head and meet Joe's eyes. "He'll never forgive me for telling you."

Joe cupped her cheek with his hand, stroking her cheekbone with his thumb. "I'll keep you safe."

She put her hand over his, letting the warmth seep into her skin. Then she turned her head slightly to press her lips against the edge of his palm.

His hiss of indrawn breath told her that her tentative efforts at feminine charms had not gone unappreciated. She tasted the salt on his warm skin and tried to keep the tears at bay. It wasn't fair of life to give her a taste of what could be when she had no chance of ever being invited to sit at the table.

But she would take that moment for herself no matter how much worse it made her hurt down the road. In her heart, she knew she'd regret it more if she walked away without having kissed him.

Seizing her lingering bravery, Cali pounced. Joe didn't waste any time in responding to her awkward efforts. His mouth coaxed and caressed hers, tasting and savoring her like a gourmet dish. She pulled him closer, intoxicated by the hint of spices and sweetness from his lips. The close-cut bristles of his hair scraped against her fingertips as she held him close as his fingers tightened in her hair.

Their bodies were still separated. A single step would bring them together, yet Cali couldn't bring herself to move forward or away. Her body felt paradoxically heavy, as if her limbs were encased in lead. At the same time, she also felt as if she could fly free into the sky without the grounding touch of his lips on hers. She could trace every drop of blood thrumming through her veins, flushing in anticipation and sending tiny jolts of excitement crashing along her nerves.

A trickle of salt water soured the kiss. She broke away, only then becoming aware of the cooling dampness on her cheeks. Joe brushed away the tears, planting gentle kisses on her cheeks.

"Don't worry," he whispered. "We'll figure it out."

She pulled back. "I can't do this."

"Colleen—"

The false name on his lips shattered her illusion.

"We can't do this. Joe, I'm not your fated love. I'm not your one." She pulled his hands away from her face.

"You don't know that." He wrapped his hands around hers, and the old sense of being trapped came back.

Jerking her hands loose, she took refuge in her anger. "I do. You said it yourself about still noticing other women. You came to me because you wanted to get to my boss."

"That doesn't mean—" He reached for her again, but she evaded his grasp, rising unsteadily onto her feet.

"No. I'm not useful to you anymore, and I've betrayed the man who saved me. I can't do this. I'm sorry."

"Colleen, your eyes." Joe stood up. "They're turning brown."

Dammit! She'd let herself relax too much. She stumbled back from him, stepping squarely on her uneaten hotdog and nearly falling to the ground.

Joe tried to catch her as she scrambled backward, covering her eyes with her hand. Regaining her footing, she turned and fled, bumping into the gawkers surrounding the two of them. None of them tried to stop her as she made her escape.

She could hear Joe shouting after her, and she put on fresh speed, needing to get enough distance between them to shift. She nearly fell as she ran around a corner, knocking over a street vendor's display of counterfeit purses. The man's shouts joined Joe's as she yanked open the door of a tiny pawnshop.

Inside, among the deserted and dimly lit shelves, she stripped off her blouse, pulled a long-sleeved T-shirt from her bag, and yanked it on. Then she concentrated, darkening her skin and hair as much as she could.

Just in time. Joe burst into the shop, looking around wildly.

"Is there a problem, señor?" Cali asked, keeping her expression and voice as bland as possible.

"Did a woman come through here?" The stricken look in Joe's eyes nearly melted her resolve. But the deceit was necessary.

She shook her head, trying to seem bewildered at the question.

Joe cursed and banged back out the door, calling Colleen's name. Cali closed her eyes and let her knees finally give way. The shoe was falling, but there was no floor to anchor it, only endless darkness and loneliness. Sinking to the dusty linoleum, she lost herself in grief.

"Did you find her?" Michael asked as Joe came trudging back to the polie station.

Joe shook his head, unable to speak past the lump in his throat. She was really gone. Just like that.

Andrew stood silently behind Michael, thankfully keeping his sarcastic mouth shut. If the shaman had said something, Joe might not have been able to resist the impulse to hit him. He wanted to lash out at someone so they could feel the same pain that ripped his own soul apart, but he held himself back. "She told me Dalhard is planning to escape tonight. Which answers the question about whether or not she's one of his mind-controlled puppets."

"All I got from her was grief and pain." Michael pulled his gloves back on. "I think she loves you and she's doing this to protect you."

Not helping. Knowing she'd loved him and left anyway dug sharp spikes into Joe's heart. That meant it could have worked if she'd been willing to give it a chance.

"She is definitely *lalassu*," Andrew said. "Of what bloodline I cannot be sure."

"Her eyes started to change. They've always been forest green, and they started to darken to brown." Joe lifted his head in sudden hope. Maybe Dani and her family would be able to help him track her down.

"Eye shifts don't ring any immediate bells, but I'll ask Virginia and Walter. Meanwhile, we need to put together a plan to stop Dalhard." Michael looked around at the uniformed men and women coming and going. "Would the police be able to help us?"

"The police wouldn't know what to do with him. But the Bureau of Special Investigations might." Joe told Andrew and Michael about his new job offer.

Michael's eyes went wide. "You can't seriously be considering working for them?"

"If it means I can put that scum away where he can't hurt Colleen or anyone else anymore, damn straight I'm thinking about it." Joe could barely open his clenched jaw wide enough to speak.

"Deciding on career prospects based on anger and revenge is not generally considered a prudent strategy."

Joe swung around at Andrew's words, but the shaman raised his hands in surrender.

"We can't fight amongst ourselves if we're going to stop Dalhard. Come on—we have work to do." Michael coaxed them both to go with him. Joe took a deep breath, trying to put on his battered cop persona and take refuge in the practical. But he couldn't help casting a lingering look back at the smears of ketchup and mustard marking Colleen's panicked flight

.

"I assume the press conference was satisfactory." The clipped male voice on the other end of the line sounded nothing like the rolling cadences that the polished politician usually used.

"It was. Your performance was impressive." Karan allowed himself the indulgence of a brief smile. His efforts were bearing significantly more fruit than he had allowed himself to hope for. His operatives had retrieved the missing data drives from Boomerang's new headquarters, leaving only one portion of the list out of his hands. "The transfer has been arranged?"

"Yes." Neither man was so stupid as to go into further details over the phone no matter how encrypted the line was supposed to be.

"Then the terms of our deal are completed." Karan hit the button to end the call. Pressing his thumb to the back, he popped open the cover to pluck out the SIM card. A surprisingly small amount of pressure snapped the fragile chip. No one would be running any traces or making further calls on that line.

Relaxing, Karan settled into his new office chair, a high-backed leather wingback—not quite the throne he deserved, but it would do for the moment. His desk curved neatly around him, every inch of the polished rosewood within easy reach. Dalhard chose to intimidate with an industrial décor, surrounding himself with glass, steel, and heavy stone.

Karan preferred the comfort and simplicity of a more natural approach. Anyone who got close enough to him to reach the inner office would not be foolish enough to be distracted by appearances.

I should begin searching for a capable assistant of my own. Business was brisk, on both the legal and illegal side of the ledgers. After running everything from the background for years, Karan had found it painless to step into the position of ultimate authority after his boss's arrest. He knew he did not have anyone's true loyalty, only the convenience of mutual goals. He needed someone invisible and reliable to be a second set of eyes and ears.

Of course, those eyes and ears would be attached to a brain, and he could never entirely trust another person. It was best to keep matters firmly in his own hands for the time being.

He unlocked a narrow, low drawer in his desk and pulled out a dull grey laptop. That machine was not connected to any other. The radio and other communication internals had been removed, making it impossible for anyone to peek inside the hard drive.

Names, birthdates, photos, and other personal information began to spill across the display. Karan's slender fingers caressed its smooth screen, triumph warming his cold and practical soul. He selected one of the more comprehensive files and opened it. One of the president's campaign photographs stared back at him.

"A promise is a promise." Karan clicked on the file, removing it from the database and sending it to a secondary one even deeper in the protected system. He had promised the president's personal file would not appear on the list that would be released to Special Investigations. But the file would not be destroyed either. Only a fool got rid of such useful leverage.

It was not even a particularly interesting file. The man had minimal gifts, simply a heightened awareness of electrical currents and radio signals. He could not even manipulate them but only detect their presence. But as panic about the *lalassu* and their gifts swept over the world, anyone who could not claim pure human blood could potentially be caught up in the inevitable purges. Karan could not help laughing in delight. He had power over the most powerful man in the world. *Exactly as it is supposed to be.*

Chapter Twenty-Four

Wearing Boomerang's persona like a shield, Cali trotted down the subway steps to the new headquarters. She needed to set up plans to keep her people safe if Mr. Dalhard succeeded in his escape and decided to enact revenge on her for her betrayal. Part of her still wanted to deny it was a possibility, but she hadn't survived her childhood by looking away from unpalatable truths.

Such thoughts vanished as she discovered the hidden entrance standing wide open. She and Hood had rigged a heap of broken machinery on a low, rolling platform in front of the door. Her knives dropped into her hands, reassuringly cool and shining steel. Unlike guns, they never jammed or ran out of ammunition. They were always ready for action.

Inside, the room was trashed. Boxes were slashed open and dumped out, scattering papers and technology across the cracked concrete floor. The special padding she'd ordered for the floors had been ripped to shreds.

"Hood! Harley!" she shouted, terror building.

"Over here." Hood's deep rumble had never sounded so welcome. Cali hurried around an overturned desk to see Hood resting against it, blood painting the side of his face a brilliant crimson. Harley held a rag torn from his shirt against his husband's head.

Cali dropped down to kneel beside them, ignoring the protest of her abused knees.

"No concussion. The cut isn't too bad, but it needs stitches." Harley answered her question before she could summon the courage to check for herself.

She could take care of it if the medical kit was still intact. She found the grey, hard-sided container kicked into a corner. The contents were jumbled as if someone had rifled through, but everything was still there. She brought it back. "We'll have to clean it out first."

Harley eased the cloth away to reveal a long, narrow gash running from Hood's temple to behind his ear. Cali took the bottle of sterilized water from the kit and ripped open a packet of sterile cloths. Blood still seeped from the cut, but Harley was right. With a few stitches, Hood would be fine, assuming there weren't more injuries. "What happened?"

"They burst in and started ripping the place apart. Hood tried to stop them, and one of them hit him with a rifle." Harley prepared the suture kit.

"Who were they?" Cali studied the gash, wondering if she should shave the edges to prevent stray hairs from getting caught up and infecting the wound.

"No idea." Hood grimaced as she picked up the razor. "They wore body armor with masks, and they never said a word to us, not even a threat not to move or talk. All they took were the drives, although they were happy to destroy everything else."

"At least they left you alive." Cali took a deep breath to still her trembling hands. Then she began to carefully shave a narrow strip around the gash. A sudden thought froze her. "Did they hit my apartment? Is Speranza okay? What about Eva?"

"Eva and Speranza are fine. Eva's at the safe house, and Twitchy Jane is staying with Speranza. I called them both from the pay phone down the street." Harley helped with wiping away the shaved hair to keep the wound clean.

Cali exhaled in relief. Twitchy Jane was even more paranoid and suspicious than her. She'd probably take a raid from an unidentified professional group as par for the course. And the woman was a crack shot with a gun if it came to that. "How did you get Speranza to agree to having someone new stay with her?"

"Skillful and diplomatic persuasion." Harley handed her the needle. "By which I mean I nagged and cried until she gave in to shut me up."

Hood smiled at the joke then grunted in pain as Cali made the first stitch. “There’s a reason you never went to medical school.”

“And yet I still somehow seem to get more practice than an ER nurse.” She’d started with stitching up her father’s wounds as a child. These days, she mostly worked on her own people to keep them from attracting official attention.

Hood brought up the elephant in the room. “We can’t stay here.”

“I know. We’ll have to destroy what’s left. Moving obviously drew the wrong kind of attention.” Cali concentrated on keeping the stitches small and even. “And then we have to go after the list.”

Harley straightened in surprise. “With what? Our wit and charm?”

“I still have our intruder’s cell phone. I didn’t want it getting lost in the chaos of a move.” Cali snipped off the final stitch. “I’m pretty sure the last call was to whoever sent today’s visitors to us. I’m sure you can work your magic on it, Harley.”

“Is the list worth risking our lives for?” Harley wasn’t one to be distracted by flattery.

“We can’t allow that kind of information to be in the wrong hands. Too many innocent lives are at risk,” Hood answered, to Cali’s surprise. She agreed with him but hadn’t guessed he felt so strongly.

“Harley, I’m going to need the digital lock-breaker kit that you’ve been talking about.” Cali needed something to allow her to break into the computers without a remote link.

Harley nodded, helping his husband to stand. “I can do that. I’ll also put together something that will destroy the database. If we’re going to do this, we might as well go into overkill. They’re going to be after us either way.”

“I’ll make sure I’m the only one with a target on my back.” Cali felt so weary that she could drop where she stood, but that wasn’t an option. There was too much to do. Enough work to bandage a broken heart, it seemed.

As the sun began to set, Dalhard surveyed the low cinderblock walls dividing the tiny cubicles that the government dared to call living quarters. This was the last time he'd have to stare at their institutionalized blandness. The thought brought satisfaction in a plan well prepared. Everything was poised to move at his signal.

Almost everything. The harsh taint of irritation marred his anticipation as he remembered Cali's refusal to participate. After all he'd done for the girl, he'd expected more in the way of loyalty. Her reaction was just more proof that allowing those he worked with to retain independent thought was a mistake. Though, perhaps he shouldn't be so harsh. He'd once believed in the importance of appearing to play by society's rules just as strongly as she did. He'd make sure she understood his disappointment, and if she continued to resist, he would eliminate her as a threat.

It would be a pity. The girl's talents as a spy were unmatched, something he'd seen immediately the first time he realized what she could do. He'd arranged for an encounter on the street and offered her sanctuary, knowing it would buy her loyalty. It was a shame it hadn't lasted, but once he got his hands on her, he'd have his tool at his disposal again.

He studied the guards in the surveillance booth. They were distracted, talking to each other, probably about the president's ridiculous announcement. *After all the work I've done to keep the* lalassu *secret.* Dalhard shook his head, reminding himself not to dwell on the past. Success in business meant adapting to unexpected realities. There were opportunities in this place.

The shift change was due in half an hour. The men in the booth were relaxed, their minds turning to home or getting something to eat or whatever mundane pleasures they pursued. They foolishly assumed any threat of danger was over. They hadn't even noticed the broken lock on the door to their booth. Dalhard's lips curved in a mocking smile. *A shame they won't have time to learn from their mistakes.*

Men lounged around the common area, pretending to play cards or watch the television perched high on the wall but really waiting for his signal. Dalhard stood up and nodded at them.

Chairs screeched and banged as the inmates rose en masse. Without hesitation, they swarmed the guards' booth. Four men got inside and pinned the guards down before the officers could sound an alarm. Another man ran in with a makeshift knife. He stabbed the guards repeatedly, silencing their cries.

Dalhard hung back, prudently avoiding blood spatter. The convict with the knife presented him with the keys, grinning maniacally with blood dotting his face like macabre freckles.

The cell-block door yielded quickly. The inmates surged into the hall. Dalhard allowed the others to clear the way like an orange-clad phalanx of bodyguards. They swept toward the exit in a rush, like a tsunami wave. Caught up in the bloodthirsty tide, Dalhard stepped over three corpses. The lights dimmed, and a klaxon blared. Someone hadn't struck quickly enough.

The noise didn't slow the inmates down. They burst out of containment like pus from an infected wound. The yard echoed with screams and shouts as it filled with angry men rushing the perimeter. Gunshots cracked like thunder as the tower guards opened fire.

Dalhard hung back, moving slowly. The guards would be focused on the frenetic movements of the other inmates. He made his way to the garage, watching the metal lattice of the front gates disappear as men climbed up, trying to get over. Disappointing. Clearly, they'd forgotten the plan or had no faith in it. Still, it worked as a distraction.

The gates began to open, parting slightly before toppling to the ground under the escapees' weight. Time for the next phase.

Boom-Boom had palmed a set of keys for the prison van earlier. Dalhard and his chosen escort climbed inside as the engine roared. Men scattered as the van raced over the collapsed gates, passing the living and dying with equal-opportunity disdain.

"Well done," Dalhard said. The men grinned idiotically, lapping up his approval like the lower wolves they were. He was their alpha, and they would do whatever he wished. They would be the seeds of the army he would raise against Karan and the Harris siblings and whoever else thought they could oppose him. Powers might be useful, but no one individual could stand against a hundred determined attackers. Or a thousand. Or ten thousand. Eventually, any position could be overwhelmed with enough resources.

A sudden bang ripped through the van. They skidded toward the side of the road. Boom-Boom swore as he fought with the wheel, the van tipping dangerously to one side. Dalhard braced himself as the vehicle began to roll, turning completely before coming to rest mostly back on its wheels and in a ditch.

He released his seatbelt as the side door crumpled, and someone jerked him out of place. A young woman stood there, her black hair flying loose and her face twisted in fury. Danielle Harris. *How convenient.*

His men attacked, launching themselves at her. They drove her back, letting Dalhard climb out of the crashed van. Another prison van skidded to a stop on the road above them. More orange-clad convicts spilled out to join the fray. Dalhard smiled at the display of loyalty and leaned against the van to watch the battle.

Danielle fought well. He still found her presence and power intoxicating. It was a shame she was so limited in her thinking, making her completely unsuitable as a partner.

Flashes of non–orange-clad bodies caught his attention. He cursed inwardly. *Too caught up in Danielle to pay attention.*

A gun blasted. Dalhard recognized Detective Cabrera, who was shouting at the convicts to return to the prison. Laughter cackled out between Dalhard's lips. Did the fool really think they would give up so easily? The men who'd fled the prison on foot were catching up and joining the fight, more every minute. Even if the detective used every bullet in his gun, he'd be overrun. Abruptly, Dalhard sobered. He couldn't afford to lose through overconfidence again. Time to take the situation in hand. He needed a suitable hostage.

There. He spotted the young man with the long hair and the ridiculous gloves whom Danielle had so rudely defended against Dalhard during their last encounter. The young man struggled with a large, tattooed convict, dodging the other man's meaty blows and delivering surgical strikes that showed he was familiar with martial arts.

"Take that man alive, and bring him here." Dalhard pointed at the target. Immediately, four men swarmed Danielle's partner, overwhelming him. *Now, to get the others' attention.* Dalhard claimed a knife from someone and stalked to where the young man struggled against his captors. *Good, he knows enough to be afraid.* Dalhard slashed through his victim's shirt, leaving a long, bloody slice across his ribs.

"Danielle," he called out, as if summoning an assistant to a forgotten task.

Her eyes went wide, and she shoved aside her opponents. Before she could take another step, Dalhard shoved the blade into his victim's abdomen.

"Michael!" she screamed.

"Dani." The detective grabbed her and held her back. Dalhard approved. Cabrera recognized the wound wasn't lethal. But the next one could be. Both of them glared at him, their hot hate soothing his soul.

Dalhard noted a young Native man taking advantage of the convicts' inattention to disappear behind the overturned van. It seemed not all of Danielle's allies were devoid of prudent thought. He turned his attention back to Danielle. "Surrender, or he dies."

He couldn't quite keep the glee out of his voice. The little bitch had cost him far too much without having to pay for it. Now she would face the bill for her choices.

"If he dies, you're a heartbeat behind," she promised. Behind her, Cabrera kept his eyes focused on Dalhard's hostage and the knife. Dalhard recognized a man preparing himself to strike.

Some discouragement, then. Tsk-tsking, Dalhard drove his blade into the young man's thigh. His victim gasped but didn't scream or shout out—a pathetic display of defiance. It was a shame there wasn't more time to break them all properly. But he had a schedule to keep.

Not as stoic as her lover, Danielle shouted, "What do you want?"

"So very many things. For now, I want you both on the ground and unarmed."

The policeman dropped his gun on the ground and slowly knelt, hands in the air. He didn't have the same air of desperate violence as Danielle, but he wasn't ready to give up yet. Dalhard respected him more than Danielle, who glared daggers from her pretty eyes as she knelt.

One of the convicts picked up the gun and aimed it at the two of them in a way that suggested he had some experience with firearms. *Initiative. Well done.* He had time for one very important lesson. "Hold her down."

Four men pinned Dani to the ground, one on each limb. Their expressions told him they were hoping for a different sort of game. A glint of metal caught Dalhard's eye. One of the convicts held a hammer, probably stolen from the shop.

Dalhard pointed at the man. "Break her leg."

The policeman shouted for them to stop, but the inmates ignored him. Grinning, the man with the hammer swung down hard on Danielle's knee. As she screamed, Dalhard chuckled in satisfaction. Being obeyed without using his powers might be risky, but it satisfied.

His hostage began to shout and struggle, ruining Dalhard's enjoyment of the moment. The policeman fought to be free as well. Perhaps it was time to simply shoot them all. "Give me the gun."

A roar answered his request. Frowning, Dalhard raised his head in irritation.

Rising up from behind the crashed van, a pale giant of a bear towered over the dented roof. Opening its mouth, it roared again. The sound reverberated through Dalhard, stripping away his power and experience to leave him small and helpless. His mind froze as the bear dropped down onto all fours to charge.

Dalhard ran with the remnants of his army. When he reached the van at the top of the embankment, orange-clad men clogged the door. Dalhard grabbed one and threw him down the hill, clawing his way into the sanctuary of the vehicle. As soon as he dared, he shouted at the driver to move. More and more convicts crammed into the vehicle as it began to roll, spilling latecomers onto the asphalt behind them.

Dalhard watched from the rearview mirror, wondering if the animal would chase them. Instead, it seemed content to cuff the men left behind into unconsciousness. Primal panic receded, and common sense reasserted control. He'd delivered a preliminary serving of justice and could return to his original plan. The world would suffer far worse for its indifference to his desires.

Chapter Twenty-Five

Vincent poked sullenly at the half-congealed macaroni and cheese in his empty apartment. He supposed he should turn on some lights to alleviate the gloom, but he couldn't be bothered. *Sending Evonne to the farmhouse was the right decision.* Between the announcement and the Beast's planned escape, being with Vincent wasn't a safe option for her.

He'd ripped the telephone out of the wall and shut down the television and wireless connections. Without communication, the Beast couldn't contact him and trigger mindless obedience. Andrew might be convinced the shamanic rituals could wipe out the Beast's influence, but Vincent refused to risk it. The fact that the shaman hadn't tried to convince him to retreat with Evonne offered enough evidence about the lack of guarantee. The scars in Vincent's mind were too deep.

This isn't right. He'd give anything to squish that stubborn little voice inside him. Of course things weren't right. They'd never be right again. But he could only stare at the ceiling at night, hearing his little voice inside. *This isn't right.*

A knock at the door sent his adrenaline jolting into the stratosphere. Vincent crept backward, trying to avoid making a sound. Maybe he could get out the fire escape before the Beast realized that he was in the apartment.

Another knock. "Vincent, please. It's me."

Evonne. He took a deep breath and recognized her unique scent—wool oil with a hint of wood smoke. *Dammit.* She was supposed to be long gone.

"I'm here." His voice sounded as if he'd been knocking back shots all night.

The key turned in the lock, and the door slowly opened. Evonne held her hands up, palms out to show they were empty. The scent of her fear stung his nostrils and his pride. Even though he'd insist on the same precautions, they still hurt. "You forget something?"

"We've been trying to call…" She glanced down at the frayed cord wrapped around the telephone.

"Feeling a bit nostalgic for the eighteenth century." Vincent shrugged.

"Dani and the others tried to ambush Dalhard as he escaped. It didn't go well, and now they need your help. I borrowed your sister's car and came to get you." Evonne held up the keys.

That told Vincent all he needed to know. Dani hated other people driving her baby. Evonne had only driven a handful of times in her entire life, all of them since coming to Perdition. The only way Evonne would get near that car was if his sister was completely incapacitated.

They hurried downstairs to where the GT convertible gleamed under the streetlights. Vincent held out his hand to Evonne. "Give me the keys."

Evonne tossed them over. "I did okay getting here."

"It's not that." The engine roared to life. "If I drive, it guarantees she'll be fine. Because if she doesn't get better, then she can't kick my ass for doing this to her baby."

They sped through the streets. Vincent might not have his sister's lead foot, but he could definitely put the pedal down when necessary.

Navigating the route from the city to his family's farmhouse was something he could do in his sleep. He sped down the rural highways and turned onto the narrow gravel roads, wincing as the stones popped upward to ding the paint. *Be okay enough to yell at me.*

The farmhouse blazed with lights when they arrived. A sedan was parked across the lawn, sprawled in front of the porch steps with its doors wide open. Deep maroon bloodstains covered most of the pale grey upholstery in the back seat. Vincent leapt up to the porch and hurried into the kitchen. "Mom? Dad?"

His father's wheelchair was parked behind the minimal cover of the kitchen island. His relieved expression didn't distract from the shotgun propped on the stone counter. "I'm glad you came. Andrew is working on the others in the back. Your mother is with Gwen. She's hysterical."

Evonne went past him, headed for the back of the house. Vincent could hear muffled moans and shrieks coming from Gwen's isolated room. Except the stone walls should have blocked any sound from coming through. "What happened?"

"Dalhard was ready for us. He didn't just break out—he released most of the prison. He brought dozens of other convicts with him." His father shook his head, scraping his fingers through his thick black hair. "We weren't ready for that kind of assault. Go on. We can talk later, but for now, Andrew needs your help."

Vincent didn't waste any more time. He hurried through the kitchen and down the narrow hall into the family room, which had become a makeshift hospital.

At first, he couldn't make sense of what he was seeing, but then pieces began to come into focus. Andrew crouched over Michael, reddened hands frantically working. Dani was stretched out nearby on a pallet, her gaze locked onto Michael as if he might die if she blinked. Her designer jeans had been cut away, and a heavy icepack covered her exposed knee. Eric sat on the couch, his pale skin and dark eyes suggesting he'd suffered something of a relapse. Evonne held a small bowl and was coaxing Eric to eat. Joe, bleeding from a number of scrapes and cuts, had collapsed into the chair beside the others. From the reddish splotches on his skin, he'd also have a fine crop of bruises come morning.

Andrew looked up. "Good, you're here. Your sister needs a cast on her leg, and then someone needs to check the detective for injuries."

Vincent started to protest, but the shaman cut him off.

"You took field medical training. If I hear one word about how you can't help, I will put you through the wall and then use your corpse for spare parts."

Not the moment to argue, then. He knew where his family kept the medical supplies. Hospitals kept records, and the Harrises didn't do records well. Their first aid kit included surgical thread, sterilization packets, and plaster.

Vincent grabbed the supplies and knelt by his sister. "How bad does it hurt?"

"It's fine." She tried to wave him away, keeping her attention locked on Michael.

"As the leading user of the word *fine* to cover a multitude of issues, I'm going to have to call bullshit on that." Vincent pulled off the icepack and swore. His sister's knee was swollen to twice its normal size and a mottled reddish brown. He touched it carefully, trying to determine if the kneecap was intact.

Dani's breath hissed, and she grabbed his leg, her nails digging in painfully.

"I don't care if you're a grand-muckety-muck divine conduit. I'm your little brother, and I will smack you down if you hit me." Vincent examined the kneecap. He expected her to glare at him, but she still watched Michael, her teeth gnawing through her lower lip.

Vincent managed to pop the kneecap back into alignment, proving the gods weren't done playing with him yet—otherwise, the pain would have caused his sister to reflexively eviscerate him. He propped up her leg to allow room to maneuver around it. He found an old sock with the tip cut off and slid it over her knee to protect her, making sure the fabric stayed absolutely smooth. Next, he wrapped medical padding around the joint, taking care not to impair circulation.

Finally, he started applying the wet plaster, sealing her knee into place. He was about halfway done when Dani suddenly lifted herself onto her elbows. "Michael?"

Oh, shit. If Michael died, his sister would go ballistic—as in an end-of-the-world, duck-and-cover apocalyptic reaction. Vincent turned, the plaster cooling on his sticky fingers.

Michael's eyes were closed, and his skin was pale. But his chest slowly rose and fell as he breathed. Andrew stepped back, scrubbing the drying blood off his hands. "I've done all I can. If he makes it through the night, he'll be okay."

Dani's exhalation of relief echoed through the house. "Thank you."

"I'm sorry I waited so long. I honestly thought Dalhard would spend more time gloating." Guilt twisted the shaman's mouth downward. "I shifted to the fur as soon as I realized what was going on."

"Yeah. He's gotten more direct since last time." Dani winced, finally seeming to notice the plaster coating her leg. "What the hell is this?"

Vincent applied a new strip to the growing cast. "My art homework. I should get an A in interpretive sculpture, don't you think? I call it *My Sister Should Shut Up and Let Me Finish.*"

Dani laughed—weak and feeble but still a laugh. "You are such an asshole."

"I learned from the master." He bowed his head to her.

"What do we do now?" Joe asked. "The men with Dalhard mowed through us like we were nothing."

Vincent examined the suddenly fascinating wood grain in the floor. He should have been there with them.

"If you'd been with us, Bro, you'd only have gotten hurt too," Eric said suddenly from the couch.

Taking refuge in sarcasm, Vincent forced himself to continue. "True. Being shot is not a fun way to spend an evening."

"Tonight was more about blunt-force trauma." Eric leaned back. "I don't know what we can do. Obviously, the jail can't hold him, so we can't go to the police even if they had the manpower to go after him."

"The US Marshals are the ones who handle escaped prisoners," Joe corrected absentmindedly.

Eric continued, ignoring Joe. "Every day he's out, he's going to build up more of an army of his zombies. He'll be unstoppable. We have to take him down quickly."

"'Cause we did such an awesome job this time." Dani hissed as Vincent started smoothing down the plaster for an even coating.

Slumped in place, Joe looked utterly defeated. "I should have let Vapor kill him." His quiet words dropped into the discussion like a boulder into a puddle. Everyone focused on the policeman.

"He wanted to when I was in Alaska. I refused to help unless he gave me a chance to take Dalhard in. I wanted to let the justice system handle it instead of turning to vigilante methods." Joe's fingers pressed into his temples.

"And the moral of the story is"—Vincent got up to clean the tacky residue from his fingers—"people suck."

"That's unfair." Evonne rose to her feet.

"What part of this says *fair* is a concept that applies to us?" Vincent turned on her, suddenly angry at her naïve condemnation. Life didn't care if people played by the rules or not. It reached in and screwed people over just because it could.

"We need a plan. I've been trying to connect with the Goddess, but I'm only getting vague messages. Something like, 'Your call is important to us—please stay on the line.'" Dani relaxed back onto her pallet, glancing quickly to check on Michael.

"Surprisingly unhelpful for a deity," Joe muttered, earning himself a glare from both Dani and Andrew. Vincent hid a relieved smile. Sarcasm meant there was still some fighting spirit left.

A muffled shriek from Gwen's room interrupted the argument before it could go any further. Evonne had barely gotten to her feet when Virginia emerged from the kitchen. She trailed her fingers along the wall, her milky grey eyes staring blankly ahead.

"If psychic powers always prevented us from making mistakes, the *lalassu* would have been discovered generations ago. Humans err, and so must we." Vincent's mother turned her unseeing gaze on Joe, reminding them all of her clairvoyant abilities. She could predict things a short distance into the future—about twenty minutes at most. "I don't want to have any more blood spilled in here tonight."

Would the fight have switched from verbal to physical? When he was a boy, Vincent believed his mother's powers were infallible. Lately, he wasn't so sure. Otherwise, why would she have allowed them to get involved with Dalhard without warning them away?

"Is Gwen okay?" Dani asked.

"She's very upset. Chuck is trying to get through to her with a message." Virginia's slender hand snaked out to check Eric's forehead.

Our family really needs to stop using dead people as our primary message system. Chuck was the ghost of a ten-year-old boy who had been dead since the thirties. He passed information to Gwen and Bernie, both of them powerful mediums. Vincent wanted to make a joke about switching to texting but held himself back. *See, I do so have a filter.*

"I think something has gone wrong with Bernie. But making sense of what a hysterical child said after the message has gone through a decades-dead ghost and Gwen's alternative view of reality is proving to be a challenge. All I can be certain of is that Bernie and her mother need help." Virginia's blind eyes turned unerringly to where Michael lay. He paled at the mention of his former client, who was now hiding from Dalhard.

"I'll go to her." Eric started to struggle off the sofa, but their mother's iron grip kept him in place.

"You'll stay put until I tell you otherwise." Andrew crossed his arms and glared down at his patient. "I'll take care of it."

"You can't leave Michael," Dani objected. "What if he gets worse in the night?"

"I can go. It's not like I'm useful here anymore." Joe stood up, bracing against the wall a little more than one would expect from a volunteer.

Aw, hell. Heroism is contagious. Vincent raised his hand. "I'll go with him. Bernie knows me."

Virginia smiled at her son. Vincent glared at his mother. He couldn't be sure if she was unaware of his scowl or was choosing to ignore it. No one knew exactly how much her powers showed her.

"I'll see if I can get an address," Virginia said. "You can leave in the morning."

"With respect, ma'am, if this is an emergency, the faster we get there, the better." Joe straightened.

Vincent winced at his purposeful enthusiasm. Didn't the Boy Scout get it? There was no guarantee that the good guys were going to win. Tonight had proved as much. In real life, when the determined and ethical went up against the powerful and amoral, good intentions and purity of thought ended up bloody on the floor along with their defenders.

Chapter Twenty-Six

I know something you don't know. Naya's digital taunt hovered over the contract that Karan was trying to read. Special Investigations was offering handsome terms for the use of Dalhard's accumulated stable of *lalassu* and significant finder's fees for others on the list. Karan had delivered a copy to them immediately as a sign of good faith. The government's money would set up the next phase of Karan's plans.

He considered ignoring the hacker, but alienating him or her would not be a wise choice. Still, he need not encourage such interruptions. **I have a great deal to do. If you possess useful knowledge, you could simply email it to me.**

Naya replied, **Where would the fun be in that? You shouldn't worry about the Special Investigations contract. It's set up in your favor.**

Karan had no intention of taking the hacker's word on it. **What is it you wish to tell me?**

Three things, the hacker typed. **First, Shawna Goddard was arrested by the Bureau of Special Investigations this afternoon and transported to a temporary holding facility.**

Should he recognize the name? It would be convenient if he could look it up on the list, but after Naya's intrusions, extra security precautions had been necessary, and all significant information had been moved to an unconnected computer. Inefficient but necessary.

Naya answered, **Shawna Goddard has a long list of fraud-and-extortion charges, mostly stemming from running psychic scams. She fled the States and lived in Montréal, Canada, for the last two years. Last fall, she moved without warning the day after the warrant was filed for André Dalhard's arrest. They picked her up in**

Little Rock, South Carolina.

Karan still saw no reason why he should be interested in Shawna Goddard. The timing suggested she was *lalassu*, but as she was already in custody, she was of little use to him.

Naya continued. **When Special Investigations searched Goddard's apartment, they found clothing for two women and a child along with books on childhood schizophrenia.**

Then Karen understood. Childhood schizophrenia and psychic work could mean the Goddard woman was connected to Bernadette Anderson. The hairs on the back of Karan's neck stiffened in anticipation of concluding the hunt. If he could find the child, she would be invaluable as an undetectable surveillance system. **Was a child found?**

No. Two teams are searching the surrounding area. They won't get far. Shall I presume the child holds some interest for you?

Karan considered his options. Thus far, he had been working closely with Special Investigations, planning their unveiling along with the *lalassu*. He did not want to burn those bridges, but a reliable and malleable medium was a tempting prize. **Yes.**

Naya replied, **I'll make sure she's transferred to your custody. I can guarantee Special Investigations won't cause problems.**

What will such help cost me? Karan tapped his fingers on the desk, impatient to learn what Naya would demand.

A partnership between you and me. Working together.

Partners could be both resources and vulnerabilities. Karan was not certain that he required the former, and he definitely did not want the latter. **I would consider it. What are your other two pieces of news?**

The hacker typed, **I've located the Fuentes family, and they do not have the missing portion of the list. They claim to have given it to Detective Cabrera. Which leads me to my third piece of news: André Dalhard escaped from prison two hours ago. Special Investigations was on the way to transfer him to a secure facility.**

Karan's own sources had informed him of Dalhard's escape, and he had personally arranged for his former boss's transfer as part of his deal with the president. Naya's information might be redundant, but it showed promise and was worthy of some small reward. **I will transfer**

appropriate recompense into your accounts if you provide the information.

I'm not sure I'm ready to trust you.

Karan could not fault the hacker's caution. No matter how insulated bank accounts were, they offered a great deal of information to those who knew how to look. **It is odd that you have asked me for trust and yet are not willing to grant it. You are the one who invaded my home and business, and yet you do not trust me.**

Naya replied, **Don't be so sensitive. Your mother always said you worried too much.**

Karan was far too disciplined to allow his sudden increase in suspicion to appear in his face or body language. His mother had indeed chided him not to worry so much about the future and trust in the gods. But she had also been dead for centuries along with anyone else who could have passed on such information. If this Naya Jeevan thought to use memories of Karan's family against him, the hacker was sorely mistaken. **Identify yourself.**

In time. When you understand how much you need me. You've already begun to learn that you can't keep track of everything on your own.

The hacker was insightful and patient. A dangerous opponent on multiple levels. Karan reached to shut off the computer.

Naya typed, **Wait. You can trust me. I may have broken into your system, but I haven't caused you any trouble. I've been helping you.**

Karan lowered his hand, avoiding looking at the tiny dimple housing the web camera. The attempt to turn off the computer had been a test, and the hacker failed it. The *wait* revealed that the camera had been compromised, allowing Naya to see what Karan was doing. **I will not trust someone who hides from me. If you want a partnership, come in for an interview.**

There was no further answer from Naya. Karan waited for fifteen minutes and then turned off the computer, that time without an onscreen protest. His intruder had made the first mistake and given Karan both the advantage and important information. The hacker watched him through his own computer's camera and had deep connections within the Bureau of Special Investigations. In fact, Karan would be willing to bet significant money that Vapor had been caught up in one of Special Investigation's sweeps for *lalassu*. Which meant he was likely being held in a government detainment facility. Finally, the hacker had knowledge about Karan's family, perhaps received directly from Vapor.

The hacker showed skill and promise. But Karan would not make the same mistakes as André Dalhard and forget that subordinates could develop goals of their own that did not always match those of their employers.

Still no answer. Joe stared at his phone as if it would spontaneously provide a solution for how he could get Colleen to talk to him again. Her phone kept going directly to voice mail. He needed to warn her about Dalhard and make sure she was all right.

He'd sent his mother a message to warn her that he'd be out of touch for a day or two. Hopefully, it would prevent an accumulation of rotting leftovers and a scolding lecture when he returned. He'd also told Modnik that he was following up a lead on the escaped prisoners. She'd been so overwhelmed that she'd barely listened, giving him twenty-four hours to pursue it. He tried to tell himself that one cop's presence or absence wouldn't make a difference, but it didn't stop the guilt from whispering that he was letting his fellow officers down.

The phone was cool in his hands, and he wondered if giving Colleen's number another try would be too much like something an ex-boyfriend stalker would do. He didn't think she'd really wanted to walk away. Something had made her believe she had no other choice. He suspected her actions were connected to Dalhard and his escape. Which brought his thoughts directly back to worrying if Colleen was okay.

"You know, I don't think it's traditional to give someone a booty call as you're leaving town." Vincent's eyes never left the road ahead as they sped down the interstate.

"It's not a booty call. I just want to make sure she's safe." Joe made himself tuck his phone back into his jacket. He'd left three messages so far. What if she wasn't answering not because of the breakup but because Dalhard had found her? The man would be angry about Colleen leaking his escape plans. Joe clenched his fists in his pockets to avoid seizing the wheel and forcing the car to turn around and go after Colleen. That could end up putting her in more danger if he led Dalhard to her.

"This the chick you were talking about? The one working for Dalhard?" Vincent asked, concentrating on the road.

Joe's back straightened in surprise. He'd never heard Vincent refer to Dalhard by name before. It was always the Beast.

Vincent's nostrils flared. "Don't make a big deal about it. I've been able to say and hear his name for a while now. But I don't want to forget that he's not a man—he's a monster who takes over people's minds. Which is why I'm glad to hear your girl is out of contact."

"And why would that be?" *Don't get mad until I hear the reason.*

"Because she might have set all this up for him," Vincent replied bluntly.

Okay. Now I can get mad. Joe's muscles ached as they tightened. "There's no way."

"Really? I would have said there was no way that I would betray my family and go fist to fist with my sister, but it still happened. The girl could have deliberately leaked the escape plan to set up an ambush for us. If Andrew hadn't been there tonight, you all would have been dead, and there would be no one to stand against him." Vincent delivered his conclusions like knife wounds, plunging inside effortlessly so the victim only felt the hurt when the blade ripped free.

Every one of Joe's instincts insisted Colleen wouldn't have set them up. But he had no real evidence to back that up. Even if she didn't want to do it, Dalhard could have hooks in her mind. *Michael said that Colleen walked away to protect me.* His teeth squeaked as his jaw clenched painfully. If Dalhard did his Siren thing on her, Joe wouldn't rest until he'd gotten her free.

"You planning to hit me?" Vincent asked.

Joe relaxed his hands and jaw. "Not yet. I think I'm more upset at myself than anything else. I haven't been making the best judgment calls." He'd lied to his sergeant and left Perdition when it was about to try and cope with a mass prison escape and rioting. His personal firearm was in the hands of one of those escapees. He'd gotten involved with a possible suspect and accomplice. And he was on his way to rescue a little girl whom no one else would believe and keep a promise to a gravely injured friend. Joe rubbed his head, hoping that his loyalty wouldn't bite him in the ass.

"I don't suppose there's a *lalassu* bloodline that can time travel, is there?" Joe asked, only half joking.

"No, that's more of an alien thing," Vincent replied with a straight face.

Really? Joe looked up at the sky.

Vincent grinned. "I'm bullshitting you. Aliens aren't real."

"Like I'm supposed to know," Joe muttered. "Last year, you weren't real." That meant he was stuck with the decisions he'd already made, so he had to start coping with them. "How long a drive again?"

"About ten hours. You should sleep. I'm going to need you to take over the wheel in a few hours if we don't want to have to stop."

"I'm still too wired to sleep." Joe could feel his nerves twitching—the aftermath of the adrenaline rush from the fight. Vincent nodded, not pushing the issue.

Silence weighed heavily in the car as distant lights crept past. Joe took a deep breath and asked the question he'd been wondering about. "Umm, don't take offence, but how reliable are these messages coming through Gwen?"

Vincent smirked. "You mean because she's crazy?"

Joe refused to be rattled. He had a right to ask.

"About as reliable as any 9-1-1 call. We know there's trouble, but I wouldn't count on the details too much. Gwen's been better since Dani reconnected with the Goddess—less asking us to go fix shit from colonial times or the Civil War."

According to Gwen, Chuck had told her that Bernie and Martha had been on the run since the president's announcement. Virginia tried to reach Shawna, the medium helping them, and discovered the number had been disconnected. Chuck claimed that Shawna had been snatched off the street by armed men and that he'd warned Bernie and Martha to flee.

The logistics made Joe's head hurt. "Chasing down burglars and murderers was a lot easier than this."

"Anytime you want to go back, just say the word."

"Give me a break." Joe eased the seatbelt away from his throat. Those things always crept up like a chokehold. "You grew up with this stuff. I didn't."

"No, you grew up in a house where you could go out and play with your friends without having to worry about them finding out your big secret." Vincent snorted. "You didn't go to bed wondering if your parents were going to wake you up in the middle of the night and tell you to grab the go-bag under your bed because we needed to leave town in a hurry. You didn't watch your baby sister go crazy before she even learned to talk because the damn ghosts would never leave her alone—"

"No, I just had to dodge the gang recruiters and watch my parents work themselves to the bone trying to support us." Anger had control of Joe's mouth and made him drop his usual filters. "When I was twelve, my father and I were out, trying to give Mamá some peace, and I got to see him shot by some punk kids in a drive-by. And then I got to go to school with his killers for the next three years because there wasn't enough evidence to convict them."

Oh shit. He didn't tell people about that. Not ever. He braced himself for Vincent's sarcastic assault on a wound that still throbbed despite the years.

Vincent didn't say anything right away. Joe's fingers curled inward as the tension simmered and grew with each passing breath.

"Tough shit."

It took Joe a moment to process what Vincent had actually said. There had been no dismissal in his tone—no sarcasm, no attempt to one up. It had been a sincere, if crude, expression of sympathy.

"Is the bonding moment done? I'm not up for much more without adding some beer into the mix." Vincent glanced over.

And the old Vincent was back. But the long hours ahead seemed a lot easier to face.

The Turn

CHAPTER TWENTY-SEVEN

The sound of smashing glass from the street below made Cali wince. An early-morning dustup several blocks over had ended up with guns blasting and police sirens wailing. That minor incident had triggered a general revolt from the neighborhood, and now groups were wandering the streets, chanting and looting. The news couldn't give any useful information except to report similar outbreaks occurring in Chicago, New York, Miami, and Los Angeles.

Cali turned away from Speranza's window. No sense in making a target out of herself. The kids were happily occupied in coloring their books as well as most of the kitchen table. Speranza was napping to rest her ribs. And Hood wasn't calling Cali, which made her twitchier than Jane.

News of the prison escape had torn through the underworld in record time. There hadn't been a mass breakout of more than a half-dozen prisoners in North America since the Civil War, but more than sixty of them had broken free this time. Rumors hinted at substantial casualties among the guards and escapees.

And yet none of the prisoners were making themselves known. Not a single one had turned up at home or in a familiar locale. They'd all vanished into the darkness.

Which meant Mr. Dalhard was in charge. Cali had heard him lecture on the stupidity and laziness of the common criminal. They got sloppy, they made the easy choice and went for the familiar, and then they got themselves caught. If he was keeping them out of trouble, it meant he had a purpose for them. And it probably wasn't rehabilitation.

Mr. Dalhard had left a message on Colleen's phone. Only four words: *I'm disappointed in you.* Then nothing. She'd turned off the phone and removed the battery to avoid having it traced back to her.

When Hood found out, he'd insisted that she lie low with Speranza and the girls. Cali argued that she would be a risk to them if she stayed there, but Hood was persuasive when determined. The crew needed information, and she couldn't be the one to collect it. Once they knew more, she could come up with a better plan. Harley was busy hacking into the corrupt detective's phone while Hood checked on Joe for her.

"Cali, I'm hungry." Carlotta dropped a pink marker and what looked like a decent imitation of a Jackson Pollock painting.

"Sure thing, sweetie." Cali pasted a fleeting smile on her face and pulled out the Tupperware of sliced vegetables and fruits.

"I want cookies." Carlotta folded her tiny hands. "Zara does too."

Zara perked up at the word "cookies" and pulled the pacifier out of her mouth in anticipation. She swept the mess of markers and papers to the floor.

Uh-oh. "I'm pretty sure that you're supposed to have your veggies first." Cali had dealt with professional blackmailers without blinking an eye. Too bad those experiences didn't seem to apply when dealing with someone under four feet tall.

"No. Cookies." Carlotta wasn't going to budge.

"'Ookie." Zara added her two cents' worth.

If I say no, they're going to cry and wake up Speranza. And if I give them cookies for a snack, Speranza will kill me. Actually, her neighbor would just look at Cali with the expression that said that any idiot should have been able to negotiate without giving the kids cookies. Which would sting even worse.

"How about your veggies first and then a cookie?" Cali heard the quaver of fear in her voice and knew she'd lost.

"Cookie now!" Carlotta wailed. Zara started screaming too, banging her chubby fist on the table.

"Shh. Your mom is still sleeping."

"Not anymore." Speranza walked calmly out into the living area, moving much more freely than she had the previous day. "What's going on here?"

"I. Want. Cookie!" Carlotta managed to shout through hiccups, a feat which impressed and slightly terrified Cali.

Speranza carefully picked up Zara, who immediately quieted. "And when do we have cookies?"

Bereft of her ally, Carlotta caved. "After supper."

"Is it suppertime?" Speranza continued in merciless parental logic.

Carlotta shook her head, scowling. Her mother leaned over to kiss the top of the little girl's head and motioned for Cali to get the snack ready.

"I'm sorry they woke you." Cali served the pint-sized plates of food. Speranza put Zara down, and both girls began to munch away with every sign of contentment.

"I've been awake for a little while now." Speranza glanced at the window. "It sounds like a war zone. Is your Mr. Cabrera all right?"

"I… I don't know. And I don't think I'll be finding out anytime soon." Cali felt traitorous tears threatening to spill.

"What happened?" Speranza didn't come closer, although Cali could tell she wanted to. She always respected Cali's need for distance.

"I told you we're too different. And I had to make a bad choice." The words stuck in her throat.

"What did you choose?" Speranza's voice held the same tone she'd used on Carlotta earlier.

"I tried to protect him, but it meant betraying someone else, someone who's been like a father to me. And it didn't even work. Now everything is in a mess, and I don't know what will happen." Cali clapped her hand over her mouth to stop the outpouring of words. Speranza needed her to be the strong one. The young mother had enough to deal with.

"I have some experience with that." Speranza smiled gently. "Come and sit down before you wear through the floor."

Cali hadn't realized she was pacing. And right in front of the girls.

"Is Auntie Cali okay?" Carlotta asked with wide eyes.

"She'll be fine. Her heart is very confused right now, and she needs to talk to me about it. You finish your snacks, and then you can color some more." Speranza sank into the couch with a grateful sigh.

Cali joined her. "I'm sorry. I'll pull myself together."

"Denying how you feel won't help. I should know." Speranza adjusted a pillow to provide more support for her back. "It took me a long time to understand that I could love Rodolpho and still need to leave him. The happy times don't somehow balance out the fear or the pain."

Cali couldn't help staring at Speranza. Her neighbor had never wanted to talk about her ex-husband's abuse before.

"I talked to the girls last night. I explained why we were hiding from their father. Something is wrong with his mind, so we can't trust him not to hurt us, no matter how much we love him." Speranza smiled at her girls. "I think it was a relief for all of us to finally have it out in the open."

"That's a big change from before." That topic was exactly the distraction Cali needed.

"You can thank your friend Jane." Speranza chuckled. "I realized I was becoming more like her, always afraid and wanting to hide it. But hiding only made all my fears bigger. And I was teaching the girls to see the world as a terrifying place. I want more for them than that."

"Does this mean you'll be leaving town?" She would miss them, but if it meant they were safer, Cali wouldn't stand in the way.

"I still have no intention of letting him push us out of our home." Speranza's spine of steel returned. "But I will call the police next time he comes to harass us, and even if they refuse to listen, there will at least be a record of what he has done. I will reclaim our lives rather than hide behind these walls."

"I know you will." Cali had no doubts.

"Now, what about you? There is more than the detective on your mind. What about this man who you say is like a father to you? I've been watching you, and I can see you are uncomfortable with what he has asked you to do."

Cali stared at her hands, which were locked together to keep from trembling. "It's not what he's been asking. He's been changing. He's not the man I thought he was."

Speranza nodded. "It can be difficult to accept that the demons are truly a part of someone we love. And it doesn't stop us from being drawn to them, so we have to learn to ignore that connection."

"Life was not supposed to be this complicated. I can't stand back and let Mr. Dalhard hurt people. I'm going to have to stop him. But I don't know what to do after."

"You don't need to know that yet. Just concentrate on the first step, exactly as you told me to do." Speranza smiled, clearly pleased to have the advice tables turned. "And the first step is talking to Mr. Cabrera again."

"That's more complicated." Cali looked down at her hands again.

"You like him. He likes you. He's a good man. What is so complicated?"

Cali couldn't raise her voice louder than a whisper. "I've lied to him. A lot."

"Then you will have to tell him the truth. That's embarrassing but not as horrible as dreading it."

Cali studied her clasped hands as if memorizing them. "What if he hates me?" She'd hate someone for lying to her the way she'd lied to Joe.

"Then you will know. What if he could forgive you but you walked away? Wouldn't that be worse?"

With all of Speranza's history, she still had a surprisingly romantic outlook. But Cali knew better. Life wasn't a romantic comedy where couples overcame impossible odds before the credits rolled.

"Auntie Cali, your phone is dancing." Carlotta interrupted.

Cali shot up from the couch to grab Boomerang's buzzing cell phone. Hood's number flashed. "Any news?"

"It's not good," Hood replied. "The police station is overrun and overwhelmed. They know that Dalhard organized the escape. He is considered extremely dangerous, and the police have orders to shoot. There were guys here from the Bureau of Special Investigations, but they appear to have withdrawn. And no one has seen any sign of Joe since lunch yesterday."

Cali's aching fingers tried to dig into the Formica countertop. *Lunch yesterday.* She was one of the last people to see him.

"His boss is afraid that Dalhard may have found a way to take him out," Hood continued, each word driving into her like nails into a coffin. "Harley found Joe's cell phone. It's traveling through Virginia."

“Then he’s alive.” Cali exhaled the too-stale air trapped in her lungs.

“Or one of the convicts took his phone.” Hood crushed the dream before it could fully bloom. “The cops found something near the prison. One of the prison vans crashed into the ditch with signs of a struggle all around it. There was blood on the grass but no bodies.”

No bodies. There was no reason to remove or hide Joe’s body in the middle of a prison escape. So the odds were good that he’d survived. But he could have been hurt. Her emotions kept flapping like a flip-flop caught in an escalator, moving too rapidly to even begin to process.

Hood continued, piling on more worries. “It’s not just Dalhard. Word on the street is that Dalhard Industries will pay handsomely for Joe’s location. I think they know he has the last portion of the list.”

Even if he was all right, Joe wouldn’t stay unharmed for long. “How’s Harley doing with Hampton’s cell phone?”

“He’s tracked the last number called to a burner phone. We expected that, so he’s checking into when and where the burner was active. So far, it looks like local calls once he gets rid of the anti-trace garbage.”

“Get me a location,” Cali ordered. Whatever else was going on, they couldn’t allow Karan to keep the list. She could do that much to help Joe and his friends.

Chapter Twenty-Eight

"I don't like being out of touch," Joe grumbled as the car crunched to a stop on the gravel drive beside a battered and mud-speckled truck. Vincent had insisted on turning off their cell phones after a final check-in as they crossed the Virginia–North Carolina border. The sign at the front proclaimed "Rose on the Grave: An Afterlife Adventure Bed and Breakfast." It looked like a decommissioned stone church, complete with a graveyard, and Joe couldn't imagine anyone voluntarily wanting to stay there.

"Once we hook up with Bernie, we'll have the perfect undetectable communication with back home." Vincent started scooping fast food litter out of the back seat and into a plastic bag.

"Messages relayed by ghosts between your sister and a child are not my idea of the perfect system." What if Colleen reconsidered and tried to call? As much as he understood the dangers of being tracked via their phones, his fingers itched to pop the battery back in and check his voice mail.

Vincent actually smiled at Joe's comment before poking at the doorbell. "Sorry, did you want to ring for Frankenstein?"

And Sarcastic Man was back. Joe ignored the taunt and tested the front door. Locked. Taped to the door, a small hand-lettered sign explained that Rose on the Grave was temporarily closed and directed visitors to call at a later time. Joe wondered if anyone was even there.

He heard footsteps approaching, and the latch clicked open to reveal a pretty young woman with honey-blond hair caught up in a long ponytail.

And he felt nothing. Zero hint of attraction. Why had he reacted so strongly to Colleen, Boomerang, and Cali while no one else even raised a quaver of interest? Joe felt as if he was scrambling to put together a puzzle, but the picture kept changing.

"I'm Jessica. You're Bernie's friends." She opened the door wide for both men to step inside. The lack of discretion made Joe twitchy. They could be anyone as far as she knew.

"Don't worry." Jessica closed the door behind them. "Chuck told me who you were before you arrived."

"You know Chuck?" Joe asked, looking at Vincent in confusion.

"I don't hear him as clearly as Bernie, but I can still get some impressions. Bernie is waiting for you in the main hall." Jessica stood aside.

This girl was too open with a stranger, even one verified by Chuck. She might not think precautions were necessary, but Joe wasn't going to follow suit. He summoned up his third-most charming smile and dug for information. "A place like this must take a lot of upkeep."

"I imagine so." Jessica crossed the duskily lit lobby to the large double doors opposite the main entrance. "But I don't work here."

Then who does? The business was closed. Joe's cop radar pinged as she pulled hard on the massive wooden door. "Do the owners know you're here?"

"She does. She's just suffered a rather large disappointment and is taking a break to process it. Trust me, I'm not a break-and-enter type." Jessica winked. "Bernie's waiting for you."

A young girl of about twelve looked up from her notebook as they stepped inside a long, vaulted hall lined with narrow stained-glass windows. "Joe! Gwen says to tell you that Michael is doing okay."

Relief loosened the cramped knot in Joe's stomach. "Thanks, kid. What're you working on there?"

"Taking messages." Bernie passed over the spiral notebook. Joe opened it to reveal dark sketches of faces peering out at him. Scattered through the page were notes like "Wife—insurance policy—third drawer at work" and "Don't let my brother get my bike." Joe flipped it shut and took a closer look at the little girl.

"Are the ghosts bothering you?"

Bernie shrugged. "When I don't want to be bothered, Chuck makes them wait. It's nice to talk to them sometimes. I don't have many alive friends to talk to."

His heart went out to the child. She'd spent so much of her life surrounded by therapists and doctors instead of friends.

A moment later, she brightened in one of her odd switches of personality. "We're going to be going to a new place, someplace we can stay. I want to get two cats and a dog. And maybe a parrot and a hamster."

"Slow down, Bernie. You might want to check with your mom about all that," Jessica said. "Martha is finishing packing."

In a few seconds, the girl had gone from too dark and mature to having the bubbly enthusiasm of a six-year-old. Martha had her hands full even if she did understand her daughter better than when she'd thought Bernie was schizophrenic instead of psychic. After years of medication, otherworldly visits, and isolation, Bernie would always need special care and attention.

"The faster we get out of here, the better." Vincent tugged on his jacket collar.

Bernie eyed Vincent, tilting her head to one side. "Hi, Vincent. You look awful."

"That's not nice to say." Jessica's hushed whisper echoed clearly.

"It's true." Bernie shrugged, returning to her drawing.

"Can't argue with her point." Vincent shoved his hands into his pockets.

"Jessica, I think I have everything." A heavily muscled young man with short brown hair emerged into the dining hall from an open door at the far end. He carried a duffel bag, a small suitcase, and a coil of orange electrical cord. All three crashed to the floor when he caught sight of the strangers in the room.

Joe's hand went to his holster, but the man held still, his eyes on Jessica.

"Greg, this is Vincent and Joe, Bernie's friends," Jessica said, and the man visibly relaxed.

"He's looking a lot better. He was all smudgy before because of the demon." Bernie frowned as the tip of her pencil cracked free of its wood enclosure. "This is broken."

"Demon?" The hair on the back of Joe's neck tried to stand up and run for it.

"Ah… it's a long, weird story." Greg rubbed the back of his head, not quite meeting their eyes. Joe would have sympathized if he weren't busy wondering whether or not he should pick up a few of Aunt Agata's charms for his own place. It had taken him a long time to accept superpowers as real. Demons were a whole other story. But maybe the demon talk was like Vincent's alien joke.

"Jessica, my pencil is broken." Bernie tugged on Jessica's arm, trying to direct the grown-ups' attention to the truly important issues.

"We live on weird." Vincent snorted. "What happened? You get possessed?"

So much for the joke theory.

Greg blinked as he picked up the duffel bag, clearly unprepared for such a matter-of-fact approach. "Um, yeah."

This is not my kind of conversation. Joe wondered if he should offer to go help Martha to escape witnessing any more uncomfortable revelations.

Jessica and Bernie both suddenly lifted their heads and turned toward the half-open double doors. Joe tensed, reaching again for his gun, although he couldn't see or hear anything.

"Chuck says they're coming." Bernie shoved her notebook into a backpack.

"I'll go help Martha. Get our stuff to the truck." Jessica pressed a quick kiss to Greg's cheek before hurrying to the back of the hall.

"Who's coming? Is there anything we need to take care of before we leave?" Joe wondered if he was fleeing yet another crime scene.

"I'm guessing the same men who picked up Shawna—the Bureau of Special Investigation." Greg grabbed the suitcase in his free hand. "Christie, the owner, already left. We need to get out of here before they arrive. Can one of you get the door?"

Joe volunteered, picking up the electrical cord. His arm snapped tight under the unexpected weight, and he took another look at the other man's broad arms. He was probably a contractor or someone who worked a lot with his hands. They went outside to the truck and loaded the gear into it. As they closed the tailgate, the others came out. Jessica locked the front door and hid the key underneath the planter to the left.

"I'll have Chuck talk to you, Jessica." Bernie hugged the blond woman. Martha stood a little behind them, her dark-blond hair pulled back into an uneven braid and her hands twitching as if she wanted to hurry her daughter along but also didn't want to deprive her of that moment.

"Thanks, Bernie. Take care of yourself and your mom." Jessica gave Bernie a final squeeze before pushing her gently toward Vincent and Joe's sedan. Martha guided her daughter into the car, waving at Jessica and Greg.

Joe got into the driver's seat, and once everyone was safely inside, he pulled away from the haunted bed-and-breakfast. The truck followed them down the drive, turning the opposite way at the main road.

As they came to a four-way stop a few miles away, Bernie suddenly spoke up again. "Turn right here."

"The highway is straight ahead." Joe pointed at the sign.

"We have to turn." Martha sat beside her daughter, arms around her. Joe stared at them for a moment in the rearview mirror before complying.

"Turn into the driveway there. Hide the car inside the garage." Bernie's calm directives sounded out of place coming from the mouth of a child.

To their left stood a large home with a detached garage whose door was wide open, revealing plenty of room for the sedan alongside the tools and a few bicycles. Joe turned the car and slowly backed it in. Pinning themselves down inside the garage felt like walking into a trap.

He looked nervously toward the house. No one seemed to be peeking from behind the curtained windows, and he couldn't hear any dogs barking, but that didn't mean no one had seen them pull in.

"Having fun yet?" Vincent's eyes scanned the road rapidly, and despite his casual words, his hands were curled into fists.

Seconds ticked by like minutes, measured in sweat trickling down Joe's scalp and neck. *This is stupid. I shouldn't take orders from a preteen even if she does talk to ghosts.*

He was about to tell them so when Bernie announced. "There they are."

A pair of black SUVs slowed and halted at the four-way stop before continuing down the road toward Rose on the Grave. There weren't any flashing lights, but the uniformity and tinted windows screamed government vehicles.

Joe exhaled slowly. If they'd seen the fugitives, they certainly would have noted their car and probably would have stopped them. Clearly, ghosts could be more helpful than he'd initially thought.

Joe woke up from a fitful nap, his neck cramped from sleeping in the front seat. He blinked at the clock. It was nearly midnight. "Everything okay?"

Vincent shook his head. "All good."

Glancing back over his shoulder, he saw Martha and Bernie asleep in the back seat, propped against one another. Bernie snored loudly, her mouth wide open. "Michael will be happy to see Bernie again."

"He shouldn't get too attached," Vincent replied grimly. "They won't be able to stay."

"Sure they will…" Joe trailed off as he realized Vincent was right. They'd failed to stop Dalhard, and the attempt had cost them dearly. Michael and Dani were both out of commission, Vapor was missing, and Eric was still recovering. That meant that a feral in a wheelchair, a blind clairvoyant, a crazy medium, a shape-shifting shaman, and a woman who could detect weakness in fabric were the only assets currently at full strength. There was no way they could protect Bernie.

"We have to keep them away from Special Investigations too." Joe considered the options. Although the organization appeared to be suspiciously full-fledged, they couldn't have too many people and facilities in place just yet. "They're probably concentrating on urban areas for now."

"That and small towns where there's always someone eager to rat out the people who don't belong." Vincent raised an eyebrow at Joe's questioning look. "Hey, man, I spent most of my life on the run. I learned pretty fast who was likely to cause us trouble."

Having spent most of his formative years within an eight-block area between school and home, it wasn't something Joe could comment on. Everyone in his neighborhood knew everyone else, or at the very least, they knew Mamá. After Papá was shot, their house stayed full for two weeks. There was always someone stopping by to offer condolences. Joe would have given anything to have the chance to hide then, to have a few moments alone to try and figure out his feelings of survivor's guilt and fear.

A sign for the next town flashed past them, promising a place to refuel their stomachs and the car. Joe pointed. "Why don't you pull over, and I can drive for a bit?"

Vincent's hands tightened on the wheel as if he wanted to refuse. He was probably hanging on to stubborn pride. But he nodded and began to slow down for the exit. "I can't decide if they're going to be the lucky ones or not."

Bernie and Martha? Joe didn't ask. He suspected Vincent would continue, and a moment later, he was proven right.

"I keep asking myself, what chance do any of us have to hide? How hard are they going to come after us? With our names on a list, we're all sitting ducks if they decide they want us badly enough."

"We'll have to fight it," Joe said.

"How? File counterclaims as they lock us up in camps? Go to war against humanity and the government? Our only hope was silence, and that's gone. We can't win. The best we can hope for now is survival."

Chapter Twenty-Nine

Scratches in the parquet floor marked Cali's exact path as she prowled back and forth along the long dark hall in her apartment. She'd left once Speranza and the kids were ready for bed, but the restlessness twitching through her body told Cali that sleep would not be in the cards anytime soon. It was almost thirty-six hours since anyone had heard from Joe. His cell phone had disappeared from the grid, and any calls went straight to a full voice mail. Hood organized their people to watch the police precinct and Joe's apartment, but neither showed any sign of him.

I've made a horrible mistake. She couldn't hide from it, not anymore. Walking away from Joe wouldn't protect him or her. She was already too emotionally entangled. *Mr. Dalhard might already have hurt him. I might never get the chance to fix this.* She stopped pacing and braced her hand against the wall. Her heart and lungs constricted, painfully refusing to continue. Her knees slowly gave way beneath her as she curled into a ball on the floor. Making herself breathe, she forced herself to think it through. *Even if he's alive and I go after him, I'll have to tell him the truth about who I am and what I've done.* Could he ever understand her pride in her skills as a thief? He was a cop after all. She held tight to her logic, needing it as a shield to keep her from rushing out the door.

Her stomach growled, tempted by the scent of Speranza's latest casserole resting on the empty kitchen counter. She should eat and go to bed, but the closet no longer felt like a sanctuary, and her gut twisted too tightly to allow food inside. After hearing about the details of the escape, she'd been running on caffeine and willpower. She made herself stand up again, swaying unsteadily.

I can't go on like this. I need to make it right. Joe might hate me. The thought threatened to unhinge her swollen knees and send her sprawling in a faint like a corseted historical heroine. *It doesn't matter. I've earned whatever he chooses to feel about what I've done.* The decision wasn't about the two of them as a couple anymore. She owed him, and she couldn't pay her debts if she stayed away. She needed to find the courage to do what was needed.

Like you did with Mr. Dalhard? Her horrible inner voice jabbed its poison deep into her soul.

"I didn't have a choice," she muttered aloud. As much as she wanted to deny it, Mr. Dalhard had changed. He cared more about the thrill of uncompromising violence than protecting his people.

Does he really, or did you just take the first excuse to run away? Again.

Cali refused to keep arguing with herself. More poison always waited beneath the surface, ready to spew at the slightest touch. No matter how much she tried to ignore it or tell herself that her inner voice was only leftover distortions from her childhood, it always waited, ready to steal her pride in her accomplishments and tarnish any dreams. Holding it at bay exhausted her, but succumbing was worse.

In the end, she only had three choices. She could go back to Mr. Dalhard, she could try to find and protect Joe, or she could run from the entire mess and abandon everything she cared about. Bu running wasn't really an option. She'd never be able to live with herself if she ran.

Mr. Dalhard had succumbed to whatever darkness haunted him. She recognized it from watching her father descend on the same path. No matter how much she might want to pull him back, it wasn't possible.

That left Joe. If she wasn't already too late and she could find him, she could make sure he walked away from Mr. Dalhard's plots. It wasn't even a decision—it was the only choice she could live with. So why was she still paralyzed by this horrible fear?

"I need to get out of here." She might not be ready to face Joe, but she needed to get moving or she'd brood herself into catatonia. Lifting wallets at the casino and picking up enough cash to pay Speranza's bills for another week suddenly seemed like the perfect distraction. Maybe the activity would even wear her out enough to sleep. She grabbed her jacket and hurried out of the apartment and down the stairs.

Too fatigue-fogged to pay her usual close attention to her surroundings, she didn't hear the pounding steps coming up the stairs until it was too late. Halfway down, she came face to face with a huge man, and they both froze, staring at each other.

Bushy black hair spiked out from his scalp and jaw, framing skin flushed red with fury and alcohol. His clenched fists looked bigger than her head as he grabbed the skinny metal handrail, confronting her. Rodolpho.

I can't let him get upstairs. Speranza's new start was still shaky. Cali wouldn't let that asshole terrorize them yet again and wake them out of much-needed sleep.

"I recognize you. You poisoned my Speranza against me." He jabbed a meaty finger in her direction.

This would be so much easier if I'd been paying attention. "You need to leave." Cali held her ground despite the rush of rank alcohol-tainted breath hitting her. He shouldn't be able to stand up with that much liquor in his blood. *I can scare him away.* Her knives weighed down her forearms, reassuring reminders that she wasn't helpless. She left them sheathed. The sight of a blade would only escalate matters. Besides, in his drunken state, he might not feel it if she cut him unless she struck someplace lethal, which brought its own complications.

"You will not keep me from my wife." He charged up the stairs at her.

Cali dodged his clumsy grab, retreating to the narrow landing above. If she got past him, would he be angry enough to follow her instead of going after Speranza? *I'd bet my life on being faster than he is.* Unfortunately, his thick body blocked the entire stair. "She's not your wife anymore. That's how divorce works, moron."

She grabbed the metal rail on either side and kicked him with both feet, knocking him back.

Anger flushed his ruddy face, turning his swollen features purple.

"Take the hint—let her go." Cali's arm muscles were twitching, ready to release her blades.

"She's mine." His snarl could have inspired guard dogs to new levels of nastiness. He moved forward again, one beefy hand on the rail and the other braced against the wall. "We are meant to be together. What God hath joined together, let not man put asunder."

"Maybe you should have thought about the sanctity of marriage before you hit her." Cali's tiny store of patience had evaporated. Debate was pointless. Bullies never cared about logic. The man standing in front of her only wanted to lash out at others to make himself feel better. He was exactly the same kind of insecure asshole as her father.

Long-buried anger tightened her fists and mouth. Her father had beaten her as if each blow elevated him above his frustrations, as if blood and bruises could buy a way into the life he craved. Rodolpho did the same to Speranza. Someone needed to show them what it felt like to have to live in fear. Cali's father might be long past any potential vengeance, but this bastard was right in her sights. If he wanted to play the fear-and-intimidate game, she'd show him how it was done.

Don't let him grab you, the old instincts whispered, snapping back into place. Cali tugged the knife out of her sleeve and palmed it, keeping it hidden from Rodolpho. *In a minute, you're going to be the one afraid and helpless.*

She retreated back one step. For her plan to work, she'd need a few seconds to concentrate, and she couldn't do that while dodging. She crouched and hissed, curving her nails like claws. "Don't you know who I am?"

Rodolpho's mouth dipped down in a confused frown before reasserting itself in an angry snarl. She knew what he saw was a skinny young woman, his ex-wife's friend, someone he thought he could hurt with impunity.

Not tonight. She might not have done this since her father made her run religious scams when she was six, but she remembered the transformation. She flushed her skin with blood, turning it bright red while darkening her hair as much as possible. That was easy. The hard part was forcing small jutting lumps of flesh up from her temples. It hurt, and it wouldn't be very convincing in the light, but in a shadowy staircase, it would do.

Rodolpho gasped, his right hand rising to his forehead to make the sign of the cross as he confronted what appeared to be a devil. His widened eyes and mumbling mouth told Cali this was the moment she needed.

She slashed out at him with the knife, opening a long gash down his arm. He howled as the blade parted his sleeve and flesh with surgical ease. Clutching at the bleeding cut, he stared at her in disbelief.

Let's get theatrical. She sniffed at the bloody blade and stretched her lips in her creepiest smile. "First taste."

Like any self-indulgent bully, Rodolpho never questioned why a demon would be interested in him. He stumbled backward, shouting at her in Spanish. Cali took a single deliberate step toward him, and he ran, barely managing to get his feet under him as he pounded down the stairs. Cali smiled in triumph. With any luck, he'd fall and break his neck, ending the problem.

But not really. She hadn't solved anything. All she'd done was to become as big a bully as her father. She let her aching flesh resume its natural shape and shade as she sat down on the stairs, suddenly exhausted. Rubbing her face, she leaned against the rough wall. Humiliation burned, making her want to crawl back into her hole and never come out.

Closing her eyes against tears, she stayed curled up on the stairwell for a long time. *I can't ever do that again.* She had to hold off that impulse no matter what it cost.

Karan read through Special Investigations' report twice before allowing himself the indulgence of an emotional response. He dropped the papers onto the floor and stalked to the window overlooking the bay.

Idiots and incompetents, he seethed. Was it truly too much to expect competent aid in one's subordinates? Their sloppiness had allowed the girl and her mother to escape. The investigators found evidence of the family at Rose on the Grave Bed and Breakfast, along with signs of a hasty exit. The owner of the ridiculous attraction was in custody, but there were traces to suggest other people had been involved. None of it altered the fact that once again, the child had escaped.

Rather than set up roadblocks to prevent anyone from entering or leaving the area while they searched, the investigators had simply descended en masse. They ignored his warnings, and the girl had detected their presence. So much for Special Investigations' vaunted claims of experience in dealing with *lalassu*.

That was not what he had planned. Karan depended on Special Investigations to act as the stick while he proffered the carrot of employment to those deemed useful. After a generation or two, the *lalassu* working for him would naturally look to him as a leader. Between his private forces and those in the government, it would be child's play to take over a significant territory. As they had in ancient times, the *lalassu* would rule, with him at their head. He had not yet decided if he would whisper from the shadows or claim his place in the sun, but there was time to work out such details.

I must be patient. He had infinite time after all, provided he learned from his mistakes. During the last World War, he had amassed a substantial secret coalition of *lalassu* who were ready to take advantage of the chaos of intercontinental warfare. But the coalition had scattered like roaches when he needed them. The policy of secrecy allowed them to seamlessly switch sides once more rather than forcing them to commit. He needed his supporters to be in the open, where they would have no choice except to continue his bidding. Or at the very least, they would suffer alongside him if they chose to hold back.

Karan considered his silent, powered-down computer. Naya Jeevan might be alarmingly competent, but eliminating such threats would mean surrounding himself with idiots and failures. He decided that tea was necessary while he considered his options. As he prepared it, he strove to keep his mind focused only on the necessary steps. His ritual might not be as elaborate as a proper Japanese Tea Ceremony, but it served a similar purpose. As he dropped the leaves into the steaming water and savored the rising scent of green tea and jasmine, his mind cleared.

He could not trust Naya Jeevan. That was an unalterable fact. But at the same time, he needed the intruder's aid. Another unalterable fact. So what he needed was a way to ensure cooperation under any possible circumstance. In most cases, he preferred blackmail or holding loved ones hostage. It was a shame he did not yet possess sufficient information on his intruder for such methods.

But he was not completely without resources. For whatever reason, Naya Jeevan had chosen to approach him and wanted desperately to work with him and be trusted by him, which gave Karan potential leverage. The hacker had already incarcerated Vapor and provided valuable intelligence. He or she had even spoken out on Karan's perceived mistakes. Those actions were all bids for approval.

Approval would not be sufficient leverage, but the desire for it gave him another avenue to explore. Naya Jeevan must have weaknesses, and in order to discover them, Karan had to allow the hacker within the inner circles. Decision made, Karan powered up the computer again and typed a single word into the chat window. **Partners.**

Chapter Thirty

Cali glanced up and down the empty hallway outside of Joe's apartment, listening intently for any warning clicks that would signal someone leaving one of the neighboring units. Her lock picks were palmed out of casual sight, but the longer she lingered outside his door, the greater chance of being noticed. She inserted a torsion wrench and swiftly began manipulating the internal pins with her worn hook pick. A few seconds later, she heard the deadbolt slide home, and she quickly slipped her tools back up her sleeve.

Joe's home didn't match her preliminary mental picture. She thought he'd have a state-of-the-art entertainment system propped on top of milk crates and a sofa whose most admirable quality was that he'd gotten it for free. Instead, soft leather and polished wood gleamed in the early dawn light filtering through the windows. The walls were painted a rich, sensual burgundy that set off the long black-leather sectional sofa, creating a powerfully masculine atmosphere. Despite the essence of alpha male, it didn't feel threatening. Instead, it coaxed a visitor to relax and anticipate—

Stop that! She throttled her imagination back under control.

There were no signs of a struggle. The brass lamps on the low side tables stood straight and proud, their halos of creamy fabric pristine instead of bent or smashed. The speckled white granite countertops shone in the kitchenette, and every cupboard door and dark-stained drawer was firmly in place. Cali opened up the door on the far wall and found a walk-through bathroom leading to Joe's bedroom.

She saw no sign of struggle but also no sign of anyone having been in the apartment for the last two days. That made her an idiot for trespassing in search of an overlooked clue. Or for believing she could ride to his rescue. He had a family, friends. He didn't need her.

Hesitating with her hand on the knob to Joe's bedroom, Cali cursed herself for a fool. If she let herself, she'd bury her nose in his clothes to pretend he was close. Even though she'd been the one to push him away.

He's not here. Rifling through his things would only be a violation of his privacy. She owed him more than that. Maybe she could have Harley check the hospitals again.

A key twisted in the open lock, jolting her into stealth mode. She turned off the bathroom light and stilled her breathing. Kneeling down to keep her head below most people's range of vision, she peered through the narrow gap between the bathroom door and the frame.

The front door opened, and Joe stepped into his apartment, gun drawn as he swept the room. Cali smiled in elation and relief. He was alive! Dark circles hugged his eyes, and his dark hair seemed to leach the color from his tan skin, but there were no signs of injury. No bandages, no bloodstains or bruises, and no awkward movements. Cali had still never seen such a welcome and inviting sight.

"I'm getting paranoid," Joe muttered to himself, closing the door. He tucked his gun back into the holster and hung it up on a hook near the door. His leather jacket followed.

The awkward reality of her situation suddenly occurred to Cali. She was crouched in Joe's bathroom, virtually guaranteed to be discovered. She couldn't sneak past him to the door without getting caught. She steeled herself. *I came here because I realized I made a mistake.* Trying to hide would be another cowardly error. She'd come here to tell him the truth.

Joe poked around in his kitchen, sniffing at some containers in the fridge. Cali pulled her glasses out of her bag and firmly fixed Colleen's features in place. *At least his gun is out of immediate reach.* He must have detected some sign of her presence or he wouldn't have come in with it drawn, but he wouldn't shoot her before she could start to explain. Possible gunshot wounds after she explained were still a separate issue.

"Joe." She kept her voice low and soft as she slowly opened the door, not wanting to startle him.

He held still, hand creeping to the knives in the butcher block. "Colleen, is that you?"

"It's me." Stepping out of the bathroom felt like leaving cover while under fire, but she made herself do it anyway. "I…" *Don't have a clever excuse.* "Needed to see you."

She dropped her gaze to the carpet, not knowing where to begin. Perhaps if she'd kept her focus higher, she would have seen Joe move.

Suddenly his arms were around her and his mouth was on hers. Too surprised to stiffen, she quickly melted under his plundering kisses. The hard frame of the bathroom entrance dug into her back as Joe's tongue tasted and explored, dipping into her. She moaned against him, letting her hands reassure her that he was truly there with her and physically intact. The warmth of his muscles under his thin cotton shirt crept under her skin, relieving the perpetual chill.

"I've been so worried about you," he whispered in her ear, teasing her earlobe between his teeth.

"I was scared you'd been hurt." Her breath bounced off his shoulder, and she dared to gently nip at the curve of his neck with her lips. From the sudden increase in heat and size bulging at her hip, he liked that.

His kisses nibbled at her neck, his powerful hand cradling her cheek. The sensation short-circuited any rational thought. It felt like flying—dizzying and overwhelming and wonderful. There was something Cali was supposed to be doing, and she'd remember in a minute once she stopped feeling so amazingly good.

Reality crashed back into her as Joe began to unbutton her blouse. She gasped. "Wait."

His mouth and hands stilled immediately though he still leaned against her, struggling to catch his breath.

Cali's breathing wasn't entirely even either. "I'm sorry."

He delivered another gentle kiss. "Never apologize for saying what you need. I shouldn't have pounced, but I've been imagining the worst since you disappeared on me."

"I owe you an explanation. Possibly more than one." She couldn't stop her hands from slowly exploring him, feeling the muscles shift and bunch under his clothes.

"You're *lalassu.* I may not know what bloodline, but I know what it means when someone's eyes shift color." He cupped her face with his hands, his thumbs brushing delicately against her eyelashes. "Though I like green to brown a lot better than the black to red."

Red eyes? What? Her attempts to stay focused kept getting interrupted by the sensual pleasure of his warmth under her fingers and the comforting, masculine scent. Her brain wasn't going to function with him so close, but she didn't want him to move. "It's more than that."

"Whatever it is, we'll figure it out." Joe punctuated his promise with another brain-melting kiss. He rested his forehead against hers, his body pressed against her entire length. Protecting her.

"You may not want to once you know the truth." Cali's fingers tightened in his shirt, pulling him closer. Her brain might insist on giving him a chance to reject her, but her body had other, more possessive ideas. "Mr. Dalhard wanted me to get close to you, find out where your secrets are buried." She swallowed. "Or who he could threaten to hurt you."

Joe stilled against her. "What did you tell him?"

She shook her head. "I didn't tell him anything. I don't like what he's become, and I don't trust him to make the right decision with any information I give him. He isn't happy with my choice. He's even less happy now since he knows I told you about his escape plans."

"Did he threaten you?" His dark eyes pinned her in place more effectively than any restraint.

"Not yet." To her utter embarrassment, tears began to spill out, and her hands started to shake.

"Hey, don't cry. You're not alone anymore. I'm always going to be here for you." He kissed her forehead, his hands drifting down from her face to caress her shoulders.

"You can't promise that. I know he hurt people during the escape." She should tell him about being a metamorph, but she soothed her conscience with a promise of *later*. He knew she was a *lalassu*. The specifics could wait.

Joe's hands tightened on her. "He took my friend, Michael, hostage. He cut him pretty badly and ordered the others to smash Michael's girlfriend's legs with a hammer. He was going to kill us all."

Bile-tainted denial rose in Cali's mouth, but she swallowed it down.

She'd already accepted that Mr. Dalhard was no longer the man she remembered. The details only confirmed the necessity of standing against him.

"I know that's hard to hear—"

"No. I needed to." She met his eyes. "The Mr. Dalhard I knew was a man who found a fourteen-year-old girl running a three-card-Monte game in Las Vegas. He gave me two hundred dollars and his card. He told me to get a safe place to sleep and to call him when I needed more cash. I honestly thought he was a pimp, and I planned to stay away as long as I could."

"What about your parents?" Joe asked.

"Mom took off when I was little. I can't quite remember when. She and my father both had a habit of leaving me alone in the apartment for days while they enjoyed the Vegas nightlife. Dad started taking me with him as a prop for his con games after my mother left. He taught me to steal and manipulate. He died of an overdose when I was nine, leaving me on the streets." That was her life story boiled down into a few words. She'd skimmed over the beatings for failing to pick pockets or trick a mark, the hours of demented training, and the constant fear of wondering when life would violently catch up with them. "I was surviving on my own, but I wanted a chance at something beyond the streets. After the money that Mr. Dalhard gave me ran out, I followed him for two weeks, spying on him. He caught me and offered me a job, an apartment, everything I wanted. I thought he wanted a mistress, but instead, he only made me promise to stay off the streets and get an education. He used to stop by every few weeks, check on my progress with my tutors, and make sure I was okay."

"He really did save you," Joe said slowly in wonder.

"That man isn't the same one who hurt you and your friends. Somewhere, he changed, and prison only brought out the worst in him." Cali took a deep breath. "I can't let him keep hurting people."

"I'm sorry. I wish he could have stayed that man for you." Joe held her close.

"I just don't want him to hurt you." She leaned in and kissed him again, enjoying the rasp and catch of the short bristles of his unshaven skin against her fingertips.

Joe caught her hands and pulled back, cradling her wrists against his broad chest. "I know you've been through a lot, and I'm trying to be a gentleman, but I want you so damn bad right now. I don't know if I can stop myself if we keep going."

I'm not afraid. The lie wouldn't fall from her lips. She was terribly afraid of the fire between them. She craved it, but it could consume the last of her defenses, leaving her naked and vulnerable.

"If it were up to me, you'd be naked in my bed right now." His thumbs rubbed against her hands, flattening them against his chest.

Cali swallowed, the chill air caressing her through her open blouse.

"I'd lay you down, and then I'd start exploring you with the lightest touch you can imagine. I'd see how long you could stay still as I teased you." His wicked grin told her that he had every faith in his ability to drive her past the threshold. "I'd begin right here."

He released one of her hands and let his finger skim from the hollow of her throat down to the valley between her breasts. Cali shivered and closed her eyes.

"You have no idea how tempting you are. And if I couldn't feel you trembling, I wouldn't be able to do this."

The sudden loss of warmth from his presence left Cali frozen. She opened her eyes to see that he'd moved two steps back. His eyes were glittering and his cheeks were flushed, letting her know that he was equally affected by their separation.

"I told you I wouldn't do anything you didn't want even if I tried to persuade you." His hungry eyes followed her numb fingers as she slowly began to rebutton her blouse.

"I know." Too much stood between them to go any further. No matter how much she burned for it, these flames threatened to scorch her to ash and leave nothing behind.

"I should find you someplace safe to stay. My mother—"

Cali interrupted. "I still have things I need to do. I think I can find where Mr. Dalhard is hiding."

Joe's entire body tensed, and for a moment, Cali thought he would go primal caveman on her and forbid her from doing anything but cower in fear. Then he put his hands on his hips and exhaled up at the ceiling. "I don't like it, but I won't deny we need it. Will you stay in touch to keep me from going crazy?"

She nodded, pulling out a new burner phone from her bag. She dialed Joe. "I promise I'll keep it with me all the time."

Joe checked to make sure the number was properly stored before tenderly putting the phone away. "There's one more thing I need from you—a promise to come back here tonight. We can go over everything together and decide the next steps over takeout."

And she could tell him the rest of her secrets. "I'll be there."

Chapter Thirty-One

Joe stepped out of the sergeant's office, resisting the temptation to check himself for scorch marks. He'd hoped to avoid Modnik, but she'd spotted him coming in and demanded an update on his lead. Having to admit it hadn't panned out ignited an uncharacteristic fury. He'd tried to stand quietly as the sergeant vented her frustrations over the previous twenty-four hours, but he was too energized from Colleen's surprise visit that morning. He couldn't play the part of a chastened employee when a besotted grin kept creeping back onto his face.

At least the city was quieting down. Reports of looting and fires were coming in less frequently. Maybe everyone had exhausted themselves in their panic and it would all begin again once people got some rest. Meanwhile, he'd been given a new assignment and partner by the sergeant. Being paired up with Rob Salazar was a small price to pay for his rescue trip down south. And to sweeten the bitter pill, they were investigating Detective Hampton, who still hadn't made any contact.

Unsure whether or not to hope the man was taking advantage of the chaos, Joe wouldn't argue with the assignment. It could end up pointing straight to Karan Samil and André Dalhard. If they found Hampton squirreled up in a bar somewhere, then it would cement the man's reputation as an unreliable asshole. And if he was truly missing, then he deserved the truth to come out, crappy cop or not.

Joe found the rookie stirring sugar into his coffee in the break room. "Hey, Salazar."

"Hi." Salazar took a big gulp of caffeine. He stared at a blinking screen saver for a long moment before shaking his gaze loose. It was the second time he'd fixated since Joe had walked into the room. The rookie probably hadn't slept in the last twenty-four hours.

"Are you good to keep going?" Joe asked. Sleep deprivation could cause Salazar to miss clues. And if something unexpected happened, it could get them both hurt or killed.

"I look worse than I feel. Better to get this done before the next wave crashes on us." Salazar drained his coffee. "I got Hampton's keys out of his locker."

"Then let's start at his apartment."

On the drive over, Joe could tell that the rookie wanted to ask him something. Salazar kept drawing breath to speak before looking out the window or down at his hands. Joe paused at a red light. "Something on your mind?"

"Everything seems to have turned upside down." Salazar stared out the window at the blackened remnants of what had been an electronics store. "I'm not sure what to believe anymore."

"Because of what the president said? Or because of what seems to have happened to Hampton?" Joe kept his attention on the road. The streets seemed deserted for the time being, but that could change quickly.

"Both. It doesn't seem possible. People with those kind of powers would be noticed."

"You'd be surprised by what people can ignore or dismiss." Joe certainly had been willing to turn a blind eye to how Michael got his information.

Salazar drummed his fingers against the windowsill. "My uncle used to tell us that he had magic powers. He did the usual pulling coins out of our ears and stuff, but he always insisted he could do real magic as well as parlor tricks. He would take my sister and me on walks. We'd beg him to make things explode with his mind, and he'd pretend to object and then cave in. He always insisted on using an almost-empty water bottle since he said it wouldn't hurt anyone. He'd buy a bottle of water, and we'd drink most of it. Then he'd stick it on the path ahead of us and stare at it. A few moments later, the bottle would rocket up into the air and blast into pieces, and we'd be so impressed."

"Sounds cool." Could Salazar's uncle have been one of the *lalassu*?

"I thought so. Until I caught him slipping little packets of dry ice into the bottles." Salazar's grim smile held no amusement. "When it melts in the water, it produces huge amounts of carbon dioxide."

"Sending the bottle into the air and eventually exploding it." A magic trick. Not supernatural, only sleight of hand.

"It made me realize how easily someone could be distracted. It's too easy to look in the direction that everyone is pointing. Detective Hampton reminded me of my uncle. He always had a plausible explanation for what he asked me to do, but he'd warn me off if I started checking too deeply." Salazar straightened. "I think this one is his place."

Hampton lived in a decent neighborhood. People were still out walking their dogs and getting groceries. The area didn't appear to have suffered from rioting or looting except for a few overturned newspaper boxes. Joe and Salazar let themselves into his apartment building and his unit.

The smell of rotting food hit them. Joe held his breath as he and Salazar cleared the apartment. No one was there, just the evidence of a long-term slob. If the man didn't have rats or roaches, he was lucky.

"Should we toss the garbage?" Salazar asked, his knuckles pressed against his nose. "You know, clear it out so we can breathe?"

Joe shook his head. Until they knew what had happened, the apartment needed to be treated like a crime scene. Nothing could go in or out without being logged. "See if you can find some bank statements or something."

They found a pile of unopened bills shoved into a pizza box along with half a slice of stale pepperoni. It turned out that Hampton had seven credit cards, all maxed out. Scanning through, Joe didn't see anything hinting at a particular refuge or a place out of town. Everything was local, mostly bars, takeout, and 1-900 numbers. Then something caught Joe's eye.

In the last two months, Hampton made three massive payments on his credit card debt—over twenty-five grand in total. He'd also started having charges at the local casinos. "He didn't get this kind of money on a cop's salary. Looks like Hampton had a side business going."

Salazar raised his head. "I've got his phone bill here. We can run his phone records and see who he called."

"Good thinking." Joe glanced around. "I think we've learned all we can here." *Even if we're walking away with more questions than answers.*

"He ran away?" Speranza struggled to change the diaper on a squirming Zara.

"I think I surprised him." Cali couldn't help a certain smugness. "I thought you should know."

"It's strange to think of him being so close without us knowing. It makes me wonder how often he's been here silently." Speranza picked up Zara and held her close, causing the toddler to wail. "I'm sorry, *querida.* Time for a nap."

Zara accepted her mother's apology along with her pacifier and quickly curled up in her crib. The women left the room, Speranza carefully closing the door. Cali's phone buzzed.

"I'll go see what Carlotta is up to." Speranza hurried down the short hall to the living area. Cali's heart rate increased as she recognized Hood's number.

"We've got him." Hood didn't wait for her to say hello.

"You found Karan?" It didn't seem possible, but Cali was ready to believe in a miracle or two.

"Harley traced the phone calls to an address in the Sandy Hook Bay area. We've pulled up the plans. Looks like it's an upscale residential address, a victim of the housing-market crash. It's been empty for several years and hasn't been officially resold but is now up to date on power, water, and heating. Along with several interesting security upgrades." There was no masking the vindictiveness in Hood's voice. When he'd been a street-level enforcer, he'd been known as the Pitbull because of how relentlessly he went after his enemies.

"That's got to be it. Do you have the layouts?" If they could get in that night, they could eliminate at least one of the threats facing them.

"On their way."

Cali heard the beep indicating a new message. "Give me a little time to study them, and then we can put together a plan. In the meantime, see if someone is available to stay with Speranza and the kids tonight."

Pocketing Boomerang's cell, Cali felt Colleen's new phone buzz with an incoming text. Smiling, she pulled out the new burner to check the text message from Joe:

Hey, staying safe?

Fine. You? she texted back.

I may need to take three showers to get rid of the smell from the apartment I just visited, but otherwise no issues, he wrote. *Looks like all's quiet.*

The news reported riots continuing in other cities, but Perdition seemed to have gotten itself under control after a single night of panic. Something niggled at the back of Cali's subconscious, tugging to get her attention. Before it could fully form, Joe's next text distracted her:

I'm going to make one more stop before I'm finished for the day, and I'm nearly there. The sergeant is giving everyone extra time off to rest before nightfall. Still up for dinner?

Of course. See you soon. It should be easy to tell him about her metamorphic powers now that the really awful stuff was all out on the table. She wondered if she should tell him first or show him by shifting. If he already knew about *lalassu*, he probably wouldn't freak out. Cali tucked away the phone and had an extra spring in her step as she emerged into the living area.

"I take it there is good news." Speranza smiled as she poured milk for Carlotta.

"There is indeed. Work stuff." Cali swung her arms, unable to contain her energy. "I'm going to have to go out tonight."

"We'll be fine. You've already done more than enough for us."

"Hey, I thought we were on the same page. We're helping each other." Cali gestured at the fridge. "If you didn't feed me, I'd starve, remember?"

Speranza's smile suggested she wasn't buying Cali's argument but wasn't going to push the point either.

"I like having Cali here." Carlotta displayed her winning smile and an impressive milk mustache. "I want her to stay."

"I like being here too, munchkin." It was a little taste of normal, and Cali didn't get too many of those moments.

Speranza leaned over the counter to wipe her offspring's mouth. "I like her too. But she has her own life and can't always be here with us. We have to learn to protect ourselves."

"Like ninjas, blasting the bad guys with my ninja powers." Carlotta's arms waved as she made appropriate sound effects.

Cali laughed. "Just like that."

Carlotta stopped, grinning. "I'm still hungry, Mommy. I want a Popsicle."

"Agreed. Since it's such a good day." Speranza winked and opened the freezer. Cali couldn't remember the last time her friend had been in such a good mood.

"I want a red one." Carlotta scrambled down from her seat and ran around the counter to join her mother at the fridge.

Speranza poked through the box of frozen flavors. "We have purple, white, blue, and orange. We're out of red."

Carlotta's lip quivered. "I want red. It's my favorite."

"I know, but we've eaten them all. How about purple?"

"I want red." The little girl's face flushed, and dewy tears squished out of the corners of her eyes.

With a sinking feeling, Cali knew Carlotta was only seconds from a meltdown, which would ruin the day and wake up Zara. Carlotta already dealt with too much disappointment in her life. Something as easily fixed as available Popsicle flavors shouldn't be one more. "Why don't I run to the store and pick up a red Popsicle?"

Carlotta's face unscrunched, and she peered at Cali suspiciously. "Really?"

"Really. If your mom says it's okay."

Speranza seemed torn between using the missing flavor as a parental lesson and indulging her daughter. "Are you sure?"

"Of course I'm sure. It'll only take me a few minutes." *And it will buy us some peace.*

"All right. Carlotta, you should thank Cali."

"Thank you!" Carlotta ran out and threw her chubby arms around Cali. Cali awkwardly returned the hug, secretly touched by the little girl's affection.

"No problem. One red Popsicle, coming up." Cali shooed the child back to her mother and opened the door.

Only to find Rodolpho standing there, a black revolver in his hand.

CHAPTER THIRTY-TWO

I forgot to check the peephole. Everything slowed for Cali. Rodolpho lifted the gun toward her. Speranza's shouts echoed with Carlotta's screams. Cali's brain kept processing every detail with incredible speed, from the glint of sunlight on the counter to the smudge of mud on Rodolpho's boots to the ticking of the clock on the wall. The hyperawareness threatened to paralyze her. But one horrible fact jumped into prominence. If she couldn't close the door, Speranza and Carlotta would have to cross the weapon's path to get to the safe room. She pushed at the door, slowly narrowing the open gap.

"Demon!" Rodolpho shouted.

His first shot thundered in the small space. Normal time resumed as the door shuddered under Cali's hands. A distorted bubble popped out as the steel absorbed the bullet's impact. She slammed her weight into the door, trying to seal it shut. "Run!"

Speranza didn't need more prompting. She ran for the bedroom, cradling a screaming Carlotta in her arms. Cali tracked them by the girl's dwindling shrieks. Rodolpho wrestled with Cali for control of the door, his meaty hand wrapped around the edge. His weight pushed her back. Without something for her to brace against, he'd be inside. She planted her feet on the slippery floor and shoved hard.

"I'll destroy you all!" Flecks of spittle flew into the apartment.

Cali jammed her shoulder against the door. She dropped a knife into her hand and sliced at his thick fingers.

He roared and backed up. Cali slid as the door almost closed. *Just a little more.* He slammed back into it. She braced, half kneeling on the floor. A second blast from the gun deafened her. Shards of ceramic from the cookie jar showered over her. *If he gets in here, he'll kill us.* She needed a plan. In her apartment, there were weapons and traps. At Speranza's, nothing was prepared. She was helpless. Rodolpho outweighed her by at least sixty pounds.

He's going to get in. She couldn't win a contest of force. He would force his way in no matter what. *It needs to be on my terms.* Carlotta's screams abruptly cut off, which meant the family was safe in the soundproof panic room. No more worrying about collateral damage. She threw herself backward into the middle of the room.

Without her weight pushing back, the door flew open. Rodolpho crashed forward into the apartment. Cali rose to her feet, knife ready to throw. *Shoulder hit, he drops the gun.*

"Police! Don't move!"

The shout distracted her. *Am I hallucinating? That sounds like Joe.* It cost her the perfect strike. Rodolpho scrambled to his feet, gun still in hand. Cali backed up, knowing he would shoot at any second.

Her hallucination was convincing. She could see Joe behind Rodolpho. Another cop stood beside him in the doorway. Both had guns pointed at Rodolpho. Joe shouted, "Drop the weapon."

Rodolpho roared, and Cali realized it was no hallucination. Everything slowed once more into frightening clarity. The madman began to turn, lifting his gun. Steps echoed in the hallway. Joe's fingers tightened but not in time.

Not today. Cali's hand snapped forward. She'd done that move so often she could hit a target in her sleep. Time crawled as the tiny steel blade flew. Rodolpho's gun rose, moving to aim at Joe. The other cop's eyes got wide, and he shouted. Joe realized his danger and tried to move out of the way. Cali's knife buried itself in the fleshy folds of Rodolpho's bared neck.

He dropped to his knees, the gun bouncing on the parquet floor. Cali's conscious mind finally caught up with what she'd just done. Horror welled up like the blood beginning to leak around the edges of her knife. She'd killed him. *I did that. Oh my God, I did that.*

Joe's muffled voice tried to break through, but Cali couldn't process the words or even look at him. Her entire world narrowed to Rodolpho's crumbling form. *I'm sorry.* She'd never thrown a knife at another person, only at practice targets. She'd worked diligently, determined never to be vulnerable again. But she hadn't imagined it would feel so overwhelming to strike back.

Something sharp smacked into her, pricking her skin. Cali jerked her gaze up as painful currents locked every muscle into rigid agony.

"Cali!" Joe saw Cali go rigid. Her blond hair darkened and then went lighter in quick succession. Her nose and cheekbones shifted like a poorly done CGI character. Even her skin tone changed, from pale to deep tan and back again. In the space of a few seconds, she kept flicking back and forth before dropping to the ground.

"Oh my God." Salazar's astonished exclamation barely registered in Joe's awareness.

Joe's mind couldn't make sense of what he was seeing. He'd come to Speranza's apartment as a final stop for the day. He'd wanted to check in and see if he could convince her to press charges against her ex-husband, whom he recognized from the man's police files. Joe hadn't expected to walk into a gunfight.

"*Lo siento! No lo hice con intencion.*" Speranza Mechoso dropped a Taser gun from her shaking hands. Without the electricity pumping through her system, Cali stopped twitching and went dangerously still.

Ignoring all his training, Joe vaulted over Rodolpho to check on her. He yanked the prongs out of her before the residual electricity could cause any more damage. Gently lifting her, he tucked her limp head against his shoulder and pressed his fingers to her throat. To his relief, a steady pulse thrummed. She was alive.

Salazar took the Taser gun from the weeping Speranza. Her protests of not meaning to do it weren't exactly reassuring. Visions of the last few seconds kept flashing through Joe's mind. Cali had saved his life. She'd thrown the knife to stop Rodolpho from shooting.

"What was that?" Salazar demanded. "What is she?"

Joe's anger flared, and his arms tightened around Cali. "She is a person, and if you can't remember it, then you can get the hell out of my crime scene."

The rookie flushed. Joe supposed there must still be some human decency in there, but the *what is she* was hard to see past. *What*, not *who*. Because she was different, Cali had been dismissed as a thing instead of a person.

Speranza knelt beside them, reaching out to Cali with trembling hands. "Is she all right?"

Cali moaned and shifted, answering the question.

"We need to get her to the hospital." Joe didn't want to let Cali go. She felt right, cradled in his arms. Thoughts of Colleen tried to break through and inject some caution-inducing guilt, but Joe couldn't abandon the woman who'd saved him.

"Joe… no doctors. No hospital." Cali's weak protest was barely audible.

Speranza burst into tears, clutching at Cali's arm. "I am so sorry!"

Cali reached over and patted Speranza's white-knuckled grip. "I know. Go check on the girls."

Things improved immediately once Speranza could focus on a familiar task. Cali stiffly turned her head toward Rodolpho. "Is he dead?"

The man moaned, one hand fluttering up toward his neck. Salazar knelt to check on him, preventing Rodolpho from pulling out the knife and bleeding to death. "I called the ambulance."

"I can't go to a hospital." Cali pulled free of Joe's embrace. She pointed at the bleeding wound. "Keep pressure on it."

Salazar picked up one of Zara's blankets off the floor and pressed it against the knife. The cheerful giraffes and elephants quickly disappeared under a spreading red blossom. Cali braced her hand on the low table. Realizing she was about to try and stand, Joe jumped to his feet and offered support.

"Thank you." Her cold hand gripped his tightly. It felt familiar.

"You should get yourself checked out." Joe put his other hand on her shoulder to steady her, worried at her refusal to get help. She could have hurt herself when she dropped to the floor. Or she could have been hit or grazed by a bullet without realizing it.

She pulled out of his grasp immediately, grabbing the counter to brace herself. "Trust me. Doctors and I aren't a good mix. I'm not in their textbooks."

Joe made himself stand back despite his protective instincts going into overdrive. He had no right to argue with her. But he couldn't entirely let it go either. "You're *lalassu*, aren't you?"

"There's a name for it?" Salazar interrupted, eyes wide.

"There is." Cali fixed Salazar with a glare. "Planning to turn me over to the Bureau of Special Investigations?"

"That's what we're supposed to do. So you can be registered." Salazar didn't back down. Maybe the sound of approaching sirens gave him courage.

Joe couldn't let the discussion keep going. In Salazar, he saw himself as he'd been a few months earlier. Too many people would face the *lalassu* with that same expression of confusion and disgust.

"And after we're registered, what do you think happens to us?" Cali snapped. "When people know what we can do, it paints a big target on our backs and a scarlet letter on our fronts. No one wants to help a freak, but there are plenty of people who want to use one. We've been underground for generations to avoid this exact situation."

Joe crouched beside the injured man and looked Salazar in the eye. "We don't have time for this. She needs to be gone before the ambulance arrives. They all do."

"You can't be serious!" Salazar's hand went to his holster. "She threw that knife, ready to kill this man. They're all witnesses!"

Joe recognized Salazar's fight to fit the fantastic into the boxes of the familiar world. "I know. And I know what I'm asking you is against all the rules, but there are times when the rules get in the way of doing what's right."

"The rules are the rules." Salazar released his gun and returned to stopping the bleeding. That was progress.

"Okay. Let's look at this another way. You saw what happened. She used a weapon to stop a gunman from killing you and me and possibly the family who lives here. It was a clear and present threat." Joe spread his hands wide. "Would you say it was self-defense?"

The rookie nodded.

"Then how will it help to drag Cali into a system that isn't prepared for her? She'll disappear into Special Investigations for the crime of having been brought to their attention. And what about the mother and two kids in the back room who have been terrorized by this man for years? Do they deserve to be dragged through the media and the courts?" Joe hoped he wouldn't hear his own words echoed back to him in an Internal Affairs investigation.

The rigidity in Salazar's shoulders softened, and he slumped. "What do you want to do?"

Speranza emerged from the back, carrying one daughter and holding the other's hand. A full duffel bag hung over her shoulder. Joe pointed at the family. "We get them all out of here so that they're not in the official report. You and I heard the shots and found the man like this. He's got a record, and with everything else going on, no one is going to be in a rush to push this."

He finally got the courage to look at Cali again. She stared at him as if astonished at his defense. To be fair, he was a little surprised at the depth of his arguments. But it was the right thing to do. It might go against every protocol and ethic he believed in, but it was the only way to serve real justice.

Speranza hung back, clearly trying to prevent the girls from seeing their father bleeding on the ground. Cali went to them, using a stuffed animal to block the baby's eyes. Joe approved. Children shouldn't see such things.

"What's it going to be?" Joe asked Salazar. The sirens blared from outside the building.

The rookie looked at the women and children and exhaled a ragged breath. "Go."

They hurried away, vanishing up the stairs a few moments before the EMTs arrived. They were far more interested in stabilizing Rodolpho to get him to the hospital than in preserving evidence. Joe dropped a discreet hint or two about the man's suspected role in beating his ex-wife on multiple occasions. When the EMTs secured Rodolpho to the gurney with heavy restraints, Joe enjoyed a moment of extreme satisfaction.

Joe didn't recognize the cop who arrived a few moments later to take statements.

"We came to check on the victim of an assault. When we got here, the door was open, and he was lying there with the knife in his neck and the gun in his hand." Salazar displayed the gun he'd dropped into a Ziploc bag.

He did it. The situation between *lalassu* and humans wasn't doomed. With time, they'd get it sorted out. Joe added, "I've reached the assault victim, and she and her children are fine. They weren't in the apartment."

The officer took their contact information but didn't seem particularly interested in further details. As expected, a surprise stabbing wasn't a big priority with everything else going on.

While the EMTs and the officer consulted, Joe took a moment to text Colleen and let her know he would be delayed. She sent back a message immediately, telling him to take his time. She wasn't going anywhere.

Once Rodolpho was on his way to the hospital, Joe and Salazar managed to drag the apartment door back into place. Craters from bullet impacts had warped it, but they got it secured. The landlord would have to replace it. If Joe had his way, Speranza would only be coming back here to pick up her family's things before moving somewhere else.

"How long have you known?" Salazar asked. He didn't have to clarify.

"A few months ago. The *lalassu* are people with abilities that seem to come from myth and legend. But they're still just people. Like Cali said, most of them live in fear of being exposed and exploited. They're not interested in being threats."

Salazar shook his head. "This is all too complicated for me."

"I don't have all the answers. All I know is that right now people are panicking, and they won't be able to see past the label. I don't like this, believe it or not. I'm caught between how to do my job and why I do my job. In this circumstance, the two things aren't compatible, and I have to choose. So I'm choosing to uphold justice by preventing persecution." Joe took a deep breath. "If you change your mind and decide your conscience takes you in a different direction, then you can tell them I coerced you into lying."

"Even when the other cops, especially Hampton, were calling you crazy, no one even hinted that you were corrupt." Salazar leaned back against the wall. "Right now, I don't know enough to know if this is the right call. I'll trust you, but I need to be kept in the loop."

"You sure? The loop is how I ended up tangled in this mess." Joe wouldn't drag another unwitting person down the same rabbit hole that had swallowed him.

"I'm sure. The world is shifting, and I don't want to be caught off guard." Salazar seemed certain enough of his choice. "I'll take care of the paperwork; you take care of the people."

"Thanks. It's good knowing someone has my back again." Joe held out his hand, and the rookie shook it before heading down the stairs.

"Is the bromance moment over?" Cali sounded amused as she adjusted the shoulder strap of her small backpack. She and Speranza were waiting with the kids on the landing above.

"I think it's safe. And now I'll get you someplace safe." He had the perfect place for them.

Chapter Thirty-Three

"I didn't sign up for this shit to hide in the dark."

The muttered comment was loud enough for Dalhard to overhear. Which meant it was a challenge.

Disappointing though not unexpected. After the thrill of the escape, he and the other convicts had gone to ground in a squalid warehouse. It once housed illegal immigrants or kidnapping victims. He wasn't sure which and frankly didn't care. The rudimentary plumbing and long rows of basic cots weren't much worse than the prison they'd left. Especially considering the handcuffs hanging from each cot's rail.

The idiots chafed at not being able to pursue their small-minded pleasures. *They should be grateful to me for keeping them from being caught.* Once again, Dalhard needed to remind them of why he was in charge. And it wasn't because of his superior planning skills.

He rose to his feet, and the low buzz of conversation immediately stopped. He smiled, surveying the group. "You would prefer it back in prison?"

He scanned the group. Most of them met his gaze briefly before looking away, signaling their submission, but one kept his head low, trying to avoid notice. *There.* The youth's name escaped him, but Dalhard recalled that the boy had been convicted of stabbing four people to death during a fight. He wore a brilliant orange-and-yellow scarf tied over his shaved head, and dark tattoos peppered his pale-brown skin. Dalhard stopped in front of him, enjoying the anticipation of the inevitable.

The youth checked the men on either side of him, but none offered any encouragement. They refused to meet his eyes, their bodies turned to block him out. The boy decided to bluff it out, lifting his head and grimacing to reveal a mouthful of meth-rotted teeth. "I just wondered what the plan was, y'know?"

"I see. Growing bored, are we?" Moving fast, Dalhard snatched at the youth's collar, hauling him up off the cot with only one hand.

The youth shouted, battering at Dalhard's iron grip. None of the other convicts rose to intervene.

Dalhard smiled. "It appears everyone else understands the virtue of patience."

"Lemme go, man!" he yelped, choking as Dalhard tightened his hold.

"Myself, I don't have much patience. Particularly with those whose lack of discipline could threaten my plans," Dalhard said conversationally. "You are here because it is convenient for me. No other reason. Understood?"

The youth nodded, gasping for air.

Dalhard released him, dropping the boy unceremoniously to the ground. "Is anyone else feeling restless?"

None of them would look in Dalhard's eyes anymore, not even for a second. If they had been wolves, they would have been pissing and cringing to display submission. Their groveling was intoxicating. None of them even tried to help the boy as he wheezed against the filthy concrete.

Dalhard turned his back and slowly walked back to his isolated cot. Asserting dominance through physical strength was far more satisfying than using his persuasive gifts. He flexed his fingers, curling them like claws. He'd never imagined using them in such a direct fashion nor that he would enjoy it so much. Perhaps he should have. He'd always enjoyed the implied threat behind his powerful physique after all.

The door at the end of the warehouse opened. Boom-Boom swaggered in, greeting his fellow convicts in an exaggeratedly friendly fashion. Following him were five dark-skinned men who glared and conspicuously fingered the guns tucked into their waistbands.

"Gentlemen," Dalhard called out. "Thank you for coming."

They scowled at him, not answering. Dalhard would have laughed in their faces, but it would have made his task harder.

"Boom-Boom say you got business for us." Irritation and barely concealed contempt poured out from the speaker's sullen expression.

Good, a spokesperson. Dalhard reached out and offered his hand.

Reluctantly, Sullen took it, sealing his fate. Dalhard's persuasive influence flowed through the skin-to-skin contact far faster than anything he'd been able to do before. *Prison did teach me efficiency.* In the past, it had taken him several minutes to overwhelm someone's mind, and it often left people unable to think and move on their own initiative. Some prudent but necessary experimentation had allowed him to discover shortcuts.

The sullen expression vanished from the man's face, replaced by wide-eyed wonder. Dalhard smirked, offering his hand to the others.

A few minutes later, it was over. Five new devotees were ready to drop to their knees and worship him if he ordered it. That was tempting, but he had more practical instructions to deliver. "Gather your people and your weapons. Tell them to lay low until they receive a signal from me."

"What happens then?" Sullen asked eagerly.

"When our forces are gathered, then we claim our rightful due." Dalhard waved away their confused expressions. Whispered explanations in the group set off a chain of grinning and slapping each other in anticipation.

"What next?" Boom-Boom stepped forward.

"Find me the rest of the gang leaders. I want them all under my banner." How could he have missed it before? Weapons, hardened men and women—the streets held everything he needed for his revolution. Let Karan bow and scrape for the upper crust. When the blood started to run, they would panic. They depended on insulation for their power, and when that insulation was stripped away, those of the so-called elite would be revealed as bleating sheep. "The time for hiding is almost over."

"You really think we'll be safe here?" Cali asked as the car pulled up in front of Joe's family's home. Huddled in the back, Speranza and the children didn't say anything. On the drive, Joe had begun to have second thoughts, wondering if Colleen would be upset at him bringing Cali to his mother's. He hoped she would understand as long as he kept everything professional. Mamá would want to match make, but he could keep her distracted with the children. He checked his phone again. He'd texted Colleen again with an update, and she hadn't replied yet. He worried she was disappointed and upset with him. As soon as Cali and the others were settled, he could go to Colleen.

"This is my mother's house. She'll take care of you until we figure out what else to do." Joe tried to sound confident, as if he had plenty of practice sheltering fugitives. *Maybe I should get used to it.* "Come on. I bet she's got some *tortas.*"

The little girls perked up at the idea of food. Joe ushered them all up the short front walk, carrying their bags. He guided them to the kitchen entrance on the side. As soon as he opened the door, a wave of scents wrapped around them: fresh bread, beans, spices, simmering pork, and beef. *Home.*

"Pépé!" Mamá bustled around the half-full table to greet her son. She knelt in front of the two girls. "Who's this?"

"I'm Carlotta, and this is my baby sister, Zara."

Joe smiled. Kids always came first at Mamá's house.

"Ah, Carlotta. Nice to meet you, *gordita.*" Mamá winked at her. "You can call me Inéz."

"Thank you, Señora Cabrera," Speranza said stiffly.

Joe jumped in before feathers could get ruffled. "Mamá, this is Speranza. She and her girls need a place to stay for a few days."

"Of course, Pépé. They can stay in Abuelita's old room. But before they do, there is one very important rule in my house. Do you think you can follow it?" Mamá turned a skeptical eye on Carlotta.

"What is it?" The child's face pinched in suspicion.

"No one goes to bed hungry in my house." Mamá produced a pair of sugar-and-cinnamon–coated churros. The girls helped themselves, grinning broadly. Mamá winked again. "Why don't you go and see what games my Pépé's cousins are playing in the front room?"

Speranza's fingers twitched toward her children as they ran off, but she let them go. Joe gave himself an internal victory high five. *First hurdle down.* Mamá didn't even seem curious about Speranza possibly being his mystery girlfriend. Maybe he'd worried too much about that.

"You look exhausted." Mamá patted Speranza on the shoulder. "Go and get some rest before dinner. If the girls need you, we'll call."

Speranza hesitated as Mamá called for Tía Ximena to show her the room. His aunt came in from the dining room, her grey-and-black hair neatly fastened to the top of her head and her arthritic hands folded over her floral apron. She took Speranza in hand, leaving her no choice but to follow as his tía clucked and chattered in rapid-fire Spanish.

"Be careful, Mamá. She's been through a lot." Joe kept his voice low.

"Even more reason for her to get some sleep." Mamá turned to Cali, her eyes lighting up. "And who is this?"

Red alert. Need to derail those assumptions. His mother's nose for sniffing out hidden attraction was unbeatable. "This is Cali. She's Speranza's neighbor, and she got caught up in what happened." Joe wished he could come up with a discreet way to explain that Cali was not the woman he'd mentioned to Mamá—preferably without having to explain it to Cali as well.

"I see." Mamá wiped her hands on her apron. Joe knew she'd picked up on the feelings he was trying to hide. He could practically hear the lecture building behind her narrowing black eyes. Cali would be an unsuitable wife—too blond and too standoffish. She was obviously ill at ease in Mamá's house, which bordered on insulting. And she was either trouble or in it.

But that all remained unsaid. Mamá would be a gracious hostess to the demons of hell, though she might insist they wipe their hooves first.

Cali offered a verbal olive branch. "I'm sorry to drop in like this. Joe said this was the safest place he could think of. Would you mind if I washed up, and then maybe I could help with supper?"

He would be thoroughly interrogated later. But for the moment, Mamá allowed Joe to take Cali upstairs.

"I don't think she likes me," Cali whispered casually as if it were a joke. Joe saw her twisting at the cuff of her long-sleeved shirt and knew she wasn't as comfortable as she pretended to be.

"She doesn't know what to do with you. The children are easy, and Speranza is a mother who needs a break. Your story isn't quite as clear."

Joe opened up the door to his old room. His posters of cars and motorbikes were still neatly tacked in place on the walls.

"I suppose it isn't." Cali wouldn't meet his gaze but stared at the walls and floor. She carefully placed her backpack on the bed. "There's just so much to say. I don't know where to start."

That was an understatement. Joe took a deep breath, reminding his body not to indulge. This wasn't the girl he'd committed to. But thinking about Colleen's kiss only made the situation more awkward. All his traitorous body cared about was how good Cali's butt looked in her jeans and how easy it would be to slip his hand inside her loose shirt.

Maybe a little space would be a good thing. "Take a bit to think about it while you clean up. The bathroom is across the hall."

Cali nodded, making her escape.

Joe took a deep breath. He needed to understand Cali's place in what was happening without overstepping any boundaries that he'd regret. And he was going to have to make some kind of explanation to Mamá, although he didn't have one at the moment.

First things first. He needed to call Colleen and make sure she was okay. He refused to cancel their dinner together even if they started later than planned. He dialed the number.

Something began buzzing in Cali's bag.

Joe frowned, glancing at the closed door across the hall. Should he let her know about the call?

Colleen's voice mail answered, and the buzzing immediately stopped.

Joe slowly lowered the phone. It had to be a coincidence.

He hung up and dialed again.

Cali's bag obediently began to buzz again. Joe slowly opened up the battered leather backpack, using the sides of his fingers as if processing it for evidence. He found three hard rectangles in the bottom of the bag, one of which was buzzing and flashing. It stopped as he lifted the three phones out.

Multiple phones were never a good sign. *Maybe she runs a small business. Or several small businesses.* Even in his head, the excuse sounded lame.

Joe hit redial one more time.

The one on the right immediately lit up and buzzed. His picture appeared on screen, leaving no doubt. Cali had Colleen's phone.

Panic hit. Was Cali working with Dalhard or Karan? Had she hurt Colleen? Joe remembered the effortless efficiency of Cali's knife throw. It hadn't been a lucky shot. That level of skill took serious training, and since he doubted she belonged to some kind of military special unit, that left a street-level assassin.

Any reticence about searching through Cali's things fled. Joe dumped out the backpack. Among the few clothes, he found an envelope full of twenties and fifties, easily close to a thousand dollars, an expensive watch, and a hard eyeglass case. And identification for Calista Wyman, Adele Goldman, Kelly Roland, and Colleen Avila. His fingers trembled as he picked up Colleen's ID. While he'd been preventing Cali from being taken in for a crime, he should have been protecting Colleen.

He popped open the eyeglass case to see Colleen's familiar brown clunky glasses. His legs sagged out from under him. Holding the case as delicately as he could, he plopped onto the bed. *I can't panic. She needs me. Work the evidence. Figure it out.*

Taking a deep breath, he went through the small pile of things again. Another familiar face on the driver's licenses caught his attention. The license for Kelly Roland had Boomerang's picture. Why would Cali have a fake ID for his data thief?

The bathroom door opened, and instinct took over. Rising, he dropped Colleen's license and yanked out his gun, aiming it at Cali. She froze in the hall, hands raised, as Joe snarled, "Who the hell are you?"

The River

Chapter Thirty-Four

For the second time in less than an hour, Cali found herself staring down the barrel of a weapon. Her phones and identifications littered Joe's bed among her clothes. *Shit.* Putting her things in a bag rather than her pockets had seemed like a good idea back at the apartment.

"What have you done to her?" Joe's eyes were wild and wide enough for a ring of white to shine around his dark irises. He shook the gun to emphasize his question.

"Who?" Cali asked, trying to keep as still and calm as possible. If she moved even a little bit, he was close enough to a hair-trigger reaction that he might shoot.

"What have you done with Colleen?" Joe's face crumpled briefly before hardening into resolve. "If you've hurt her—"

"I haven't hurt her. I swear." Cali licked her dry lips. "I can explain, but I'd feel a lot better about doing it if you'd put the gun down first."

"Start talking," he growled. The gun didn't budge.

This was not how she'd pictured this conversation, but she did have plenty of experience in crisis-level improvisation. She began slowly. "You know I'm a *lalassu.* My bloodline is rare. I'm a metamorph."

"What is that? Like a skinwalker?" Joe's hands tightened on the gun. "What does it have to do with Colleen?"

"A skinwalker can change between a human and an animal. A metamorph can change their appearance to look like someone else." Hoping he didn't decide to shoot her, Cali darkened her blond hair to a sandy brown, thickened her nose and cheeks, and dampened the brown flecks in her hazel eyes, leaving only the green. "I am Colleen."

Joe's hands were shaking. "It's a trick."

"It's not. I'm the same woman who was in your apartment this morning. And the same one who had Tony's coffee with you when we first met." *He has to believe me.*

"Take off her face. You don't deserve to wear it." Joe wasn't calming down.

Cali let her features relax back to her natural ones, fear clenching her stomach hard enough that she was afraid she might vomit if the situation got any tenser.

"So you're telling me that it was all a lie. Colleen doesn't even exist." He started to laugh. "I finally fall in love, and it's with a woman who isn't real."

"Pépé, is everything all right?" Mamá's voice accompanied the creak of the stairs.

Joe glared at Cali. She held her breath, still struggling to process his declaration that he loved her. *No, he loves Colleen.*

"If you hurt my family—"

"I would never hurt them. Cuff me to the desk if you don't trust me, but put the gun away before someone gets hurt." She held her breath, wondering if he would listen.

He lowered the weapon and gestured to the child's desk in the corner. Cali hurried over, her knees creaking and popping as she sat down. Mamá's footsteps grew louder, and Cali held out her wrists for the handcuffs.

Joe holstered his weapon and snapped on the cuffs, snaking the chain through the drawer handle. It wasn't much of a restraint, but if it kept the gun locked down while they talked, then it got Cali's vote. She shuffled the chair forward so the cuffs wouldn't be immediately obvious from the door, although it meant painfully stretching her shoulders and elbows.

"Pépé, I heard shouting. What's going on?" Mamá appeared at the top of the stairs, darkening the hall.

"It's nothing important." Joe stood at the door, blocking his mother's view of the inside of the room. Mamá peered around him, clearly suspicious.

Cali smiled at her, twisting farther to keep the cuffs out of sight. "It's fine. Just a misunderstanding."

Mamá's expression cleared, and she swatted Joe across the arm. "You know better than to treat a guest and a woman in such a way. I raised you better."

"I know, Mamá. I'm sorry. I need to finish talking to Cali. Please."

Since Cali could hear the tension in his voice, she doubted his mother was fooled. Her sharp eyes swept over Cali's awkwardly bent arms. "You call me if he forgets his manners again."

"I will, Mrs. Cabrera. I promise." Her cheeks were starting to hurt from the effort of keeping her smile in place.

Joe's mother shot them another suspicious glance as she turned away, but she made her way back down the stairs, leaving them some privacy. Cali looked up at Joe, the cold steel biting into her wrists. "What now?"

"Now you start talking." He pulled the gun out again but fortunately didn't point it at her. Instead, he sat down on the bed, glaring at her as if she'd murdered Santa Claus with puppy corpses.

"I created Colleen to work for Mr. Dalhard. She could go into any company and be unremarkable. No one ever paid her any attention. I designed her very carefully to be unnoticed." Cali wondered if Joe could understand. It wasn't too different from undercover work. "After his arrest, he needed someone unremarkable to serve as a courier, spy, and messenger. Colleen was the best choice."

"Why her?"

"Because she's not attractive or particularly feminine. Administrative work tends to take two forms at the higher levels. There are those who are very attractive and those who are very competent. If a woman is pretty, then she faces a bunch of assumptions about high-powered executives and their secretaries. People don't tend to trust them or take them seriously. Being anonymous allowed me to get more work done." Cali saw Joe's hands starting to relax and allowed herself to hope, despite the growing ache in her joints.

"That's pretty old-school thinking, isn't it?" Joe leaned back, resting his wrist on his knee, gun pointed at the floor.

"People like to think those assumptions died in the fifties, but they are still very much with us. No one will say it out loud, but they still tend to make the same judgments. You were the only one who ever paid attention to me as Colleen, if you don't count barking orders." Cali swallowed, wondering if he would believe her next words. "I wished I really was Colleen."

"Guess that makes two of us," Joe replied bitterly. "I have to say, you did good with the whole sob story about your parents and Vegas. I swallowed it all."

His accusation stung her. "It was the truth. I've never told anyone else about what I went through. Not Mr. Dalhard. Not my partners. Not anyone."

"You can understand why I'm skeptical." Joe picked up one of her IDs. Boomerang. "Is this you too?"

Cali nodded, and Joe let out a bark of weary laughter.

"You've been stalking me all over the place. Guess I know now how you made such a quick getaway at the hospital. You just became someone else and walked away whistling."

Cali looked down, not wanting him to see the tears in her eyes. His cruel words smacked her harder than her father's fists ever had. She swallowed, summoning up her old armor. "I guess I did. Now you know the truth."

"Now I know. And I've got no idea what to do next." His knee bounced in agitation. Cali kept her eyes on it, unwilling to face his anger.

"I could walk away, and you won't see me again." She didn't have the steel plating to survive another blow to that particular concrete block. The shoe had dropped to where there was no picking it up again.

"I'd like that, but I still need your help with your former boss. Dalhard is out there." There was his bitter chuckle again, slicing at her heart. Joe continued. "I need her help too, tracking down the stolen list of *lalassu.*"

Which her? Cali raised her eyes just high enough to see him holding out Boomerang's ID. "I don't have the list anymore. Karan stole it back except for the portion that Fuentes gave you."

"We can't leave it in his hands." Joe stood up and started to pace.

He said we. Hope lifted her head. "I know where he is. I can take you there."

Joe glared at her as if she were a particularly disgusting bit of goo that he'd discovered on his dress shoes. "Very convenient. Why would I believe you?"

Cali's heart shriveled beneath her business shell. *It's over.* She'd lost him with her lies, and he'd never see her as anything other than a fake. Summoning up Boomerang's protective arrogance, she recrossed her legs and leaned back as nonchalantly as her awkward position allowed. "What other choice do you have?"

Leaving Cali cuffed to the desk, Joe went downstairs, his mind still shaky from realizing that Cali, Boomerang, and Colleen were all the same person. That Colleen, the woman he'd thought he would build a life with, was nothing more than a cover.

He needed to figure out a plausible excuse for Mamá for taking Cali away again so quickly after bringing her there for sanctuary. He couldn't leave her here alone with his family. *At least she's secure for…* his inner thought trailed off as he realized she could get out of the cuffs as easily as Boomerang had in the hospital. Her offer to be restrained was meaningless. She could be climbing out the window while he walked down the stairs.

Preoccupied with his thoughts, he only noticed something was wrong when the quiet sank in. The kitchen was deserted—no women gossiping over food preparation or kids dashing in to sneak an early bite. The door between the kitchen and the rest of the house was closed. Joe stared, trying to remember if he'd ever seen it shut before.

"I told them I wanted to talk with you, Pépé." His mother folded her arms over her chest, somehow managing to tower over him the way she had when he was a child.

Joe reminded himself that he was a grown man who did not have to worry about being in trouble with his mother. That reassurance changed absolutely nothing.

"You lied to me." His mother stabbed her finger toward him.

"I made a mistake. I needed you to go back downstairs quickly." Joe scrubbed both hands across his head. "It turns out Cali isn't who I thought she was."

"And who is this *fulana* then?"

That was not a complimentary term. Joe swallowed, upset at the insult but not ready to jump to Cali's defense. "She's mixed up with some very dangerous people. I'm going to take her out of here."

"And what about the others?" Mamá pointed toward Abuelita's old room off the dining room and the backyard, where he could hear the shrieks of children playing.

Joe hurried to reassure his mother. "Speranza's exactly who I said she was. Her ex-husband beat her. He's gotten himself badly hurt, and she and the kids need somewhere to stay for a while. They don't have anything to do with Cali except that she's been helping to take care of them."

Mamá sniffed. "So what will you do with the *fulana*? Arrest her? Report her?"

"I can't. She says she can help me stop something that could be even more dangerous. I don't want to trust her again, but if she's telling the truth, I can't walk away." Joe locked his fingers together, resting his elbows on his knees. "If she's right, then we could prevent a lot of pain."

His mother understood. Sometimes a deal with the devil kept innocents safe. "Then you must take the chance, Pépé. And while you do, keep yourself and your heart safe."

I think it's too late for my heart, Mamá. Joe straightened and rubbed his palms across his thighs. "Guess I'll have to grab a to-go plate."

His mother's stern eyes softened, and her fingers flew to her mouth. Joe wished he could curse out loud. She'd always been too perceptive for him to hide anything from her for long.

"Oh, Pépé." Mamá ran her cool fingers along his cheek. "She was the one, wasn't she?"

He should deny it. But instead, he found himself nodding as his head drooped.

"I'm sorry, *tesoro.*" She only called him that when things were really bad. Joe sagged, and his mother wrapped her arms around him, comforting and sturdy—the implicit maternal promise that nothing could hurt him as long as his mother held him.

But his mother couldn't always stand guard. And Joe needed to protect her and the rest of the family. He extricated himself. "I'll be all right, Mamá. Heartbreak builds character, right? Girls like that."

She didn't reply, but her mouth thinned into a narrow line.

"Maybe Tía Ximena's neighbor's daughter will want to help me get over it." *I'm babbling. I need to get out before I start promising grandbabies.*

"Don't give up on love, Pépé. Not because of her. Promise me."

"I'm not giving up," he said. Even though he couldn't imagine ever trusting someone with his heart again.

Chapter Thirty-Five

Joe did his best to ignore Cali as they walked to his car. To his surprise, she'd still been cuffed to the desk when he'd gone back upstairs. Out of the corner of his eye, he noticed her rubbing her wrists and shoulders. Her joints crackled and popped as she moved slowly down the sidewalk. Just like Boomerang's had in the hospital. More proof of a truth he still wasn't ready to accept. His heart ached, and his primal instincts demanded that he hunt down his woman. Except Colleen had never existed. Somehow, he'd ended up falling for three illusionary facets of the same woman.

She seemed as anxious to avoid contact with him as he was to avoid her. They got into the car without a word. She gave him terse directions as they drove deeper and deeper into Perdition. She didn't look at him once after they got in the car but kept staring out the window with her spine ramrod straight. He'd heard GPS recordings with more animation in their voices. *I guess this is the real Cali.* Cold, practical, and hard as a diamond.

"This is it. Pull over here," she instructed.

Last Down? Joe recognized the dive of a sports bar. Everyone knew it as a hub for illegal gambling and probably other sordid exchanges, but there wasn't enough proof to make it worth officially going after. Why hadn't she just told him where they were going?

Cali opened up her backpack and pulled out a heavy designer watch. As she held it, her hair darkened and her lips became fuller and redder. She didn't have the glam forties-pin-up flair with her hair pulled back in a ponytail instead of styled. But the transformation left him unsettled and creeped out. If they gave an Oscar for Best Impersonation In Real Life, then Cali would have won. She moved differently, spoke differently, and gave every sign of being an entirely separate person than the woman she'd been a few minutes earlier. Method actors would flock to learn from her.

She clasped the watch around her wrist. "Ready to go?"

"Give me the knives." He held out his hand.

"Wh-what?" Her confident stance wavered.

"I'm not going in with you armed." He held his breath, waiting to see if she would resist.

Rolling back her sleeves, she pulled three short blades out of clever arm sheaths tucked tight against her forearms. If he hadn't seen them for himself, he never would have guessed they were there. She placed them carefully on his palm. "Satisfied?"

In answer, Joe opened the door and stepped out of the car. Cali emerged as if striding onto a red carpet. Ignoring him, she stalked off toward the entrance.

If she thinks those kind of games will keep me off balance, she's got another think coming. Joe followed her easily, hanging back out of immediate reach. He kept her knives tucked in his jacket pocket.

Inside, the bar was mostly deserted except for the hard-core gamblers. The only real sources of light were the dozen televisions above the bar, each tuned to a different sporting event. Joe spotted hockey, baseball, basketball, golf, horse racing, and—was that cricket? Joe had heard of it but never seen it played.

One of the regulars, a portly man whose Hawaiian shirt strained over a paunch filled with onion rings and bad gambling choices, noticed them, and his eyes went wide.

"It's all right, Chomp. Strictly business today." Cali patted him on the shoulder as she went past.

It didn't work. Chomp grabbed his racing form and hurried out of the bar as fast as his legs would carry him.

"Poor man. He's been skittish for the last few months. He disappeared for a few weeks last summer, and since coming back, his tolerance hasn't been the same." Cali sounded like a bored society matron relating a minor scandal. She lifted her hand toward the darkened booths in the back. "My people are already here."

Joe followed her. It took his eyes time to pick out the dark-skinned man in his charcoal suit from the deeper shadows. Cali took a seat opposite him and patted the cracked vinyl beside her. Joe sat down slowly, making sure he could still draw his gun quickly if needed.

"Your weapon is not necessary, Detective." The man's heavy Jamaican accent was distinctive. From the powerful build of the man's torso and arms, Joe wasn't entirely inclined to believe his statement. If it came to a fight, Joe would need every edge he could get.

"Hello, Hood. Where's Harley?" Cali asked cheerfully. Joe was surprised she didn't do an air kiss.

"Right here." Another man showed up, substantially skinnier and narrower than Hood but with wiry muscles, carrying a heavy leather folder. "We got everything you need, Boomerang."

"Good. Let's have a look." Cali accepted the folder and began to unfold blueprints and schematics.

Hood stared at Joe, his hands steepled in front of his lips.

"Detective Cabrera has an interest in this," Cali said crisply, absorbed in the diagrams.

It hit Joe all over again that Colleen was gone, vanished into the real Cali. It really had all been a lie, and now that he knew the truth, she could abandon the pretense. The realization hurt like the growing ache after being slugged in the gut. *If she can be professional, so can I.* "We need to recover the list as soon as possible."

"Karan must have given the list to Special Investigations. They've made a number of surprising arrests." Harley smoothed out the corner of a blueprint. "Aren't we closing the barn after the horses are gone?"

"I know Karan, and he's not one to share more than he needs to. Even if Special Investigations thinks they have the list, he will have kept a master list for himself. Once we have his list, we can go after the government's copy." Cali tapped the blueprint. "This is probably Karan's office. The list will be there."

"It will be difficult to access. The windows have redundant alarms and sensors." Hood ran his finger and thumb down either side of his mouth.

"We should go through the main house instead of breaking in through the windows." Cali outlined the various security features along with conjecture about other places where Karan could be storing the data.

"Our best chance of success is if Karan isn't there. But he works odd and irregular hours precisely to make it difficult to predict when he will be home."

"What if we used a clairvoyant—someone who could tell us when he left without having to be in sight?" Joe lifted up a map of the area. "There has to be somewhere to hide in the neighborhood without being too obvious. Then we can go in once we get the word."

"A clairvoyant would certainly be helpful. Do you happen to know one?" Harley leaned back in the booth.

Joe ignored the sarcasm. "She says she's short range, so we'd need to get her close. But we'd want that anyway to reduce travel time."

"My, my, Detective." Cali clucked her tongue. "So quick to use *lalassu* talents." She and Hood began to discuss the best way to find a suitable hiding place, leaving Joe to wrestle with his conscience. He'd suggested Virginia as a potential solution, but Cali's words made him aware of how quickly his thinking had changed. When Michael had first approached him, Joe insisted on being kept in the dark and protecting his friend's gifts. Now, he accepted *lalassu* talents and didn't hesitate to use them if circumstances warranted. *Which makes me no different than Special Investigations.* The realization didn't sit well with his conscience, making him all the more determined to walk away from that strange, corrupting world.

Vincent was the first one to notice when Michael began to twitch from a bad dream, risking tearing out his stitches. To be fair to Dani, she'd long since fallen asleep in the armchair beside her lover's bed. After what she'd been through, her body wouldn't wake up for anything short of invasion or earthquake.

"Hey, Bookworm." Vincent shook Michael's shoulder lightly, careful to avoid touching the man's bare skin. No sense making it easy for his future brother-in-law to pick up secrets. *I never could have done this with Dani.* His sister had faster reflexes than him, and Vincent bore the childhood scars to prove it.

Michael's eyes opened, blindly searching. After a moment, he focused on Vincent. "Where's Dani?"

"Two feet to your left." Vincent pointed with his chin to where Dani was slumped against the bed, her disheveled hair concealing her death grip on Michael's hand.

"Is she okay?" Michael started to sit up and winced.

"Lot better than the guy with the stab wounds. You pop your stitches, and I'm not sure what Andrew will do to you. And then Dani will have to kill him, and it'll be a total mess. So how about keeping it quiet?" Vincent shrugged as if he didn't care one way or the other. If Michael wanted to pretend to be invulnerable, Vincent wasn't planning on being the one to sew him up again.

Michael tilted his head to one side to study Vincent, who resisted the impulse to pick his nose or do something else disgusting under the scrutiny. Movement in the hall caught his eye. Vincent's head snapped up to track the source. Bernie.

She stumbled in the dark, her oversized T-shirt cutting a pale swath in the dim light. As she got closer, Vincent could read the black letters that spelled out "Professional Wheelie Machine." It was probably Vincent's father's. The little girl's bushy brown hair stood up in a halo around her head.

"Chuck said you were awake." She wandered closer to the bed, her eyes tracing unseen patterns over the walls. "This house is too noisy to sleep."

It was dead silent. Walter and Virginia, Vincent's parents, were sound asleep hours earlier, and so was Bernie's mom, Martha. A few enterprising insects chirped outside, but otherwise, the loudest sounds were the leaves rustling in the wind.

"Too much talking," Bernie continued, her mouth twisted in a frown. "Gwen said I could sleep in her room, but it's too creepy."

Wake up, and start using the lump above your shoulders for something other than hat storage. Vincent felt stupid for missing the obvious. Bernie must be hearing the ghosts who came to try and attract Gwen's attention.

"It would be quieter in there for you." Michael's gentle voice was offset by the tightness of his jaw.

"It's cold, and it smells. I never want to get stuck in a room like that."

Vincent couldn't argue with Bernie's accurate, if tactless, evaluation. Gwen had lived in her isolated room with no lights or electricity or piping of any kind for over ten years, making sure there was no way for the ghosts to get in.

"I'm going to go someplace nice. Chuck promised," Bernie announced.

"Remember, Chuck isn't always good at keeping his promises." Michael's mouth tightened as he eased himself into a more comfortable position. The movement woke Dani. She snapped upright, hands moving into a defensive posture before her brain woke up enough to recognize everyone.

Vincent hid a smirk as Bernie dismissed his sister and focused on Michael. Dani liked being all badass, but quick reflexes and superstrength didn't impress the little girl. *Watch. Now Dani will transfer all her irritation to me and Michael.*

"You should be resting." Dani's hands moved rapidly in a diagnostic dance, checking Michael's temperature, pulse, and stitches.

"I'm fine. Bernie's worried." Michael held out his bare hand to the little girl, and Vincent sucked in a quick breath. If she touched him, Michael could get overwhelmed with her emotions. He could tell from the translucency and paleness of Michael's skin that he didn't have a lot of resources to deal with an overload.

Bernie stayed where she was, her face settling into a mature sadness that looked out of place on her immature features. "Chuck says it could hurt you."

Michael's hand dropped down to the mattress, and his face twisted as if someone had just kicked a puppy in front of him.

"Aw, hell. Here." Vincent grabbed a pair of pink rubber gloves from the bucket nearby and shoved them at Michael.

His pitiful smile of relief more than made up for Dani's glare. *As if she expects me to give a little more support for the grown-up point of view. The kid's been through enough, and adulting sucks.*

Gloves in place, Michael opened his arms to Bernie. She curled up beside him, gently avoiding his injuries. Dani hugged her arms together as if afraid she might interrupt the moment.

"You have to go tomorrow." Michael turned his head to face Dani. "Did you know?"

"It isn't safe for Bernie and her mom to stay here," Dani replied. "They're going to the sanctuary at Ekurru. They need someplace isolated to ride out the storm."

Standard Harris plan. Hit first, and when that doesn't work, send the problems out of sight. Vincent wondered if his family would ever come up with a Plan C.

"It's going to be a long drive. And Grumpy Face is going to come with us." Bernie wrinkled her nose and stuck out her tongue, making it clear what she thought of the shaman. Vincent grinned. He loved the nickname, especially since it irritated the crap out of Andrew.

"Is Ekurru a good choice? Dalhard knows about it." Michael looked anxiously between the two siblings.

"The sanctuaries in New Orleans and Seattle are compromised. Anything else would need a passport and official travel, making it even easier to snatch her." Dani rubbed at her forehead. "Everything I'm getting from the Goddess suggests Ekurru is their best option."

"She didn't warn us about the president's announcement or Special Investigations." Michael tightened his grip on Bernie.

Damn, that's close to blasphemy. Michael was digging himself into dangerous territory. Vincent waited for his sister's explosion.

"You should get that." Bernie nodded toward the old rotary phone resting on the table.

Michael frowned, but Vincent had spent too many years with psychics to be freaked out when the phone began to ring a moment later. "County Morgue. You stab 'em, we slab 'em."

"Hi, Vincent," Joe said. "How's everyone doing over there?"

"I think we're in the 'and hijinks ensue' portion of the program.

Michael's fine, my sister is annoying, and Bernie is freaky. All business as usual." Vincent grinned as Dani rolled her eyes. Bernie grinned back at him.

"I actually need to talk to your mother."

Damn, the fuzz wants to talk to the 'rents. I must be in trouble. Vincent waited, mentally counting down from five in his head.

At two, his mother appeared in the doorway, wrapped in an old robe with her grey-streaked braid dangling over her shoulder. "Tell the detective that I agree, and you and I will meet them tomorrow morning. It's late, and we should all get sleep."

She left, and Vincent relayed the message.

"But I didn't actually ask." Joe sounded stunned.

"Get with the program. Psychics save time. See you tomorrow. Pretty sure we'll know where." Vincent hung up and then frowned. "Wait, how did I get recruited?"

"It's not like Mom can drive." Dani shrugged. "Well, she probably can, but she shouldn't."

"Don't worry." Bernie yawned. "I'll send Chuck with you to keep you out of trouble."

Vincent knew he shouldn't take comfort in the idea of being accompanied by a ghost with anger-management issues. As he watched Bernie, Michael, and Dani settle back into sleep, somehow he couldn't help feeling the first stirrings of hope.

CHAPTER THIRTY-SIX

Do you still want to meet?

Naya's message caught Karan by surprise. After a full day of silence since his impulsive invitation to be partners, he assumed the hacker was refusing. **Yes.**

There was another lengthy pause. Something had undermined the hacker's confidence. Karan longed to push but knew better than to disrupt the delicate rapport. If Naya Jeevan attempted to flee, Karan would not yet have sufficient information to pursue him or her. He needed to coax out more details.

The hacker finally came back with a response. **Very well. I will meet you at Right Hand Man this afternoon. One p.m.**

May I ask what brought about this change of mind? Karan asked. The lightest snare to wrap around his quarry, one which it would not feel until the trap closed around its neck.

I knew this day would come. Once we meet, you'll understand why I kept my secrets so close.

Could Naya Jeevan be someone he knew? Karan leaned back from the computer. The hacker claimed not to be Vapor and had shown him as a captive. But Karan had no true evidence of those claims aside from his old partner's continued absence during unfolding events. Vapor would be incapable of playing such a deceptive role for such an extended length of time. Resisting the temptation to meddle was outside the man's character.

For the moment, Karan would continue to play along with his intruder's game. But he would make certain to have a number of contingency plans in place by that afternoon. **I look forward to finally putting a face to the name. Right Hand Man, one p.m.**

Joe scanned the news as they waited for Virginia to let them know it was safe to break in to Karan's house. Harley had discovered that Karan's neighbor was in Europe on business, giving them a perfect vantage point.

Something wasn't right. There were still riots and protests across the country, the ones in larger cities sparking smaller ones in various communities. But Perdition still seemed immune. Theorists suggested their proximity to New York meant that the larger city drew off any troublemakers, but that struck Joe as garbage. Perdition always had plenty of trouble of its own.

He'd noticed another disturbing trend. All crime was down, from purse snatching to armed robbery. In some cases, the number of incidents had dropped to zero. Not one assault outside of domestic incidents. The illegal gambling rings had shut themselves down and, most frighteningly, so had the drug trade. Junkies had been cut off, cold turkey, for at least twenty-four hours. Low-level dealers had nothing to offer, and the higher-level ones seemed to have vanished. The hospitals and clinics were being overrun not just with people in the throes of withdrawal but with half-crazed addicts searching for a fix, any fix.

Salazar agreed to cover for Joe with the sergeant, making realistic excuses for his continued absence. The rookie hadn't been happy about being left out of the raid, but Joe had convinced him that the extra body wouldn't be helpful and could only get in the way.

Cali sat by the bay windows overlooking the water. She hadn't glanced at him once since arriving, and her face could have been carved of marble for all the life it showed. She still wore her Boomerang disguise, and Joe found himself wanting to ask her to be Colleen for a few minutes. *Why? So I can say good-bye to my imaginary friend?* He had to keep reminding himself that none of it had been real.

Virginia lifted her head, her milky eyes turning toward Karan's home.

"He's left. There's no one in the house now."

"Time to go to work." Cali rose gracefully to her feet, holding her burglary bag. Joe had never seen such a comprehensive set of break-and-enter tools.

"Vincent, keep everything ready for a quick departure if we need to," Hood said. "Detective, with us."

Joe insisted on going in with Cali and Hood, although he knew nothing they found would ever be admissible as evidence. He needed to be a witness to what they did and what they found even if it could never be used in a court of law.

They walked swiftly across the wide expanse of lawn between the two luxurious houses. Committing a crime in broad daylight with no attempt at concealment was counterintuitive, but Joe could see how their confidence would reassure any witnesses. They looked as though they belonged and were thus unremarkable.

Cali disabled the elaborate security at the front door in less than fifteen seconds—faster than any of the lock-pick trainers from the police academy. If her story about her father was true, Joe guessed she would have needed to learn quickly.

There were motion-and-noise sensors throughout the house, ones that would trigger cameras and alarms. Joe, Hood, and Cali hugged the walls and moved slowly, trying to appear to be part of the background. Sweat trickled along Joe's temples and crawled down his back. He tried to avoid leaving damp handprints on the wall and wiped his hands on his pants.

Time stretched out, each minute seeming to take an hour as they made their way to the office. Cali hadn't been able to find any evidence of cameras in there. Evidently, Karan wanted to keep what was done in that room a secret.

Cali knelt and began to pick the complicated mechanical lock. Joe shifted in place, trying to find something to do with his hands. The lock seemed too simple to guard Karan's inner sanctum. Joe wondered uneasily if they were being lured into an elaborate trap.

Once inside, they each began to search. Joe opened up the file cabinets while Hood went through the shelves and Cali searched the desk.

It all seemed very efficient and impersonal, making Joe more and more uncomfortable with each passing second. Maybe he should have gone in to the precinct and done his shift. He wasn't being useful, and he doubted he could prevent Hood and Cali from crossing any lines.

The file cabinets were stuffed with copies of thick contracts full of tiny, dense print. Skimming through the legalese, Joe found one hefty tome outlining a consultancy partnership between Dalhard Industries and the Bureau of Special Investigations. The date caught his attention—three days before the president had made his announcement. He took a quick picture with his phone.

Cali clicked her tongue softly, alerting them to a find. Joe carefully closed the drawer and hurried over. She held a laptop and was scrolling through a long list.

That's it. Joe swallowed an exclamation of triumph. Cali copied the list onto a thumb drive they'd brought. Then she pulled out a second drive and plugged it into the computer, giving Harley remote access to the machine.

The screen blinked once, and then a bar appeared, labeled "System Overwrite." The rest of the screen went blank, and the bar filled in once, twice. After the third repetition, Cali unplugged the drive and nodded at Hood. Her partner held up his cell phone, which was blank and dark. Harley and Virginia had promised to contact them if either saw any evidence of Karan making copies of the file for multiple locations. Thus far, it looked as if the man's paranoia was working in their favor.

Karan arrived at Right Hand Man precisely at one. He smoothed the front of his suit jacket, not wishing to reveal any of the uncertainties running through his mind. Being in a situation where he did not have complete control over all the possibilities was rare. Unaccustomed nerves kept threatening to crack his calm exterior. His bodyguards flanked him at a discreet distance as he entered the abandoned office.

The staff at Right Hand Man had received two weeks paid leave after Fuentes's abrupt departure. Karan scoured the records to make certain no other unexpected rebellion lurked in their ranks. *If the man had only given me what I requested, there would have been no need to go to distasteful extremes.*

A man in a dark suit waited in Fuentes's old office. "Mr. Samil. My name is Investigator Lockett. I'm here to escort you to your meeting with Naya Jeevan."

"And where will you be escorting me?" Karan might not have been born in a high caste, but he had mastered the accent of aristocratic disdain.

"To a secret Special Investigations facility. However, Ms. Jeevan requested I show you something first." Investigator Lockett held out a tablet. "Your office's internal alarm went off a few minutes ago."

Karan accepted the tablet, not sure whether to be irritated or concerned. No alert had come to his phone, which meant either this was a ruse or someone highly skilled had circumvented his alarms. The tablet screen showed a live feed from the camera secreted in his desk, his last line of defense against intruders.

Boomerang. Karan's fingers curled tighter around the tablet. Her face was unmistakable as she studied his laptop. Her role in stealing the data for Dalhard already placed her on thin ice, but to break into his home to thieve back what he had successfully stolen was unacceptable. He refused to get caught up in a high-stakes game of fetch with her. *This ends now.*

Stepping back from Investigator Lockett, Karan sent a message to a contract professional who went by the moniker Mr. Smith. Karan had given Boomerang some leeway, acknowledging their mutual history with Dalhard. But she had refused to acknowledge his warnings. Leniency was not something he was in the habit of offering twice.

Mr. Smith acknowledged the request. Karan sent the man's standard urgent-priority fee to a holding account, ensuring his contract would be dealt with immediately. A few moments later, he received the proper confirmation codes.

"The matter has been settled." He handed back the tablet to

Investigator Lockett. "Shall we proceed to our meeting?"

The visual feed abruptly cut out. A surge of excitement threatened Karan's composure. Either Lockett's boss was monitoring the conversation, or Boomerang had found the camera. The former suggested much more exciting possibilities. Karan had caught the investigator's slip, referring to his boss as Ms. Jeevan. One more fact to tuck away: Naya Jeevan was a woman.

Investigator Lockett escorted Karan and his bodyguards to the elevators. *Interesting.* Ms. Jeevan held a position of authority within Special Investigations. No wonder she had been able to hold Vapor. He followed Lockett to the offices he had procured for Special Investigations several months earlier.

As he expected, they emerged onto the correct floor, two levels above Right Hand Man. The plaque near the elevators announced the offices belonged to a small real estate tax firm, a standard deception for government agencies wishing to fly below the radar. Investigator Lockett opened the secure doors and gestured for Karan and his escort to precede him.

Ms. Jeevan was certainly doing her best to treat Karan as an honored guest. He was not immune to the lure of flattery, but he had practice in steeling himself against it. Still, the level of deference was pleasant.

Investigator Lockett escorted them to a pleasant lounge at the back of the facility, overlooking the city. But Karan had no interest in views. His attention remained on the young woman standing by the window, her back to them.

She wore a well-tailored navy-blue suit that flattered her slender figure. Karan did not recognize the design and wondered if it was custom work. The pants nearly concealed her high-heeled boots. Even with the artificial boost, she was several inches shorter than him. Her thick, dark hair was styled in a sleek cut just above her shoulders. Her dark-skinned and slender hands bore no jewelry, nor did they fidget. All of that pointed to a person who paid attention to detail and left nothing to chance. *This must be the infamous Naya Jeevan.*

She turned, and her lips curved in a genuine smile of pleasure. "Welcome, Brother."

Chapter Thirty-Seven

"Karan will be after this." Cali held up the slender red data drive as she sat down in the booth at Last Down. "He won't spare any expense to get it back."

As the first words to break the swollen silence hanging over their group, they cut right to the point. Joe had wondered if anyone in the group was going to be able to push past the discouraging weight of all the lies. Vincent and Virginia had already gone back to the farmhouse. Maybe that was why Cali had waited to share her thoughts. There was no one left to argue with her. Except him.

I should have made her hand it over to them before they went. More proof he wasn't cut out for criminal life. Joe had brooded so much over committing a felony that he'd failed to consider the aftermath.

Hood returned with drinks for all of them—glasses of water. No one felt like celebrating. He took his place beside Harley in the booth. "We will help you protect it."

"No. You and Harley have each other and Eva to think about. Not to mention all the kids on the crew. I'll broadcast that I have the list, which should keep anyone from coming after you." Cali tucked the drive back into her pocket, her hand brushing dangerously near Joe's thigh. He clenched his fist, trying to ignore the contact.

Harley cleared his throat. "Then you'll need this."

He slid a tiny black thumb drive across the table. The exterior portion was barely twice the width of Joe's fingernail. It would be practically invisible when plugged in. "What's that?"

"Nothing you need to worry about. It's something to help me get the other copies of the list back." Cali's clipped delivery stabbed nails into Joe's conscience with each syllable.

Hood's eyes and mouth narrowed. "You don't have to face them alone."

"If I do, then no one else gets hurt." Cali ran her finger along the water-beaded side of her glass. "Please, I couldn't live with myself if something happened to either of you."

Joe shoved aside an instant fantasy of having her slide that cool finger down the side of his throat and past his collar. "I know people who can take care of the list."

"Can they afford to be targets? Whoever has this list will have to keep running." She toyed with her glass, not looking at him.

"I'm not letting you take off with it," Joe said.

"Fine. We'll argue about it later." Cali suddenly stood up. "I'll be back in a minute."

Joe grabbed her wrist, ignoring the sudden growl from Hood and his guilt over how Cali stiffened instantly at his touch. "Leave the drive."

"You really don't trust me." She pulled the candy-apple-red drive out of her pocket and slapped it onto the table. "There. Now can I go to the bathroom?"

Joe let her go, shifting his attention back to his water and wishing the glass held something a lot stronger. He knew he was behaving badly, but he needed to be smart about this. His friends were counting on him. Getting fooled again wasn't an option.

Cali suddenly reappeared. "Joe, I know you think I'm just a liar and a manipulator, and I deserve it for what I've done. But will you make me a promise? Will you watch over Speranza and the girls to make sure they get someplace safe from Rodolpho? I've put money aside for them. Hood will be able to show you where."

Either she was the best actress ever in the history of the world, or she meant every word she said and actually cared about protecting her neighbor.

The jingle of someone entering the bar rang loudly in the silence. Cali swallowed and straightened, her eyes turning cold and haughty. She turned to walk away.

"I'll do it." Joe said gruffly. Whatever the history between him and Cali, Speranza and her children were innocent.

Cali stopped, her back rigid. She didn't bother to turn as she replied. "Thank you."

Joe became aware of Hood's baleful glare and asked, "Problem?"

"I'm not certain if you are a complete asshole or only an idiot," Hood replied calmly as if presenting a purely intellectual challenge.

"Probably both." Joe took a long swallow of water. "What happened between me and her isn't any of your business." He had enough eager family members ready to cause havoc in his life.

"I have known Calista for a long time. I suggested she take on the persona of Boomerang so she could set aside her life on the streets when the time came. Do you know why they call her Boomerang?" Hood leaned back against the booth, his eyes boring down on Joe like the barrels of loaded weapons.

Is there a way I could stop you from telling me? Joe shook his head, hoping it would be a short story.

"People used to come to her after being robbed. When someone took their grandmother's ring or a wallet with their children's baby pictures. As you know, there is little the police will do for such small thefts other than file a report for insurance claims. Except no amount of money could replace the emotional value."

Joe held his tongue despite an instinctive pressure to defend his brothers in blue. It was true—there weren't the resources to investigate all the little thefts. There were too few officers and too many avenues for the goods to disappear.

Hood continued. "Boomerang would find the items and steal them back. Then she would return the items to the owner for a nominal fee, usually only a few dollars. She earned her name as someone who would reliably return. I won't lie and claim she was entirely altruistic. She also ran card scams and cons as well as picking pockets. But she lived for the chance to see someone's face light up when she could return the things that meant the world to them."

"People change." Joe wasn't about to get sucked into another fantasy. His fingers clenched around the data drive hard enough for the edges to bite into his flesh. The criminal with a heart of gold was a Hollywood myth. *I've already had my heart hurt enough by believing in the romantic dreams. Real life isn't like that.*

"True. Mr. Dalhard found her and paid for an apartment and education. I thought we would never see Boomerang again. Month after month, year after year, she came back and continued to find items for people. And she recruited other kids from the street, giving them the same chance that she'd been given. They help her in her searches." Hood's lips curved in the faintest of smiles. "She is a good person despite all that has happened to her. She deserves better than your scorn."

Cali scrubbed at her face, trying to remove all evidence of tears. She would not appear weak in front of that man. If he wanted to believe she was scum, then that was on him, not her. Despite her internal pep talk, her lip quivered, and her chin crumpled again.

She closed her eyes, leaning back against the uneven painted concrete, hoping the chill would suck the heat out of her skin. She'd heard people talk about having lost their hearts, but she hadn't expected to feel it so literally. Her chest felt empty and hollow, as if there was only a bloody cavity where her heart had once beat.

Enough. All I have to do is get the drive back, and then I can walk away, and I'll never have to face him again or think about what a fool I was. She splashed cold water on her face and studied herself in the mirror, adjusting the redness in her cheeks and eyes. It would be a strain, but she could manage.

She peeked out of the washroom, half hoping that Joe would be waiting to apologize, the other half dreading more accusations. He wasn't waiting outside, but someone else was who made her broken heart irrelevant and sent her pulse into high gear.

The man stood by the squat ATM, leaning against the wall. He could be waiting to do some kind of shady business with one of Last Down's patrons. The heavy, dark sunglasses he wore—despite the dimness of the corridor—would be consistent with that. As would the thick leather gloves.

Cali swiftly reviewed her memory of the bar when they'd entered. Only one other customer had been there, an older woman in a worn suit, avidly watching the races. If the man in the sunglasses had wanted to talk to her, it would have been far easier and less noticeable to join her in her front booth than for both of them to walk down the length of the bar to the washrooms. Which meant he was probably there for her and the others.

She stepped back from the door, resettling it into place as smoothly and quietly as possible to avoid attracting his notice. *Maybe I can call Hood.*

Her half-formed plan died as the washroom door banged open. Sunglasses Man stepped inside, gun in hand.

"I don't have any money." Cali kept her eyes fixed on the weapon—a standard semi-automatic pistol, easily available and difficult to trace.

"Please do not waste my time with games. I know who you are, Calista." There was a faint trace of an accent but not one Cali could place. The man's gun stayed steady on her. "It is nothing personal. You are my assignment."

Not many people knew her birth name. Cali tensed her arm before remembering the arm sheaths were empty. *No knives for this fight.* She swallowed and played for time. "You don't want to kill me here. Too many witnesses."

"I agree." His words crushed her faint hopes as he pulled a syringe out of his jacket pocket and laid it carefully on the top of the broken tampon dispenser. "I initially planned to drug your drinks, but plans change. You will hand over the data and inject yourself now."

Cali slowly pulled out her pockets, showing they were empty. "I don't have it."

She tensed, wondering if he would shoot her. Instead, his shoulders twitched in a mini-shrug. "That is unfortunate. It means I will have to deal with your companions as well. You will still inject yourself."

"What's in it?" Cali stalled as she frantically tried to come up with a plan for escape. She couldn't count on Joe and the others for rescue. If she screamed, she would be shot. If she ran, same result. *Think!*

"A barbiturate cocktail. At first, you will become sleepy, and I will take you out the back door as if you've had too much to drink. By the time we reach my car, you will be slipping in and out of consciousness. A few minutes later, you will be unconscious, and thus you will not feel the bullet when I shoot you." He smiled coldly. "Do not make the mistake of believing I do not see what you are doing. You hope to escape or be rescued, as anyone would in this situation. I am telling you what will happen so that you understand your only choice is between a painless, quick death or the agony of being shot right here and now. I have no need to be cruel, but I will complete my contract."

"Just business, that's what you said." She kept her hands steady, not wanting to spook him with any sudden moves. "Don't suppose I could make a counteroffer?"

"If you do not tell me where the drive is and inject yourself in the next three seconds, I will assume you are choosing the bullet." He sounded as if he actually would regret it. *A polite and nonsadistic assassin. You really can find everything in Perdition.* She yanked hard on her hysterical thoughts. *No time for anything better.*

She jumped up, pushing herself off the narrow sink to launch herself at him. Most attackers expected a victim to drop or run. Going up and toward them usually threw them off balance.

Her gamble paid off. He fired as the sink cracked and fell, spraying water into the air, but the bullet passed beneath her. She slammed into him, knocking him onto the floor and the gun out of his hand.

He recovered quickly, grabbing her face and ramming his forehead into her nose and cheek. Red-hot pain cracked across her cheek and eye. Her vision dimmed as she scrambled to hit him back.

She felt something solid under her knuckles as a second blow caught her head again. Her skull bounced painfully against the floor. She couldn't see anything, and she flailed, hoping to find him.

A click warned her that he'd recovered the gun. She scrambled backward on her hands and knees, trying to get out of the bathroom before he could fire.

Crack. The gunshot echoed and blasted, ringing in her ears. Half blind and mostly deaf, Cali scrabbled at the wall, trying to find the door.

Someone grabbed at her arms, and she struck back blindly. She heard a buzzing that almost sounded like words as her attacker held her immobile. Blinking, she managed to clear her vision enough to make out Joe's blurred face hovering above her.

"Joe?" She only knew she'd spoken by the vibrations in her throat.

He helped her to stand up. Dazed, she looked down to see her attacker lying on the ground, staring sightlessly at the wall with a growing pool of blood spreading across the floor. *He could have killed me.*

Joe said something, but her ears were ringing too badly to make out the words. He must have realized, because he gently grasped her elbow to lead her out.

Leaving sounded like an excellent idea. Cali took a step and immediately collapsed as agony ripped through her leg. Only Joe's quick grip kept her from doing a face-plant on the bloody linoleum.

I've been hit. Her jeans were torn at her left calf, the edges wet and shiny. *Blood. My blood.* Dizziness threatened to introduce her to the floor again.

CHAPTER THIRTY-EIGHT

"Priya." Karan inhaled sharply, shock overcoming centuries of self-training. It had to be a trick. His sister had been killed in India centuries before by the son of their father's master. Karan had spent more than five years plotting revenge on the arrogant snot.

"I expected this to be a surprise. It's gratifying not to be disappointed." The smile matched his sister's, as did the way she brushed back the hair from her temple, discreetly showing off the silver bangles decorating her slender wrists.

How could this imposter have learned Priya's gestures? *I should go.* He grasped the door handle. This sort of indignity was not worth his time.

"Wait. Please." The impostor held up her hand. "I am truly your sister."

"I sincerely doubt that," Karan replied through gritted teeth.

"I can't blame you. It seemed impossible myself, Ekie." The woman gestured to a low table off to one side. "Please, sit and listen to me. I have *vada*. It doesn't quite taste like mother's, but it's close." She lifted a silver dome, revealing the crunchy circles of fried chickpea batter.

Karan nodded stiffly. His mother had made vada as a treat for him and his sister, something to keep them going through a long day of cleaning other people's homes. His family used to call him Ekie, short for his birth name, Ekaant, which meant *solitary* in Hindi. "You have done an admirable amount of research."

Her teeth gleamed as she laughed, pouring them each a cup of tea. "I knew you would be suspicious of me. You never trusted other people." Her smile faltered. "You were right about Hiral. He only wanted a mistress, and when I refused him, he became very angry. He beat me so badly that I thought I was going to die. The last thing I remember is him dragging my body to the river."

Karan stilled. His plan for vengeance had been executed over several days. His sister's killer began as a proud man, certain of his invulnerability and blessed stature in the eyes of the gods. After four days of methodical torture, Hiral had been broken, bloody, and begging. He confessed to beating Priya for her refusal and to dumping her body into the river where it would not be discovered. No one could know that. No one had been present, and Karan had killed his enemy shortly thereafter. His certainty that this was a deception began to crumble.

"I woke up sometime later. A woman and her husband dragged me from the river. They helped me to heal but told me not to go back to my family." Priya's smile thinned into anger. "They convinced me that none of you would accept me anymore since I had been disgraced. After a time, I gave up hope. Years passed, and I learned a terrible secret—that I was touched by the gods."

Much as I did. Karan considered her story. Could she be telling the truth?

"My owners grew old and died, but I remained a young woman. Their children saw me as more of a trusted part of the family than a slave. Would you believe me if I told you that it wasn't entirely terrible? I missed my family, but I thought you were all lost to me. I learned to find my own snatches of happiness. I stayed after earning my freedom. I had a place, even some power. Of course, it was all fleeting." Priya stirred sugar into her tea.

"They turned against you when they learned you were immortal." They had done it to him as well. People were not kind to those they envied.

"Exactly. I escaped and made my own way. I discovered my skill at organizing large groups of people and information. I could build trade networks spanning countries and continents. I could not stay in any one place for long, but I could move on to a new place and pretend to be my own daughter or niece. About fifty years ago, I became involved with a group here in the States. They discovered my gifts and asked me to help them find ways to deal with other gifted individuals. Eventually, they became the Bureau of Special Investigations." Priya sipped at her drink and bit into a crunchy vada. "Which brings me to how I became aware of you, my brother."

Karan motioned for her to continue.

"Six weeks ago, we captured a *lalassu*. We'd tracked him for a long time. He was a hacker who manipulated information and forged records to help other *lalassu* blend."

"Vapor." It wasn't a guess.

"Imagine my surprise when he told us about you. I couldn't believe it. And now you have a decision, Ekie—or shall I call you Karan? If we trust each other, we can do great things in this world. If you don't, we could end up destroying each other. Which shall it be?"

When Joe saw the blood on Cali's leg, he ceased to be a police officer and began to panic like every other person he'd seen standing over a victim who was a loved one. *I have to get her out of here.* He picked her up to take her to his car.

The bartender tried to stop him, but Hood and Harley held him back. Joe probably should have expected interference. Despite the dingy housekeeping and less-than-savory clientele, Last Down still wasn't the kind of place where a man could carry a bleeding woman out the doors without a challenge.

"We should take her to the hospital." Hood reached for her.

Joe stepped back, pulling Cali closer to him. "No hospitals. She doesn't like them."

"I'm not going to let her go with a man who could barely look at her twenty minutes ago," Hood rumbled. "If you hadn't taken her knives, she could have defended herself."

The knives. He'd forgotten about them, tucked into his jacket pocket. Guilt dropped through him like a plunging weight. His arms tightened around her as he realized how he'd left her helpless.

Cali stirred in his grasp. "'S okay, Hood."

Pride added warmth to Joe's churn of guilt. Despite being denied her weapon of choice, she'd still fought her attacker enough to give them time to come to her rescue. She never gave up.

"You don't have to go with him." Harley stepped between Hood and Joe, his attention all on Cali.

Her eyes opened, and she turned away, squinting. Harley moved, shading her eyes from the bright sun. Joe held her steady. She seemed alert, which had to be a good sign.

She licked her lips. "Joe can take me home. Go and get yourselves and Eva someplace safe. Scatter the crew until this is over."

"Are you sure?" Hood asked, his accent strong.

She nodded. "I'll be fine. We need to go."

Joe caught the first echoes of sirens. Hood helped him to get Cali into the car, squeezing her arm briefly before retreating with Harley. Joe pulled away from the curb, not wanting to attract any more attention.

"Where am I going?" he asked.

"I have an apartment in the same building as Speranza," Cali said softly. She tried to pull aside her bloody jeans to check the wound and winced. She snatched her hand back, tightening it into a fist.

"You need a doctor." Joe was second-guessing his choice. Could she treat a bullet graze properly? It didn't seem life threatening, but he knew how much that kind of wound hurt. There was a lot of blood seeping through her jeans. He didn't even have enough experience to guess what could go wrong without proper medical attention.

"I'll be fine. I have what I need at my place. And this won't be the first time I've stitched myself up." She rolled her head against the headrest to look at him. "Just get me home, and then you can go."

Her words stung, but he deserved it. When he'd seen her bleeding on the floor of the bathroom with that psychopath preparing to shoot her, all the complications had melted away. "I'm not going anywhere."

A hint of a smile danced at the back of her eyes, giving him hope that he hadn't screwed things up beyond redemption. He drove as quickly as he dared. Cali directed him to park in the street behind the building so they could access a back entrance.

She began to get out of the car, but he scooted around and picked her up again without waiting for an argument. Shrugging, she handed him a set of keys from her pocket. Luckily, it was obvious which keys opened the locks, so Cali was able to rest as he carried her up four flights of stairs.

When they reached the apartment, he hefted her against his shoulder to free up a hand to unlock the door. He shoved it open with his foot, carried her across the threshold, and stopped. There had to be a mistake.

The apartment was abandoned. The main room was empty, without even blinds on the windows. Old newspapers were scattered over the scratched parquet floors. He stepped forward, wondering what to do next, and heard the crunch of glass under his shoe.

"Be careful of the traps." Cali whispered in his ear.

Joe kicked aside the newspaper he'd stepped on, revealing shattered pieces of light bulb glass. Comprehension dawned. *This is the right place.*

He'd heard the outline of her life story, but it hadn't struck home before that moment. What had happened to cause her to surround herself with deception and traps? He couldn't imagine coming home and still not feeling safe. She needed a home—a beautiful place that made her feel warm and welcome and secure. He wanted to build that for her. "Where now?"

"Bedroom," she whispered, slurring the word in a way that got his adrenaline pumping in fear. "Be careful. Tripwire in the hall."

He spotted the slender wire and stepped high over it. No further surprises awaited him as he navigated the dark hallway, Cali balanced in his arms. There were only two doors, one of which opened into another empty room. He opened the closed door and, to his surprise, found a bathroom. At least that one showed signs of use, with clothes hanging along a rack on one wall and some toiletries stacked on narrow shelves.

The other room had to be what she meant, but he'd be damned if he'd tend her in that barren hellhole. Maybe he could rig a pressure bandage on her leg, buying time to get her to Vincent at the farmhouse.

"My kit is inside my room." Her words were clearer than before. "Just get me inside."

The bedroom was just as deserted as the main room. *She can't really live like this.* There were homeless people who created more of a sense of *home* than she did. He'd been in dive hotels that were more welcoming.

"Open the closet." Cali told him. "You'll have to put me down first."

He freed one hand again to yank on the sliding door. It refused to budge.

"I can lean against the wall." Cali braced her arms on his shoulders, lowering her good leg to the floor. She leaned against the wall, her skin pale enough to make the darkening bruises obscenely noticeable. Joe reluctantly let her go, fighting an irrational certainty that she was more vulnerable standing six inches away than she'd been in his arms.

He tried the closet door again using both hands. The heavy mass shifted slowly. It wasn't made of the standard cheap pressboard. From the coolness, he guessed it was metal. *A giant metal sheet made to look like a regular closet door.*

The closet was surprisingly large, a walk-in that could qualify as a second room. A squat, old-fashioned trunk rested against one wall under a neatly folded futon. The back wall held a minifridge and tiny microwave. A few clothes sat on the shelves above the bare hanging racks. Near the bottom of the wall was a long magnetic strip holding a dozen tiny knives.

"Thank you." Cali started to inch her way down the wall.

Joe caught her and helped her inside the miniature fortress, propping her up against the futon and trunk. He started looking around for something to use as a pressure bandage.

"I'm not going anywhere. I'll be fine here." Cali pulled a flat plastic case out of the trunk and opened it to reveal a comprehensive medical kit. She selected a needle and surgical thread with practiced ease.

Joe knelt, the implication of what he was seeing striking home. This was Cali's sanctuary. She couldn't trust the vulnerability of a bed, choosing instead to barricade herself in the closet while she slept. She'd never had a safe place she could trust. Not even a place to dream.

She'd mentioned stitching herself up, but Joe assumed it was more metaphorical than literal. She cut away the jeans, baring the long gash in her calf. Then she pulled out a syringe and injected herself. After a few minutes, her entire body relaxed, and Joe guessed it was a local anesthetic.

She tilted a small lamp to direct a circle of light directly on the wound and offered him a handful of antiseptic wipes. "Can you help me clean it up?"

Joe began to wash away the drying blood, exposing the wound. "How often have you done this?"

"Dad wasn't big on doctors. They cost money and won't keep their mouths shut about things like knife and bullet wounds." Cali's timid smile twisted into a rueful grin. "He figured small, nondrinking hands would be better than his."

"Sounds like parent of the year." Joe kept his voice light even as his inner white knight wanted to go crusading on the man's head. He avoided watching as she began to stitch up the bullet graze. Somehow, it looked much smaller than it had in the bar.

"He was all about teaching me useful life skills. At least it meant I could survive when he finally miscalculated on his tolerance for alcohol and heroin." Cali snipped off the final thread. "That should do it. Pass me a bandage from the kit, please."

Joe took the suture kit from Cali and covered her hand with his. "I'm sorry."

Cali blinked rapidly before shrugging and looking away. "Hey, whatever doesn't kill you only makes you stronger and all that."

"No. You don't have to pretend it was okay. It wasn't. And I wish I could take away all the horrible things that happened to you. Including what I've said to you." Joe brushed stray tendrils of hair away from her face. Her skin was always so cool under his touch. He could never mistake her for anyone else. Not again. He took her hand in his. "Can we start over? Detective Joe Cabrera."

CHAPTER THIRTY-NINE

His powerful hand, wrapped around hers, dominated Cali's vision. She wondered if she dared to believe him. Could she pretend any other option was possible, given how many boundaries had already fallen?

"Calista. I don't know what my last name was at birth." She drew in a shuddering breath, gulping courage to continue. "I've never let anyone see where I sleep before. Or even come inside my apartment. Not Hood or Harley. Not Speranza. No one."

"Then I'm even more honored. I'll keep you safe, Cali. I promise." He brought her hand to his mouth and kissed it.

Cali hadn't given it much thought in the past, but if asked, she would have said the hand kiss was a rather boring social convention only used by affected elitists. However, Joe's technique could have romantic converts sweeping the nation. His thumb kneaded her fingers, awakening and exciting the nerves under her skin. His kiss was perfectly placed with a hint of suction just beneath her knuckles. She'd never heard of that area being particularly sensitive, but somehow, the contact set up an erotic resonance between that tiny nook of flesh and the slick folds beginning to throb between her legs.

Her breath caught, and her neglected hand clawed against the floor as if trying to find a grip to avoid being swept away. Joe's lips left her hand, and he leaned forward, his free hand coming up to caress her hair. Cali closed her eyes, acutely aware of how his thumb still teased her fingers. Every graze echoed in her rapidly melting core. His other hand combed through her hair, running along the curve of her skull. When he found the tender place where her head had struck the floor, even the sharp jab of pain couldn't break the sensual spell tightening her skin.

"You've got one heck of a goose egg there, but I don't think you have a concussion." Joe's words didn't quite fit her expectations, and Cali couldn't understand them for a moment. She opened her eyes as he released her. His tan skin was flushed with ruddy undertones, and his fingers shook.

"I should take care of that. It'll be easier if I do it." He took the swatch of gauze from the medical kit and smoothed it over her calf, sealing it in place with surgical tape. Thanks to the anesthetic, his touch didn't hurt. His fingers lingered along the curve of her muscle, and for once in her life, Cali didn't want the intimate contact to stop.

His muscles bunched under his shirt and along his neck, evidence of the struggle to control himself. Despite his efforts to return to a nonchalant and professional pose, sweat glistened on his skin, and his breathing was shallow. He shifted in place, presumably to alleviate the uncomfortable pressure of arousal. His gaze kept darting toward the swell of her breasts or the long curve of her legs and then moving back to her face as if determined not to take advantage. He would be familiar with how the body could become physically excited after an adrenaline rush. If she chose to assume their actions so far were because of that phenomenon, he would never press it further. The night would end with a kiss on the hand and nothing more.

Except, she didn't want to dismiss those feelings. She'd cut herself off for too long, and for once, she was going to allow herself the luxury of not thinking about the future.

She reached out to him, letting her fingers drag down the front of his shirt. Micro tremors quivered in his muscles at her touch.

"Cali, I promised you that I wasn't going to push." His voice was hoarse, and his eyes were locked on hers.

"I know." She rolled her grip and slowly bunched the fabric of his shirt. The hem rose to reveal a taut strip of skin and a tantalizing promise of firm abs.

He covered her hand with his, stilling her movement. "Are you sure?"

"Yes." Licking her lips, she edged closer to him to make it easier to pull his shirt over his head.

"Then you're going to let me take care of you." He got his feet under him and slid his hands underneath her, lifting her easily.

Cali clung to him, uncertain if he meant to take her out of her sanctuary. Instead he shoved the medical gear to one side with his foot and then balanced her against him to free up a hand. He grabbed her futon and shook it out to cover the floor.

"I can help—" she began.

"You've been hurt. And this is our first time. So me taking care of you is not a negotiable point." Joe gently lowered the two of them, making sure Cali was settled where she could lean against the back wall while he knelt between her splayed legs.

Hardly daring to breathe, Cali held still, wondering what he would do next. His smoldering eyes pinned her in place.

"Hold still. I don't want you tearing your stitches." He yanked his shirt off in one smooth motion. Cali's mouth dried as she realized something had shifted in the last few seconds. The polished, professional cop was gone, and someone much more passionate and animalistic had taken his place. He looked at her as though he could devour her and have her loving every second of it. That was what lurked below the surface, creating the raw magnetism she'd first noticed about him.

"Are you okay?" He hesitated. "We can stop if you want."

Cali swallowed. "I don't want to stop, but I don't have much… any experience with… this."

Enlightenment dawned behind his eyes. He opened his mouth, and Cali made herself finish before he could interrupt. *No secrets.*

"I saw a lot of stuff. My dad used to bring women back to the apartment, and there was nowhere to hide from it on the street. I fought off guys, and I kept them away. I didn't want any part of what I'd seen, not until now." Her fingers pleated tiny folds in the futon.

"Then we'll take this slowly. Anything you don't like, just say so. Understood?" Joe hooked a finger into the hem of her T-shirt. "Let's start by getting these clothes off."

If she did that, he would see the scars on her back. *No. I won't let that get in the way.* Taking a deep breath, she straightened. "Help me turn around. There's something I need to show you first."

He shifted her easily, keeping her injured leg steady to avoid any further injury. After settling her in place again, with her back to him, his fingers trailed along her thighs.

Cali shivered, closing her eyes again. Before she could lose her nerve, she lifted her shirt over her head and pulled her hair over her shoulder. She heard Joe's gasp of shock. That reaction wasn't exactly a surprise. Her back resembled a topographical map, pale lines of scar tissue overlaying each other, a legacy of her father hitting her with whatever he could get his hands on.

"It's all dead. I can't make it do anything." She darkened her skin, knowing it would make the pale stripes stand out even more.

Joe's hands ran along her spine, the warmth of his skin soothing her. "I still can't get over watching you do that. Of all the things I've seen *lalassu* do, this seems the most fantastical."

"Really?" She twisted around to see if he was joking, but there was no mistaking the admiring burn in his eyes.

"Really." His mouth twisted in a lopsided smile. "I know you want to hide your scars, but to me, they only show your strength." He slid her shirt down her arms and tossed it to the side, leaning in to taste the skin of her shoulder with a gentle, probing kiss.

Cali sighed, leaning her head back and letting her hair fall over him.

"Besides, I'm much more interested in your front." His arms skimmed around her waist, slowly unbuttoning her jeans. Nibbling on her shoulder, he eased the jeans down carefully and slowly. Cali could have ripped them off, along with her stitches, and never noticed. Her body thrummed too loudly for caution.

Joe peeled her pants off, his warm hands sliding down her thighs and calves until she was free of the clinging denim. Then he eased her back until she was lying on the futon in her bra and panties. He moved to hover above her, watching as intently as if he intended to engrave that moment onto his memory.

"Where to begin?" He chuckled, looking around. "These will do."

Cali craned her neck as he grabbed some papers she'd been reviewing from the top of her tiny fridge. "For what?"

He rolled up a single sheet into a narrow tube and tapped it against his palm. "I'd prefer a feather or a rose, but a little improv can make for a memorable experience. Close your eyes."

Cali obeyed and was rewarded by the light rasp of paper against her skin. It began at the hairline of her temple and traced along her cheek, circling around her lips and then traveling down the line of her throat.

"Too many people rush through lovemaking. It's an acquired skill. And like any sensual experience, it's best to start light and allow yourself to enjoy all the layers." Joe's voice rumbled close to her ear as the paper began to coast along the outline of her bra, leaving a tingling wake of excitement and tightening her breasts.

His mouth closed over hers as the paper began a leisurely route along her ribs. He kept the kiss light and teasing, darting his tongue along the outline of her lips. The paper began to skim along the line of her thighs, and Cali gasped at the jolt of sensation running through her.

"A leg woman, I see." Joe pulled away from her lips, and she opened her eyes in protest. He knelt between her thighs, an amused and sensual grin on his lips. "Trust me on this. I'll be careful."

He tossed aside the paper and lifted up her uninjured leg, resting her calf on his shoulder. Then he used the back of his nail to trace a line from the hollow of her knee down the inside of her thigh.

Cali's eyes snapped shut as her back arched against the futon. Joe did it again, that time using two fingers to follow the sensitized nerves and letting his fingertips brush against the damp surface of her underwear. She moaned deep in her throat and blushed, embarrassed by the strength of her reaction and completely unwilling to stop.

He began to run his fingers along the responsive skin of her other thigh while his tongue began to explore the first. Working his way down, he alternated soft nibbling kisses with swipes from his tongue. Panting, she clutched at the futon as if it were an anchor as he came closer and closer to the junction.

"So beautiful," he murmured as he slipped his fingers past the fabric barrier. Cali bucked her hips, all too ready for his caresses. She might not have experience with a partner, but she had been willing to experiment on her own. The difference between the two gaped wider than the Grand Canyon. She'd expected to need to give directions, but Joe seemed to be able to read her like a master conductor directing an orchestra.

His fingers slipped inside her while his thumb rolled her sensitive nub of flesh. Her legs tightened around him, and he held tight to her injured leg, keeping it steady as his other hand coaxed her body tighter and tighter. Her hips bucked against him as he pushed her farther and higher than she'd ever explored on her own. A cry ripped out of her throat as she found the throbbing burst of release.

"That's my girl." His cheerful compliment could have been condescending if she'd been capable of irritation.

He slid her underwear off, slowly working the soaked fabric free. Still quivering from her orgasm, Cali wasn't sure what to expect next. When his lips touched her damp lower curls, she tensed in surprise.

Surprise quickly vanished in a wave of pleasure as he coaxed her body back up the swiftly collapsing crescendo. She grabbed at him instinctively, not wanting another empty clenching of her erotic muscles, and begged. "Inside. Please."

He bit his lip, clearly torn between conflicting desires to protect and to desire. She cupped his face in her hands, still shaking. "Please."

With that word, his primal male took charge, ripping open a condom packet and shucking his jeans. He caught her gaze and held it, requesting a final permission. Cali nodded and gasped at the first delightful stretch of her inner passage. He moved slowly but steadily, leaving a tiny pinch of pain that quickly dissolved into ecstasy.

She clung to him, kissing his salty damp skin as he drove relentlessly into her. His breath pooled and puffed on her skin in time with his thrusts. The time for conversation was gone, and she dug her nails into his scalp and shoulder, cradling him close.

New tension built from their combined friction, and she wasn't sure whether his bellow followed or preceded her own throaty cries, but it didn't matter. He propelled her into a shattering series of explosions rippling through her body, heart, and soul, leaving her boneless and satiated.

She was still floating on the trembling aftermath as he kissed her tenderly, offering gratitude and appreciation for their mutual enjoyment. He whispered, "You okay? We didn't rip anything?"

Cali shook her head, not ready for words to tug her back to reality.

She didn't care if she was only feeling the calm of the shoe flying in the air before it hit the ground. *Throw the damn shoes away into a bottomless pit.* The moment held no dangers, no threats, and no disappointment. It was a spun-sugar cocoon of perfection and connection, and she intended to make sure it lasted as long as possible.

Joe twisted his head to check the bandage on her calf before claiming her lips for a slow afterglow kiss. Their bodies cooled as they lay entwined, trading kisses and lingering caresses. Joe chuckled. "I can't wait to try that again on my bed. You're going to be spectacular against my red silk sheets."

Niggling doubt sent the first cracks through her fragile contentment. The idea of sleeping somewhere other than her little sanctuary brought a flush of panic to the surface. Cali drew Joe closer, hiding her face against his shoulder to breathe in his scent. She felt safe with him for the moment, but how long could it possibly last? *I won't let my fears get the better of me.*

"You're thinking awfully loudly." Joe kissed the hollow of her neck before pulling back to study her. "Not having any regrets, are you?"

The hint of genuine fear in his words prompted her to find her voice. "No. No regrets. That was… definitely worth the wait."

The twinkle returned to his eyes, her very own North Star to guide her. A repeating pulse of vibration quivered against her leg. "I think your pants are trying to get your attention."

Joe grinned as he withdrew. The cool air rushing over her skin reminded Cali that no matter how much they'd enjoyed that moment, the world still waited to rain down on them. Maybe, just maybe, there was a chance for happiness to stick around. She curled up her legs, wincing as she realized that the anesthetic had worn off from her calf.

Joe pulled out his phone, and his face locked into an expression of apprehension. "Cabrera here." He listened briefly, his eyes closing. "Damn it, get out of there however you can. Head south out of the city. I'll send you the address where to go."

Cali stayed silent as he hung up and began grimly searching for his clothes. "What's happened?"

"Dalhard's escapees attacked the police precincts—all of them across the entire city. He's taking the cops hostage where he isn't shooting them. We need to leave as quickly as we can."

Joe's grim assessment destroyed whatever lingering laziness remained. *Mr. Dalhard's planning to turn the officers with his persuasive powers. With them and the gangs, he'll have an army, armed and ready for anything.*

All In

CHAPTER FORTY

Joe held Cali's hand tightly as they hurried down to the street, half dreading walking out into riots and anarchy. Instead, it looked like a normal day with people going about their business as usual. He scanned the street, trying to find some sign of impending disaster.

"Joe, you're attracting attention," Cali said softly from behind him. "We can't help them if we get caught."

He made himself slow down his movements. "I don't understand."

"Did your contact say that Mr. Dalhard was at your police station himself?"

Joe sucked in a breath of gasoline-tainted air as the implication hit him. If Dalhard was at the station, then Salazar could be zombified. They couldn't trust him or his account until they were sure that Dalhard hadn't tampered with his mind.

Spotting an SUV with tinted windows cruising down the street toward them, Joe hurried the two of them into the doorway of another tenement. That car wasn't local, and he was willing to bet it held men with weapons.

His heartbeat rose steadily as they waited for the SUV to pass. If it was Dalhard's people, and they identified him or Cali, the bullets would fly. Joe's free hand rested on her shoulder, ready to pull her into the shelter of his body at the first pop of gunfire.

"They're moving on," Cali said softly. Joe glanced down to see her holding a small pocket mirror at waist level, using the reflection to track the vehicle.

"We need to get out of the city. Guaranteed, we're both on the list."

Joe wanted to call his mother and warn her but knew better than to draw attention to her.

Cali nodded, tightening her grip on his hand. He should have been concentrating on what was going on, but he couldn't stop a flush of smug pleasure at how she no longer tensed with fear at his touch. Being able to return a portion of the tactile pleasure that should have been her birthright made him feel like a genuine hero.

They made their way to Joe's car. Drying brown stains marked the passenger side, reminding him of how desperate he'd been only a few hours earlier. Cali pulled her hand out of his. "Give me the keys."

"I'm fine to drive." He'd done all the extra training in offensive driving techniques. If it came to needing to evade pursuit, he was the best qualified.

"You should sit in the back." Cali's gaze flicked around the street. She was clearly nervous at speaking out in the open. "No one is reacting to what's happened."

"I'm not following." Swallowing his impatience, he waited to hear what she had to say.

"The takeover of the police should be lighting up social media like a twenty-four-hour parking lot. Instead, no one seems to be aware of it except us." Cali pulled out her phone. "Mr. Dalhard is suppressing the information."

"He probably doesn't want to start a panic. Or trigger a federal reprisal." It made strategic sense.

"Which means he'll probably have roadblocks up to keep people from leaving. He'll have a pretext to keep people in their homes." Cali tapped rapidly on the screen. "Like rumors of a mass shooting and terror attack." She held out the phone with the breaking story flashing on screen.

Shit. She was right. Joe popped the trunk and handed over the keys. He pulled out the heavy wool blanket that he kept for winter emergencies and got into the back seat. Maybe they'd be lucky and manage to get out before Dalhard could set up a secure perimeter. If they were horribly unlucky, then Dalhard's people would be looking for him and Cali specifically. If he stayed out of sight, and Cali shifted into some new persona, they should be able to get through the barricade. If their luck was disastrous, the roadblocks would be airtight, and they'd have to fight their way past them.

The engine grumbled as he gave Cali the directions to get out of the city and head toward the Harrises' farmhouse. Joe searched online and found dozens of stories about the fictitious terror attack that said shots had been fired at different locations and the city was on lockdown. The same reassuring message kept repeating: the police were handling it, and citizens should remain where they were to keep out of harm's way. He had to admire the cleverness. If the citizens saw men running around with guns, regardless of whether they were gang members or cops, it would fit into the lie.

"Head down," Cali hissed.

Without pause, Joe shut down the phone and dropped himself into the long foot well between the driver and passenger seats, draping the blanket over him. It was not a comfortable fit. His knees were wedged into his chest, and the blanket blocked his airflow.

The car began to slow, and Joe tried to keep his breathing even and his body relaxed. They came to a stop, and he could hear voices talking to each other outside the car. Cool air spilled into the interior as Cali rolled down the windows.

"License, please," a bored female voice asked.

"What's going on?" Cali replied, her voice breathy and higher pitched than normal.

Joe could almost hear the nonexistent gum cracking, and he was once again impressed at Cali's ability to take on a persona.

"With the attack, we're looking for some fugitives." The woman had an official-sounding voice. "Have you seen any of these individuals?"

"No, ma'am." Cali sounded properly awed by the woman.

"If you do, it's critical to contact us immediately. We're recommending people remain in town for their own safety. You can turn your car around here."

"I have to check on my mother. She's old and recovering from surgery. She needs someone to take care of her." The mixture of innocence and uncertainty in Cali's voice made her sound young and vulnerable—exactly like a law-abiding citizen caught between official instructions and personal obligations.

"I'm going to have to check on that. What's the number?"

Cali rattled off a set of digits, and Joe repressed a curse. He was wedged too tightly between the seats to be able to draw his gun easily, and if he tried, he'd only alert the officer outside. He tensed, preparing to muscle his way through if necessary.

"Hello, ma'am, this is Officer Leman. I have your daughter, Adele, here… yes, ma'am, I'm afraid there's a bit of a situation, and we're not advising people to leave the city. Would it be possible for her to come and see you tomorrow morning? I see… that does sound uncomfortable… yes, I understand. I'll allow her through, but she'll have to remain with you until the situation is resolved. Thank you, ma'am." The officer paused. "Go ahead, but you'll need to stay with your mother, understood?"

"Yes, ma'am. Thank you." Cali eased the car forward, making several sharp turns, suggesting that some kind of physical barrier had been set up to prevent cars from crashing through the roadblock.

After a few minutes, she told him it was safe to get up. Joe threw back the blanket and clawed his way back up to a seated position, his back and legs screaming protest at him. "How the hell did that work?"

"Hood. We have a system set up. He's an incredible mimic." A pleased smile hovered at the corner of her mouth. "First rule for me, always have an escape plan no matter how unlikely the circumstance."

"I'd say you were paranoid, but under the circumstances, I'll stick with *well done*." Joe peered backward out of the rear window. "I'm surprised they let us through."

"I saw four cars ahead of us. One went through, and the other three turned back. So I knew there was a chance. Most people want to help someone who's right in front of them even if it means bending the rules." Cali's smile disappeared. "He's put out pictures of me, Boomerang, and Colleen. You too."

"I'm a terrorist now? I resent that." Joe checked his phone and was relieved to see it had service again.

"What are you going to do about your contact?" Cali asked, keeping her eyes on the deserted road.

"We'll meet up with him. When we get to the Harrises', Michael should be able to tell us if Dalhard got to Salazar." Joe rubbed at his eyes. If Salazar really had taken his warnings to heart and kept away from Dalhard, then his story would make sense. A rookie with no known connection to Joe might have been overlooked. But if anyone figured out they'd been working together, then Salazar would be the perfect trap. "Pull over, and we'll switch drivers."

"You could just tell me where we're going." Cali's dry observation didn't stop her from slowing the car and rolling onto the shoulder of the highway.

"It soothes my male dignity if I drive," he teased, needing to lighten the mood.

As he climbed into the driver's seat, his phone rang. Salazar. Joe tensed as he answered.

"I made it out. Now where do I go?" The rookie sounded much less panicked than he had in his earlier call. If he wasn't a zombie and he survived Dalhard's takeover, Joe predicted a fine career ahead for the young man. He was coping better with the surprises than Joe had.

"Head along Highway 95. We'll meet you at the gas station where it intersects with the 278. Got it?" Joe closed his eyes, hoping he was making the right call. Cali squeezed his hand.

"What do we do then?" Salazar asked.

"Then we're going to plan to take our city back."

Holding the crystal goblet to the window, Dalhard savored the ruby glow of his Merlot after a hard day of mental work. The view was only slightly spoiled by the crimson splotches staining the Italian tiles and hand-woven wool rug. He'd always admired Benjamin's taste in wine and décor, which was why Dalhard had chosen the man's penthouse apartment. He took a sip of the wine, rolling the velvety flavor on his tongue to enjoy the mature subtleties.

He could have used his abilities to persuade Benjamin to surrender the townhouse or at least not put up a fight when Dalhard arrived with an escort of armed police officers and gang leaders. Instead, Dalhard had decided to use him as a test, to see if any of his former social circle would embrace the new ways of the world. He'd hoped that Benjamin might be corrupt enough. The man had five different mistresses as well as a frigid wife who lived overseas. His companies owned half the slums in major cities across North America and turned a healthy profit by ignoring building codes, maintenance, and any complaints.

What a shame the man had attempted to bully and threaten rather than accept his place. Dalhard leaned back in his chair, pleasantly recalling the shock and despair on Benjamin's face when he finally understood the truth. His money and social position meant nothing, and he held no true power.

The flickering glow of flame warmed the darkening cityscape below, making Dalhard feel rather like a medieval king overlooking a bonfire. His people had secured the downtown core of Perdition with barely any effort, rolling over ad-hoc resistance with crushing efficiency. He now controlled the police, the power grid, the local media, the surveillance cameras, everything. The commoners huddled in their homes, waiting for his leadership. He'd even graciously allowed those caught at work to evacuate to their homes. With them gone, the borders of his little kingdom were sealed tight, with loyal supporters manning concrete barriers. *An excellent test run.* His eyes turned greedily to the distant glow of New York City.

He would have airlines, naval yards, international media, and anything else he needed to go global. No one could ever dare to threaten him again. Unless Karan proved to have another ace up his sleeve or the Harrises decided to launch a suicidal heroic counterattack.

That thought spoiled his enjoyment of the moment. *Surely Danielle has taken her people and run rather than face me again.* The stark horror on her face as he'd stabbed the blade into her lover's gut still made Dalhard smile. *No, they've been neutralized. But I need to know what other* lalassu *might be lurking out there.*

Calista, such a disappointment. She'd failed to pass the list to him, and her endless nattering about trusting the system and due process had long since ceased to entertain. Her success as a thief was unquestioned, so she had to be holding the list herself. *I need to give her a reason to give it to me.* She was softhearted, no question. She would likely surrender it rather than see others hurt. And once she was within his grasp, he could erase the inconvenient conscience lingering beneath her loyalty. She would take her place at his side once more.

Karan was the true threat. *I would never have guessed that my secretary harbored such deep ambitions.* That had been a rare and unique mistake in character judgment. The man had no ties to the community, no loved ones to leverage, and skill at vanishing like a ghost. *I need a trap to lure him out.*

"Boss. We got a problem." Boom-Boom knocked awkwardly on a wall, looking ill at ease in such luxurious surroundings.

Exhaling in long-winded frustration, Dalhard put down his wine and gestured for his former prison mate to continue.

Boom-Boom crossed the room and fumbled with the television controls. A press conference filled the screen. Dalhard recognized Drew Fangato, the recently appointed head of the so-called Bureau of Special Investigations.

"—want to reassure the American people that there is no immediate danger from these gifted individuals. We are undertaking an extensive registration process to avoid surprises for local and federal law enforcement. These people were only threats so long as they could hide in the darkness. Once we shine the light of public awareness on them, they will quickly find themselves neutralized." With his curly dark hair and earnest expression, Fangato looked more like a Boy Scout than a public official.

Dalhard smiled. Special Investigations was selling a comforting lie. Knowing about the *lalassu* and being able to deal with them were two quite different propositions.

"With the help of the National Guard, we have restored order to our cities. In a few cases, we have temporarily instituted a curfew, but this is a limited measure and not a cause for concern." Fangato showed no sign of self-consciousness in using euphemisms for martial law. Dalhard's respect for the man's political skills rose. "I know you have questions about the rumored terror attack in Perdition, outside New York, and Special Investigations is committed to investigating the reports of a mass lockdown by the local police force. At this point, we do not have sufficient information to make a statement, and I would ask the press to respect that rather than speculate."

"Is that the problem you were worried about?" Dalhard turned his attention back to Boom-Boom.

"It means word got out." Boom-Boom glared at the screen, which had switched back to several men in suits earnestly arguing with each other about what should be done about the menace of gifted individuals. Locked up for more than twenty years, Boom-Boom had missed the explosion of the Internet and social media. He had no idea how many routes there were for rumors to fly.

"The situation is under control." Dalhard sipped his wine again. The conversation had soured the flavor.

"But if they call in the damn army—" Boom-Boom abruptly stopped talking when Dalhard allowed his irritation to show.

"They can know exactly what we have done and what we plan to do, and it would make no difference." Dalhard enunciated each word with threatening precision. "Go and enjoy your well-earned break. Tomorrow, the next phase begins."

CHAPTER FORTY-ONE

This was a bad idea. Cali folded her hands behind her back to keep from fidgeting and revealing her nerves. Joe stood beside her while Salazar waited by their cars. He wasn't showing any signs of Mr. Dalhard's influence, but they still needed to have Michael check out the rookie's mind. Assuming they ever got in the door.

"Why in hell would you bring her to our house?" Dani glared at Cali with a fervor people usually reserved for traitors and door-to-door salesmen. Despite the thick cast over her leg, she managed to project an impressive level of threat. Cali remembered seeing the woman's picture in Mr. Dalhard's office and thought Dani was intriguingly attractive with her dark hair and olive skin, but the picture hadn't captured the crackling energy animating every move. No wonder Mr. Dalhard desperately wanted to claim her.

"It's not like we have a lot of choice here. The city is overrun." Joe wasn't showing any sign of doubt. He folded his arms over his chest and glared at Dani. "There isn't time for this bullshit. We need to figure out what to do next."

"We're not some kind of damned refugee headquarters. And *she* is only coming in over my dead and cooling body." Wood creaked around Dani's grip on the doorframe.

Good call, Joe. Take me to people with a personal grudge against the man I work for. Used to work for. Cali sought out the comfort of Joe's grasp, entwining her chilled fingers with his. Movement behind Dani caught Cali's attention. Dressed in a loose robe with a pattern of bright yellow stars, an older woman with grey-streaked dark hair and milky eyes raised her head to stare directly at the two intruders. Cali recognized Virginia from the Sandy Hook break-in. *Right, blind but psychic.*

"Events are moving swiftly, changing too quickly to see." The older woman picked up a tablet from the countertop without fumbling and used the touch screen to pull up a newsfeed. Cali ignored it. They'd caught Fangato's announcement en route.

"Thanks for the fortune-cookie update." Dani snorted and glared at Cali. "Are you learning impaired? I said get going."

Salazar stepped forward. "With respect, ma'am, I think Detective Cabrera is right. We all need to work together against this André Dalhard."

Cali was impressed at his courage. Salazar had accepted Joe's briefings about the existence of the *lalassu* surprisingly well. He'd even accepted the necessity of being scanned, although he insisted he'd avoided contact with Mr. Dalhard.

"Do I look like someone who gives a shit about your opinion?" Dani's snarls were sounding less like someone protecting their family and more like someone trying not to show how frightened she was. Cali could see little tremors in the other woman's hands, a sign that she was nowhere near as confident as she wanted to appear.

"Dani, manners." The older woman navigated smoothly around the kitchen island, moving closer to the door. "Let them in."

"Thanks, Virginia." Joe pitched his voice to carry past Dani, who showed no sign of moving.

"Hell no," Dani growled.

Cali tried to calculate a plan, but there were too many unknown factors and too much potential for disaster. *Dani carries herself like someone practiced in using brute force to overcome every obstacle, which should give me a chance if I use her own strength against her.*

"Michael will want to know what they have to say." Virginia patted Dani's arm, her blind eyes focused on Cali. "And they need his help."

"Michael needs to rest, Mother." The venom in Dani's voice suggested this was more than a recent argument.

Cali found it hard to believe the squabbling bunch could possibly be leaders in the *lalassu* community or have evaded Mr. Dalhard for so long. *There must be something more.* She checked on Salazar and was dismayed to see his hand firmly attached to his weapon. At least it was still in its holster, but they were running out of nerves. Sooner or later, someone was going to make a mistake and blow this powder keg.

"None of us can go up against Dalhard alone, Dani. We need to work together or he'll take us apart like last time," Joe said. Cali could feel the tension in his arm building through their clasped hands.

"We'll get taken apart even faster with his spy telling him everything," Dani said.

"She's not his spy," Virginia clucked her tongue. "Look at her, Dani. She's lost right now. And we shouldn't talk about it on the porch while flies get into the house. Let them in."

Dani reluctantly stepped back, allowing Cali and Joe inside the kitchen. Virginia smiled, her occluded eyes meeting Cali's. "You're a quiet one, aren't you, Cali? And you, Mr. Salazar, it's always a pleasure to meet a fine young man. Would you mind if I called you Robbie as your mother does?"

Cali's mouth dried. She kept forgetting that Virginia wasn't limited by her handicap. Swallowing, she tried to come up with a nonchalant response. "Thank you for speaking to us."

Salazar didn't even manage that dignity, though he did snap his jaw shut after a few moments of gaping. "That would be fine, ma'am."

"My pleasure, dear. The cookies will be ready in a few minutes." Virginia picked up a metal spatula from the counter and took it over to the sink. She pulled a barbecue fork out of a drawer and put it down where the spatula had been. "This will be better. I'll need the spatula later."

"Stop showing off, Mother." Dani braced her arms on her hips, leaning against the wall. Virginia shook her head, a faint smile on her face.

"Why don't you take a turn? Or is your reputation only so much hot air?" Cali kept her voice bored and with a hint of disbelief. Meanwhile, her mind was calculating and noting everything, trying to fit it into place in case they needed a quick exit. Virginia's psychic powers would make surprise difficult, but Vincent had claimed they were only short range. If Cali and Joe could move quickly enough, then they should be able to get past her.

Dani reached back and grabbed the barbecue fork. Holding it in one hand, she twisted it into metal origami. "Showed you mine."

"Holy shit," Salazar gasped.

"Wait for it." Joe leaned back against the counter.

Cali shifted into Boomerang's form. "I trust it is self-explanatory."

"Told you." Joe nudged his gaping partner, clearly entertained.

"A Protean. I don't believe we've seen one in the records for a hundred years." Virginia sounded pleased. Dani folded her arms and glared at them.

Protean? Is that the word for what I am? Her mother hadn't stuck around long enough to share family lore, and if her father knew, he hadn't bothered to pass it on. Cali shoved aside her questions to focus on the issue at hand. "Mr. Dalhard is going to strike out at you. Even if you evade him, Special Investigations is acting far too coordinated for my taste. We can't afford to be distracted, and we need all the information we can get."

The belligerence faded from Dani's mouth, replaced by uncertainty. "Things are even bigger than you realize. My connection to the Goddess is supposed to give us a heads-up about things like this. We should have had a chance to prevent it. But the messages were vague, talking about big changes and stepping into the light."

"That's frustratingly cryptic." Joe leaned on the counter. Virginia pulled out a tray of fresh chocolate chip cookies from the oven.

"It gets worse." Dani's lips twitched in a rueful smile. "Right after Dalhard ambushed us, I got a visitation. The Goddess told me we were on the cusp of a new age and that the days of hiding were done. She didn't help us to stop this because she wanted it to happen."

The timer on the stove dinged into the silence. No one quite seemed to know what to say. Except perhaps Virginia, who offered up a plate to the stunned Salazar. "Cookies?"

The list of names kept scrolling, seeming endless. Joe produced Fuentes's portion of the list, and Cali put it together with the other portions. The database was far more extensive than she'd guessed. That was the bad news.

The good news was that Salazar wasn't hiding any hooks from Mr. Dalhard's powers. The rookie snored on the sofa, worn out from trying to reorganize his understanding of the world.

Virginia appeared with sandwiches. "At least it's not all of us." After several hours of reviewing the data, they were used to her frequent caloric offerings. She put a plate beside the sleeping Salazar. Virginia's adoption of the rookie was one of the few bright spots from the last few hours.

"What do you mean?" Michael asked. Cali liked Joe's friend with his shy and unassuming manner. Of course, his girlfriend, Dani, was aggressive enough for the pair of them.

"The list. There aren't enough names. There are about five thousand people on it, and that's only a fraction of us." Virginia moved unerringly through the room, picking up dirty dishes. Vincent got up and began to help, but she encouraged him to go back and sit down. He'd been avoiding Cali since she'd arrived, barely even acknowledging her existence.

"Are you saying you have a bigger list than this one?" Cali asked. If that was true, she'd need to do some rapid recalculating.

"Oh, nothing like that. It's more like a phone tree. I can send out an alert to a number of people who have their own lists of contacts, and so on and so forth." Virginia balanced a plastic tumbler on top of crumb-filled plates. "Sometimes, we don't even know who we're contacting. We just leave messages on dead drops. It's not as quick, but it's safer for avoiding discovery. A full list would be more efficient for our efforts."

Salazar's snores suddenly ceased. He sat up, rubbing his eyes. When he saw everyone's eyes on him, he pretended to take a great interest in his sandwich. Virginia patted him on the head again as she headed back to the kitchen with the dirty dishes.

"It's too dangerous to leave in the government's hands." Joe's fingers squeezed Cali's reassuringly.

"You really think that taking the list away from Special Investigations will stop them from persecuting us?" Dani rolled her eyes.

"It will stop them from doing it in a methodical and efficient manner. If they have to search to find *lalassu*, they will move slower, and you'll have a chance to gain public acceptance." Cali delivered her answer in the clipped tones of a disappointed schoolteacher and selfishly enjoyed watching the other woman bristle. If Dani wanted to belittle someone's opinions and experience, she'd picked the wrong target.

"Eric, you think you can help us to figure out the places Special Investigations set up shop—where they might have the list?" Joe asked, clearly changing the topic.

Cali fingered her empty mug and decided it might be prudent for her temper and alertness if she procured a fresh cup of coffee. As Dani and Michael joined Eric and Joe at the computer, she beat a strategic retreat.

Virginia wasn't in the kitchen, but Cali quickly found the coffeepot and began pouring a fresh cup.

"The coffee here sucks." The male voice startled her enough that only quick reflexes saved the carafe from smashing on the floor. Cali spun around to see Vincent in the doorway, his hands raised in the universal signal of nonthreatening intentions.

"Beats the alternative." She finished pouring herself a cup and offered him the pot.

"Here." Vincent stood up and grabbed a heavy, sky-blue covered dish from a corner cupboard. "If you put enough sugar in it, you can almost believe it's not made of battery acid."

Cali took his advice, stirring in three spoonfuls of sugar. *Sugar is good. Sugar will keep me awake too.* Vincent hovered nearby, fidgeting with the silverware. Paranoia broke through Cali's exhaustion. Had he decided she was an enemy?

"You said you worked for André Dalhard." Vincent glanced over his shoulder at the dark hall.

Checking for witnesses? Adrenaline and exhaustion warred for control of her thick tongue, so Cali settled for a nod. She took a firmer grip on her mug, ready to dash the hot liquid into Vincent's face if he struck.

Vincent stayed silent, all of his attention on the fork he kept spinning in his fingers. Cali stepped back to where the cabinets would interfere if he threw it at her.

Finally, he broke the silence. "How long?"

"I've known him for eleven years. Twelve in October." Cali's chin lifted defiantly. She didn't care if it wasn't prudent to share her past. She'd rather be condemned for who she truly was than for a lie.

Vincent still wouldn't look at her, only at the fork. "He took over your mind?"

"No. He's never used his powers on me." Cali wondered if it was safe to take a sip from her mug or if Vincent would use the distraction to attack.

He finally lifted his eyes, and Cali took another step back at the anguish they held. He put down the fork. "How can you be sure?"

"He said he valued my mind as it was and didn't want to risk altering it." She decided to trust her luck and take a sip, desperate for the artificial boost to her reflexes and thoughts. "He didn't need to do anything to me to ensure my loyalty. He saved me."

"He said he would save us too." Vincent turned away, staring at the uneven darkness outside. "He offered us more money than we'd ever seen and a place to belong. I was willing to throw everything away for the chance."

Cali couldn't think of anything to say to that.

"I want to blame him. But I can't. It wasn't all him twisting my mind." He faced her again, weariness tugging down the corners of his mouth and eyes. "They don't know how much I still want to go back."

"He saved me," Cali repeated softly. "He got me off the street, gave me choices I never thought I'd have. I'd have done anything for him. Somewhere, something changed."

"He asked me and my brother to kill a man. Part of an audition before offering us a job." Vincent shared. "I don't think he changed all that much."

Cali wanted to deny it, a child's cry of protest. "Maybe not. Maybe he always hid behind a mask, and what we're seeing now is the truth. Or maybe he was once a good man and temptation lured him down the easy road, slipping down the slope into becoming a monster. I don't know if it matters in the end."

"Because monsters need to be stopped." Vincent raised his mug as if offering a toast.

"No. Because whatever his intentions were, what he's doing is dangerous and wrong. Calling him a monster denies the dark possibilities inside all of us." Cali clutched the mug, the heat from the coffee seeping into her fingers.

"I'm okay being a monster. Monsters can be useful. And at least I'm better looking than Frankenstein."

Cali laughed harder than the joke deserved. The break in tension left her giddy. "Thanks. I needed that."

"It's what I do." He shrugged, but Cali saw the glimpse of pleasure before he tried to hide it. "Come on. Time for the next round."

Chapter Forty-Two

Joe watched as Cali pointed out potential flaws with the different entrances in the building that they suspected Special Investigations was using as its headquarters in Perdition. He'd always assumed movies were exaggerating when thieves entered through the ventilation units or elevator shafts, but Cali seemed to consider it no more unusual than walking through the front door.

"We need to keep our team surgical." Cali ran her fingers along the rough floor-plan sketch they'd attached to the wall, braving Virginia's irritation at thumbtack holes in her wallpaper. "Having more people also increases our risk of discovery. And they all need to be mobile."

The last sentence was a shot at Dani, who had been vocal about not being left behind despite her broken kneecap. Joe had no doubt she could still fight, but she no longer moved with supernatural speed. She was barely faster than Joe.

Dani's hands tightened into fists, but her father, Walter, rolled up to her in his wheelchair and put his hand on her knee. "Don't risk your recovery on this. If this doesn't work, we're going to need you to be at your best later, particularly if the Goddess has turned against us."

Joe suppressed his reflex response of assuming anyone claiming a direct connection to a god was delusional. The Harris family was unsettled enough by Dani's message. If their Goddess had chosen not to stop Special Investigations from coming into existence, then they couldn't count on her to help them in the conflict with Dalhard.

"Actually, I don't think she's turned against us." Eric's interruption surprised them all into frozen silence. He'd been drowsing in the corner beside Salazar as the debate raged on. "Dani, she said it was time to step into the light, right?"

Dani nodded, letting her brother continue.

"Maybe it's a time of transition, like the Black Plague or the collapse of the British Empire. Maybe the *lalassu* need to be in the open for the next stage of progress to happen." Eric looked out the window to where dawn light painted the first pale streaks of color across the sky. "Maybe she can see something we can't."

"That's a lot to take on faith." Dani rolled her shoulders as if stretching under a burden.

"Isn't that what people are supposed to do with their gods—have faith?" Eric held his sister's gaze. She looked down, biting her lip.

"I'm more of the get-up-and-fix-it school than someone who waits for *deus ex machina.*" Cali straightened, earning a surprised smile of approval from Dani. "However, it's already morning, and we're all exhausted. We need to catch a few hours of sleep if we want to have a chance."

"Good idea. We're a little short on beds right now, but I'm sure we can find something." Walter took charge, shepherding his offspring out.

Joe went over to Cali and took her in his arms as he'd been wanting to do throughout the night. She rested her head against his shoulder, her warm breath tickling the base of his throat. He held her tightly, reassuring himself that she was still all right. "How are you holding up? Any pain?"

"I'm running on coffee fumes and stubbornness. But otherwise, no problems, if that's what you're asking." Her cheek rounded in a smile, pushing into his shoulder. "I wish we could reason with Mr. Dalhard."

"You don't have to go. You could stay here." Even if it made things riskier, if he could spare her that trauma, he would. She shouldn't have to fight against the man she still probably saw as her savior.

"I've already stepped over that line, Joe. You all need me and my skills if this is going to be successful. Besides, I'm going into Special Investigations, not after Mr. Dalhard. You're the one who has to confront him." Her arms tightened around his waist as if she wanted to protect him too.

"Don't worry. I'll keep it hands-off. This body is only for you now." He grinned as she began to laugh against his neck, her whole body rumbling with amusement.

"The female population of New York will go into mourning at the loss." She lifted her head to brush her lips against the line of his jaw, igniting an instant hard-on and desire to drag her off to the nearest private flat surface.

"I'm reformed, baby. Officially off the circuit." He captured her mouth with his, backing her up until they hit the wall. Letting her go, he tucked his hands into his back pockets, not wanting her to feel trapped.

From the way she still clung to him, opening her mouth to deepen the kiss, his efforts were appreciated. He'd never thought that kissing without using his hands could be so erotically charged. Her fingers roamed freely over his body, tracing his chest and shoulders before sliding down his sides and cupping his butt. He ground his hips against her, growling in appreciation as he tilted his head to one side to nibble at her jawline, working his way to her ears. "Keep it up, and you're going to push my control to its limits."

"Then maybe I'll have to find a way to keep you in your place," she whispered against his ear. "There must be a set of handcuffs around here somewhere."

"Top drawer of the desk in the back."

Vincent's dry commentary broke them apart as if magnetically repelled. Flushed with arousal and embarrassed, Joe tried to discover if it was possible to kill someone with a glare.

The other man shrugged, unmoved. "I'd say get a room, but almost everyone in this house has superhearing. We're all gonna know anyway. The dining room table is pretty sturdy. Have fun."

Joe huffed a lungful of air at the ceiling as Vincent left.

"At least he didn't offer us our choice of options. Padded, gold-plated, maybe an animal print?" Cali planted one final short kiss in punctuation.

"Don't tempt him to come back." Joe reluctantly stepped back. "Let's find a place to crash."

"Together?" Cali asked, tucking a blond strand behind her ear.

"Trust me, I'm not into exhibitionism. But take pity on my masculine nerves and let me hold you while we sleep. Let me know that for now, you're safe and we're together." He lifted her hand to his lips and gave it a lingering kiss.

"Let me just shut this down. No sense wasting power." She leaned over the laptop, giving Joe a spectacular view of a first-class behind. Perfectly curved for a satisfying double handful.

"All done." She closed the computer and glanced back over her shoulder, her mischievous smile suggesting her position hadn't been entirely accidental. Joe recaptured her hand and led her in search of a little privacy. *Hopefully with superior soundproofing.*

"Ready?" Cali asked Vincent as they arrived. If their information was accurate, the building housed both Right Hand Man and the Bureau of Special Investigations.

"If I said no, would it make the slightest bit of difference?" Vincent eyed the glittering façade of glass and concrete.

"Not really. No." Cali kept her expression poker smooth.

"Then I'm ready." Vincent grinned but still hesitated, his hand on the door. "You know, the last time I walked into this building, I ended up running away with a bullet in my leg."

"Great story. Maybe share it another time when we're not breaking in to a secure government facility?" Cali motioned for him to get moving.

"I don't understand why Joe likes you. He must be into pushy women," Vincent grumbled, but they got through the door. "I like a nice docile girl myself, someone who will appreciate my many manly virtues."

Cali smiled. "Is there ever a point when you stop cracking jokes?"

"If I do, start running." All traces of humor vanished from Vincent's face. Cali bit her lip, wishing she could call the comment back. She knew what he'd been through at Mr. Dalhard's hands, and she shouldn't have made a reference.

The two of them made their silent way to the sixth floor, just below where Special Investigations should be. That level was completely abandoned—the previous tenants had relocated a year earlier, and no one had moved in since. Cali easily found and disabled the surveillance cameras still dotting the ceiling, setting them to endlessly repeat a single frame of their previous recording. "Gotcha. All of the cables lead upstairs. This is definitely the place."

"I'll send a letter to Congress. My tax money should buy top-quality stuff, not this shit." Vincent stripped off his suit jacket and pants and tucked them into a plastic bag. Cali did the same. The ducts would be choked with dust, and they needed to appear presentable on the other side. Vincent lifted Cali to the ceiling vents. Building blueprints showed that they connected to the floor vents in the level above. In theory, going through them would be simple.

In practice, the vents were cold, dark, and full of grainy dust and other litter. Not to mention cramped. Cali wasn't sure if her partner's muscular frame would fit through, but he proved adept at shimmying and scraping his way through with a minimum of noise. Her injured leg ached, but she was used to ignoring pain, and she kept moving.

They didn't have far to go. After a few minutes, Cali found their exit point. They'd hoped the office would be unoccupied, and luck was on their side. She carefully popped out the ventilation grate and slid it to the side before crawling out of the vents. Vincent followed, and they shook the dust out of their hair.

"I can't believe that worked." Vincent scrubbed his fingers through his hair, dislodging a halo of dust.

"Never underestimate institutional oversight." Cali pinched the front of her shirt to shake loose her own accumulated load of debris.

"Nice legs, by the way." Vincent pulled out his clothes from the plastic bag.

"Not the time." Cali slid on her pants and jacket as quickly as possible. She'd keep her own face for this, not wanting to be distracted by the effort of holding a shift.

"Thought if I said it downstairs it might be awkward. But a deserved compliment shouldn't be held back." He shrugged, a wicked gleam in his eyes.

Cali rolled her eyes. How someone could manage such innocent lechery was beyond her. Replacing the grate in the floor, she quickly sobered. They needed to act as if they belonged. She tucked her hair back into a boring professional bun and opened the office door, striding confidently down the hall. Vincent followed at her heels.

A few people were at the office, working on computers or carrying files from one location to another. No one seemed alarmed at Vincent and Cali's presence or even gave them a second glance. People were busy with their own jobs.

Their target was the main server. If Special Investigations had the file, it would be on those computers. Cali hid a smile as they arrived and she saw a physical lock. Special Investigations counted on its elaborate security to keep unauthorized people out but didn't want to risk an electronic invasion of its computers.

Unfortunately, it was a far more complicated lock than the standard. Cali worked on it for nearly a full minute, teasing the tumblers into position, while Vincent kept watch. Eventually, it yielded a triumphant and satisfying click.

Slipping inside, Cali quickly opened up the computer terminal while Vincent began searching through surveillance for any sign they'd been spotted. She slid in Harley's tiny drive and activated the login bypass. Immediately, the screen started to flicker with username and password attempts. Cali held her breath, but the computer soon acknowledged her as an authorized user.

She searched through the databases, looking for the list. "Got it."

It was time for the nasty surprise that Harley had prepared for her—a simple virus that would crawl through every connected system and overwrite the information again and again, effectively removing it from any possibility of recovery. Cali activated the program without a twinge of regret. A list of *lalassu* was too dangerous to leave out there.

"You have got to be kidding me." Vincent's exclamation caught her by surprise. He stared intently at one of the surveillance monitors.

"We're done." Cali quickly scanned the camera feeds. There was no sign that they'd been discovered, no surge of activity or influx of people. But it wouldn't last long. The virus would announce their presence within minutes.

"No, we're not." Vincent growled, pointing to the image of a man tied to a chair in an otherwise empty room. Scars or tattoos peeked through the dark, unkempt hair. "Come on."

"We don't have time," Cali hissed. She didn't like the idea of leaving someone in the hands of Special Investigations, but she liked the idea of being caught even less. Vincent ignored her, hurrying down the halls. Sweat crawled down Cali's back. She was all too aware of the ticking clock.

"This area is off limits." The guard held up his hand to stop them. Cali tried not to stare at the gun holster tucked under his arm. They needed to project confidence to assuage his suspicions.

Cali smiled, ready to bullshit her way through. "I'm sorry, but—"

Vincent slammed his fist into the guard. The man flew backward hard enough to rattle the walls.

So much for the subtle approach. Cali shoved her picks into the lock as Vincent and the guard grappled. The door popped open, revealing the man from the monitor. Now that she was in the same room as him, Cali questioned the wisdom of rescuing him. Even tied to a chair, he gave off a palpable aura of competent menace.

"Inside." Vincent ordered the guard. Somehow, he'd managed to get the guard's gun during their struggle. The guard obeyed reluctantly, watching them closely with his muscles tensed, ready for any opportunity to turn the tables.

Vincent handed Cali the gun. "Keep it on him. If he moves, shoot him."

The gun was heavy and awkward in Cali's grip, but she braced her wrist and pointed the business end at the guard. Vincent knelt beside the chair and snapped the plastic restraints with his bare fingers.

The man in the chair stood up, rubbing his wrists. "Your consistent tardiness never ceases to amaze me, Vincent."

"Hey, if you want to wait for the next rescue party, you can be my guest, Vapor."

CHAPTER FORTY-THREE

"So is there a real Wonder Woman?" Salazar asked as they arrived at the precinct.

Joe suppressed an irritated growl, reminding himself that Salazar's curiosity about the different *lalassu* bloodlines was an improvement over fear. After nearly an hour of constant pop-culture references, Joe's patience had boiled dry. "No. Let's concentrate on what we have to do."

"Sure." Salazar nodded.

Joe wished he had the same confidence. He'd asked Virginia to ask Gwen to use ghosts to check on his family. Gwen reported that they were all fine and no one seemed unhappy or frightened. Karan and Dalhard hadn't gone after them, assuming Gwen's interpretation could be trusted. Getting back through the roadblocks had proved surprisingly easy. Joe kept a spare uniform in his trunk, and apparently, the right clothes were all the credentials they needed.

Someone should tell all the wannabe villains out there that mind control cuts down on usefulness. Maybe it was like forcing someone to work double and triple shifts. No matter how good they were, competence eroded under the constant grind.

Dalhard was here in the city, running his tyrannical coup with an iron fist. The streets were deserted except for intermittent patrols of cops and gang members, all conspicuously armed. The media dropped hints of army mobilization and planned attacks on Perdition. Every time Joe heard one, his stomach twisted tighter at the thought of mind-controlled officers firing on government troops and both sides taking casualties. Civilians would be caught in the crossfire. And the worst part was that if Dalhard got through, he could turn the attacking troops against the rest of the country.

They needed to take him down before it had a chance to play out. None of the records told whether or not a Siren's influence continued after death, but Joe hoped the psychic override would vanish if Dalhard died. His gun felt heavy in his hand, carrying the weight of a moral decision that Joe could never feel qualified to make. *Except I still have to make it. There's no one else who can do it.*

His phone rang, and Michael's number came up on the display. Joe frowned. "Hey, I thought we were going radio silent."

"We have a problem," Michael replied grimly. "The list is gone."

Salazar sat forward but kept quiet when Joe shook his head, concentrating on the conversation. "What do you mean, gone?"

"Someone accessed the computer and then carefully went into the files and removed all the information. It looked like it was still there until we went to access it. And you can guess who the chief suspect is."

"Cali wouldn't do this." Right on the heels of his denial, Joe remembered her fiddling with the computer before they crashed early that morning. A chisel of doubt started to chip away at his confidence.

"She's been pretty clear about not wanting us to have the list." Michael paused in a way that Joe recognized as his friend steeling himself to say something unpleasant. "What if she's still working for Dalhard?"

"She's not," Joe insisted. "Besides, wouldn't Virginia have sensed Cali destroying the list?"

"Not if she was asleep when it happened." Michael sounded reluctant even as he destroyed Joe's hope. "Joe, you know what Dalhard can do and what he means to Cali. Do you really think she's turned against him so quickly after so many years?"

Yes. He wanted to say it. Needed to say it. But he couldn't force the word past his lips— not past the reasonable doubt clouding his certainty. Instead, Joe made himself concentrate on the big picture. "It doesn't matter. We still need to take down Dalhard."

He hung up the phone, his head and heart aching equally from the accusation. If Cali had destroyed the list, he could almost understand her choice. But what if Michael was right and she'd kept a copy to give to Dalhard? No ready answer surfaced for that one.

"Are we aborting?" Salazar asked.

"No. We've got a job to do. Let's go." Joe got out of the car and headed into the police station. He and Salazar needed to blend in with the other controlled zombies and find Dalhard. After that… Joe's hand found the handle of his weapon again, cold and uncompromising. After that, they would remove the threats. All the threats.

"Can you walk?" Cali asked Vapor, hearing shouts from outside the cell. Above the door, the camera's red light blinked out. All computers networked to the server were down. There was no more time for a quiet escape. She kept the gun trained on the guard.

Vapor nodded slowly, rising unsteadily to his feet. Vincent ducked under the other man's arm, supporting him. "We're about to have guests."

"Then let's go before we get trapped." Cali hurried the two men out and relocked the door, sealing the guard inside. Only then did she hear the steady tread of approaching footsteps.

"Vincent, get Vapor out of here." She pointed to the fire stair at the end of the hall. It should lead them out of the building. "Don't wait for me."

To his credit, Vincent didn't waste time arguing. He and Vapor left while Cali went to meet whoever was coming. She kept the gun in plain view but held loosely.

Two men in suits came around the corner, weapons in hand. Cali immediately dropped the gun and held up her own hands in surrender. "Trust me, you want to talk to me."

It was a calculated risk. They might open fire, preferring a dead scapegoat to answers. Cali was betting her life on the appeal of the latter outweighing the former. She suppressed an exhalation of relief when the two men lowered their own weapons.

"Who are you?" the older of the two asked.

"My name is Calista, but I usually go by Boomerang. And I have a solution to one of the problems you're facing—André Dalhard." She left her form alone but drew on Boomerang's arrogance and confidence, wearing it like a protective coating.

"Very well, Ms. Calista. You have our attention. I'm Investigator Lockett, and this is Investigator Davis of the Bureau of Special Investigations." The older man tucked his gun back under his coat. "May we escort you to our head of operations?"

She inclined her head regally. If she could occupy their attention for long enough, Vincent and Vapor would reach safety. Davis stayed behind her while Lockett walked in front. It didn't escape her notice that Davis kept his weapon out, though she pretended to ignore it with all the aristocratic disdain she could summon.

They took her to a large and comfortable conference room. Scanning it, Cali guessed they assumed the main door was the only exit and entrance. The windows were solid panes of glass with no mechanism to open them, probably shatterproof given the height. However, the walls were only prefabricated panels, easy to pop out or slice through with a sufficiently sharp knife. Her own blades reassuringly weighted down her forearms.

The door opened to reveal a slender Indian woman with sepia skin and long dark hair tied in a neat braid. Her heart-shaped face and delicate features belied the ruthless authority in her eyes. The evaluating stare she inflicted on Cali was that of an equal. She would not be underestimating Cali.

"You've certainly caused a great deal of trouble." The woman sat down on her padded office chair as if ascending a throne. "Destroying our computer system is hardly a friendship-inducing method of introduction."

"Neither is sending an assassin or soldiers," Cali countered. "If you desired a copy of the list, then offering me a fair price would have been a more traditional first step."

A ghost of a smile haunted the other woman's serious expression. "Special Investigations had nothing to do with Mr. Smith's contract."

"But you wouldn't have objected if he had succeeded. For now, consider this a warning about attempting to steal from me and my people." Cali folded her hands primly on the polished wooden table. "Because of your heavy-handedness, you no longer have the list and whatever other information was on your computers."

"So this is purely a business matter?" The other woman lightly scratched her jaw with a long fingernail. "Not a rescue attempt?"

Only long practice allowed Cali to keep her composure. The woman lifted one finger, and the door opened, revealing the guard that Cali had locked in Vapor's cell.

"Your efficiency is impressive. As is your commitment to distracting us. All quite clever. However, we were prepared and waiting for your companion on a lower floor." The woman allowed her first true smile to stretch her lips since she'd entered the room.

"I doubt that." Cali leaned back in her chair, allowing her own amusement to show.

"You think I'm lying? You may have disabled our cameras, but I expect word of the capture at any moment." Despite the woman's cool social mask, her fingers twitched closer together as if tempted to form a fist. Whoever she was, she did not like being dismissed.

"I don't doubt your people were waiting. Someone in your position doesn't stay there without some strategic talent." Lifting her chin, Cali delivered a withering smile. "But I doubt anyone is prepared for what my companion can do."

"I'm quite familiar with Vincent's skills." A new voice entered the verbal duel, and Cali froze. Karan.

He sauntered into the conference room as if joining them for a casual meal. "I see you have met my sister, Priya."

"She's a delightful conversationalist." The words stumbled from Cali's numb lips.

"I believe we've been discussing the ethics of counterespionage and theft. I'm so glad you could join us, Brother." Priya's polite reply did nothing to disguise her sadistic pleasure at Cali's discomfort.

"You are only alive right now to provide us with the list that you so inconsiderately destroyed." Karan stood behind his sister like some kind of summoned demon.

"What about André Dalhard?" Cali asked.

"What about him? Special Investigations will handle him." Priya shrugged.

"How?" Cali leaned forward, resting her elbows on the table. "Whoever you send, he can turn them against you. He already has a considerable army, and it doesn't mind shedding blood for a profitable cause. Add in the cops, and now he has a recognized authority that will help him to control the ordinary populace. He won't stop there. I'm sure he's already got his eyes on bigger targets."

"Special Investigations—"

"Special Investigations isn't ready for this scale of attack." Cali interrupted Priya's attempt at dismissal. "I'm going to assume you've been working under the table for a number of years, with all the freedom that implies. Now you're working in the public eye, and how do you think it will look if Special Investigations' first major operation goes down in flames? Can you afford the negative publicity so early in the game? First impressions and all that."

Priya remained stonily silent. She flicked her fingers at the open door, and her people hastened to close it, leaving Cali alone with the two siblings. Cali kept her face smooth. Priya might not be ready to admit it, but Cali could see that her point had struck home. They would let her go. It was only a matter of negotiating the fine details.

"None of your people can get close to him. I can. He's never controlled my mind." Cali flicked her eyes to Karan. "It's something he does with those whose opinion he values. You need me, which is why you're going to let me walk out the door."

"We can find an alternate course of action." The malevolence in Karan's glare left Cali no doubt that he would rather see the world burn than let her go.

"Not in time." Cali refused to back down. She imagined hurling her knives into Karan's smug face. He'd destroyed her life when he'd betrayed Dalhard, and the lure of immediate vengeance sang sweetly in her mind. But if she went after him, she would throw away any hope of stopping Mr. Dalhard, and the people he hurt would be her fault. "Your sister is already feeling the pressure."

"We could use her companions as hostages," Priya suggested thoughtfully. "To guarantee her cooperation." A radio squawked at her belt, and she pulled it out.

Cali kept her expression impassive as she overheard the static-laden report of failure. Vincent had gone through the waiting ambush like a bowling ball, and he and Vapor had disappeared in their vehicle. It was time to seal the deal and secure their freedom and hers. "I don't require leverage to do my job. You have a simple choice. Either let me go after Mr. Dalhard, or we can waste further time and resources attacking one another."

She wondered if the siblings would leave the room to discuss the situation, but neither made any attempt to communicate. They didn't even look at each other. Priya nodded as if completing a calculation. "Very well. A temporary truce, then."

Cali stood up and buttoned her jacket.

"Aren't you interested in knowing where he is right now?" Priya called out as Cali's hand closed around the doorknob.

A final attempt at manipulation. *Fine, I'll bite.* "I prefer to take my time to plan effective strategies."

"An excellent approach," Karan replied. "Of course, it means allowing Detective Cabrera to walk into an ambush."

CHAPTER FORTY-FOUR

At first glance, it seemed like business as usual at the police station—plenty of activity and movement. But Joe quickly saw through the façade. The cops at their desks weren't bantering to relieve the boredom. They weren't even interacting. They were all doing their jobs with straight-faced efficiency and purpose, moving from one task to the next without pause. The men and women walking around were carrying much heavier weaponry than Joe would have expected to see outside of a war zone. Assault rifles hung off every shoulder as if they were that season's lethal-accessory choice.

A large whiteboard stood prominently in the middle of the room. Joe recognized his own picture as well as those of Cali, Boomerang, and Colleen, placed like wanted posters in the middle. The rest of the board was taken up with names neatly aligned in columns. Some were crossed off, and others were marked with an asterisk. Joe hung back, not wanting to attract any attention. If anyone realized he and Salazar weren't controlled, they'd never get close to Dalhard.

The rookie tapped Joe's shoulder, directing his attention to one of the interrogation rooms. Muffled shouts penetrated the thick soundproofing, and Joe tensed. The door opened, and officers dragged out a young man with tears streaming down his tan cheeks. "Please, just give me another chance. There must be a mistake."

"The test confirms your status." An older man in a government suit emerged from the interrogation room. Flipping through papers in the file, he didn't even bother looking at the begging man. Joe held his breath. *What kind of testing? What status?*

"But I don't even have any powers!" The young man tried to break free from the relentless grip of his captors. "I've never done anything to hurt anyone."

Various Spanish curses ran through Joe's head. They had a test for *lalassu.* Maybe the suit was some kind of psychic reader. But it meant Special Investigations wasn't relying on the list.

"Gifted individuals are held for processing." The older man turned away, indifferently bureaucratic. The door closed behind him. Joe's clenched jaw threatened to shatter his teeth. He couldn't walk away and leave that boy to be sent somewhere just because of a quirk of DNA. But interference could cost them their only chance to deal with the real source of the problem.

Salazar nudged Joe. Sergeant Modnik stalked toward the interrogation room, her mouth pushed into a determined frown. A surge of hope lifted Joe's spirits. Even mind controlled, Modnik would never tolerate that in her department.

The sergeant snapped to a halt in front of the officers holding the boy. "What's going on here?"

"It's confirmed, sir. He's one of them," the officer on the right reported, grinning triumphantly.

"Excellent work. Take him downstairs with the others, and come back for your next assignment." Modnik delivered an approving pat on the back and made her efficient way to the whiteboard. She put an asterisk next to one of the names as they dragged away the screaming boy.

"It's a witch hunt for *lalassu.*" Joe's stomach tried to crawl down the inside of his leg. It had already begun. People were being rounded up and held because others were afraid of them. "We have to find out where they're keeping the information."

Salazar nodded. They'd agreed that he would ask any questions instead of Joe. No one would suspect him, whereas Joe's face was plastered on signs as Most Wanted. Joe ducked behind a pile of evidence boxes, pretending to search through them for paperwork. Salazar raised his hand to catch the sergeant's attention.

Catch it he did. She narrowed in on him and headed straight for the rookie. "Officer Salazar. Is there a problem?"

"No, ma'am. I finished my shift on the roadblocks, and I'm ready for my next assignment." As instructed, Salazar kept his voice and face as neutral as possible.

In her natural state, Modnik would have been immediately suspicious. She could keep track of all her people's positions and assignments. She would have realized that Salazar hadn't been assigned anything since the attack on the precinct.

But Modnik under Dalhard's control was a considerably blunter instrument. "Report to Mr. Dalhard in my office. He'll want an update on the roadblocks."

Salazar nodded. "Yes, ma'am."

Modnik moved away, shouting instructions at someone else. Joe rose to his feet, slowly unholstering his weapon. Dalhard's location had been confirmed. *One shot, and this could all be over.* Or they could die in a hail of bullets if the mind-controlled minions weren't released at Dalhard's death. Both he and Salazar wore bulletproof vests, but protective helmets would have aroused suspicion. *Here's hoping they stick to the center-of-mass targets.*

Death had never been an appealing option to Joe, but it was even less so now. The universe owed him after his father's death, and Joe was cashing in. He and Cali would both walk out of the current situation and be together. No questions, no other options.

Taking a deep breath, Joe followed Salazar toward the sergeant's office, one of the few private structures in the precinct outside the interrogation rooms. Sweat curdled through Joe's hair and down his back. In a few more seconds, he was going to take a life. Not in the heat of the moment. Not to protect his fellow officers or a civilian from an immediate threat. He would walk into the room and shoot a man. It was murder by any legal definition, and Joe somehow doubted that *he was mentally controlling everyone* would be accepted as a defense even after the president's announcement and the establishment of Special Investigations. Pulling the trigger would end everything he'd worked for. He would never be a cop again.

But everyone will be safe from Dalhard. I should have stepped aside and let Vapor execute him in Alaska. Everything that has happened since then is my responsibility. So I have to be the one to do it. Joe stepped through the door. As they'd agreed, Salazar faded back, staying just at the door to give them both a chance to escape afterward.

A line of police officers waited for Dalhard's attention. The man himself sat behind the sergeant's desk, ignoring the uniformed woman in front as she gave her report. He doodled on a notepad and checked his watch. He wasn't paying attention, and Joe had a clear shot.

He lifted his weapon, aiming it at Dalhard's head. His finger tensed on the trigger, ready to fire. People began to shout, pushing each other out of the way. Dalhard's head lifted, frowning.

Do it! Joe screamed at himself, ordering his reluctant muscles to squeeze the trigger.

Except he couldn't. Somewhere deep inside, he couldn't make himself shoot an unarmed man who wasn't offering any physical threat no matter how much evil he knew that man could do and had done. Joe couldn't be the executioner.

The gun was grabbed out of his hands. Someone pushed him roughly to the floor, yanking his arms behind his back. Joe crashed hard onto his face. His cheek blossomed into sharp, radiating pain. *Probably broken.* And through it all, Dalhard's laugh echoed in the closed room.

Joe gritted his teeth as he was hauled more or less upright and dragged to the sergeant's desk. They made him kneel in the small space in front. He didn't hear any further commotion behind him but didn't dare look back to see if they'd taken Salazar as well. Hopefully, the rookie had enough brains to continue playing along with the other zombies.

"So much effort only to choke at the last minute." Dalhard pushed back his chair and rested his knuckles on the desk, looming over Joe like a giant gorilla. "What happened, Detective? An inconvenient resurgence of conscience? Lack of nerve? Or perhaps you failed because deep down you didn't truly want to succeed."

Joe couldn't answer. Rage locked his jaw together so tightly that he couldn't have spoken if his life depended on it—rage both at the man in front of him, who had destroyed so many lives, and at himself for not taking the opportunity to end it.

"You see, I've learned an important lesson. In the end, brutality is the only true power." Dalhard flexed his hands as if eager to crush Joe's bones under his fingers. "In the end, money and social position cannot shield people from someone who is both determined and vicious enough to go after them. Wealth and status are lies that only protect when both sides follow the rules."

Joe had met plenty of thugs and wannabe wise guys over the years who would have agreed with Dalhard. All of them had been certain that the path to the top could be built with blood. Of course, blood made for a pretty slippery foundation. There were always more predators waiting to yank down the so-called kings of crime.

Dalhard spread his lips in a mirthless grin. "I'm starting to understand why so many people make the foolish mistake of explaining instead of taking action. It's satisfying to demonstrate just how wrong my enemies were, how shortsighted and weak willed. But I know my words won't persuade you."

Joe threw his weight to the side, hoping to break free. If Dalhard touched him and took over his mind, then Joe would tell the man everything. About Cali. Where the farmhouse was. How Dani and Michael were recovering from their injuries.

Those holding him were prepared for escape attempts. They knocked him down and used their weight to pin him. No matter how hard Joe struggled, their grip stayed firm. *No! I won't let this happen.* He wished for a cyanide capsule to swallow—anything to deny Dalhard that victory.

"This was not our agreement."

It couldn't be Cali. She was with Vincent. She wasn't supposed to be anywhere near the precinct. A boot slammed painfully into Joe's kidney. Joe drew on his training in order to fight through the paralyzing agony. He tried to kick back, but his captors held his feet. Weight pinned each limb, and more heaviness knelt on his back. He could barely move his head to see what was happening.

"Neither of us has been particularly steadfast with the agreement." Dalhard was looking toward the door. Joe couldn't see from his angle. It had to be a trick. Cali wouldn't negotiate with Dalhard. She was supposed to be safe. He squirmed, trying to see. He needed to know she was safe.

"Haven't I?" She stepped into view, and Joe's heart sank. It was Cali, shifted into Colleen, though without any of Colleen's meekness. "You asked me to procure the list of *lalassu*, find Karan Samil, and keep an eye on Detective Cabrera. I've accomplished my side."

It's a trick. It must be. She couldn't have lied with her heart and body. Joe clung to the swiftly eroding foundations of his certainty.

Cali continued. "I insinuated myself into the detective's investigation. I removed the list from his allies. And I've discovered that Karan is with the newfound Bureau of Special Investigations."

"Impressive indeed. Perhaps I misjudged you." Dalhard didn't seem entirely convinced.

"I didn't say I approve of everything you've done. Had you taken me into your confidence, I could have helped you to avoid several serious errors." Cali glanced around at the men and women crowding the office. Cop and gang alike received equally disapproving judgment. "My continued cooperation has a price."

"And what is the bill for your loyalty, dear? Money? A small country to rule as your own?" Dalhard's mocking reply sparked obedient laughter from his zombies.

"Joe Cabrera," Cali replied. Joe's heart soared. He'd known it was a trick. This was all a stratagem to rescue him.

"Simple enough. Once I've taken over his mind, I'll implant everlasting devotion to you." Dalhard signaled to Joe's captors to bring him closer. The weight vanished from his back, and they lifted him back into a kneeling position.

"No." Cali held up an imperious hand.

Dalhard tilted his head as if trying to translate a foreign language. "No?"

"You won't be able to take him over, not completely. There will always be a piece of the original Joe screaming in the back of his head. Eventually, he'd break free or go mad." Cali's eyes met Joe's, full of forest-green sympathy.

"I've learned a great deal over the last few months. You would be surprised at how deep I can go now." Dalhard gestured at the others. "Shall I order them to bark like dogs?"

"You don't know him like I do. His mind is too strong to break." Cali came closer to Joe. He watched carefully, wondering where she planned to go with that angle. Granted, her tactics were keeping Dalhard away from Joe for the moment, but what was the second step—lure

Dalhard out? Or maybe Vincent was waiting to free Joe. Even if he got loose, they would still need to fight their way out of the precinct. *I'll have to shoot my fellow officers for the crime of having had their minds taken over by a madman.* After the last few minutes, Joe knew he couldn't do it. But he'd protect Cali and make sure she got out.

"I can't allow him to wander merrily on his way. He's already caused me too much trouble." Dalhard took his seat behind the desk again.

"I know," Cali said softly. She was close enough for Joe to smell the lingering scent of the antibiotic ointment they'd used to clean the bullet graze in her leg. She knelt down stiffly, her lips thinning in pain. She cupped his cheek, unshed tears darkening the green in her eyes. "I'm sorry, Joe. I wish I had a better escape for you."

He tensed, ready to move at her signal. But she stayed perfectly still.

"I know you'd rather die than be under Mr. Dalhard's control." A single tear glistened in the fluorescent light as it rolled down her cheek. "I'll make sure your family is safe after you're gone. He won't have any reason to go after them."

Wait. What?

Chapter Forty-Five

"A touching, sentimental gesture, but I need him alive," Dalhard said.

Joe stared into Cali's eyes, hoping for a wink or a twitch—some kind of signal. She couldn't be planning to let him die. *Yes, I'd rather die than be controlled by Dalhard, but I don't want it to be the first option up for grabs!*

"No, you don't. I have the list and the location for the Harrises. My price for both is a quick and painless death for him." Cali got to her feet and stepped back from Joe. Her hands were tightly locked into trembling fists. "You can take me over once he's gone."

This can't be true. Could she be so twisted by her upbringing that this seemed like a good idea to her? He strained against his captors, needing to reach her. "Cali, you can't give him what he wants."

From his angle, he could see her face as she stared at her shoes. Guilt. Regret. Resignation. Her arms wrapped tightly around her waist as if she wanted to disappear.

"I'm not a fighter, Joe. Not like Dani or you." Voice pinched with grief, she pleaded with him. "I'm a plotter, an escape artist, and a thief. I sneak, I go sideways, I go around. Right now, I don't have any other options left to try. I tried to catch you before you came in here, but I was too late. Now it's all too late." She turned away from him to face Dalhard, and her voice hardened. "Do we have a deal?"

Reality hit home like a sledgehammer. She was really going to do it. Joe fought harder, anger bubbling over at his own foolishness. She was giving up, going back to her old life. "You can't do this!"

If she'd been willing to fight, they could have stopped Dalhard. Joe believed it with all his heart. Instead, she'd surrendered everything and thrown them all to the wolves. Bitter bile coated his throat and tongue as he realized he should never have trusted her. She'd been Dalhard's creature for too long.

"Do we have a deal?" Cali repeated.

Dalhard tapped his fingers on the desk. "You've been loyal to me since I found you as a child in Vegas. I could always rely on you, Calista. Until four days ago."

"I made a mistake then—" Cali abruptly stopped as Dalhard stood up.

"A very serious mistake. I asked for your assistance, and you betrayed me to my enemies." Dalhard took a menacing step toward her. Then another. And another.

Cali backed away, the color draining from her hair and her features sharpening as she transformed. Gasps of astonishment came from the others in the office. *Now she knows. You can't make a deal with the devil and expect him to keep it.* Joe didn't take any satisfaction in Cali's lesson. He needed to concentrate on getting himself out of there if he could.

"I don't believe I'm inclined to grant your request. Instead, I'll make sure that both of you are incapable of betraying me in the future." Dalhard reached out to grab Cali.

Sharp, cracking bursts sparked from the garbage can by the door.

On instinct, every cop moved to take cover—including the four holding Joe.

He rolled and came up on his feet. Someone grabbed his arm. Desperate to stay free, Joe began to swing his fist. He barely managed to stop when he recognized Salazar.

The rookie's tight grip led Joe through the chaos to the door. The two men charged through, breaking past the wall of bodies. Joe couldn't stop himself from looking back, but there was no sign of Cali.

"We have to move!" Salazar hauled on Joe's arm. They ran through the confused ranks of cops trying to react to the sudden noise and chaos. The escaped prisoners and gang members opened fire with their assault rifles, spraying the ceiling and walls with bullets.

Joe and Salazar burst out of the narrow back entrance, stumbling on the smooth pavement. The alley was barely wide enough for a police van and only open on one end. They were beginning to move toward the street when a silhouetted female figure appeared at the alley's mouth.

Cali spotted them and ran toward them, blond hair flying. She hurled herself at Joe. "Thank God!"

He pried her arms loose from his neck and stepped back. Glaring at her in disgust, he wished he still had his gun.

"Joe?" Her small, hurt voice would have struck right to his heart if he didn't know what an actress she could be.

"You betrayed us all." The hurt and anger inside Joe lashed out, seeking to inflict equal damage on its source.

"No, Joe, you don't understand. It was all her plan," Salazar babbled. "She grabbed me at the door and gave me the firecrackers, and we were going to Taze the ones holding you—"

A hint of doubt started to chisel away at Joe's righteous wrath.

More gunfire came from the precinct. Salazar looked between Cali and Joe, searching for direction. "I'm sorry. I couldn't get the firecrackers lit in time."

Cali bit her lips, her eyes flicking between the alley mouth and Joe. "It's not your fault. The two of you get out of here. Don't worry about me."

"We can't leave you." Scandalized offence made the rookie's words squeak.

Was it true? Joe didn't know what to believe anymore, and his battered heart wouldn't survive another change of face. "We're going."

Salazar objected. "But—"

"Go!" Cali pushed at the rookie. "They're coming."

Shadows blocked the light from the street. "Correction. We're here."

Dalhard stood there, flanked by two men in gang colors and carrying automatic rifles. Cover was scarce in the alley, part of the security choices to minimize the risk of transferring high-threat prisoners.

Joe held still. Cali and Salazar did likewise.

"Luckily for you, I was being truthful. I do need you both alive at least until you've told me what I want to know." Dalhard advanced, his escort keeping pace. "You know, Calista, I hope you're right. I hope some tiny kernel of you both survives what I'm about to do to you. I hope you both spend the rest of your miserable existences knowing true helplessness. It will be short, but I'm certain it will feel like an eternity. And when you die, it will be knowing that all of your efforts were useless and you were turned against everything you wanted to protect." The furious hatred in the man's voice slapped at them like a physical assault. But Joe refused to cower, and so did Cali.

"The list is gone. I've destroyed every trace of it. There won't be any easy collecting of the *lalassu*." Cali nearly growled the words, her voice trembling with anger.

They'd planned to destroy the records at Special Investigations. And Michael said that the copy at the farmhouse had been destroyed. Joe wanted to believe she spoke the truth.

If he hadn't been watching closely, he would have missed Dalhard's mouth tightening in a microscowl before expanding into a fake smile. "We have other methods of finding *lalassu*."

"Maybe." Cali stood tall, her chin lifted high. "But how long will it take them to organize against you? You needed to move quickly. Even now, your empire is starting to crumble at the edges."

That time, there was no hiding Dalhard's scowl. "We'll soon find out the truth."

Joe tensed to fight. Dalhard would need to come close enough to touch them.

"Don't shoot them unless they try to escape," Dalhard ordered.

Five feet. Three feet. Two.

As Dalhard reached out, Joe swung. Digging up strength from every corner of his mind and soul, every horrible act the man had committed, every heartbreak he'd caused, Joe's fist crashed into Dalhard's face hard enough to crack his knuckles and send splatters of blood flying.

Dalhard staggered back. Joe followed, striking again. That time, he caught Dalhard in the gut, driving the air out of his lungs.

Gasping, Dalhard tried to fold, but Joe wouldn't let him. He punched again, aiming for the lying teeth that had caused so much trouble.

Crack.

That hurt. Enamel was harder than bone covered by skin and flesh.

Joe's shock and pain gave Dalhard the half second he needed to fight back. Spitting blood, the man slammed into Joe's shoulder, knocking him down.

Joe's head smacked into the pavement. Dalhard's weight crushed Joe's chest, preventing him from getting his breath. But he retained enough awareness to grab at Dalhard's suit cuffs, trying to keep the man's hands away from his skin. If Dalhard touched him, the game was over.

"You think you can attack me!" Dalhard snarled as they grappled.

Joe struggled, fighting back against his opponent's mad strength. The slick suit fabric kept slipping through his fingers.

"I'll destroy you and everything you ever loved. Anything you even thought about loving. I'll burn it all to the ground—" Dalhard abruptly stopped. His arms went limp, and he leaned back, his brows knitting together in puzzlement.

Joe seized the advantage. He shoved Dalhard off him. Rolling to his feet, Joe instinctively reached for his empty holster. *Damn!* There had to be something he could use for a weapon. His head snapped back and forth, scanning the area. He needed to find a weapon fast before Dalhard came after him again.

Except Dalhard wasn't coming.

Joe's mind slowed and expanded, coming out of its narrow, fight-or-flight focus. Dalhard still sat on the pavement, staring numbly ahead. His mouth opened and closed, but no sound came out.

At first, Joe couldn't understand the small flash of silver around Dalhard's chest. He blinked, wondering if his head injury was bad enough for hallucinations. But it wasn't a visual trick of a damaged brain. It was the hilt of a tiny silver knife winking in the dim light.

Dark crimson blotted Dalhard's pale shirt, growing larger with each second. Bright-red blood beaded on his lips as his mouth continued to move soundlessly. Joe finally realized the truth. The knife had pierced Dalhard's lung, making it impossible for him to draw breath and speak. He'd been rendered silent, unable to pass on whatever final sadistic commands he'd planned.

Everything seemed to be happening in slow motion. Joe lifted his gaze to check on Cali, standing a few feet away. A second knife gleamed in her hand, ready to throw. She stared at Dalhard, her chin crumpling but her eyes determined. Joe took a step toward her, ready to hold her, kiss her, listen to her, whatever it took to make her hurt disappear. She'd said she wasn't a warrior, and he'd seen how devastated she was when she'd attacked Rodolpho. Yet she'd taken Dalhard down without hesitation. *To protect me.* He should have trusted her.

A thud behind him signaled the return of regularly scheduled reality. Dalhard had pitched forward onto his face, dead eyes fixed and sightless.

Shouts burst into life from inside the police station, the din penetrating the muffling walls. Demands to know what was going on squawked from nearby police radios. Joe couldn't spare a thought for the armed men at the mouth of the alley or his comrades inside. Nothing mattered except Cali.

"I couldn't let him hurt you," she whispered, the knife clattering to the ground.

Joe pulled her into his arms, holding her tightly to apologize for ever doubting her. Her skin was chilly against him, and he wrapped himself around her. "I'm so sorry."

"I couldn't let him hurt you," she repeated.

"It'll be okay." Joe kissed the top of her head, inhaling her sweet scent.

"Not to interrupt the moment, but why aren't they attacking?" Salazar directed their attention to the two men with rifles. They both stood awkwardly, staring warily at each other and at the tiny group in the alley.

"He said not to shoot unless we tried to escape. We're not trying to escape," Cali explained wearily. "It'll take some time for them to recover from his influence."

More shouts came from the precinct. With Dalhard gone, people were waking up.

One of the gang members bolted, vanishing into the street. The other backed away slowly before running in the opposite direction.

"So that's it? It's all over?" Salazar asked.

"Not even close," Joe replied. It was only the beginning. They'd need to spend months, if not years, cleaning up the mess, not to mention dealing with Special Investigations and the newfound revelation that the *lalassu* were real.

But Dalhard's leftover mess wasn't the only beginning. Joe might have begun to doubt whether or not he would ever follow his father's footsteps in finding true love, but he no longer had any doubts about the woman in his arms. She was everything he'd never realized he needed and more than he'd ever dreamed of asking for. And if she let him, he would spend the rest of their lives making sure she never had any doubts about his love for her and his faith in her.

"Are you okay?" Cali asked, murmuring deliciously against his chest.

"I'm more than okay." He pulled back just enough to see her eyes. "I'm in love."

Salazar coughed. "I'm gonna go."

Cali laughed weakly. "Are you sure it's not our romantic surroundings talking? Or maybe getting hit in the head?"

Joe shrugged. "Granted, standing beside a cooling corpse isn't how I planned to do this, but I'm not letting you out of my arms until you agree to marry me."

For a long horrible moment, he thought she was going to refuse. That would make his romantic declaration both awkward and a potential legal issue, since he had just technically refused to release her.

"Part of me wants to make a joke right now, but I can't." She kissed him softly. "I love you too, Joe Cabrera, and if you still feel the same way tomorrow, then I'll marry you."

Relief and joy sparked through him. "Trust me, I'm not about to change my mind. Although my mother might beat me senseless if I don't make a proper proposal with roses and a ring. Preferably with a circle of family witnesses."

Cali bit her lip. "Is it too late to mention that I'm not into public spectacles?"

"You say the word, and we elope to Vegas. It will crush my mother's doting heart, and I will undoubtedly hear about it for the next several decades, but if it'll make you happy, that's what we'll do." Joe kissed away the tiny dent marring her bottom lip. "I'm yours now to do with as you will."

"I don't want to break your mother's heart." Cali twisted her fingers in his shirt. "Will she really be okay with you choosing me? I don't think she likes me much."

Joe took a deep breath, as much as he could with the bulletproof vest still snugly wrapped around his ribs. "She'll come around. It's mostly that she's always been protective of me, especially after my father died. Once she sees how much I love you, the whole family will adopt you."

"I never had a family who looked out for one another. It'll take me some time to get used to it. Because I'm yours too." She stole a final kiss from him. "I wouldn't ask you to choose between me and your family. Or do anything else that would make you unhappy or hurt. And on that note, we're going to have a doctor check you out and make sure that you're all right."

"Lead on." He moved to the side, keeping one arm tucked around her, because only an idiot let go of the perfect woman when he found her. And Joe's Mamá had not raised an idiot.

Epilogue

"Make faces for us, Tía Cali!"

Cali laughed as the neighborhood children swarmed her when she emerged from Mamá's kitchen, carrying a tray of sweet, decorated skull cookies. Dozens of tiny hands reached up to tug at her clothes and claim the place of honor at her side. Beaming faces grinned up at her, the yellow dust of marigold pollen shining on their cheeks. She put down the tray of cookies on the overladen picnic table and turned to face the tiny horde. "Wouldn't you rather have some treats instead?"

"Please! Make a face for us!" Carlotta begged prettily, echoed by the rest of the children. Cali glanced at Speranza, who was carefully "making up" a little girl, using a marigold flower as a powder puff. The scars of her ex-husband's reign of terror had faded with his death, letting laughter paint over the lines of fear.

"All right." Cali clutched her ears as the kids shrieked in eardrum-piercing excitement. She snagged a large cloth napkin from the table and held it up in front of her face. Shifting her blond hair to dark and her eyes from hazel to dark brown, she dropped the napkin. "Boo!"

The children pretended to be frightened, running and scattering as Cali allowed her features to relax. They quickly came back, demanding more, cheered on by the adults. Cali spotted Dani and Michael in the forefront, healed from their disastrous ambush on Mr. Dalhard's escape. Dani pretended to scoff but couldn't hide an amused smile when Michael clapped almost as loudly as the children for each of Cali's "faces." She pretended to ask their opinion on different ludicrous looks, making her nose grow like Pinocchio's or plumping her lips like a cartoon character's. Each face was met with applause and shrieks.

"Hey, Tía Cali needs to get back to help!" Joe pretended to scowl at the children, none of whom were fooled for a moment. They simply ran off to enjoy some new game. Cali watched them go, rubbing her sore cheeks and nose. Joe sat down beside her, his arm automatically snaking around her shoulders to tuck her against his side. "You can say no to them, you know."

"I could, but why disappoint them if I don't have to?" She leaned her head against his shoulder, scanning the crowd to see if she could spot Vincent. Evonne and Eric were talking together over loaded plates in the corner, but Vincent wasn't in sight, although he'd come to the party. "I never thought I'd be showing children what I can do instead of hiding it. I want to enjoy it while it lasts."

"The way you indulge those brats, you're going to end up doing it for the rest of their lives." He tipped her chin up to steal a kiss, teasing her lips with a promise to revisit the highly pleasant explorations from that morning.

Cali reluctantly broke free. "I should get back to help Mamá."

"She's in her glory right now, complaining about too many cooks in the kitchen and too many kids running around underfoot, but she wouldn't trade a second of it." Joe grinned. "Trust me—you're fine out here."

She wasn't quite as sure. Over the last six months, she'd made an effort to bond with Mamá and the tías. She'd helped Tía Agata hang charms. She'd shared the herbal treatment she used for her own aching joints with Tía Ximena. She'd spent more time stirring and serving food than she'd ever done in her life. But while Mamá accepted her into her home and her son's life, Cali still felt a divide between them. A primal force held Mamá back and hovering, waiting for Cali to break her baby boy's heart. Not that Cali had any intention of doing so, but she wished she could take back that awful night when she'd broken the family's trust in her. "I'll still see if there's something I can do to help."

Joe shrugged, snagging a cookie and then another lingering kiss. Waggling his eyebrows at her, he grinned. "So you'll hurry back."

Cali smiled and reluctantly left the picnic tables, letting her fingers trail along Joe's outstretched arm as she walked away. She stopped on the threshold to let her eyes adjust to the cool dimness inside, a welcome change from the bright fall sunshine outside.

In the kitchen, Tía Agata and Tía Ximena were arguing in rapid-fire Spanish. Cali was still learning and couldn't even get the gist of what they were arguing about but guessed it concerned the roast they were dressing. Mamá was conspicuously absent, although her black-bean stew bubbled in the red pot on the stove.

Cali made her way to the dining room, where a large Day of the Dead altar dominated the floor. Decorated with brightly painted skulls and brilliant yellow marigolds, pictures of different loved ones were lovingly placed where they could keep an eye on the proceedings. Candles flickered, and plates of offerings rested alongside photos. Mamá stood at the altar, placing a bowl of stew in front of a picture of a handsome young man in a leather jacket. Cali recognized Joe's father.

"Ah, Cali. Come here and let me introduce you to Antonio." Mamá beckoned her over, and Cali quickly obeyed. Mamá's plump hand squeezed hers tightly. "Antonio, this is our Pépé's great love. I was not so sure at first, but I see him watching her the same way you used to watch me when you thought I wasn't looking. She makes him happy, and she loves him with all her heart."

The broken little girl hiding deep inside Cali's psyche responded to the declaration of maternal warmth. Mamá coughed and tightened her grip on Cali's hand.

"She is everything we could have wished for him. You would be so very proud of our boy, Antonio." Mamá beamed.

"He's a wonderful man," Cali said softly.

"I have a present for you, Cali." Mamá lifted a sparkling ring from the plate in front of the picture of a wizened woman staring, unsmiling, into the camera. "This is the wedding ring from my Antonio's mother. She was very respected and wealthy in her village and very proud of having a diamond ring for her wedding. I think she would admire your strength and determination. I would like you to have it." Mamá folded Cali's hand around the ring.

Shocked, Cali met Mamá's warm gaze. "Are you sure?"

"I'm sure, *guerita.* You are a very welcome part of our family." Mamá clasped both of Cali's cheeks with her hands and bestowed a maternal kiss on each. "Now, sit down, and tell me what's been troubling you."

There was no fighting it. Cali allowed Mamá to take her to the chairs lining the dining room walls. Once seated, she opened up her hand. The ring winked in the candlelight. "I've never had a family before, just my friends. I'm not quite sure how this is all supposed to work."

"Family isn't only blood. It's love, and it works the way everything works—sometimes good, sometimes not so good." Mamá waved a dismissive hand.

Families of love. Cali thought of Hood, Harley, and Eva on the road to investigate rumors of a new, isolated, supermax prison being constructed for *lalassu.* She wished they could be there that day, but that was the other part of being a family: protecting one another. And they were all going to need protection. Karan and Priya had been quiet since Mr. Dalhard's death, but Special Investigations was still seizing *lalassu* across the country.

Mamá touched Cali's hand, bringing her out of her worried thoughts. "Try on the ring. Let me see."

Cali slid the antique onto her finger. It fit perfectly.

"Now, tell me about the man who raised you. Pépé said he saved you from starving in the streets."

"For a long time, he was my family." Heaviness clamped down on Cali's lungs and heart, turning everything sluggish. "In the end, he wasn't who I thought he was."

"Have you said good-bye to him?" Mamá asked.

Cali shook her head, holding so tightly to the ring that it bit into her hand.

"Do it, *guerita.* Tell him how you feel, what you would have liked to say. Today, he'll hear you, I'll check and make sure Tía Agata isn't burning my stew." Mamá patted Cali's knee before trundling back to the kitchen, already shouting in Spanish.

Alone in the room, watching the flickering shadows chase each other and dance across the worn hardwood floor, Cali made a decision. She got up and searched for Vincent. After a few false starts, she found him tucked into the front stairwell, determinedly drinking a bottle of vodka.

"Hey, leave me alone. I said I'd come, but I never said I'd do the crazy, happy-family thing," he said as she dragged him back to the altar in the dining room. "I'm conducting an important scientific experiment on the effects of alcohol to see if it improves my ability to tolerate this many children."

Cali ignored him, pulling out her wallet. Inside was the card that Mr. Dalhard had first given her so many years earlier. Creased and soft with age, it looked ready to fall apart at the first stiff breeze. She propped it up on the altar behind an unlit votive candle.

"What are you doing?" Vincent asked, clearly not as drunk as he wanted people to believe.

"We're going to say good-bye to Mr. Dalhard." She found a book of matches and used one to light the candle.

"And why would we want to do that?" He put down the bottle.

"Because we're the only two who miss him." Cali took a deep breath, hoping she was right. "He promised us both better lives and failed to deliver. But we still believed in him."

Vincent remained silent, staring at her. She couldn't interpret his expression and plunged ahead anyway.

"All the others, they're glad he's gone. They only saw him as the monster. You're the only one besides me who ever saw him as anything else." A hot tear slid down her cheek. "I miss the man who used to call me to see if everything was going all right at school and if I needed books or money. I miss the way he used to send me clothes because he saw them and thought I'd look pretty in them. Everyone else thinks they were bribes to keep me as his pet metamorph, but to me, it was his way of showing that he cared about me."

"He was a monster," Vincent said quietly, a basic statement of fact without the twist of revulsion the others used.

Cali nodded. "I know. There was something wrong deep inside him. But I can't help remembering all the other stuff too. It still means something to me." She turned resolutely back to the altar. "So I want to say good-bye."

I'm sorry, Mr. Dalhard. I wish I could have saved you. She fingered the worn card. Part of her had expected to feel guiltier. She'd ended his life. In the moment when she had to choose between him and Joe, she'd thrown the knife without even thinking about it. Because the man in that alley wasn't her Mr. Dalhard anymore.

"He was the first person to think I could be important instead of just Vincent the screw-up party guy."

She looked back over her shoulder to see Vincent staring at the altar. His face was drawn, prematurely aged, as he studied the photos and offerings. His fist held tight to the half-empty vodka bottle like a lifeline.

He kept talking, not making eye contact. "I'm not saying it even comes close to making up for what happened. But it made me feel like maybe I could be more. And I don't like being jammed back in the screw-up box, but I don't know where to start."

Cali reached out and took the bottle from Vincent's hand, replacing it with her own hand. A year ago, she wouldn't have been able to tolerate the touch, and now she was initiating it. She had changed. So had Mr. Dalhard. They'd both struggled to find their places in the world. His had consumed him, while she'd managed to crawl out of the pit she'd been born in. A strange sense of peace dissolved the burdens of guilt and uncertainty she'd been wrestling with.

"Good-bye, Mr. Dalhard. I hope you find peace. Like I did."

Strong arms wrapped around her shoulders, and Joe kissed her head. "He saved you. Without him, I wouldn't have you here today. For that, I owe him thanks."

Cali leaned back against Joe, knowing his strength would always be there for her. And hers would always be there for him.

"Umm, this is turning into an awkward three-way moment, so I'm going to leave you to it." Vincent let go of Cali's hand and began to walk away. After a few steps, he paused and looked back. "Thank you."

She smiled at him, noticing he'd left the bottle behind. Joe hugged her tighter as they watched the candlelight play on the altar. "Papá would have adored you. Just like the rest of the family does. Just like I do."

"Guess that really does make me one of you. Because I adore them all too. Especially you." She squirmed around to plant a soft kiss on his nose. He rested his forehead on hers, cradling her close.

The stillness shattered as a wave of children ran through the dining room, brandishing flowers and fistfuls of skull-shaped sugar candies. Cali laughed softly again, finally at home with a family of her own. No shoes left to drop.

Thank you for reading. If you enjoyed it, please consider sharing it with friends or family or posting a short review. It makes a world of difference and is very much appreciated.

Want more details? Check out Under the Covers at www.jclewis.ca for my chapter by chapter author commentary, including what inspired various scenes, background research and other details which didn't make it into the final text.

If you'd like more updates on novels of the *lalassu* and other upcoming works, please sign up for my newsletter on my website: www.jclewis.ca.

The adventures of the *lalassu* will continue in book 4, *Judgement.*

Coming in 2018.

Keep reading for more details.

JUDGEMENT

Coming in 2018

When the *lalassu* were revealed to the world over a year ago, they were met with fear and chaos. The government stepped in and created the Bureau of Special Investigations, to register *lalassu* and investigate claims of paranormal activity. As public panic grew, the government took matters a step further, creating evaluation camps in remote locations. They have explained that identified *lalassu* will be housed in these camps as a temporary measure. Once their powers have been tested, the innocent shall be released and the dangerous kept in secure facilities. But so far, few *lalassu* have returned from such camps and the stories they tell are frightening, prompting many to go deeper into hiding.

Martha and her daughter, Bernie, have been hiding deep in the Alaskan wilderness, in a secret refuge for *lalassu,* Ekurru. Learning to live in a small cabin without running water or electricity has been a challenge, but Martha is used to making sacrifices for others. She gave up her career to take care of Bernie, when her daughter was diagnosed with childhood schizophrenia. When she discovered that Bernie was actually a medium, she didn't hesitate to go on the run to keep her little girl safe from those who would use the child's gift. Her daughter means everything to her.

Which is why she is surprised when Michael, her daughter's former therapist, comes to visit them in Alaska to ask Martha to go undercover in the new prison set up for *lalassu.* Without Bernie.

Lou's family have been the Guardians of Ekurru for generations, using their shape-shifting abilities as skinwalkers to protect it from all threats. He's always been more comfortable in his bear shape than his human one, but since Martha and Bernie came to Alaska, he's been spending more time on two legs than four. This change has not gone unnoticed by his twin, Andrew, and his sister, Lily. Both are worried about keeping Lou's heart intact, especially since Martha hasn't seemed to notice him as anything more than a piece of the background wilderness.

Lou can't be sure if Martha will ever be able to accept who and what he is, but either way, he's determined to make sure that she and her daughter come out of the lion's den safely.

Coming in 2018

For regular updates, visit my blog every Monday for an update on my writing progress. Or join my newsletter at and be the first to know when *Judgment* is ready for publication.
You can find them both at www.jclewis.ca.

Thank Yous

The first thank you always goes out to my husband and sons, who have been so supportive ever since I first began this journey. Even if my boys aren't old enough to read the book, they still talk about how Mommy writes books and how proud they are. My youngest has begun writing his own stories and I couldn't be prouder.

Second thank you to my extended family, who has continued to share and recommend my work, even the ones who aren't big romance readers. You guys are my original and irreplaceable street team.

Next, thank you to my best friends, Sarah, Erin and Christina, who have held my hand when it needed holding, kicked my butt when it needed kicking, and boosted my ego when it needed boosting. And another thank you to Rick and Thump, who have asked every week about how the new book is coming. It's finally here.

Thank you to Matthew, who walked me through the prison system and shared his experiences. And to Lesley and Rosa, who opened their home to me so that I could get Joe's family just right. They've helped me take this story to the next level of reality. Any mistakes I made are my own.

Thanks to the ladies of ORWA, particularly Teresa and Susan, who have continued to support my self-publishing journey. And to Lucy for pushing me to dream bigger.

Thank you to Red Adept Editing: particularly Lynne, Jessica, Sarah and Kim. Your work is exemplary, on par with any of the big houses.

Thank you to Streetlight Graphics for yet another awesome cover and to Samianne for the amazing morphing interstitials.

Thank you to Nada and Lauren, who have continued to support me and offer words of encouragement and amazing reviews.

And the last, but most important thank you, goes to my readers. Book by book, the numbers are growing. Thank you for your emails and your reviews. They mean the world to me.

© Ryan Parent Photography

About the Author

Jennifer Carole Lewis is a full-time mom, a full-time administrator and a full-time writer, which means she is very much interested in speaking to anyone who comes up with any form of functional time-travel devices or practical cloning methods. Meanwhile, she spends her most of her time alternating between organizing and typing.

She is a devoted comic book geek and Marvel movie enthusiast. She spends far too much of her precious free time watching TV, especially police procedural dramas. Her enthusiasm outstrips her talent in karaoke, cross-stitch and jigsaw puzzles. She is a voracious reader of a wide variety of fiction and non-fiction and always enjoys seeking out new suggestions.

For more information about *Inquisition* or other books of the *lalassu*, including my Under The Covers author commentary for chapter by chapter bonus and background information, you can go to www.jclewis.ca. You can also find Jennifer on Facebook and Goodreads as Jennifer Carole Lewis. You can also follow her on Twitter at @jclewisupdate or email her at jclewis@pastthemirror.com.

23904797R00204

Made in the USA
Columbia, SC
16 August 2018